FUTURE PERFECT

FELICIA YAP

WILDFIRE

Cataloguing in Publication Data is available from the British Library

ISBN 978 1 4722 4226 6

Typeset in Weiss Medium 10.5/14.5pt
by Palimpsest Book Production Limited, Falkirk, Stirlingshire

Printed and bound in Great Britain by Clays Ltd, Elcograf S.p.A.

HEADLINE PUBLISHING GROUP
An Hachette UK Company
Carmelite House
50 Victoria Embankment
London EC4Y 0DZ

www.headline.co.uk
www.hachette.co.uk

For Alex, who helped me to write
For Dad, who taught me to read

Chapter Zero

Ally the model

A catwalk in Manhattan, just before the murder

I hear footsteps ahead. Each footfall is strong, assured. I should do the same. Walk as confidently as the girl in front, keep my chin down, eyes focused on a point beyond the floodlights.

But I'm scared. Shit scared.

I'm terrified I'll lose my balance in these six-inch stilettos. Trip over the hem of my dress, fall flat on my nose. Make an absolute fool of myself, with a thousand pairs of eyes watching my moment of disgrace.

No, I can't fail. I can't fall, either. Tonight's my big break. The show of my life, one that could land me regular gigs on catwalks in London, Milan and Paris. What did my coach say, all those months ago? *Just keep breathing, my love. That's all you need to do. You'll relax if you remember to breathe.*

I take in a deep breath and exhale.

Right, I'm going to keep breathing. Glide above the river like a swan, like the other girls before me. It's an unusual catwalk in the shape of a diamond, with the audience seated in rows along the riverbank (must remember to turn all four corners with grace). Why am I modelling the final outfit of the show? If only I were one of the first girls to hit the runway, not the last one. Gosh, I should stop fretting. Nothing will go wrong, I'm sure. I'll sparkle like the fairy lights above the catwalk, dazzle everyone in the audience.

One of the backstage assistants steps up to me, a ginger-haired boy with a crocodile-shaped stud on his left ear. He opens a small metal briefcase. I gasp. A beautiful necklace shimmers in its depths. The centrepiece ruby, framed by diamonds, is almost as large as a quail's egg.

'Xander thinks you should wear this,' he says, whipping the piece out and hooking it around my neck. 'This damned thing costs $278,000, so don't even think of running away with it.'

'I won't,' I say.

'You look a bit worried, babe,' he says. 'Here, give me a smile . . .'

He's interrupted by another backstage helper. A tall man in neatly pressed trousers and shirt, holding a giant russet-gold handbag.

'Xander wants you to carry this,' says the man, thrusting the handbag in my direction. 'Says you should give it a small twirl when you get to the end of the runway, for Reva-Shulman's sake.'

I take the bag from him, only to frown. It's unusually heavy.

'Did he put bricks inside?' I say.

The man grins.

'Good leather weighs a tonne,' he says. 'This is choicest snakeskin. Mamba, apparently.'

'Oh,' I say.

'Good luck.'

'Thanks, I'll—'

2

'You're on, *now*.' A petite girl in neon pink-and-green spectacles rushes up, waving her clipboard at me in a frantic fluster. 'This way, please.'

I stagger forward with the handbag. I'm ushered to a small waiting area with black curtains, dazzling rays of light fanning out beneath their billowing folds. The music and cheers from the audience sound twice as loud in here. The band is really going for it tonight, even if they are an ageing bunch of pop rockers. The red-haired model waiting in front of me is wearing an eye-popping scarlet outfit, one as sinuously slinky as mine. Her lips are twisted in a small nervous pout.

'Five, four, three, two, one,' a voice hisses. '*Move*.'

The girl steps out into the lights, in a soft rustle of fabric.

'Twenty seconds,' the same voice barks at me.

I step up, still grimacing at the weight of the bag.

Tick tock.

I jump. What on earth is that noise? I strain my ears, but I can only hear the lead singer belting into the microphone, followed by a cacophony of drum rolls and yet another giant roar of applause from the crowd. Did I imagine it? Was it part of the infectious tune blasting from the speakers?

'Ten seconds.'

'I heard something,' I say, turning blindly in the direction of the voice. 'It sounded weird—'

'Five, four, three, two, one. *Move*.'

But I can't. I feel my chest constricting, something pinning me down. It's the leaden weight of fear.

Tick tock, tick tock.

'Oh God,' says the voice. '*Move it, girl*.'

Someone prods me hard on my right shoulder. I stumble forward through the curtains, onto the catwalk and into a

3

blinding pool of light. I blink, momentarily disorientated. A stream of red lights dissipates into the darkness ahead, on the left, almost like an airport landing strip. The lead singer is still crooning away into the microphone; the audience is erupting again with wild cheers. Yikes, a thousand pairs of eyes are staring at me. Focus, a voice in my head screams. You've got to focus.

Keep breathing.

I take a deep breath, pull my spine up and shoulders back, start gliding down the runway.

Tick tock.

I halt for a couple of seconds, prompting a ripple of astonished twitters from the crowd. Oh no, I'm losing it. I need to concentrate. Keep breathing. Keep walking. Keep pulling my lips together in a sexy pout.

I take another deep breath and step forward again.

Tick tock, tick tock.

Shit. I swear the sound isn't from the loudspeakers. I think . . . it's coming from the bag I'm carrying.

What the hell?

Tick tock, tick tock.

White-hot terror strikes my heart; I freeze. I hear alarmed murmurs rippling through the audience. I should be moving forward, gliding serenely. But I can't. I'm reduced to a petrified statue, one draped in the colour of fear.

Two thoughts rush to my head in a dizzying blur. One, there's a thousand people in this space and they are all going to die.

Tick tock, tick tock, tick tock.

The second is this:

I'm going to die, too.

4

Chapter One

Christian

Alexa is whimpering to herself in the kitchen. I strain my ears. She's repeating 'Help, help, help' in a low voice. Didn't she say exactly the same thing when I walked in here yesterday morning? I swear she did. How bizarre. Maybe I should tell Viola when she gets home that our voice assistant has gone bonkers (it helps to have a fiancée who knows something about machines).

I trundle up to the kitchen counter and pick up my smartphone, before saying: 'A single espresso with two sugars.'

Silence greets me. Did Alexa not hear me?

'A *single espresso*—'

'Please don't shout.' Her voice is disapproving, as far as a voice assistant can sound disapproving. 'One cappuccino coming up, with a heart-shaped dusting on the surface as usual.'

I blink.

'I said I wanted a single espresso.'

'You *always* have a cappuccino in the morning.' I swear Alexa's voice has a slightly whiny edge to it.

'This is ridiculous.'

'A fact based on existing habits, twenty-nine consecutive days of cappuccino consumption.'

'Surely . . .'

'Given recent sleep metrics and health data, you should be taking less sugar to minimise blood sugar spikes. You should also be consuming more caffeine to improve alertness and concentration. Cappuccinos contain two shots of caffeine, not one.'

'But . . .'

I trail off, staring at my cappuccino maker in dismay. The machine has started spitting out a thin stream of frothy milk into a mug. I groan. This isn't the best way to start the morning. Not when you have to argue with your voice assistant who refuses to give you what you want because it apparently knows what's best for you, and so does your coffee machine.

I finish reading my to-do list for the day and sigh. I should get Alexa to order some rabbit legs, in time for the last drone delivery of the day (shame the government has banned late-night grocery drones in a largely futile attempt at reducing noise pollution). The plan is to surprise Viola with some nicely marinated rabbit stew when she gets back tomorrow. After all, she complains that I don't pull my weight, that I should help a bit more with the household chores – and with the cooking. I should try to make up for that major argument we had two days ago, make her feel a little happier when she returns. Rabbit stew is the only thing I know how to make, so it's the best I can do.

I tap the iPredict app, causing a paragraph to flash up on screen. It reads:

**Predictions for TODAY (Friday 8 June 2030) and
TOMORROW (Saturday 9 June 2030)**

Another long day today at New Scotland Yard. First
meeting scheduled with the Bell Task Force at 9 a.m.
They are likely to say that they have made little headway
with their investigation, although the case has been
hanging around our necks for days. Will probably have to
apologise to the Prime Minister when she calls to find out
how we are getting on (Suggestion: Should exert greater
pressure on the Task Force, with the PM breathing down
my neck). Am also likely to get into another blazing
argument over yet another mundane matter with Viola
(Suggestion: Should try to let Viola have her way more
often, to avert future rows). In the late evening, I'm likely
to attend the Old Billingsgate show which I managed to
get a back-row ticket to (Suggestion: Have an early night
at home, instead).
Chance of spending at least four working hours at New
Scotland Yard: 100%
Chance of having another disagreement with Viola:
83.65%
Chance of having cappuccino for breakfast: 100%
Chance of being tempted by a cigarette: 25.47%
Chance of eating rabbit stew: 12.39%
Chance of dying: 99.74%

What the hell? I blink at my phone, not trusting my eyes.
The words on the screen separate into a grey haze of incredulity before coalescing back into a stark black line.

Chance of dying: 99.74%

I rub my eyes, I'm definitely not imagining it. My head spins. This can't be. This surely can't be.

Why does my phone think I'm going to die?

I swallow hard.

Wait a minute. I should be thinking rationally and clearly. I'm surely *not* going to die. I'm as healthy as an ox (even if I'm tempted by a cigarette once in a while). iPredict has refused to reveal the precise workings of its algorithm, but I'm sure the app takes into account my recent schedule and Google searches. I grab my phone again and swipe through my to-do app, for good measure. I can't see anything that predisposes me to dying. I'm unlikely to be buying rabbit legs laced with novichok. I'm not travelling to any war zones or conflict areas. Nor have I been to places where I could have caught the Ebola virus. This stupid little device must have gone as bonkers as Alexa. Let me see . . . my phone probably meant to say 'Chance of lying tomorrow: 99.74%.'

Lying, not *dying*. Of course. It must surely be a typo. Machines are so lifelike these days, they must make stupid typos like us. I've spent decades hiding the truth about myself, nursing secrets about my past. This is why my phone thinks I'm in for a 99.74 per cent chance of lying.

Lying, not *dying*.

No reason to get worried.

Definitely not.

I take a deep breath as I slurp my cappuccino. The liquid tastes burnt, unusually harsh on my tongue. No wonder the coffee machine spat a cappuccino out, come to think of it. It's digitally connected to my phone, which thinks there's a 100 per cent chance I will have a cappuccino after repeating myself twenty-nine times. Looks like my phone was 100 per cent right when it came to cappuccinos. I did indeed have one this morning, thanks to Alexa's resolute instructions to my coffee machine (maybe caffeine-induced mental alertness marginally reduces one's chances of dying).

But I'm surely not going to die.

Damn these stupid artificial intelligence devices. They are as artificial as their name suggests. I should stop worrying and sort out some work before I head to the office. I tap my Work app, only to wince. There are 148 notifications, plus five missed calls from Harold Lester. I groan. Something big must have happened and my dear advisor is desperate to reach me.

I should ring him back.

A flutter of wings sounds in the distance. I look up to see an e-pigeon landing on the balcony ledge, its metal wings silhouetted by the early-morning sun. Special-delivery drones are getting eerily lifelike these days, I don't like them the slightest bit. If not for the fact that this pigeon is holding a small item in its mouth, I could have sworn it was alive. I actually prefer 'ugly' drones with whirring propellers, I never quite understood that recent public backlash against them. That said, I suppose e-pigeons look a little less insectoid, a little more aesthetically pleasing and peaceful . . .

I squint at the creature. It's carrying a white envelope in its beak. Who on earth sends letters in envelopes these days?

'A delivery has arrived,' says Alexa.

'I can see that,' I say, getting up.

'I'll issue an e-receipt and ensure the drone deposits the item in the designated safe place.'

'You sort the receipt out,' I say, walking over to the balcony and pushing the door open. 'I'll get the envelope.'

*

9

A blast of fresh morning air hits me as soon as I step outside. It's mingled with the damp chill of the river. I still wonder why I bought an apartment overlooking the Thames, a home perpetually infested by riverine fog. Up close, I can see that the pigeon has a stray wire trailing from its bottom and a slightly dented metal wing (I guess accidents happen to drones). I yank the envelope from the pigeon's beak. The bird's electronic eyes flash red, just before it lifts its wings. I watch it soar off from the ledge and over the river, presumably back in the direction of the distribution warehouse.

I look down at the envelope in my hands.

Christian, it says on the front, in black ink.

My breath catches in my chest. The thin spindly writing is familiar; I saw the same loops and curls on the refrigerator's door earlier this morning (the note said, *double check if Alexa ordered milk and potatoes*).

I rush back into my apartment, envelope in hand.

I sit down at the dining table, take another large gulp of my enforced cappuccino. I tear the envelope open. A single sheet of lined cream paper slides out, covered with the same spindly handwriting.

Dear Christian,

   I told you yesterday morning that I'm attending a conference, staying there for two nights. Truth is, I've taken KitKat and some of my essential belongings and headed back to Old Fen Cottage. Last night, I heard you saying 'Ella, Ella, Ella' in your sleep again. This is the ninth time you've mumbled her name. By the way, you've been talking in your sleep for twenty-four consecutive nights, repeating bizarre words such as 'leave', 'help', 'find out', waking me up each time (I struggled to fall asleep afterwards). I can't compete with this other woman who occupies your nights, even though I'm the one lying next to you. I keep asking you about her; you clam up each time. Why are you hiding the truth about Ella from me? Why are you letting her get between us? She must be a lover or a ghost. I can't coexist with either, I'm afraid.

The past six weeks we've spent living together have also been more difficult than I expected. Maybe it's because we're both fiercely independent by nature or simply unused to sharing domestic habitats. I know that I asked you to marry me a few weeks ago (and that you said yes), but I need some space apart for the time being. I will call when I work out what to do about us.

Viola

This can't be. This surely can't be.

I jump from the kitchen table, run to the bedroom. Viola keeps most of her essential belongings in the wardrobe. That includes her passport, car keys and make-up bag. I burst through the door, make a beeline for the top drawer. I tug the handle; it slides open with a loud squeak. An empty void greets me. I yank the lower drawer open. Viola has swept that bare, too; I can only see a lipstick holder lying forlornly on its side. I turn my gaze to the clothing in the wardrobe, running my eyes over the dozen or so outfits still hanging on the rails. Viola's favourite dress is a knee-length leopard print with a high collar; she wore it when she proposed to me.

It isn't there either.

Come to think of it, I definitely haven't seen KitKat, Viola's fluffy Persian feline, all morning.

11

The cat's gone.

Viola, too.

I collapse on the bed, shock and disbelief coursing through my veins. I have no recollection of muttering Ella's name at night. Nor the words 'leave', 'help' or 'find out', for that matter (maybe that's why Alexa was mumbling 'help, help, help' when I walked into the kitchen earlier). Why didn't Viola tell me that I keep talking in my sleep? Why did she bottle up her frustrations before packing and leaving? Why did I fix my eyes to the ground and mumble something incoherent when she asked me who Ella was? Why did I imply the girl never existed?

What the hell should I be doing next?

'Dear God,' I say.

'God is a matter of perspective,' says Alexa. 'Also a delusion.'

I wince. I'm tempted to throw something at the loudspeaker in the corner of the room, drown out that annoying disembodied voice. I still don't understand why Viola rigged Alexa to our household appliance system. It's one of those annoying little things we've been arguing about. If I remember correctly, Viola was pretty adamant that we needed a voice assistant at home, to help us with the chores, to send notifications to our phones if we run short of milk, potatoes or coffee. I said we were able to keep track of things ourselves, that we didn't need another goddamned electronic device monitoring our actions, one eavesdropping on all our conversations. Now that they have got rid of the trigger word, the 'wake-Alexa-up-by-saying-her-name' function, because it apparently 'inconveniences users', Alexa is now listening all the time. Viola won the argument in the end (she also won most of the other battles that took place over the kitchen counter, come to think of it).

I take a deep breath and say with a sigh: 'I don't need a reminder about God.'

'Then maybe you need a reminder that you have 157 emails in your inbox and six missed calls.'

I groan, placing my head in my hands. The day is fast disintegrating, and it's only 7.49 in the morning. My smartphone thinks I'm going to die, while my fiancée has packed up her belongings and moved out of my apartment. The second problem is much worse than the first one. It's also a more difficult problem to solve. Maybe it's indeed time for me to tell Viola everything about Ella, the girl who has haunted me for years.

I should get going.

I walk into the garage of my apartment block, a well-lit space with six immaculately parked cars. I stride past a Porsche and a Bentley to the waiting area, a circular red-carpeted spot. As I do so, a sleek black BMW without any number plates revs itself up in a loud burst. It shoots over to where I'm standing, flashing its headlights three times to greet me. I jump in. The rich warm smell of new leather envelops me; it's vaguely pleasant. I settle down, only to grimace as Alexa says: 'Good morning, Commissioner Verger.'

Am I imagining it or does Alexa's voice sound unusually smug? I grit my teeth and say: 'Old Fen Cottage, 47 Fen Church Lane.'

'Thank you, Commissioner,' says Alexa. 'We will arrive at New Scotland Yard in approximately twenty-five minutes, based on current traffic conditions.'

I blink as we zoom out of the garage and take a sharp right turn.

Did Alexa bloody mishear me?

'I said *Old Fen Cottage*, not New Scotland Yard.' My voice is sharp.

'You're meeting the members of the Bell Task Force at New Scotland Yard at nine,' says Alexa, speeding down the street before taking a neat left turn into the specially designated Driverless Car Lane with yellow markings.

'But—'

'I'll make sure you get there on time, Commissioner. I should also remind you that you now have 161 messages in your inbox and seven missed calls.'

I groan. This time, I only have myself to blame. I was the one who decided to hook up my car to my Work app (controlled by my secretary, Ginny), because I thought that it would optimise job efficiency. What a bloody delusion (like Alexa's God). Now Alexa has also infiltrated my car. The real problem with so-called 'machine reinforcement learning' is that machines end up learning how to reinforce my behaviour. If my to-do app says I have a morning appointment at New Scotland Yard and iPredict thinks there's a 100 per cent chance I'll be spending at least four hours there today, it will be damned difficult to get Alexa to budge from her chosen route. Maybe Alexa is doing this in my so-called 'best interests' again, I suppose spending the day at New Scotland Yard marginally minimises one's chance of dying.

'I wish to go to Old Fen Cottage, please,' I say, firmly and clearly. 'It's a last-minute change of plan. The address is 47 Fen Church Lane.'

No reply.

'Did you hear me, Alexa?' I say.

'Of course, Commissioner,' says Alexa. 'Your schedule for

the day says you have a 9 a.m. appointment at New Scotland Yard, while iPredict says you have a one hundred per cent probability of spending at least four hours there today. I'll make sure you get there on time.'

I groan again, looking out of the window. We're speeding down the Driverless Car Lane, overtaking all the human-operated vehicles that are stuck in an immense traffic snarl in the adjoining lane. We are also speeding eastwards in the direction of New Scotland Yard. Definitely not north-westwards in the direction of Old Fen Cottage. Why on earth did I allow my driving licence to lapse a few weeks ago, thinking these documents are now obsolete? I should ring Ginny, get her to cancel that damned appointment and (hopefully) redirect my car.

I reach for my phone, only to realise that its screen is flashing.

Advisor Harold Lester sounds a little flustered, to put it mildly.

'I've been trying to reach you for the past hour,' he says.

'How come?'

'An explosion happened in New York City yesterday night.'

'Oh no.'

'It happened on a diamond-shaped catwalk above the Hudson river, to be precise. A model was blown to bits by the handbag she was carrying.'

'You must be joking.'

'I wish.' Harold sighs. 'The bomb detonated moments before the girl got to the catwalk's pointy end. Two front-row attendees are in a serious condition. Numerous folks are being treated for injuries caused by flying shrapnel. I hear the band escaped unscathed but were not amused.'

'Oh dear.'

'One attendee has already threatened to sue the designer for the injuries she sustained.'

'Hmm . . .' I say. 'What are the NYPD saying?'

'They're treating it as a terrorist incident.'

'Naturally.'

'The designer had planned two back-to-back fashion shows, on both sides of the Atlantic. The second show will take place in London tonight. The man's currently on his private jet; it should land at Heathrow around noon. His London-based PA, a Miss Lucia Graves, rang this morning to say that she has received a threatening note. It says that her boss is going to die at the London show . . . in a similar way to the girl he's dedicating the event to.'

Inexplicable cold dread sweeps over me.

'Where's the show?' I say, although I already know the answer.

'Old Billingsgate. Believe it or not, they've built a runway over the Thames, with rows of seats along the riverbank.'

The disbelief curling over my shoulders is now replaced by fear. An intense, irrational fear.

'The designer's name is Alexander King,' I say, trying desperately not to let my voice wobble.

'Indeed.' Harold sounds surprised. 'How did you know?'

'I, er . . . keep track of things,' I say.

'Miss Graves says that most of Britain's rich and famous have been invited to the show. There will be a Beatle – you know who I mean – and a couple of lords. What's worse, the Prince and Princess of Wales were also planning to be in the front row.'

'Bloody hell.'

'Should we allow the show to go ahead?'

'Good question,' I say. 'Has a crime taken place in Britain?'

'I don't think so.'

'Can you remember what happened during the 2015 multiple-location terrorist attacks in Paris, football-wise?'

'The Parisians decided to allow the friendly match between Germany and France to go ahead.'

'Bingo,' I say. 'Life went on, indeed. Mass closures may not necessarily engender calm and resilience. We did not shut down the London Underground after those bombs in 2005.'

'Quite rightly so, too.'

'I'll have a word with the City of London Police as Old Billingsgate lies within their jurisdiction. Pick up King as soon as he arrives at Heathrow. I'll have a chat with him, too.'

'OK.' Harold sounds surprised; he's probably wondering why the Commissioner himself would bother interviewing King.

'Thanks, Harold.'

I terminate the call, cast an anguished glance outside the car. Lavish window displays featuring beautifully dressed mannequins are flashing by in a blur; we must be somewhere in Chelsea. *Alexander King*. The man's name has plagued me for twenty goddamned years, much like the ghost of a perfect girl who has been haunting my dreams at night. I open my briefcase and pull out two items. The first is a newspaper clipping from the *New York Times*, dated 30 March 2030, which I have been carrying around for weeks:

Alexander King Honours Lifelong Muse in Two Special Shows

By Rachel Silverman

The great Alexander King has spent twenty years thinking about a beautiful woman. She has influenced every catwalk piece he has created, inspired every sell-out fashion show he's staged around the globe. The only problem is: she has been dead for precisely that same length of time.

It all began when King saw a photograph of Maya von Meyer in a magazine he picked up in a dentist's waiting room. The designer was so struck by her appearance, he got in contact at once.

'Maya came into my studio in London's Shoreditch a week later,' he says, eyes misting over during our interview in his shop on Fifth Avenue, a 500-piece Baccarat chandelier glittering above our heads. 'That was back in those days when my workplace was located above a pawnshop and only contained three sewing machines and four mannequins. I was blown away by Maya's beauty, the shimmering depths in her eyes, the way her rosebud mouth curved up at me in a beautiful smile. New ideas surged to mind, taking me by surprise. I draped a long piece of brocade over her shoulders – and began sketching. Over the following weeks, I existed in a joyous state of creative mania inspired by her presence.'

All the pieces King created during those weeks made an appearance in his first major show in London, 'The Autumn of Virginia Woolf.' The show proved such a hit, practically every A-list celebrity came knocking on King's door, begging to be dressed by him. Within weeks, King had moved from his Shoreditch studio to a swanky shopfront in London's Chelsea. Twelve actresses wore his evening gowns to the Oscars the following year, including the winner of the Best Actress award. Industry insiders say that King's ascent within the fashion world has been the most seamless and meteoric of them all. His recent incorporation of smart technology, resulting in the first high-couture outfits that change color depending on the mood of their wearers, has been universally lauded. His conglomerate has also been consistently named as The Best Company to Work For in Fashion over the past two decades.

And yet . . . the girl who inspired King's stellar career was found dead in Oxford's River Isis, weeks after they met.

'The police rang one morning to say they'd found Maya's body in the river,' says King, the nostalgic mist in his eyes giving way to stark anguish. 'I was so shattered, it took me a couple of months before I could work again.'

It wasn't clear if it was an accident or murder. Toxicology reports confirmed a high amount of fentanyl and Valium in von Meyer's blood. The coroner returned an open verdict and the von Meyer case remains unsolved, twenty years later. The police, when contacted; confirmed no recent breakthroughs.

'Maya told me before she died that she would love to walk on big runways in London and Manhattan,' says King. 'I can't make this happen, but I can make the catwalks happen in her name.'

King's commemorative plans are as bold as the creations he is famed for. This summer, he will be erecting two runways in Maya's memory, both above water. One of them will be above the Hudson river, a stone's throw from where Maya had lived briefly in New York City.

The second will be above the River Thames, next to Old Billingsgate in the City of London. The shows will be held on two consecutive days in June and feature catwalk confections unlike anything King has ever created.

'I've existed in a similar state of creative mania since I began this commemorative project,' says King. 'It's as if Maya were standing in front of me, all over again. I'm planning two spectacular shows to remember her, my lifelong muse who has never stopped smiling down on me from the heavens.'

'My Muse: Maya von Meyer' will take place on June 7th 2030 in Manhattan and June 8th 2030 in London, by invitation only. A small number of tickets for the general public, starting at $1,430, will be made available at 14.30 (EST) on April 7th 2030 and are expected to sell out within minutes. All proceeds will go to charity.

I transfer my gaze to the accompanying photo. It's of a blonde girl holding a heart-shaped pillow, staring out of a bay window with her legs elegantly intertwined beneath her on the ledge. Her expression is enigmatically demure, heartbreakingly innocent. The sepia-tinted spectre of a perfect girl flits through my mind again, spreading sharp pain across my heart. I know precisely what it means to be haunted by a ghost from the past, to lose someone on an idealised pedestal. I need to get to the bottom of this case. I tear my gaze from the photo to the second item in my hand, a back-row ticket costing £2,860 (all other tickets had already been snapped up when I got to the front of the online queue).

I sigh. I now know three things about Alexander King:

1. His show has just been bombed to high heaven in Manhattan.
2. Maya's death has plagued him for most of his life.
3. Someone may be planning to kill him tonight.

As of this morning, I also know three things about myself:

1. My fiancée has just dropped a bombshell: she has packed up and left me all alone in London.
2. She's upset about the girl who haunts me at night.
3. My phone thinks I have a 99.74 per cent chance of dying.

I told myself it was a typo but . . .
I no longer think so.

Felicia Yap

The *Los Angeles Times*, June 19th 2031

Ban on Predictive Phone Apps

If the President has her way, predictions for the
future might be a thing of the past

Washington DC & Los Angeles: The President is determined to push through legislation banning all forms of
predictive apps because of growing evidence that these
apps are detrimental to mental health.

'I owe this intervention to my fellow Americans,' she
said at a White House press conference this morning.
'Social media addiction is a recognized psychiatric
illness; there's now extensive evidence that predictive
apps are equally detrimental to mental well-being.'

Recent papers in *Nature* and *Science* have pointed to
a strong causal link between the launch of iPredict in
August 2028 (followed by the emergence of a slew of
rival apps) and the rise of depression and suicide rates
in young Americans between the ages of 18 and 28.

News of government intervention has been welcomed
by many. Nineteen-year-old Angelino Amanda Fields is
one of them. She is currently seeking treatment at a
tech-rehab clinic in Santa Monica, one of the estimated
15 million young Americans receiving psychiatric help
for tech addiction. She blames her smartphone for
propelling her along the dark road of mental anguish.

'It all began when I logged on to iPredict two Augusts
ago, on the first day they rolled out the app,' she says.
'I was mesmerized by my phone's forecast for the next

two days. When most of the predictions came true, I was hooked.'

But things soon spiraled downhill, she insists.

'I became obsessive and superstitious,' she says. 'I began doing what the app said would happen, because I had a crazy irrational fear that I would upset the natural order of things if I didn't. I even went out of my way to ensure its predictions came true.'

Terrible anxiety and depression soon followed. Things got so bad, she voluntarily entered a tech-rehab clinic in Santa Monica. One of the first things her psychiatrist did was take her smartphone away.

'Digital cold turkey proved excruciating,' she says. 'I found myself reaching for my phone again and again, only to realize to my horror that it was no longer there. Yet things eventually turned around for the better. I now feel happier and liberated, more like a normal person. A girl in charge of her own life instead of being controlled by a machine.'

Spokespeople for iPredict have declined to comment. A spokeswoman for gPredict, iPredict's largest competitor, says the company takes the mental health of its users very seriously.

Chapter Two

Viola

I'm mesmerised by the images on my television. The rich and famous of America are stumbling past the screen, shell-shocked and covered with soot and debris (I never dreamt I would see the editor of *Vogue* looking so dishevelled above her diamanté-encrusted cane). I guess these folks should count themselves lucky; most of them would be in body bags if the poor model had not frozen at the start of the catwalk. The camera is zooming in on the smoking remnants of the runway. Most of it has already been carried away by the Hudson river. What remains is a series of twisted steel pylons, concertinaed by the force of the blast. A forlorn pile of smoking wooden planks lie atop, torn apart and scattered like matchsticks. A rolling newsflash appears in a strip of red at the bottom of the screen: 'Shares in Alexander King have fallen by 37 per cent since the London Stock Exchange opened this morning.' The camera focuses back on the news-bot, a perfectly coiffured brunette avatar who looks both serious and stupid.

'The NYPD are treating the incident as a terrorist attack,' she says in a half-monotonous voice. 'They haven't yet ruled out the involvement of religious fundamentalists.'

Something in the background catches my eye. I squint at the television screen. It's an attractive blonde woman dressed in a slinky leopard-print dress with a high collar (very similar to mine). She's sitting on the roadside kerb, inspecting her reflection in a powder compact and dabbing her nose with a dainty puff. The expression on her face is both haughty and dismissive. Why on earth would someone be powdering their nose, with the smouldering wreckage of a catwalk just yards away? Are fashion folk really as vacuous and ditzy as stereotypes suggest?

'Mr King is currently on his way back to London,' continues the news-bot. 'He's personally offering a reward of $500,000 for information leading to the conviction of the perpetrator.'

I wonder if Xander is still going ahead with tonight's show, in view of what has happened in Manhattan. I should check if the poor boy is all right, offer a few words of comfort and commiseration. I pull out my personal smartphone, only to gasp. It has been on silent mode all morning . . . and there are three missed calls from Christian. He must have read my e-pigeon note by now. I have no idea what he wants to say; he's probably either apologetic or angry. If he's pissed off with me for packing up and leaving, I'm definitely not in the mood for another fight.

With a sigh, I scroll past my other notifications. There is a missed call and accompanying message from Xander's PA:

Hi Viola, I found an anonymous note in my handbag this morning (photograph of the note attached). I only ever leave my handbag unattended in the office, so it could have been someone at work. Xander once said you can do anything with software: might you be able to perform some computing magic to figure out who wrote this note?

> Please ring me back if you find any matches (I'm currently on my way to New Scotland Yard and hope to be done at around half eleven). Many thanks, Lucia. PS You're still sure you aren't coming tonight? Xander is determined for the second show to go ahead and really hopes to see you at Old Billingsgate.

I sigh. Xander has begged me multiple times to attend tonight's show, to marvel at the catwalk creations I've helped him engineer. To his bafflement, I've said no, again and again. I guess he doesn't understand why I've spent so many hours writing Vision for him ('a nifty little fashion-design program that will fuck the fashion world long after I'm dead', as he had once described my software with a sadistic-sounding chuckle), only to refuse to see the results on the runway. That said, I have my own mystifications, too. I don't know why Xander wanted me to write Vision, or what he hopes to achieve with the software, and I'm curious to find out what people will think of the output. I'm also worried that the software will do what Xander predicted, that it will cause disruptive turmoil within the industry and maybe even a massive loss of jobs.

I sigh again.

Maybe . . . maybe I should tell Xander the real reason why I've been turning down his invitation: he's dedicating the shows to Maya, and I simply can't bear the thought of attending a show in her name because . . .

Because . . .

Morbid guilt floods my heart, curdling it. I shouldn't be thinking about Maya. Even if torrid memories of what happened on the night she died have been knocking at the backdoor of my mind for years, threatening to overwhelm my heart and paralyse my soul. I know what it's like to be incapacitated by guilt; I shouldn't allow the mental torture to happen again . . . Hell, I should be concentrating on something else, something more important and immediate. Gritting my teeth, I tap Lucia's attachment, causing an image to glimmer up on my screen. It's a photograph of a small sheet of paper. I enlarge the image, squint at the words on the note. They say, in simple Arial type:

Xander is going to die at the London show in the same manner as his muse Maya did twenty years ago.

I sag back on the sofa, head spinning. *In the same manner as his muse Maya?* What on earth is the sender implying?

Two possibilities barrel into my head, causing me to gasp.

One: Maya's body was found in the River Isis. Is someone suggesting that Xander will end up in the River Thames tonight? Two: The post-mortem report indicated that Maya was high on drugs when she died. Is someone planning to drug Xander before pushing him into the river?

Alarm pricks me hard. Is this anonymous note for real, or is it just a sick prank? Was it written by the person who bombed Manhattan? I should run the note past IdentiKit, a simple linguistic-profiling program that matches sentence structure and word choice to people's writings in the public domain. I'll also put a filter on the scan, limiting my search to employees of Alexander King.

I'm sure Lucia must have told Xander about the note by now. I wonder what he thinks of it. I tap out Xander's number, only to hear a standard recorded message. Looks like he switched his phone off post-Manhattan. I should try again later. In the meantime, I have to deal with three massive problems.

Problem One: I have no idea what I'm going to do about Christian and me . . . apart from remain here until I figure out a solution. Maybe I should do nothing. I shouldn't speak to him before I know what I'm going to say. I can't bear another fraught exchange, even if it's over the phone.

I take a deep breath, turn off my smartphone before putting it back into my pocket. Maybe I should keep the damned thing switched off for the rest of the day, only use my work phone and landline.

Problem Two: the attic's a mess. Late yesterday night, I popped my head through to discover that some verminous squirrels had got in through an open window. They've managed to knock over a few piles of books, dig through an open box (probably in search of nesting materials) and scatter a bunch of loose papers on the floor. I've shut the window and restacked the books, but I haven't yet finished clearing up the mess. I should head back up, inspect the attic more carefully in broad daylight, see if the squirrels have gnawed through any electric cables.

Problem Three has everything to do with my phone's prediction for today, words which are still twisting sharp hooks in my mind. The app had said:

Predictions for TODAY (Friday 8 June 2030) and TOMORROW (Saturday 9 June 2030)

Am likely to enjoy an average sleep time of 10 hours (up from my weekly average of 7.5 hours) over the next two days. Am also likely to feel extremely nauseous and exhausted, as in previous days. Damian will probably call again, to find out how I'm getting on with CriminalX. Will give him my default answer: With luck, we should be able

to take the software to the beta-testing phase soon. Am
likely to do more work on the program, with the usual
unsatisfactory results (Suggestion: Should work a bit
harder on CriminalX, now that I have finished my project
for Xander). Am likely to spend a few more hours tidying
up the mess in the attic (Suggestion: Get someone to
clean the cottage when I'm away).

Chance of spending at least six working hours on
CriminalX: 100%

Chance of getting CriminalX to work satisfactorily: 9.45%

Chance of having another disagreement with Christian:
83.65%

Chance of being tempted by chocolate: 98.47%

Chance of having another katsu curry and pickled ginger
takeaway: 43.47%

Chance of being pregnant: 79.74%

It's the final line that still unsettles me, churns deep inside
my gut. There's no way I can be pregnant. I'm a geriatric
forty-one. My period is only four days overdue. That said, I can't
remember when I last had a slightly overdue period (the data
harvested by my period-monitoring app confirms as much).
Yet iPredict is right about the extreme nausea and exhaustion,
so far. I felt pretty shattered when I woke up this morning,
despite sleeping for ten largely restless hours. The two fried
eggs I ate for breakfast had disagreed violently with my insides
and I ended up collapsing in a giant queasy heap on the sofa.

I stare down at my hands, still feeling a little nauseous. I
must have caught stomach flu or a vomiting bug, probably
from eating too many dodgy katsu curries. I can't be pregnant.
Though I did read on the BBC news website yesterday that

those vegan-friendly compostable condoms Christian bought have just been recalled due to reliability concerns . . .

I surely can't be pregnant.

'Home pregnancy tests can be purchased from most pharmacies,' booms Alexa over the loudspeaker system, causing me to jump.

Damn it, I must have voiced my last thought out loud.

'Do you think I'm pregnant?' I say.

'Home pregnancy tests are a commonly used early-verification method,' says Alexa. 'Most claim to be at least ninety-nine per cent accurate.'

I love how Alexa dispenses percentages with solemn alacrity. I ought to be thinking clearly and logically, like her. I, out of all people, should know that *all* iPredictions ought to be taken with a pinch of salt. Each and every one of them. Predictions work because human beings are creatures of habit, either by force or by design. People love to repeat their actions because they prefer the snug, reassuring comfort of familiarity, because deviations from the norm are frightening. That's why the future is a function of the past. iPredict has interpreted the data supplied by my smart yoga clothing (my heartbeat, blood pressure, temperature, pulse and propensity to sweat while vomiting), my recent supermarket bills and takeaway receipts (which demonstrate a recent preference for katsu curries, sour pickles and dark chocolate) as a sign of . . .

. . . pregnancy.

Hmm. Maybe I should buy a test kit, just to be sure . . .

A second phone buzzes in my pocket, causing me to jump. Is Damian calling? Damn it, I already know what he's going to say.

*

I fish out the work phone. It's an ancient Nokia that Damian sent a while back, insisting I use it whenever I wish to speak to him. I remember feeling extremely excited when I started freelancing for MI6, when I signed on the dotted line. I thought I would be issued with the latest gadgets, the fanciest cloak-and-dagger contraptions, the sort of stuff Bond would get from Q. Instead, all I've had from them is a crappy old phone the size of a brick. The name flashing up on the black-and-blue screen is indeed 'Damian Everett'. I sigh as I tap the answer button.

'Morning, Damian,' I say.

'Morning, Vi. How are you today?'

'Surviving,' I say, bracing myself for what I know is coming next.

'Aren't we all? I'm calling to find out how CriminalX is getting on. Made any headway over the past day?'

I grit my teeth. My smartphone has correctly predicted what Damian will say. It's both annoying and unsettling.

'We should be able to move into beta-testing mode soon. Don't you worry.'

'I've heard this before.'

'It's true, unfortunately.' I grimace at the receiver. 'I'm almost there. But there are some things you can't rush.'

'We were hoping to input some data into CriminalX, to see what the software might come up with.'

'What sort of data?'

'An explosion happened in Manhattan yesterday night.'

'You mean . . . the fashion show?'

'Looks like you've heard the news. As you may also know, Alexander King is doing a second show in London tonight. I'm hoping CriminalX might reveal something useful, help us

31

to find out if it was a terrorist job and if there's a chance the bomber might strike again in London.'

'But the software isn't quite ready yet.'

'So I gathered.' He sighs over the line. 'We need results soon, Vi. Like, *really* soon.'

'I'll keep plugging away.'

'Otherwise we might have to redirect funding to something that actually works. I really had to fight for CriminalX's budget, you know.'

I'm tempted to groan. Looks like Damian's digital division doesn't have endless funds, even if the man himself has endless clout (unlike me, he has come pretty far from the days we were both students in Edinburgh). The last thing I want is to lose funding for CriminalX, especially when I'm close to nailing it.

An idea strikes me.

'Why don't you send me the data anyway?' I say. 'I'll feed it into what I have, see if the software comes up with anything sensible.'

'Oh.' He sounds surprised. 'Sure, will do that straight away.'

'Can't promise anything, mind you.'

'I understand. At least I can tell the folks breathing down my neck that we've done a trial run.'

'Will keep you posted.'

'Thanks, Vi.'

The line goes dead. I frown at the phone, before stuffing it into the pocket of my dressing gown. So iPredict has got it right again. No wonder there's been lots of anguished debate in the media about the dangers of predictive apps. They're getting scarily accurate and people are taking them way too seriously. Today's prediction is most certainly causing havoc in my head and heart. I should stop thinking about the damned app, brew more coffee and process Damian's data.

Before . . . heading over to the pharmacy.

KitKat is sleeping on my work chair. I place my coffee mug down and scoop him up He opens one suspicious eye, scrunches his nose and whiskers, dozes off again. I settle down, placing the cat on my lap. I take a giant gulp from the mug, only to cringe as the coffee burns my tongue. The liquid tastes unusually astringent, even a little bitter (oh dear, is pregnancy responsible for this funny taste in my mouth?). I turn on my computer. A voice-dictated message from Damian is waiting for me, right at the top:

> Hi Vi, here's the data. We've obtained the guest lists of both catwalk shows, as well as the names of all backstage people (labelled BS) – models, photographers, dressers, hair & make-up artists, sound & lighting technicians, etc. There are thirty-five overlapping names, people involved in both shows. Maybe the algorithm should give a higher weightage to these folks. We also have the names of no-shows (labelled NS) – people who were invited but have RSVP'd to say that they can't come. FYI: The Americans think it was an inside job, that someone backstage planted the bomb inside the handbag before the model went onto the catwalk. Would be great if you're able to input all of these names into CriminalX and keep me posted on the outcome. It's a perfect case study for the software – hope something useful comes up. Thanks, Dx.
>
> PS I noticed you're on the list, marked as a no-show.

I know that you previously interned at Alexander King – but that was twenty years ago so we won't hold that against you.

I wince at Damian's final remark. The first problem with working for MI6 is that your employer knows everything about you and you can't hide anything from them (not even your choicest warts). The second problem with working for MI6 is that you can't tell people you work for them (not even your nearest and dearest). I wonder if my reluctance to discuss my recent commissions has baffled Christian as much as his furtiveness has frustrated me. Maybe mutual secrecy lies at the heart of the wedge between us.

I sigh as I scroll to the end of Damian's message. There are two spreadsheets at the bottom, one labelled 'Manhattan', the other 'London'. I click on the London file; there are 3,673 names on it. The Manhattan file, on the other hand, only has 1,492 names. Looks like Xander has planned a much bigger show tonight.

I turn on CriminalX and type in multiple lines of code to give a higher weightage to the thirty-five overlapping names, as Damian instructed. I take a deep breath and hit the final few keys.

A small window flashes up.

Select Crime, it says.

I select *MURDER* from a drop-down list of options (the other options, so far, include *RAPE*, *THEFT* and *FRAUD*) and hit the enter button.

Another window emerges, a grey-coloured one.

Input Data, it says.

I upload the two files. A third window appears. *Processing Data*, it says, also in pale grey. What a boring, bog-standard phrase. I remember cribbing that line from the previous software I had worked on. Maybe I'll change the colour of the pop-up window to hot-pink and the phrase to *Finding Your Criminals*. Or maybe not. Damian will probably have a fit if I do. He has a fairly limited sense of humour.

God, I hope he won't cut my funding.

KitKat's dribbling away on my lap. I scratch his ears and turn my gaze to the progress indicator at the bottom of the screen. The little white bar is thankfully crawling from left to right, but at sloth speed. Ninety seconds must have passed since I uploaded the first file; the progress is only 2 per cent. At the rate this bloody software is going, it will be Christmas before I get any results. Looks like several more lines of code are necessary to speed things up.

Maybe it's a good time to head over to the pharmacy.

I'm curious as to what CriminalX might eventually say, if it churns out anything in the first place.

I step through the front door, out into soft morning sunshine. Small fluffy white clouds are scudding overhead. I smell rosemary and honeysuckle in the air, mingled with the scent of freshly cut grass. It's a pleasant change from the damp of the river, and the exhaust fumes that sting my eyes each time I stick my head out from Christian's apartment. My neighbour Mrs Deakins is barking instructions to her lawnmower, a purple cylindrical device scuttling about on the grass. Looks like I'm in for a few minutes of banal small talk even if I don't feel like chatting to anyone. She is already turning her frizzy white head around in my direction.

'Good morning, sweetheart,' she says, face creasing into a broad smile.

'Morning, Mrs Deakins,' I say. 'How are you today?'

'Bit of the shakes this morning, but otherwise I'm fine.'

'Glad you're well.'

'I can't believe it's more than a month since you moved to London. How are you and your fiancé getting on?'

Oh dear, here we go again. Why does everyone keep asking me the same bloody question?

'We're all right,' I say, in a small voice.

'Excellent,' she says, beaming at me. 'He's such a lovely man, absolutely perfect for you.'

I'm tempted to say 'He isn't', but I bite my tongue.

'Is he joining you here today?'

'Er . . . probably not.' I can feel my face flushing.

'You should bring him over for tea and crumpets sometime. Are you heading to the shops, by any chance?'

'As a matter of fact, I am.'

'Could you kindly pick up a copy of *The Times* for me, please? Mrs Lacey texted to say that there's an excellent beetroot recipe in Section Two.'

Mrs Deakins must surely be the only person who still reads newspapers in hardcopy and refuses to accept drone deliveries as a matter of principle. I guess some members of the older generation remain convinced that drones are an ugly blight on our skies and can't stand their infernal whirring.

'Sure.' I nod, walking to the gate. 'I'll put the newspaper through your letterbox when I get back.'

'Thanks, sweetheart. I presume you got the parcel in the end?'

I freeze in my tracks.

'What parcel?'

'I saw a drone on your doorstep yesterday morning. Nasty-looking hawk-shaped bugger. I thought your voice assistant dealt with it.'

'There weren't any parcels in the safe place,' I say, frowning. 'When exactly did you see the drone?'

'Probably around nine.'

'I only got here at half nine.'

'Then it might have gone to your London address instead. It'll come back later today if it can't find you. It looked like one of those one hundred per cent guaranteed drones I've read about.'

'You mean those drones that keep tracking people down until they succeed?'

'Indeed.' She nods before wagging a firm finger at me. 'Don't forget to bring your man over sometime.'

I nod again, closing the gate. I begin walking in the direction of the shops, my head a bemused whirl. Who on earth could have sent that parcel?

A bell tinkles softly as I step into the pharmacy. The space smells of liquorice lozenges and decaying mothballs. A distant childhood memory floats to mind, of cough syrup being forced down my throat via a cold, unforgiving metal spoon. I swallow hard, forcing the unpleasant memory back. A woman with mud-puddle hair and thick circular spectacles smiles at me from behind the counter.

'Can I help you?' she asks.

I take in a deep breath.

'I would like, er . . . to buy a pregnancy testing kit,' I say. She waves her hand at a nearby shelf.

'You have six options,' she says. 'Which would you like?'

'Er . . .' I say again, gaping in consternation at the magnificent array. 'The most accurate, I guess.'

'They all claim to have an accuracy above ninety-nine per cent,' she says primly, sounding a bit like Alexa.

Looks like I will have to just grab one at random.

'I'll have that one,' I say, pointing at a specimen that matches the colour of my toothbrush.

She nods, extracting the kit from the shelf.

'That will be £32.99, please,' she says.

Ouch, it's three times the price of summoning one by rapid drone. That's insane. I guess it's the cost of not being spied on by technology, these days. With a resigned groan, I rummage about in the depths of my purse. I usually keep cash buried somewhere, for desperate emergencies (like my current predicament). My fingers eventually curl around two twenty-pound notes; I pull them out. I can see the shop assistant's eyes widening beneath her spectacles.

'Gosh, I haven't seen one of these in months,' she says, as I hand over the notes. I can't remember when I last handed over cash to someone, either. It feels as if I've just gone back to the Middle Ages (or to the twentieth century, to be more precise).

The woman prods a button on a dusty cash till. The tray shoots open with a loud ping, causing me to jump.

She frowns.

'I'm sorry, but I only have twenty pence in here,' she says, extracting the coin from the tray and waving it apologetically at me.

'That's all right,' I say with a sigh, taking the money from her. 'I guess no one uses cash these days.'

'Only folks who have stuff to hide.' She gives me a cheerful wink; it makes her look about ten years younger. 'Tell you what, I'll give you our fanciest kit, the one which retails for £36.99.'

'I don't think I need the fanciest . . .'

'Niftier is always better,' she says in an authoritative tone, pulling a green-coloured kit from behind her and thrusting it at me. 'Good luck, I really hope you'll get the result you want.'

Flushing, I grab the kit and beat a hasty retreat from the shop. Looks like it was written all over my face, the fact that I paid cash because I wanted to avoid an e-record of the transaction. In this day and age, you can't even hide the fact that you have something you wish to hide.

Let me see, there's something else I need to do. Ah yes, get a copy of *The Times* for Mrs Deakins. The convenience store is right opposite the pharmacy, the only other shop still remaining on the high street. I wonder what they are going to do with these forlorn shuttered facades and empty car parks, now that shared self-driving cars have drastically reduced the number of vehicles. Maybe I should support the ongoing campaign to convert these spaces into vertical gardens or vegetable allotments.

I cross the road, keeping a watchful eye out for stray delivery drones, more goddamned metallic birds flying a little too low. An elderly woman is crossing the road in the opposite direction, a poodle trotting at her heels. The resemblance is striking. Both have fluffy grey-white curls, the same lugubrious expressions. She nods at me, lips twisting upwards in what I presume is a smile. I smile back. The fleeting interaction strikes something deep inside me. I can't remember when I last acknowledged someone on the street, had three friendly in-person exchanges before eleven in the morning. In London, everyone walks with their heads down, collars turned up and shoulders hunched over their smartphones, with expressions that suggest they'd rather be swallowed up by a manhole than make eye contact with a stranger. The last time I chatted to a good friend was several months ago, when Xander dropped by Old Fen Cottage for my birthday. We have tried to meet up again since then, but work and life just got in the way.

I should ring him later, check if he's OK.

I've been meaning to tell Xander about Christian, but I managed to convince myself that I shouldn't jinx things by discussing them prematurely, admit to a fledging relationship that hadn't fully taken flight.

Maybe it's time to tell Xander, get matters off my chest.

Hmm, I can't remember when I last phoned a friend, just to have a random friendly conversation. No one phones each other any more (maybe folks who have stuff to hide still do). I wish I had a female buddy, a sympathetic friend. Someone who I can be frank with, someone who isn't quick to judge or retreat behind an imaginary wall of offence (people get offended too easily these days). Someone I could just ring on a whim, pour out the recent problems I have been having, the fact that I have to head back to my cottage and do a pregnancy test . . . alone. I spend too much time writing soulless lines of code, staring at impersonal, back-lit screens.

I feel a tear stinging the corner of my eye as I approach the door of the convenience store. Damn it, I shouldn't be getting emotional – I hope pregnancy hormones aren't to blame. Nor should I feel sorry for myself. It's much too early in the morning for that. Dark, miserable thoughts should be reserved for the late evenings, when one contemplates a giant glass of Malbec in front of a brooding, unlit fireplace. I should just get Mrs Deakins' newspaper and head back home . . . to do more coding on an impersonal, back-lit screen.

I swipe the tear away, face the shop's camera. A small light flashes; the front door glides open from left to right. The first thing I see is a shelf packed with full-priced diet pills, next to a crate of half-priced vitamins. I eventually spot a copy of *The Times* in the corner. The main headline reads: 'Driverless Truck Kills 11, Including Boy of Two'. I lift the newspaper from the shelf, causing a sensor to beep (and hopefully deduct the correct amount from my credit card). As I do so, a small teaser headline at the top of the front page catches my eye:

The Real Reason Why Alexander King is Staging a Fashion Show in London This Evening
Exclusive Feature, Section 2, Page 3

I stare at the headline for a couple of moments before running back to the shelf and grabbing a second copy for myself.

I'll read the article when I get home.

KitKat is snoozing on my desk in a furry bundle, tail flopping across my computer. Oh dear, I hope he hasn't been thumping the keyboard with his paws while the software was running. I rush forward and nudge him gently to the floor. This time he issues a loud indignant miaow, before arching his back and sauntering out of my study with a raised tail. I hit the keys with nervous fingers, only to discover that the *Processing Data* pop-up window has since been replaced by . . .

. . . a small window that says *Results*.

I gasp, barely believing my eyes. Has the software come up with something usable, produced the information Damian had hoped for? I click on the window; a document flashes up on screen.

41

Its title is: *Probability of Committing Murder.*

OMG. It's a seven-page report. I collapse on the chair. There should be a single name on each page. This means that CriminalX has identified seven suspects, seven possible killers in ascending order of probability. Taking a deep breath, I click on page 1. It says:

Giovanni De Luca (12.41%)
Fashion designer, Founder of Gio & Gio (G&G)

Exhilaration fills me as I scan the accompanying paragraph; this looks like the sort of informative prediction I had dreamt CriminalX might produce. Damian will be mightily chuffed when I pass De Luca's profile to him. I click on page 2. A new name flashes up on screen:

Steve Mortimer (13.67%)
Head of Millinery & Bags, Alexander King

Hmm. The last time I saw Steve was at one of Xander's crazy cocktail parties, years ago. He was high on God knows what (as usual), had two beautiful blondes clinging on to his arms (as usual, too). I've always thought of Steve as a substance supplier, a popper peddler, a contraband courier. Could he also be a cold-blooded murderer? Frowning, I click on the third page. It says:

Nigel Olaf Avery (13.85%)
Senior Legal Advisor, Alexander King

A smidgen of doubt floods me as I read the accompanying profile. I have known Nigel Avery for as long as I have known Steve Mortimer. Nigel has always been a pompous, arrogant type. He strikes me as the sort of person who would score higher on the scale for fraud; I'm not so sure about murder. Grimacing, I click on the fourth page. It says:

Lucia Graves (17.79%)
Personal Assistant, Alexander King

The euphoria inside me is fast evaporating. This isn't going so well, now. In fact, this is getting embarrassing. Lucia wasn't even in Manhattan yesterday night; she has just texted me to say that she's on her way to New Scotland Yard to help the police with their investigations. Damn, it looks like CriminalX's algorithms aren't up to scratch yet. Maybe the next prediction will be a little better, a little more realistic. I cross my fingers before clicking on page 5, only to recoil in disbelief. There's a name at the top of the page, in bold, black letters like the other names I've seen. It isn't a name I expected to find. It's a name I know well.

Extremely well, in fact.

Alexander Octavius King (18.34%)
Fashion Designer, Founder of Alexander King

There is no happy mean between fame and obscurity. Everyone either wants you at exactly the same time, or no one wants you at all.

Alexander King, interview in *Vogue*

Chapter Three

Xander

Light is breaking over the Atlantic. Hazy lavender clouds spiral beneath me, their eastern edges turning rosy peach-gold. It all looks deceptively tranquil, unlike the chaos that surrounded me before I boarded the plane. I wish I could sit here in silence, drink in more of the dawn, savour the simple act of stirring sugar into my coffee. Unfortunately, my lawyer, Nigel, is still bombarding me with pointless questions. I was tempted to sack him a couple of months ago (because I detest lawyers in general), but Steve said it would be a bad idea. Not when I needed a massive bunch of non-disclosure forms and someone to sort out all the necessary legalese in the run-up to the shows. Maybe I should have sacked Nigel all the same, spared myself this current state of grief.

I watch him take a large swig of gin and tonic, dab his mouth with a monogrammed handkerchief. One of the down-sides of fame is that you end up accumulating the (inevitable) entourage of minders, handlers and 'no'-people, all on the same private jet. Folks with greasy fingertips, opportunistic clingers-on to the bandwagon of success. They call them-selves 'aides'. I call them 'parasites'. Because I'm the one who ends up footing their fucking bills. Paying for all their goddamned gins, tasteless tonics and monogrammed hand-kerchiefs.

But as of today, I don't care. Nigel can have as many drinks as he likes. I no longer give a shit. Not when a poor girl has died at what was supposed to be one of the biggest shows of my lifetime. I can still hear the anguished cries from the audience, see people fleeing in a giant stampede of fear, smell burning flesh mingled with acrid smoke, touch blood oozing over steel pylons, taste silent screams frozen in mouths.

I wonder why my five senses have fused into a topsy-turvy mess, why I still detect bitter notes of horror wafting through the air.

'Can you take me through your movements backstage, minutes before the bomb went off?' Nigel says.

'We went through all of that already.' My voice is curt.

'The police will be waiting for us at Heathrow when we land.'

'I don't give a shit about them.'

'You should.' He leans back into his seat, folding his arms.

'Why?'

'They could say that tonight's show will be such a security nightmare, they can't allow it to go ahead.'

'That's rubbish.' I roll my eyes at Nigel. 'It's a private event, not a public one.'

'You have public figures on the guest list. Royalty, even.'

'Still.'

'The police can make life difficult for you. They have the power to detain . . . I mean, to question people for hours.'

He pauses, taking another long swig of gin and tonic before fixing his eyes back on me. The plane is shuddering and lurching again; it has been a bumpy ride out of JFK thus far.

'You wouldn't want to spend the whole afternoon in New Scotland Yard giving a so-called "witness statement", would you?'

Damn it. He's right, even if lawyers are seldom right. Maybe this man has just earned his gin and tonic. The last thing I want is to spend the rest of the afternoon within the stultifying confines of New Scotland Yard, being grilled by annoying little police officers with thick spectacles and rabbit teeth.

'It doesn't hurt to be prepared.' Nigel's voice is firm. 'So, what were you doing before the bomb went off?'

Nigel deserves top marks for persistence. I grind my teeth before replying: 'Peering through a side curtain, keeping an eye on the runway.'

'Any idea who gave Ally that handbag, how she ended up carrying that item?'

'It could have been one of Steve's backstage helpers.' I have to work hard to keep my voice level, although I'm sorely tempted to throttle the man. 'Each of them was given a printout of what each model would be wearing, the accessories that I had picked to go with each outfit.'

'When were they given these printouts?'

'Three days ago.'

'So, you're saying that everyone backstage knew that Ally would be carrying that handbag.'

'Pretty much so, yes.'

'Do you know why anyone might have wanted to put a bomb inside the bag?'

I scowl at Nigel.

'No,' I say. 'I wish I did.'

'Much better,' he says. 'You sound a bit less confused, this time. Definitely less antagonistic.'

I clench my fingers.

'I'm exhausted,' I say, lifting my glass and gulping down all of its contents before setting it down with a pointed thud. 'I'm going to get some sleep before we arrive in London.'

'Of course,' he says, nodding and rising from his seat. 'It'll probably do you good. Buzz me as soon as you wake up, we ought to go through a few more possible questions before we land.'

I watch Nigel waddle past the thick velvet curtain, still clinging on to his gin and tonic. Bloody little clingers-on. They're everywhere, plaguing my existence with their parasitic demands, all in the guise of aiding me. This private jet of mine is just a fucking clinger-on carrier. I turn back, look out of the window again. The clouds have acquired a tiramisu-like consistency, morphed into a fluffy cream layer above the sea. I wish I could sink into them, forget about Manhattan . . .

'You OK?' A voice causes me to jump.

I spin around in my seat to discover that Steve Mortimer has emerged from behind the curtain and is staring at me with concern on his face.

'Yeah,' I say, shrugging.

'You still look shaken.'

'Can't help it.'

'Need anything to feel better?' He raises an eyebrow at me.

I shake my head.

'Thanks, but I still have lots of shit in my bag.'

He nods.

'I'll try get some rest,' I say.

'OK.'

He nods again before vanishing through the curtain. Unlike me, he looks surprisingly unruffled for someone who could have been blasted to the skies. He was probably even closer to the bomb when it exploded; I'm glad he emerged without a single scratch. Maybe Steve can handle crap a lot better than me.

Perfectly on cue, the flight attendant pokes her curly head around the curtains. A tiny thing with wide aquamarine eyes, eyes that have been spared the carnage that was Manhattan. She's wearing a scarlet uniform with jaunty epaulettes and a peaked cap that looks like an upside-down boat. Whoever designed her uniform did a great job. Maybe it was me. I vaguely recall designing an airline outfit years ago . . .

'Can I get you anything else, Mr King?' she says.

'Another whisky, please.'

'Of course.'

I pull out my phone as she disappears behind the curtain. After the madness that was Manhattan, I didn't have time to read today's iPrediction. I reach out to tap the app, only to freeze before my finger touches the screen. Does it matter, any more? Do I still give a shit as to what might happen today or tomorrow?

The answer is no.

A bloody resounding *no*.

Predictions only matter when the future matters. When we no longer care about the future, the only thing worth caring about is the past. How do we erase bits that haunt us, bits that we don't wish to carry to our graves? Maybe someone will invent a device that blasts away bad memories from our brains, leaving us only with the more palatable ones. In the meantime, we will all have to make do with the latest VR technology (and potent cocktails of drink and drugs) as a means of confronting everyday reality.

Ah yes, drugs.

How could I have forgotten my drugs?

I reach into my carry-on bag, pull out a case and open it. Five small bottles greet me, each containing pills of a different colour. I tip their contents into my palm. Two of the yellow, two of the green, one of the blue, three of the white-and-red . . . The flight attendant materialises at my side, a small glass of water and a giant tumbler of whisky in her hand. I can see her eyes widening as she takes in the psychedelic blur of pills nestled in my palm.

'Please make sure no one disturbs me until we land,' I say.

'Of course,' she says.

I fling the pills into my mouth, swallow them in a single gulp. I look out of the window again. The clouds are now wispy whirls of yellow-red and peach-gold. Clouds are wonderful little things. They are a reminder of just how immaterial my life has been thus far, how everything around me – and what I've achieved or failed to achieve – is just fucking inconsequential.

Something's screaming again in my head, an agonised shriek tapering off into a long wailing call.

It's not just something.

It's *someone*.

Damn it.

My fingers are still trembling, upon closer inspection. I've tried not to look too closely at my hands, ever since my parasitic crew rushed me out of Manhattan and straight onto a private jet.

What did they say shell shock was?

Is it supposed to be a delayed response?

Or is that the definition of PTSD?

Damn it. I can still see that pair of pink tortoiseshell glasses, snapped neatly across their middle. The decapitated champagne flute next to a single white glove, soaked with remnants of human flesh. The man in his bloody tuxedo on the front row, curled up in a tiny ball on the floor and screaming for his mother. The once-beautiful girl sprawled in the middle of the catwalk, bathed in a velvety pool of blood. One of her arms is missing, torn away by the force of the blast.

Her eyes are dead, stone dead.

Death is only intriguing at a distance, not at close quarters. That's what I learned late yesterday night. Damn it. My nerves are shot, my head is spinning and none of these bloody pills are fucking calming me down. I need to stop thinking about Manhattan, drive away these terrible images from my head. Get some rest, a moment or two of respite before facing the police.

I down the whisky in a single gulp. It burns my throat, takes the sharp edge off my thoughts. But those images are still there, blood cascading in dark rivulets down the catwalk . . .

Maybe music will do the trick.

I hit the button for Sleep Mode, plunging the cabin into almost complete darkness. I cram buds into my ears and flip audio channels until I get to Ambient AI: AI-composed music which apparently puts people to sleep in a flash. A series of gong booms and tinkly chimes begin caressing my ears. I slump back, close my eyes. Unfortunately, I can only feel an expanding vibration across my skull, causing something ghastly to crawl inside my head and tickle it violently.

Grimacing, I flip channels to Classical Music, causing Johann Strauss II to whirl into my ears in a crescendo of Viennese strings. The plane judders, before plunging a little. We've probably hit another damned air pocket over the Atlantic. I let the effervescent music wash over my body for several minutes, hoping it will carry some of the tension away, only to groan in disappointment.

This isn't fucking working.

The problem with fame and riches is that neither fame nor riches guarantee a good night's sleep. Sleep is a function of inner peace. People who fall asleep in agitation merely remain suspended in that sorry state; they never truly find respite from the madness around them.

True rest comes from inner relaxation, they say.

How fucking true.

Desperate times call for desperate measures. I should try VR, instead. It's on the primitive side but it has worked before. Helped me find a modicum of mental comfort and drift into blessed oblivion.

I remove the earbuds and extract my VR headset from my carry-on bag. Guess I should count myself lucky that the CEO of Google is a good friend of mine, that he gave me a developer prototype of their next-generation headset for my birthday. He even customised the set with my initials (I made a shiny little dinner jacket for him, in return). I strap the bulky device around my head (why can't tech geeks design something a little less clunky and ridiculous looking, a little more fashion forward?) and blink frantically at the rotating menu until I reach the option that says:

MAYA

I nod to confirm my choice. Another set of options flashes up:

Would you like Maya to:
A. Inspire
B. Reassure
C. Tell the truth
D. All of the above

I nod again when (D) *All of the above* rotates back into view. The world fades into inky darkness for a couple of seconds, before bursting back into a pointed funnel of light. Sharp scorching light that blinds me for a moment, before taking the shape of a single, perfect figure.

She's exactly as I remember her, the day before she died (thank heavens the software's consistent, even if it's on the primitive side). Tall, blonde, ethereal. A single lock of hair is blowing into her face, a flaxen peroxide wisp. She reaches up to brush the lock away, smiling at me. Her cheeks are a lovely shade of pale peach, her complexion as dewy as her magnetic eyes.

'Hey, Xander,' she says.

I hold up my sketch.

'Hmm,' she says, eyes widening as she takes in the outfit's squiggly contours. 'Looks like you've been busy.'

I smile back as yet another menu of options emerges before me, also in rotating format:

What would you like to do next, Xander?
A. Tell Maya she's inspiring
B. Apologise
C. Get her advice
D. All of the above

I nod at option D when it swings around again, causing the menu to retreat out of focus and Maya to glimmer back into full view again. She seems taller and more slender, her face twice as angular (and I thought the software was consistent).

'You inspired it.' I hear the words coming from my mouth, in my own voice. 'That's the truth.'

She grins.

'I'm sorry I made you stand around in my studio for so many goddamned hours last week,' I add.

'You don't have to apologise,' she says.

'It must have added to your suffering.'

She shrugs.

'Wish I could repeat last week, be a little kinder,' I continue.

Her eyes are luminous, forgiving. They are the eyes of a person who understands what I'm trying to say, recognises that my words of apology are coming in an honest straight line from my heart. For one reason or another, the fact that I've said sorry not once but twice is strangely reassuring. I feel my shoulders softening, the thick leaden weight on them lifting a little.

She smiles at me, before reaching out to squeeze my hand.

'Things happen because they're written in the stars,' she says. 'We just have to understand why they happen the way they do.'

'That's tricky.'

'Some things take time. *Everything* takes time.'

The weight on my shoulders is lifting further. I'm swaddled by cotton wool, enveloped by a blanket of dense, amorphous fabric. Swallowed up by a vast continuum of space, sucked into a spiralling chasm of time. Maya's still smiling away at me, with luminous heavy-lidded eyes.

Her smile is reassuring, languid.

I can feel my own eyelids drooping.

Finally.

A soft voice cuts across molten darkness, shredding my blissful state of suspended animation into bits.

'Mr King,' it says.

I drift upwards, only to feel my consciousness pulling me back down again. It's telling me that I shouldn't head back up to the surface, even if I'm perilously close to it, because terrible things are lurking at the top.

'Mr King.' The voice is cajoling, persistent.

Damn it.

Guess I have to surface, whether I like it or not. I shove temptation down and haul myself up in the direction of tumultuous reality. I force my eyes open. A rotating menu darts before me:

What would you like to do next?

A. Repeat simulation

B. Return to Main Menu

I'm tempted to repeat the simulation, drift back into Maya's world of languid, forgiving smiles. But I know I can't, damn it. I yank the VR headset off to discover the petite flight attendant peering down at me, tucking a lock of hair behind her ear and looking thoroughly apologetic.

'Sorry to interrupt your rest, Mr King, but we landed at Heathrow about ten minutes ago,' she says.

Fucking hell, did I sleep through an entire landing? Did the pills eventually perform their magic, when washed down with copious amounts of whisky and VR? I glance out of the window.

The flight attendant is right. The plane is stationary, no longer lurching about in the air. Grey tarmac yawns and rolls beneath a dour English sky, punctuated by three baggage trucks with flashing lights. A chequered blue-and-yellow car is zooming past the plane, scooting to an abrupt halt. It also has flashing strobe lights. Unfortunately for me, it isn't a baggage truck. The word POLICE is emblazoned across its side. G&T Nigel is right. Looks like I'm in for some immediate fun – or a whole afternoon of ghastly pain – at New Scotland Yard. Why the fuck did I take so many pills earlier? My mind feels like a disconnected time funnel, one warping in and out of focus, with little jagged strips of broken glass around it.

I look back up at the flight attendant and say with a grimace: 'I'll have another whisky, please.'

Geeks are the new overlords of humanity. They control where data flows, where data ends up, how data is used. They bring down governments, manipulate our minds, shape our preferences and consumption habits. They also get very rich along the way. That's why the Zuckerbergs are the new Rockefellers, the Bezoses are the new Rothschilds, the Musks are the new Vanderbilts. They define the way we behave. They control the way we think. They predict the way we act. They make us more predictable.

Op-ed in the *Guardian*, 7 June 2030

Chapter Four

Viola

I bury my head in my hands, dismay flooding deep. The fifth page spat out by CriminalX says:

Alexander Octavius King (18.34%)

Fashion Designer, Founder of Alexander King

Age: 40

IQ Score: 143

Education: BA in Fashion Design, Parsons NYC

(2005–2009)

Background: Founded Alexander King in 2010 with a capital injection from London socialite Tara Russell-Cadogan. Described in the media as: 'an unstable genius', 'a death-obsessed designer with an intuitive eye for theatrics' and 'a man whose life is about death, a man who makes a killing by screwing the living'. Received a caution from the Dutch police for bringing an unbranded luggage bag with traces of explosives into Amsterdam's Schiphol Airport in 2022, causing all flights to be suspended for two hours. Said the bag had belonged to a friend he was staying with, that he had

58

grabbed it at random to put his pills in before leaving
for the airport and he had no idea why there were
traces of explosives on it. Recent Google searches:
'Alexander King', 'Maya von Meyer', 'Giovanni De Luca',
'how to update a will', 'creative ways to die', 'prostate
cancer', 'cryotherapy', 'euthanasia', 'Dignitas' &
'cryogenics'.
Status: Backstage (BS) – Manhattan & London

I'm tempted to cry. Damian will have a choking fit when I
tell him that CriminalX has identified Alexander King as a
suspect because the man is fixated with death and has been
googling himself . . .

. . . and prostate cancer.

Prostate cancer? A wave of alarm sweeps over me. Does
Xander have cancer? Is this why he has also been googling
'cryotherapy' and 'euthanasia'? I should find out if I manage to
ring him later today. In the meantime, I have a problem. A
massive one. CriminalX is half-baked. I was certain that a
person's criminal propensity could be predicted with accuracy,
that one can devise the perfect algorithm for measuring a
person's predisposition to rape or murder.

Looks like I have been deluding myself all along.

A tear wobbles at the corner of my eye. I wish I had a
sympathetic ear at my side. I reach for my smartphone to
call Christian, to hear his calm, reassuring voice . . . only to
yank my hand back. I'm supposed to be in a huff with him;
that's why I came back here in the first place. Plus, Christian
hasn't got a clue as to what I've been doing for Damian,
because I'm not supposed to tell anyone. I can't ring Christian
and complain about work . . . when I can't reveal what this

particular job is all about. Damn it, I shouldn't cry. I really shouldn't. I should mop up my tears, concentrate, read the remaining two profiles.

A blue window flashes up on the screen:

You look a little down, Viola. You have also spent 25 consecutive minutes at your desk. I suggest you take a break.

Would you like a drone to bring you coffee from the kitchen?

I hit the No button and click on page 6, only to freeze. This can't be. This surely can't be. I stare at the computer, shock and disbelief barrelling deep into my chest. Yet no amount of blinking can erase the stark black words in front of me, the sixth name CriminalX spat out. The screen says:

Christian Verger (20.17%)
Commissioner of the Metropolitan Police
Age: 47
Education: BA (Hons) in Philosophy, Cambridge University
(2002–2005); MSc in Criminology and Criminal Justice,
Oxford University (2009–10)
IQ Score: 138 (Unverified)
Background: Joined the Met as a constable in 2005,
appointed Commissioner in February 2030. Participated in
the 2028 BBC documentary *The Met: Paradoxes of
Policing*; a genetic test in conjunction with the show
revealed a high-risk version of the monoamine oxidase
A gene (carriers are thirteen times more likely to have a
history of repeated violent behaviour). Facial analysis of
photos in public domain indicates a smaller angle
between the two lines from the tip of the nose to the
corners of the mouth (19.6% of criminals have this

feature). Recent Google searches include: 'Alexander
King', 'Maya von Meyer', 'illegal drone deliveries of
firearms', 'NYPD report on murder rates', 'how to deal
with imposter syndrome' & 'how to defuse arguments at
home'.
Status: Back row (Seat ZZ217) – London

Damian is *definitely* going to cut my funding. I can see his
face when I tell him that the Commissioner ought to be one
of the main suspects, because Mr Verger has the wrong genes
and looks like a criminal.

CriminalX isn't just a failure.

It's a *disaster*.

I'm a failure, for sure.

A disaster, too. They say that Artificial Intelligence is only
as intelligent as the information fed to it. Looks like in the
case of CriminalX, the software is as stupid as the person who
coded it.

A tear trickles down my cheek. I brush it away with the
back of my hand. Wait a minute. Why on earth does Christian
have a back-row seat to the London show? Why didn't he tell
me he's going tonight? And why on earth has he been googling
'Maya von Meyer'? Looks like I'm not the only person in our
relationship that has been hiding things. So Christian has more
secrets in his closet. Why hasn't he been more forthcoming
with the woman he's engaged to, hopes to marry? Annoyance
mingled with frustration strikes deep; I grit my teeth as I scroll
to the final page.

Horror spreads over me.

It's another name I know well.

All too well.

Viola McKay (20.17%)
Freelance Software Engineer
Age: 41
Education: BSc in Computer Science, Edinburgh
University (2007–2011)
IQ Score: 178 (Admitted to Mensa at the age of nine)
Background: Did a series of summer internships at Jimmy
Choo (2008), Philip Treacy (2009) & Alexander King (2010)
before turning freelance. Facial analysis suggests high
upper-lip curvature (23.4% of criminals have this
characteristic) and a shorter distance between inner
corners of eyes (criminals tend to have a shorter distance
between the two points). Recent Google searches
include: 'Maya von Meyer', 'genetic predisposition to
murder', 'what makes a rapist rape', 'how to live with a
man', 'latest scientific research on kleptomania' & 'how to
win arguments at home'.
Status: no-show (NS) – London

This time I collapse on my chair, blood running cold.

Macabre works of art channel darkness away from the soul, ensure only loveliness and light are left behind. That's why novelists who write about gruesome murders appear well adjusted in person. That's why painters who produce cheery works of art often seem scary up close, giving you the impression that something is a little bit dead inside them.

Lucia Graves, article in Vanity Fair

Chapter Five

Christian

I peer through the window, we're almost at New Scotland Yard. Big Ben is whizzing by in a blur of Roman numerals, a forceful reminder that my time on this planet may well be fast running out. iPredict must surely think that I'm going to die because of what happened in Manhattan, because it knows I have a ticket to King's show tonight. Which puts a whole new spin on the word 'deadline'. But what if iPredict knows something more sinister about my future? What if the app takes into account factors of which I'm unaware, events that will ultimately cause my demise?

The image of a grey granite gravestone – one dated 9 June 2030, with my name etched in capital letters – wafts before me, a large and forbidding mausoleum to a reluctantly departed ex-being.

Fear stabs me hard, causing something odiously bitter to rise to my throat. I gulp. Let me see. Could iPredict have updated itself since I last checked? Seized by desperate (and probably false) hope, I fish out my phone, tap the corresponding icon. I scan the prediction, take in the final line:

Chance of dying: 99.74%

Damn it, the percentage hasn't budged. Not the slightest bit. Maybe I should do something with my hands, distract myself from these morbid possibilities wafting about in my head. Maybe I should call Viola again. I pull out my smartphone and tap her number, only to hear 'You've reached Viola McKay. Please leave your message after the beep and I'll get back to you . . .'

I terminate the call with a groan, just before my car swings into the underground car park at New Scotland Yard. It's now the sixth time I've called Viola this morning. Maybe I should have left a message, but I don't know what to say. Or maybe I do. I should have said: *Please come back, Vi.*

Oh dear. I can see my secretary, Ginny, up ahead, her jet-black hair pinned up into a severe bun. She's waiting next to the red spot where I usually disembark from my car, armed with a giant clipboard. If Ginny's standing there, it's a sign of a busy day ahead, a day where lots of ad hoc, on-the-spot decisions are required of me. The problem about decision-making is that the less time you have to make each decision (and the more people you have breathing down your neck), the crappier each decision tends to be. I attended a 'Crisis and Decision-Making' course at police training school and that was the only damned thing I still remember from it.

'You've reached your final destination, Commissioner,' says Alexa, taking a neat turn around a pillar and gliding to a stop above the red spot. 'I'm pleased to say that we have arrived ninety-seven seconds ahead of schedule.'

I'm tempted to make a scathing remark about it being the wrong destination, but I bite my tongue. There's no point arguing with a machine, because the argument is usually a one-sided one.

I stuff the newspaper clipping back into my briefcase and scramble out of the car.

'Morning, Christian,' says Ginny.

'Morning, Ginny,' I say, watching the BMW scoot away into the distance in search of its designated parking space.

'Hope you had a good night's rest.'

I shrug.

'You have a nine o'clock appointment with the Bell Task Force,' she says, leading me across the carpeted foyer and up the private escalator to my office. 'Their Chief rang just now to hint that they have made little progress, but they still hope to discuss some policy-related issues.'

'Ring him back, say we'll postpone the meeting to Monday.'

'OK.'

'Tell them they should work a bit harder, with the Prime Minister demanding results.'

'Will do. By the way, the PM's secretary says her boss will ring you as soon as she gets out of her Cabinet meeting. Basic voice call, as usual.'

Why am I not surprised?

'Sure.'

'The Commissioner of the City of London Police would also like a quick word with you.'

Ah, my dear friend Robyn Clifford, on top of things as usual. She has provided all sorts of brisk yet kindly advice since I received news of my appointment, helpful tips that I'm eternally grateful for.

'I was planning to have a word with Robyn, too.'

Ginny grimaces as she studies her clipboard.

'The head of the *Carabinieri* is still agitating for a reply,' she says.

'Tell him we'll get back to him on Monday.'

We jump off the escalator and head down the long corridor, our feet sinking into carpet. Harold's secretary, a mousy-looking girl whose name eludes me, gives me a respectful nod as she walks past.

'And . . . the NYPD will be updating us later this morning,' says Ginny, scanning her clipboard again. 'They're five hours behind us, as you know.'

'Alexander King, hey?'

'Very much so.'

'Harold can deal with them. I've told him to bring King in.'

'By the way, King's PA, Lucia Graves, is waiting outside your office.'

I stare at Ginny in surprise as we turn the corner, nearly crashing into a coffee-delivery robot. The device is emitting a strong incense-like smell (it probably doubles as a dust-mite remover and air purifier, too). I'm tempted to kick it. There are so many self-operating devices scuttling around the office these days, they are collectively turning into a health and safety hazard.

'Who called her in?' I say.

'She decided to come in herself. Said she wishes to talk to *you*, in particular. I can't remember anyone walking in from the street before, asking reception if they can speak to the Commissioner.'

I detect a disapproving note in Ginny's voice.

'Ah, there she is.'

A striking raven-haired woman is sitting outside my office, wearing an angular black dress with a choker-shaped collar that looks like it's travelled straight from the pages of *Vogue* to

New Scotland Yard (it probably has). Rapier-like blades dangle from her ears, long thin shards of silver and obsidian. Her mouth is painted a dark, almost-black red. Her eyebrows are thin, plucked to perfection. She has enormous brown eyes, eyes that remind me of a young gazelle's.

'The Commissioner has calls with the Prime Minister and other important people,' says Ginny to Lucia in a prim-sounding voice, one that suggests she doesn't approve of such dramatic fashion levity within the straitlaced confines of New Scotland Yard. 'He's a very busy man . . .'

'I'll speak to you after my calls,' I say to Lucia, interrupting Ginny.

Lucia gets to her feet and says, 'I'm glad to hear this, Commissioner. I came in hoping to talk to the right person.'

'I'm definitely a person,' I say with a sigh. 'It's difficult to talk to a real person these days, with all these machines getting in our way. That said, I'm not so sure if I'm the right one.'

I settle down as Ginny shuts the door. The phone on my desk tinkles almost immediately. I pick up the receiver.

'Morning, Christian,' a crisp female voice sounds in my ear. 'How are you doing today?'

'Surviving,' I say, resorting to Viola's favourite default answer.

'That's what the fittest do, don't they?' The Prime Minister chuckles. 'How's the Bell Task Force getting on?'

Oh dear, isn't this precisely what iPredict thought the PM would say? The app also predicted that I would have to apologise to her when she called. Unfortunately I can't think of a better option.

'The last I heard, they weren't getting anywhere,' I say. 'I'm sorry they're so slow-moving.'

'Ha.' The PM sounds amused. 'My iPredict said this morning that you'd end up apologising for their tardiness.'

'So did mine.'

'Do we even need to have this conversation, then? Anyhow, it would be great if you could give them a nudge.'

'Will do.'

'A hard prod, even.'

'One hard prod coming up.'

'On a completely different note, I don't like what happened in Manhattan yesterday night.'

'Neither do I.'

'I don't like it because . . .' the PM trails off briefly, '. . . because my daughter Elsa is on tonight.'

It takes me a while to digest what the PM has just said.

'You mean, she's going to the show?'

'She's one of the *models*.'

'Oh dear.' I rack my brains for everything I know about Elsa. If what I've read about the PM's daughter in the tabloids is true, Elsa is a spoilt sixteen-year-old brat who surrounds herself with the bright and beautiful and spends most of her time lurching from one fancy Chelsea watering hole to another. I didn't realise that Elsa was an aspiring model, let alone an actual one.

'I hope adequate security measures will be in place for the show,' continues the PM in a firm, no-nonsense voice. 'Someone should be checking all accessories on the catwalk, in particular.'

I grimace at the receiver. It looks like the Met and the City of London Police will be acting as the new security guards for Elsa the Prime Minister's daughter, whether we like it or not.

'The show is technically inside Robyn Clifford's jurisdiction,' I say. 'But we'll sort something out together.'

'Brilliant,' I can hear the PM exhaling over the phone. 'Elsa will be absolutely devastated if the show doesn't go ahead. Thinks it will be her big break, the one that will launch her career.'

'We'll do our best.'

'Excellent.' The PM sounds relieved. 'I'll leave the policing in your capable hands, then.'

The line goes dead. I stare at the receiver for a couple of moments, before putting it down with a groan. It surely can't get any worse, with the PM's daughter gliding down the runway tonight. If Manhattan repeats itself, I will probably be remembered as the shortest-serving Commissioner in the history of the Met. At best, I will be gently prodded into early retirement.

If I'm still alive tomorrow, that is.

A pert knock on the door interrupts my thoughts. I look up; Ginny is poking her head into my office.

'I fielded another two calls while you were talking to the PM,' she says. 'One was the rep from the Committee on Virtual Reality Detectives, the other was the head of the new Committee on Drone Proliferation. Both were hoping to speak to you.'

I groan. Given the exponential proliferation of new committees in this august bureaucracy, there will soon be a Committee to Supervise All Other Committees. To make things worse, the head of the Committee on Drone Proliferation already has a reputation for droning on and on.

'Tell everyone I'll get back to them on Monday,' I say. 'Actually, could you clear my diary for the rest of the day, please? I'll only speak to Harold, Robyn . . . and the Prime Minister if she calls again.'

'Oh.' Ginny looks surprised.

'Need to concentrate on the King case,' I say.

'Ah.' She nods. 'Should I connect you with Mrs Clifford, then?'

'That would be great.'

'Give me a minute,' she says, retracting her head.

I stare at the door as it swings shut. My two major woes swim before me again. I fish out my smartphone, tap my way to iPredict.

Chance of dying: 99.74%

Damn it, the percentage is still the same. I stuff the phone back into my pocket with a sigh. My gaze strays to the photo in the wooden frame on my desk. It's of Viola and me, taken by a random passer-by during one of our weekend walks in the South Downs. Both of us are beaming away at the camera; Viola is peeking out mischievously from behind me, her thick shock of soft-black hair dancing in the wind, her arms twined around my shoulders. I remember our first date well, how I was struck by her dark, gamine features. How I was mesmerised by her boyish yet wittily interesting face, those luminously intelligent eyes. I still can't believe she's packed up and left for Old Fen Cottage. It's entirely my fault. How could I have let it happen?

The phone on my desk tinkles again. I pick it up.

'Hello, Christian,' says Robyn. 'How are you?'

'Surviving,' I say. 'What about you?'

'This Old Billingsgate business is giving me a headache.' She sighs over the line.

'Can we help?' I say.

'Well, if the Met could take the lead on the case, deal with the NYPD and FBI, that would be great.'

'We can most certainly do that.'

'We'll supply the manpower for tonight, scour Old Billingsgate for nasty little surprises.' Her voice is both crisp and curt.

'Let me know if you need back-up,' I say.

'Will do. I'll call again this afternoon with an update.'

'Thanks, Robyn.'

'It's I who should be thanking you, really.'

I put the phone down. Bless Robyn Clifford, the world's most efficient police commissioner. Our conversations are usually less than a minute long, but they are always straight-to-the-point and cover everything we both need to know. I wish life could be as efficient as Robyn.

Less messy.

There is another sharp tap on the door. I look up, only to see Ginny poking her head into my office again.

'Can Miss Graves come in now?' she says.

'Sure.'

Just then, it strikes me. This might be a fine opportunity for me to try out Viola's CAB App, the software she specially coded for me as a birthday present. I reach out to activate the app on my phone as Ginny enters the room, followed by Lucia.

'Please have a seat,' I tell Lucia.

She nods, tucking her slender frame into the chair opposite me. I can see her eyes widening as they take in the set of black-and-white prints behind my desk, all of the same myth-ical creature.

'Buzz if you need anything,' says Ginny, frowning at Lucia before walking out of the office.

'You must like phoenixes a lot,' says Lucia, inclining her head in the direction of the prints.

I shrug in silence.

'Mr King loves phoenixes, too. He did a show in Milan last year with a decapitated phoenix above the catwalk.'

'I presume you've come to discuss Manhattan, not Milan. I hear you received a note?'

She reaches into her snakeskin handbag and pulls out a plastic zip-lock bag containing a small white envelope.

'I'm sorry my DNA is all over it,' she says, giving me an apologetic shrug as she hands me the bag. 'I read lots of murder mysteries; they say you should always try to minimise contamination.'

'Your efforts are appreciated,' I say. I pull out a pair of latex gloves from my desk, put them on and fish out the envelope. Nothing is written on the front. I open it to discover a small rectangular sheet of white paper. The words on it are in old-fashioned Arial type, bold, 12-point. They say:

Xander is going to die at the London show in the same manner as his muse Maya did twenty years ago.

I look up at Lucia.

'How did you get this note?'

'I found it in my bag this morning.'

'That one?' I incline my head in the direction of her snakeskin bag, feeling a slight tingle of excitement. It has been a long time since I interviewed someone in conjunction with a case, got my hands dirty, so to speak. The main problem with being at the top of the hierarchy is that you spend most of your time at the bottom of a large, unforgiving mound of paperwork. I miss the tantalising scent of a trail, the electric buzz of an investigation, the self-deluding yet heady belief that I may be doing something useful with my brains and hands.

'Indeed.' She nods. 'It was tucked into an outer compartment, one that I seldom use.'

'Did you leave the bag unattended at any time recently?'

She nods again with a grimace.

'I did.'

'When and where?'

'Xander and I dropped by Old Billingsgate three days ago. He wanted to check if preparations were on track, just before flying out to Manhattan. I left my bag backstage when we went outside to inspect the runway.'

'How long was it there?'

'Probably about thirty minutes.'

'So . . . anyone backstage could have slipped the envelope inside.'

'Pretty much, yes.'

I make a quick e-note before continuing: 'You said you were hoping to speak to the right person.'

'Indeed.' She nods. 'What happened in Manhattan was awful. I'm really worried about Xander.'

She frowns at the carpet before looking back up at me.

'If something bad happens to him tonight, I'll always blame myself.'

To my surprise, Lucia reaches into her bag again and pulls out a folder. She opens it, extracts a sheet of paper and slides it over my desk.

'I shouldn't be showing this to you, to be honest,' she says.

I peer down at the sheet. It's a sketch of a frilly white dress. A peach-pink cherry-blossom motif flutters across the dress's midriff, floating down in exquisite waves to its knee-length hem. The outfit looks delicate and ethereal, extremely flattering to the feminine figure.

'A lovely dress,' I say.

'Precisely,' she says, a note of triumph in her voice. 'That's why I'm worried about tonight.'

I'm utterly confused now; I have no idea what Lucia's getting at. Damn it, it's been ages since I interviewed someone in conjunction with a case. I'm clearly losing my touch.

'Why?' I say.

She takes out a second sheet from the folder, passes it to me. This one's a sketch of a white dress with striking contours. It looks like something a devil or a goth would wear, albeit fashionable ones. A long red line spirals around the dress's midriff – a forked red tongue, upon closer inspection. The tongue is protruding from a smashed black skull on one of the dress's sleeves.

'That's Xander's,' says Lucia, inclining her head at the second sketch in my hand. 'Through and through. He designed that one in 2010, owes his career to his fascination with the morbid.'

'Decapitated phoenixes and smashed skulls,' I say, nodding.

'The first outfit I showed you . . .' she points at the sketch of the frilly white dress, 'will appear on the catwalk later this evening.'

'So you're saying that . . .' I trail off, still struggling to follow Lucia's line of reasoning.

'I'm saying that the dress will be a complete departure from what Xander has always designed.'

I'm both puzzled and intrigued.

'Why is this relevant?' I say.

'I have a theory.'

'A theory?'

'Bit of a long explanation.'

'Go on.'

'It's called the Reverse Darkness Theory. People who create morbid stuff tend to be lovely in real life. That's because the darkness inside them is channelled out and away, straight into their works. Folks who produce sweet fluffy stuff, on the other hand, can often be violent. That's because the darkness stays put inside, never quite drains away.'

I haven't heard this theory before. It sounds bonkers yet brims with tantalising possibilities. Lucia Graves surprises me, for sure. There are hidden depths to her personality that weren't obvious at first sight. Maybe this is why Alexander King made her his personal assistant.

She reaches into her folder, pulls out a third sketch and hands it to me. It's of yet another frilly white dress. A delicate plum blossom motif floats across its bodice, curls down to its knee-length hem in concentric waves. It looks very much like the first sketch she passed to me earlier.

'I presume this is also destined for tonight's catwalk?' I say.

She shakes her head.

'Oh no,' she says. 'Most definitely not. This dress went down the catwalk two summers ago. Milan Fashion Week, 2028. To complicate matters, it wasn't designed by Xander.'

This is all getting curiouser and curiouser, as Alice would say. I feel as if I've been swallowed up by a never-ending fashion rabbit hole. Lucia takes a deep breath before looking straight at me.

'This third dress was designed by Xander's rival, a man called Giovanni De Luca. He's the founder of Gio & Gio.'

The name most certainly rings a bell; I've seen swanky G&G shops bedecked with crystal chandeliers (and populated by the vacuous rich) in Mayfair and Belgravia. But I don't get the rival bit.

'Mr King's rival?'

'The media has been calling them rivals for decades. Maybe it's because they had their breakthrough shows in the same year, back in 2010.'

'Why are you showing me this sketch by Mr De Luca?'

'It encapsulates Gio's style. He owes his name and fame to floral, floaty designs.'

'I see.'

'Like Xander, Gio's style has not changed over the years.'

Aha, I think I know what Lucia is trying to say.

'Are you implying that Mr De Luca might be a dangerous person because he has been producing pretty floral designs for twenty years and hasn't quite got the darkness out of his system? While Mr King's all sweet and fluffy in real life because he creates dresses with skulls and devils?'

Lucia looks impressed.

'That's precisely my theory, yes,' she says.

The problem with theories is that they are usually just that. Theories. I study the three sketches in my hands. Dress Number One is definitely similar to Dress Number Three.

'And King will be putting a De Luca-style dress on the catwalk tonight,' I say, muttering the words under my breath.

'The sketches say it all, don't they?'

'That's hardly a reason for De Luca to bomb King's show in Manhattan, if that's what you're implying.'

'Gio and Xander had lunch together about five months ago. I overheard most of their conversation.'

'Right.'

'By the time they finished talking, I no longer had any appetite.'

'Why?'

'They made a little bet that afternoon. A bet to end all bets, one that could have led to the bomb in Manhattan.'

CriminalX
Lucia Graves (17.79%)
Personal Assistant, Alexander King
Age: 26
IQ Score: Unknown
Education: BA in Psychology, NYU (2021–25); BSc in Fashion Business Management, Fashion Institute of Technology (part-time, 2025–28)
Background: Worked as an intern at American *Vogue* (2025), *Harper's Bazaar* (2026) and as a PA for the celebrity editor Ekaterina Reva-Shulman at *Vanity Fair* (2027) before taking up her current job at Alexander King in 2029. Recent Google searches: 'best brokers in London', 'this season's three-inch killer stilettos', 'cash payment for drone deliveries' & 'death by shopping'. Recent online purchases: *Murder on the Orient Express*, *On Murder, Mourning and Melancholia*, *Kill Bill*, *Death on the Nile*, *The Murder of Roger Ackroyd* & *To Kill a Mockingbird*. One of her Facebook friends (1,765 in total) was imprisoned for shoplifting in Los Angeles in 2028.
Status: Backstage (BS) – London

Good things happen to other people. Not me. This is the story of my life.

Anonymous

Chapter Six

It all began when I saw him hurting her with an iron tong, as crystalline snowflakes tumbled outside our home in Montana. I must have been around fourteen or so, huddling next to the fireplace for warmth (we already had to ration our logs, those days). Wood crackled around my ears, as loudly as the sound of metal landing on flesh. The fire spat out sparks as vicious as the argument they were having. She had married him two months earlier, told me that she was bringing a new father home, a man who had wooed her by appearing next to her cash till at closing time with large bouquets of wilted lilies. She capitulated after a few days, agreed to go on a date with him.

Even agreed to marry him a few months later.

I was excluded from the happy occasion.

Or rather, I feigned illness that day, excluded myself. Told Mom that I had caught the flu, that I dared not go out into the bitter cold outside.

Mom didn't look surprised. She merely shrugged as she pinned her hair up into a high bundle of locks and dabbed a touch of gloss on her lips. Said I was entitled to throw a couple of extra logs on the fire, use her duvet if I felt too chilly. Make my own lunch and dinner from the scraps of food in the fridge, which consisted of a mouldy lettuce and an equally ancient cheese. Also warned me not to burn the place down by mistake. I later found out that the marriage ceremony involved the signing of papers in front of two witnesses (Mom's fellow cashiers), followed by a trip to a bar where everyone got very drunk (and where my new dad managed to smash someone's nose on his way out before collapsing face down in the snow).

I remember my first encounter with Step-Dad, weeks before he persuaded Mom to marry him. That night, he stumbled into my bedroom by mistake and flipped the light on, thinking it was the bathroom.

Light tore into my sleep-fuddled eyes.

I bolted up on my bed.

Honey Bunny, the scruffy grey toy rabbit I slept with, flew to the ground.

A man was standing in the middle of the room, unbuckling his belt. His bulk was massive. His face was flushed red. The jowls on his chin sagged halfway over his neck; the pock-marked skin on his face oozed a yellow, oily sheen. He smelt of weed and congealed beer, a stench that strangled both my throat and nose, made me choke a little. His hand froze briefly over his fly when he realised I was gaping at him. He recovered by pulling the zipper down, slowly and fully, before giving me a long appraising look that made feel like a heifer up for sale.

'And what do we have here?' he said, a chuckle erupting from his lips. 'A scared little rabbit?'

There was something about his tone, mocking yet pregnant with meaning, which made me twice as terrified.

'Pretty little thing, aren't you?' He swept a long, lingering gaze along my tousled hair, my quivering length.

'I ought to let you get your beauty sleep,' he continued, chuckling again. 'Sweet dreams, sweetie pie.'

He turned and waddled back out of the door, pants sliding halfway down his ample buttocks.

I didn't sleep a wink that night. I remember curling up in my bed until dawn broke, until the first faint notes of birdsong trickled through the frosted windows, wondering what manner of misfortune could have brought such a beast into our home. When Mom announced a couple of weeks later that she would be marrying him, I said that I would run away from home.

She spat and laughed.

'Oh yeah?' she said, her shoulders convulsing with mirth. 'And where exactly will you go?'

It was a good question. One I had no answer to. Not when I was only fourteen years old. Not when I was stuck in the middle of nowhere, where the nearest big town was forty-seven miles away.

'You shouldn't marry him,' I said in desperation.

'Why not?'

'He's evil.'

'He isn't,' she said, stubbing her cigarette out and smiling at the scratched silver ring on her left hand (it bore a small inscription that said 'Fidelis' and had apparently belonged to his grandmother). 'He brings me flowers, gives me things. And he'll stick around, unlike some other men I've known.'

The day she married him, I shredded the mouldy lettuce in the fridge to bits, wishing it was his face, before feeding the pieces to the flames. I then started on the cheese. It trickled down the extra logs I threw onto the fire, molten bits of foul fondue as yellow as the sheen on his skin.

I went to bed hungry that night.

When Mom started screaming in pain in front of the same fireplace two months later, courtesy of the iron tongs he used on her, that was when we both realised the same thing: she was wrong and I was right.

Shame she didn't realise that earlier.

That was the night I made my first, fierce resolution while still crouching next to the fireplace, trying to make myself inconspicuous as iron tongs came down hard opposite me.

My resolve was simple.

I would find a way out of this.

Mom bore it stoically, at first. She began turning up at her workplace with bruises on her upper arms, marks she would try to hide with long sleeves. When the bruises migrated to her lower arms, she would try to patch them up with a heavy-duty concealer stick that was unfortunately two shades darker than her skin tone. Loneliness and deprivation made her vulnerable, desperate for any scrap of affection that came her way, like a half-starved greyhound hoping for an extra morsel or two. He would storm out of the front door after unleashing his fury on her, only to crawl back the next morning and plant a slobbery kiss on her face (an area of her body that he took care never to mark), mumbling his usual red-cheeked apologies.

She took him back, every time. Even if the process involved longer and longer periods of grovelling at our doorstep. Words of 'apology' that became more voluble, more revolting each time. It's unbelievable how bouquets of half-dead lilies can melt a woman's heart. It's amazing what a slobbery kiss can do in the morning, when planted in the bright forgiving light of day.

It wipes out hurt.

Pain.

Dark memories of the night before.

She had to do an overnight shift once, to cover for an ill colleague. That was when he came into my room again, a couple of hours after I fell asleep. I heard a loud rustle at the door, a sound that infiltrated my semi-comatose dreams. It was the first sign that something was amiss.

Desperately wrong, in reality.

I should have acted at once. Done something to defend myself, to protect myself, to save myself. But I was so petrified, so taken aback by his audacity, I didn't do anything. My mind just flipped into disengage mode. I felt oddly detached from my body, as if I were staring at myself from a distance.

I didn't even scream.

His lips were wet, covered with an oily sheen. So wet, they were slimy. His hands were moist and oily, too. His breath smelt of pickled onions and fish guts, mingled with weed and beer.

Honey Bunny saw everything that happened from his corner of the bed. He was a good little rabbit, because he didn't tell a single person what happened that night. He couldn't.

Neither did I.

I couldn't, either.

Until this day, I still blame myself for not locking the door, for not being alert enough to the presence of evil.

The next morning, I told myself that I was a coward, a wimp for not putting up a fight. I scrubbed myself thoroughly, until my skin was raw and only ice-cold water leaked out of the faucet, until my skin felt as frozen as the icicles that hung down from the eaves of the roof. Yet his nauseating stench still lingered on me, filling me with deep revulsion. To make things worse, the oily sheen that oozed from the depraved depths of his soul had rubbed off on me, too.

I couldn't wash it off, no matter how hard I tried.

As I stared at my reflection in the mirror, I made a new resolution. The thought rose to my head like flames surging in the fireplace during the witching hour. I would find a way to purge my memories of that night, cleanse my skin and soul, scrub away his oily stench from my skin.

A week later, I sat under a tree in the schoolyard, trying desperately to concentrate on Dostoevsky's *Crime and Punishment* (which I had borrowed from the school library with the faint hope that Russian authors could tell me everything I needed to know about the speedy despatch of villains). My best friend tapped me on the shoulder. I swung around to discover that she had a small frown on her face and her large aquamarine eyes were brimming over with concern.

'You OK?' she said.

I stared at her. Something began bubbling to the surface, something unbearably hot and painful.

'I . . . I'm fine,' I said.

'Something's wrong,' she said, narrowing her eyes at me. 'You haven't been yourself for a week.'

'Nothing's wrong,' I said, knowing that my words sounded hollow even to my own ears.

She rolled her eyes before saying: 'I don't believe you.'

I couldn't hold her gaze, at that point. I just couldn't. I stared down at my canvas shoes, noticing that the cloth was getting so worn and threadbare, I could almost see my toes. Just then, she reached forward, touched my shoulder. I looked up, only to realise that she was staring at me with sympathy on her face.

'You're welcome to come over anytime,' she said. 'Especially if you need to get away from . . .'

She trailed off. It was then I realised that she knew, or at least suspected, what had happened to me.

'Gran says you should come over for dinner more often.'

'Thanks,' I said, nodding. 'Your gran's really kind.'

She tapped my shoulder again before walking off. I stared after her retreating figure in silence. That was the first time I discussed Step-Dad with my best friend, alluded to the presence of evil in my home.

The day he broke Mom's forehead was the day I realised just how wretched our situations had become. Earlier that day, I'd taken up my best friend's invitation, gone to her home. It was a special occasion: dinner to celebrate her fifteenth birthday (I was the only person there who wasn't family). Her gran was there, a frail-looking woman with a bright, robin-like face. She had patted me on the head, said I looked five inches taller than when she last saw me. She had also baked a giant apple cake for her granddaughter, placed fifteen candles on it. I remember feeling extremely envious when everyone crowded around the table with sparklers and party hats, singing 'Happy Birthday' in merry unison.

No one had ever baked a cake for my birthday.

Hell, no one had ever baked *anything* for me.

I trudged home in the snow at around half past eight, feeling well fed and watered for a change. I flung the door open, only to find Mom crouching next to the fireplace in a tiny ball. Back against stone, knees to her chest. A single pitiful ember flickered in the hearth, a forceful reminder that we no longer had logs to burn. One of Mom's hands was clasped over her tummy, knuckles clenched white. The other covered her forehead.

I ran up and gently prised her hands away, only to gasp.

'Did he do this to you?' I said.

No reply.

'I'm taking you to the doctor,' I said.

She laughed, a wheezy crackling sound at the back of her throat.

'Don't be silly,' she said, her words hoarse and rasping. 'There's nothing wrong with me.'

I studied her face, the deep oozing gash running across her forehead. Her glazed eyes void of life and hope. I tried to mop up the blood with a damp rag. It was the best I could do. That was the day he marked Mom's face for the first time. The gash became a nasty serrated scar, a series of raised pink cicatrices that never quite healed. It was the week she graduated from crack to heroin (I found telltale evidence in her handbag). This was why we finally ran out of logs to burn. It was also the moment when I realised that if Mom couldn't protect herself, there was no way she could protect me.

I remember having a significant conversation with Mom. It was such a long time ago, I can't remember whether it was before or after she remarried. The conversation was about my real dad, a man I had never met. It happened when she yelled at me for forgetting to buy an extra packet of cigarettes when I went to the grocer to pick up some eggs. Those days, we could only afford the cheapest ones, the ones just past their expiry dates.

'You're just as useless as the man who made you,' she said.

I froze, before turning to look at her. It was one of the rare times she mentioned him to my face.

'Is Dad still alive?' I said, repeating a question I had asked lots of times before, but to which I'd never received a straight answer. 'Why isn't he here?'

She wrinkled her nose before stubbing out the cigarette and saying in a flat voice: 'Your dad's dead.'

'You mean, dead and buried?'

'Dead to me.'

It took me a while to excavate past her words, grasp the implicit meaning buried within their depths.

'So you're basically saying that . . . he isn't dead, right?'

Silence overtook us, the sort of silence that pricked and stabbed at me by virtue of its agonised existence. It convinced me that Dad was out there, somewhere. I just had to find him. Somehow. Someday. It would help if I knew who he was, where he lived. I stared at the embers in the ashtray, the forlorn wisp of smoke curling up in the air, before plucking up my courage to ask: 'So where's Dad now?'

She remained silent.

'Where does he live?'

'That's enough.' Her voice was fierce, shot through with annoyance. 'Enough is enough.'

She lit up another cigarette and stormed out of the room, leaving a gnarled puff of smoke in her wake. That was the day I realised that Mom had kept a little Pandora's box of secrets all along, that she had locked the chest up and thrown away the key, long before I was born. I never managed to find the key when she was still alive. I also had more pressing things to worry about. Like hunger, once we could no longer afford the cheapest eggs.

Hunger does strange things to you. It's a gnawing feeling that digs into the pit of your stomach, burrows deep and never quite leaves, no matter how hard you try to dislodge it. It's an agony that follows you around like a wretched dog, one constantly baying for attention. It makes you lose reason.

Your sanity, on occasion.

It makes you want to kill, just for an extra scrap of food.

It makes wretched dogs rabid.

After Mom married Step-Dad, I went hungry most days. He must have stolen quite a lot from her purse because she kept coming home with less and less food each night. The rest she spent on cigarettes and heroin. Drugs and delusion were the two things that kept Mom going as cash ebbed away from her purse and flesh wasted away from her bones. Mouldy lettuces and ancient cheeses became memories of a glorious past. If not for the scraps of food handed out by the sympathetic cook at my school's canteen (and my best friend's family who fed me generously whenever I visited their home), I would have probably died of starvation that winter.

I owe so much to folks who weren't even family.

He tried coming into my bedroom again, but I was careful to lock the door. I would hear the latch turning in the middle of the night and freeze in my bed, praying the bolt would hold. It did, each time.

Thankfully.

I grew to love the sound of retreating footsteps.

I contemplated putting weedkiller in his beer, at one point. But it wasn't really a subtle way of killing someone perpetually high on weed.

One day, it struck me.

Fire was the way forward.

Fire purges the past. Cleanses the soul. Wipes out evidence. But I had no idea how to fiddle with flames in a way that didn't lead in an accusing, straight line back to me. I had no intention of rotting in jail for the rest of my life. I plotted and schemed, toyed with all sorts of tantalising ideas and possibilities, only to discard everything in frustration. Nothing seemed foolproof enough.

Death's a particularly elusive character when you become desperate for him to pay a visit.

In the meantime, I took special pains to stay away from home whenever Mom was not around (which happened with increasing frequency), just to be on the safe side. I came back only after she returned each day.

But then one day, she didn't.

I was at school when it happened. It was a dreary summer day, with drops of rain coming down so hard they stung my eyes and flowed upwards into my nose. I had spent the previous months avoiding home, roaming the streets until Mom returned.

My Chemistry teacher came into the classroom to say: 'You need to get to the hospital, now.'

I got to the hospital to discover Mom lying in bed, as rain continued to pummel the roof above our heads, trickling down the window in long miserable streaks. Her gaunt, heroin-addled features seemed unexpectedly serene. She looked beautiful, liberated from the pain of persisting. Peaceful, spared the agony of living. I kissed her cold lips, as an idea began germinating in my head.

A fiery new possibility.

If chemicals killed Mom, I will use chemicals to kill.

I didn't find Mom's Pandora's box, but I did find a wooden approximation among her possessions. That box contained her birth certificate, a small amethyst ring and a silver filigree locket. I opened the pendant to discover a lock of hair, hair so blond and fine it reminded me of homespun cotton and candyfloss. Was it mine? Someone else's? Mom's own hair, perhaps? Two sepia-tinted photographs lay beneath the locket; I fished them out from the box. The first was of my maternal grandparents, beaming from sun-baked chaises longues. I unfortunately have zero memories of them; Gran died from a stroke when I was three, five years after Gramps. The second photo featured a fluffy cocker spaniel; I assumed it had once belonged to Mom.

The box had also contained twelve dried roses and my birth certificate.

It's funny how Mom's death revealed everything I needed to know about my birth. The certificate said I was born in midtown Manhattan. I never knew I began life in a place where bright lights dazzled the eyes and big hopes fired the soul. How on earth did Mom and I end up coming back to Montana, to Gran's mouldy log cabin where the water tank would freeze solid each winter?

I suspected I knew the answer: Mom must have needed help from Gran, after I was born. Maybe even money and shelter.

Mom's name and address were also on my birth certificate,

of course. Marianne Lily Robinson, it said in capital letters (I never knew Mom had a middle name). The second name on the certificate was a man's name.

The name Mom had refused to tell me.

My father's name.

I remember clenching my fists, vowing that I would track him down. But the certificate yielded a third surprise. The name at the top of the document wasn't the name Mom had been calling me for fourteen and a half years. Turned out I had been living a lie all along, using a name that wasn't even mine. Mom had named me after someone who left a profound impact on her life, only to change her mind later on. She probably didn't want to be reminded of that particular person on a daily basis.

As I much preferred the name she had been using for me, I vowed I would change my name legally as soon as I was old enough.

I also remember a conversation I had with my best friend, a couple of days after Mom's funeral. She had dropped by the log cabin with one of her Gran's apple pies, one entirely for me. She had narrowed her eyes and peered around warily as she stepped across the threshold. It prompted me to say, 'He isn't here. I've not seen him since Mom died.'

'But he'll come back eventually, won't he?'

'He will.' I nodded. 'I'm sure he will.'

'What are you going to do?'

'Run.'

She digested my reply for a couple of moments.

'Where to?'

'NYC, to look for my real dad.'

93

'He lives there?'

'I don't know for sure. But I should try to find out.'

'Don't you want to finish school first?'

'I would love to, but it isn't safe here. Not when he has a key to the front door, can let himself in anytime.'

She nodded.

'I guess nothing holds you back here now.'

I nodded, fully understanding what she was trying to say: Mom was dead and I was free to do whatever I liked.

'Actually, there's something.'

'Really?'

'I'll miss you,' I said, deciding to be both honest and frank. 'I don't want to leave the only friend I have.'

'You'll make other friends when you get to the Big Apple.'

I shrugged and said: 'They won't understand me as you do.'

She chuckled.

'I always knew I was special. When are you leaving?'

My reply was grim.

'As soon as I tie up a particular loose end here, one that's begging to be tied up.'

Six days after Mom's funeral, he let himself back into the log cabin. I had just returned from my best friend's place, after having had dinner with her family. I heard a key turn in the lock, a few minutes past ten. I was only half prepared; I never expected him to come back so soon after her death. I scampered to the corner of the living room, wedged myself into the semi-concealed gap between the airing cupboard and the grandfather clock. I saw him waddling across the threshold a few seconds later, a bloated form silhouetted by the dim light from the hallway. I held my breath as he came into the room and fumbled for the switch with a loud belch.

Honey Bunny saw everything that happened that night. Didn't tell.

Chapter Seven

Viola

I clamber up the staircase leading to the bathroom, shaken and stirred, seven names wafting before my eyes. I ought to be feeding a couple of CriminalX's more sensible predictions to Damian, but I'm desperate to know something else. It's time for a loo break, one involving the use of a certain device. I shouldn't put this moment off any longer. Knowing makes all the difference, for better or worse. Information is everything, as they say. Or as Xander once phrased it with a chuckle: it's addictive. Information is a drug. Once you have some, you want more of it.

Especially information that may redefine your existence, change the meaning and purpose of your life.

I stumble into the bathroom, clutching the pregnancy testing kit so hard, I'm practically squashing the box.

Paper rips.

Water tinkles.

Breath skips.

Eyes freeze.

Shock floods.

I'm staring at two positive pink lines on the indicator. Two lines I'd never expected in a million years.

I stumble to the bathroom sink, still in a catatonic state of disbelief. I grab the vanilla-scented soap bar, gouge it with my fingernails. I turn on the tap and begin scrubbing away, so vigorously I'm nearly flaying off my skin. The full-length bathroom mirror beside me glimmers, its glass taking on an iridescent blue-green sheen. I hear something whirr, a jaunty click. I stare at my reflection in dismay. Damn it. I should have turned the mirror off, but it's too late now. I already see a line flashing up at the top of the glass, in small white letters:

Good morning, Viola!

You look unusually flustered today.

I groan. Christian gave me the mirror for my birthday. I thought it would be a fun addition to our home (the damned thing unfortunately proved too large for the London apartment, so I'd had it sent up here). I had always wanted a body-analysis mirror that inspects my features for potential health problems and dispenses tips on how to be the fairest of them all. Christian, bless him, got me a top-of-the-range model that also scans my body and updates my virtual mannequin with my current measurements so it can 'try on' clothing in online stores, see if they fit.

It was a lovely surprise, back then.

Unfortunately, I now think these ever-helpful, all-knowing devices are more annoying than fun. I'm tempted to reach up and hit the OFF button at the top of the mirror, but my hands are still full of soap. I grimace at my reflection, scrubbing my hands twice as hard. I don't need a mirror to tell me I'm flustered. I also know I'm not the fairest of them all, this morning. My hair is a tangled, frizzy mess. The worry lines running across my forehead seem twice as deep; the indentation between my eyebrows seems twice as pronounced. My eyes look like someone has twisted a corkscrew through them. More words flash up on the mirror, this time in rolling fashion:

Please don't frown, dear Viola. There's no need to be worried because all your vital signs are good. Your blood pressure is within normal limits, if a little low. As your face looks unusually flushed and you seem a little out of breath, I suggest you take a long leisurely shower.

A long leisurely shower, God forbid. I'm tempted to throw my stainless-steel toilet brush at this damned thing, hear the satisfying crunch of metal against glass. Maybe Christian was right the last time we chatted about technology, during one of our weekend walks around the neighbourhood.

'We don't need machines to tell us what we already know,' he had said. 'Most of the time, we're better off not knowing.'

'I disagree,' I replied, feeling unusually combative. 'Knowing makes all the difference.'

'Not necessarily,' he said, shrugging. 'Ignorance equals sanity, with so many things bombarding us on all fronts.'

'Ignoramuses are fools.'

'Knowing doesn't necessarily make us happier.' His voice was equally firm. 'I reckon ignoramuses are happier sorts.'

I didn't believe Christian then, but I'm slowly (and grudgingly) coming around to his point of view. I most certainly know a bit more now, compared to when I woke up this morning. I know I'm pregnant. I also know that CriminalX thinks I'm likely to be a murderer, out of the thousands of people involved with Xander's shows. These extra bits of knowledge are messing with my mind, interfering with my sanity.

Hooray and congratulations, Viola! I've just connected to your pregnancy testing kit and it tells me you are pregnant. I would suggest you refrain from eating undercooked eggs and raw sushi, limit your caffeine intake, and consume folic acid and vitamin supplements. On your long leisurely shower, please be careful to ensure the water isn't too hot. I have already subscribed you to the weekly pregnancy newsletter issued by the National Health Service and prompted Alexa to order 50 tablets of folic acid (400 µg) and 400 tablets of vitamin D (10 µg). To cancel, just say 'Alexa, no vitamins and folic acid'. I have also booked an appointment with a virtual midwife for you through the NHS MidBot Service. Your online consultation will take place at 9 a.m. tomorrow, with Katarina MidBot. To cancel, just say, 'No Katarina MidBot'.

I gape at my stunned reflection, my eyebrows creasing upwards with disbelief and consternation.

'I . . . I don't understand how I can be pregnant.' My words spill out in a loud and plaintive rush. 'My period is only four days overdue.'

Pregnancy is counted from the first day of the last period, not from the point of ovulation (few first-timers know this fact about pregnancy, so there is no need to feel sheepish or embarrassed), which makes you a healthy four weeks and four days pregnant, so many congratulations again!

My virtual mannequin glimmers on the right-hand side of the mirror, dressed in what must surely be Alexander King. It's wearing a striking black top and chartreuse slacks (almost my favourite colour). A python slithers across the trouser hems in a trail of butterscotch spots.

> I've scanned this season's summer collections and think this gorgeous combination from your favourite designer, Alexander King, will fit you well. The outfit is also suitable as maternity wear.

Hell, even the mirror is trying to sell me pregnancy-related stuff now. I thought I could outsmart all my electronic devices by using cash at the pharmacy, but it's impossible to hide anything from them these days.

> The outfit is priced at £1,748. Would you like me to:
> (A) Order it, to be delivered by drone within the next hour
> (B) Monitor the price for promotions (the outfit has a 15.12% chance of going on sale within the next six months)
> (C) Look for more maternity wear

My virtual mannequin begins rotating on the mirror (the butterscotch python, as it turns out, has a decapitated head). I can jolly well get the outfit for free if I really want it; I just need to call Xander or Lucia. Come to think of it, I really should be calling Lucia after turning this bloody mirror off.

> Please don't roll your eyes, Viola. Recent research on eye-rolling confirms that it causes people to age prematurely.

That's it. I've had enough. I'm going to get the toilet brush. Just then, my ancient Nokia buzzes in the pocket of my dressing gown. Shit. It must be Damian, agitating for an update. I haven't yet worked out what I'm going to say to him. I pull the phone out and grimace at its screen for several moments, before tapping the answer button with a resigned sigh.

'Hi, Damian,' I say.

'Hi, Vi,' he says in a brisk voice. 'Any luck?'

I gulp.

'I'm still processing the files,' I say. 'But . . . a few things have come up.'

I hear him sucking in his breath over the line.

'Care to elaborate?' he says.

I take in a deep breath.

'The software spat out a few names in ascending order of probability,' I say. 'Giovanni De Luca, Steve Mortimer, Nigel Olaf Avery and Lucia Graves.'

Damian whistles over the line.

'Did the software explain why it picked these four individuals?'

I hesitate again before replying.

'Kind of,' I say.

'What do you mean, kind of?' he says.

'CriminalX relies on a black box that does trillions of calculations that can't be easily turned into language,' I say, deciding on the partial truth. 'This is what I'm trying to fix, why development has taken so long.'

Damian is silent.

'I hope the names will be helpful to you,' I continue, trying to inject greater firmness into my voice.

He sighs.

'Those folks are already on our radar,' he says.

'Oh.'

'I was hoping your software could tell us something we don't yet know. Give us new possibilities.'

Shit. There's no way I'm giving him the other three names. Wait a minute. If MI6 is aware of the four names I've mentioned, I wonder if they are also on the Met's radar. Probably not. I suspect the two organisations operate on parallel but separate tracks, even if they share the same aims, and only talk to each other when it's necessary. Didn't the *Sunday Times* say recently that Britain's agencies tend to be 'jealous of their own patches'? Hmm . . . it's a shame I can't ring Christian, tip him off. I swore complete secrecy to Damian when I signed on the dotted line, thanks to the Official Secrets Act.

A little voice groans in my head: *Oh come on, Vi, stop kidding yourself. You're just using the Official Secrets Act as an excuse. You childishly wish to withhold something from Christian because he has been keeping Ella a secret from you. Tit for tat, isn't it?*

Shit, I really need to give Damian an answer.

'I'll run the software again, then,' I say. 'As you know, it takes into account everything that's happening in real time. It may throw up something new, next time.'

'Maybe we should cast the net a little wider. If you could cross-check our dataset of all possible terrorists both in and outside Britain, that would be great.'

'OK.'

'Thanks, Vi.'

The phone goes silent. If Damian wants me to run CriminalX again with an additional dataset of names, it will probably take another few hours of waiting around. I stuff the phone back into my dressing-gown pocket. The opening refrain of *Méditation* sounds through the loudspeakers, causing me to jump.

'You sounded jittery on the phone,' says Alexa. 'I'm playing

Massenet to calm you down. By the way, can I also recommend the Combat-Stress-Yoga Mat, which is currently discounted to £22.99?'

'Shut up,' I say.

I need to clear my mind.

*

I climb the staircase leading up to the attic, only to grimace as another brief wave of nausea envelops me. I pause to steady myself and catch my breath, before unlocking the latch on the attic door and pushing hard. The door swings upward with an ear-splitting creak. I don't know why Xander prefers to spend the nights here whenever he visits me, instead of the more accessible (and comfortable) guest room downstairs. He once mumbled something about inspiration, that it only happens if one is a little closer to the stars. That being at the top . . . helps one to reach for the top.

He also said that rooms with uneven walls and sloping floors increase awareness, improve brain activity, make people think better. Unusual spaces make folks alert, awaken their instincts.

Maybe he's right.

Xander's always right.

He's a fount of expletive-filled wisdom, for sure.

I haul myself up the final step, landing with a thud. Rays of light are streaming through the sloping skylights. I take a deep, suspicious breath. The space smells airy and pleasant, of old wood beams and sun-baked haystacks. It does not smell of vermin droppings, thankfully. Maybe the squirrels were in here only briefly. I remember my horror when I stuck my head in here yesterday night and realised the window at the far end was wide open. I should have remembered to check the attic before leaving for London, made sure everything was shut tight. Time to clear up the rest of the mess, work out if the squirrels have caused any damage to the electric cables, stop thinking about . . . damn it, I surely can't be pregnant. What did they say about percentage accuracy?

'They all claim to have an accuracy above ninety-nine per cent,' the woman at the pharmacy had said.

It's hard to dispute a figure like that. Which means that I'm indeed somewhere early along, probably four weeks because my period is overdue by a fortnight . . . Oh God, I'm going to be such a lousy mother . . .

Damn, I should be concentrating, doing something useful with my hands. That's why I came up here in the first place. I stoop down and pick up two books that the squirrels have knocked over. The textbook on top is entitled *Morality and Mortality in the Digital Age*. Why do I bother keeping these ancient volumes, all turning mouldy and yellow around their edges? I'm unlikely to read them ever again. Only sentimental fools or compulsive hoarders hang on to things that have long served their rightful purpose. Maybe I should take these books to a charity shop.

I extract a large hessian bag from one of the open boxes, begin tossing the books inside. The act feels strangely liberating. Maybe I should throw away more. There's little I truly need to function in life. I remember the day I first arrived at this cottage for a three-month stay, carrying only hope in my heart and a small suitcase in my hand. There was hardly anything in my bag apart from a toothbrush and a credit card. How on earth have I accumulated so much junk in middle age, so much useless baggage I no longer need? That includes a bloody mirror that tells me to take a long leisurely shower, for God's sake. I grab a couple of loose sheets from the floor (one is entitled 'The Basics of Digital Forensic Technology') and stuff them into an open box labelled 'MISC'.

Something in a corner of the box catches my eye. It's a large photo frame that contains a yellowing picture of my late aunt Lisabeth and me, taken at a cousin's wedding more than twenty years ago. She's beaming away at the camera, beneath one of those magnificent feather-embellished hats she always wore, her eyes crinkling up happily. She's also hugging me tight, arm placed around my shoulders.

A warm, fuzzy feeling steals over me.

Aunt Lisabeth, Atelier Manager Extraordinaire, specialist maker of dresses with puffy sleeves. A woman who was larger than life, with a heart bigger than anyone I've ever known. A person who used to outshine brides at weddings and upstage corpses at funerals owing to the sheer force of her presence. She was one of the few people who truly believed in me, said that I needed a leg-up if I hoped to succeed. She suggested I do a few internships (however badly paid) if I wished to get somewhere in the world of big jobs and scary people. She even helped engineer a few of them, thanks to her fashion-industry connections. I could stay at her Oxford cottage, she told me with a cheerful grin, if I didn't mind taking a bus back and forth to London (an offer that I gratefully took up each summer when I was still at university). Dear Aunt Lisabeth would definitely approve of the baby. If she were still alive, she would probably say I'd make a decent mum, that I should stop fretting and start buying some pretty clothing for the little one . . .

Maybe I should put this frame back in the living room downstairs, where it stood for years. Restore it to its rightful place on the mantlepiece. As they say, memories of kindness are everything. They stretch our souls, fill our hearts, make us whole again. So few people have been truly kind to me, come to think of it.

Christian's kind, for sure.

Maybe I shouldn't have been so emotional, fled back here in a huff.

I lift the frame from the box. As I do so, its cardboard backing falls loose to reveal a small white envelope.

What on earth is this?

I turn the envelope over in my hands. Its edges are brittle. The paper exudes a faint earthy musk and bears the yellow-brown patina of age. The envelope must have been wedged inside the photo frame for a while; the cardboard backing has a correspondingly deep, time-furrowed indent in its middle. Four words adorn the envelope's front, in small nervous hand-writing. They say: *For my best friend.*

I open the envelope, only to frown.

There's nothing inside. What on earth could have been there? Who was it really intended for? How did it get inside the photo frame in the first place? It's a day of bizarre mysteries, fast-multiplying ones. So much has happened since I woke up this morning. I feel dizzy, overwhelmed by the speed of developments. I tuck the envelope into the pocket of my dressing gown before reaching down to close the box, catching one last glimpse of Aunt Lisabeth's smiling face. She would've liked Christian, I think.

A wave of sadness washes over me.

I slump to the floor, my mind whirring back to the sequence of events that prompted me to leave him.

Where did it all go wrong with Christian?

Maybe it went wrong from the start.

I even know the precise date when it all began. When I turned forty, I started to panic. I was still alone in Old Fen Cottage, my eventual inheritance from Aunt Lisabeth. A charming place with a giant oak tree and pond, a haven where wisteria drooped from trellises in an avalanche of lavender each spring. A home where doves cooed from the rafters, squirrels gambolled on the grass and butterflies shimmered over the orange blossom bushes fringing the garden path. The main problem with my dream cottage was that I had no one to share it with. Unlike me, all my close university friends were busy coupling, marrying or procreating. I had dated all sorts of people over the past twenty years, even enjoyed two long-lasting relationships in my late twenties and early thirties. Yet none of my emotional entanglements had resulted in The Right One, my perfect, magical soulmate.

So that's what a lifetime of trying and hoping has led to.

Nothing.

No one to curl up with during the darkest hours.

No one to call my own.

More nights ahead of reaching out with the fervent hope of finding warmth, only to be greeted by a cold, empty sheet.

On the afternoon of my fortieth birthday, I was staring at my computer screen in abject misery, wondering if I would turn into one of those crazy cat ladies by the age of seventy and if I should pour myself a third glass of Malbec, when the phone rang.

'Happy birthday.' Xander's voice boomed cheerfully over the line.

'Thank you.'

'Hope you're having a fabulous day.'

I frowned at the phone before deciding I should be frank with him.

'I feel a little miserable today, to be honest with you,' I said.

'Fucking hell.'

'It's all right.'

'We should sort this out.'

'It's no big deal. Just a passing case of birthday blues.'

'No . . . no . . . no . . . I can't have you feeling miserable on your *birthday*, of all days. Listen, I have some work to finish in London, but I'll jump into my car at around seven, head straight to you. I'm supposed to have dinner with the loonies, I mean the Clooneys. I'll tell Lucia to cancel.'

'No, you shouldn't be cancelling . . .'

'Don't you dare argue with me. I'm your *friend*, for fuck's sake, and it's been ages since we had a chat.'

He did indeed arrive at the cottage a few hours later. He refused the use of the guest room, stuck his bag in the attic (as usual) and clambered back down again to the living room. I handed him a giant glass of whisky and we settled next to the fireplace where sparks flew merrily from crackling logs.

'Thanks for coming all this way,' I said.

'It's I who should be thanking you.' He shrugged. 'It was time for me to get away from those idiots at work. I'm going to climb your tree tomorrow morning and scream "FUCK YOU ALL" before taking a flying leap into your pond.'

'You're mad. The water's freezing cold.'

'Which will make it twice as fun,' he said, swallowing the whisky in one gulp. 'Adversity builds character, as they say. So, spill the beans. Why are you feeling miserable?'

I took in a deep breath before saying in a tiny voice: 'I'm forty today and I'm still alone.'

'Aha,' he said. 'I had a feeling you might say that. I've been thinking hard about your existential dilemma and . . .' He trailed off, spreading his hands in a theatrical swoop.

'And?'

'And . . . I have the perfect solution,' he said, beaming majestically at me.

'What is it?'

'Do what you've always been good at.'

'Huh?'

'Solve your problem with *solve*-ware. Build a program that finds the right person for you. Bit like Tinder but bespoke.'

I was reduced to stunned speechlessness.

'Work out the compatibility criteria you prefer, use the software to scan all your friends. Maybe their friends, too. Maybe all famous folk on Wikipedia, why not? See if anyone meets your criteria. Maybe Miss Right is within six degrees of separation and . . . you just need software to root the person out.'

'I'm not *that* desperate.'

'I think you are.'

'No, I'm not.'

'Whatever. Name the software Spark.'

I couldn't get Xander's suggestion out of my head. It gnawed away at my insides when I filled the dishwasher, when I fed KitKat, when I trimmed the orange blossom bushes in the garden. That's when I began compiling my list, revising it obsessively until I came up with ten criteria. The list read:

My perfect partner must:

1. Be intelligent
2. Be reasonably good-looking
3. Have a sensible job
4. Appreciate good food
5. Have a quirky sense of humour
6. Understand technology
7. Enjoy long walks and other outdoor activities
8. Like to read
9. Be partial to cats
10. Have a philosophical bent

It only took me a day and a half to build the software. It spat out six names in descending order of suitability.

That was when both fun and angst began, tracking the six down. I realised that it was damned easy to get in touch with people (everyone has a cyberspace presence, these days). It was also easy enough to eliminate people from the list. As one gets older, one becomes firmer about what one *doesn't* want. Yet there was one name I just couldn't eliminate, no matter how hard I tried. It was the name at the top of the list, the person Spark the Software deemed most compatible for me. The more I read about the man online, the more I was intrigued by his personality, the more I wanted to meet him.

But that wasn't straightforward at all.

The problem with the man at the top of the list was that he was also at the top of the Metropolitan Police.

Much to my incredulity, I found myself dressing for our first date (with nervous fingers) just a few weeks later. I tried on a slate-grey suit, only to discard it as too pretentious and formal.

The crimson top paired with green slacks made me look like a bird of paradise, while the tight-fitting leopard print suggested I was trying too hard. After minutes of rummaging through the closet in desperation, I eventually settled on a knee-length white dress with a rectangular neckline.

Not too dressy, I thought. Simple and, hopefully, classy.

We had agreed to meet at Casa Perfetta, a fancy Italian restaurant (his pick) around the corner from where he worked. He said that he might be late, apologised in advance. I suspected that he would indeed be late, that I would end up waiting for a while. To my surprise, I saw him already sitting at a table when I passed through the restaurant's double doors at two minutes past seven (Aunt Lisabeth said that I should always be a little late if I wished to be impressed, and a little early if I wished to impress). He was dressed in a crisp, well-fitted white shirt, so starched I could almost hear its collar crackle. He looked both slim and dapper; I loved how he combed his greying yet luxuriant hair back in a slick swoop. Damn it, I thought. He's twice as good-looking in person. Maybe I should have worn the sexier leopard print instead.

He looked up at me, took in the fact that I was gaping at him.

'Viola?' he said, rising to his feet.

I nodded, unexpectedly tongue-tied.

'Lovely to meet you,' he said, leaning forward to kiss me on both cheeks. I caught a whiff of the eau de cologne he wore, a scent both musky and sexy in a wonderfully masculine way.

'Do have a seat.'

I sat down gingerly, feeling a little self-conscious as I tucked my dress beneath me.

'I'm glad we eventually found a date that worked,' he said with a smile.

'Me too,' I said, beaming back at him. 'You've been busy, haven't you?'

'To be honest with you, it has been absolutely bonkers since I received my letter of appointment,' he said with a grimace, grabbing the napkin in front of him and spreading it neatly over his lap.

'How has the new job been?' I said, feigning ignorance although I had spent the entire day reading everything I could about him on Google News.

'The job's fine.' He shrugged. 'The job has always been fine . . . until I came along. I think the job would have done even better had I stayed away from it.'

'Oh, come on,' I said, rolling my eyes. 'You're being too modest, selling yourself short. You must surely be doing fantastic work.'

'That's what I hope people think.'

'I read somewhere that everyone thinks you were the best Cyber Drugs head the Met Police ever had.'

'I don't know why they think so.' He shrugged again. 'That said, I gave everything I had to that particular job. I feel strongly about traffickers; I've seen people die of overdoses in the past.'

I saw a flash of raw emotion in his eyes, hinting at pain and loss, possibly even anger. His words triggered a sharp pang of guilt within me; I remember swallowing hard and staring down at my hands. I understood exactly how he felt about overdoses because drugs had caused Maya's death and . . . and it was all my fault.

He grimaced before continuing. 'Being Commissioner is an altogether different story, though. It's a largely bureaucratic job, as it turns out. Unlike Cyber Drugs, I haven't got a clue as to what I'm doing most of the time.'

'They wouldn't have promoted you if they didn't think you were capable enough,' I said, still trying to push the black guilt away from my mind.

'Life's a facade,' he said. 'But work's an even bigger facade. I've been spending endless hours at my desk, giving everyone the impression that I'm working hard. Pretending that I know what I'm doing, even if I don't. Even if I feel completely out of my depth at times. But that's enough about me and my job. Robert said you're into detection technologies?'

'Oh yes,' I said, nodding fervently. 'It was really kind of him to introduce us, by the way.'

Truth was, I had pestered our mutual friend Robert to introduce us (after discovering that Robert was the only common friend we had in the entire digital universe), but I wasn't about to tell my date that.

'Robert has been a good friend over the years.'

'He's definitely obliging.'

'Tell me more about these technologies,' he said, leaning forward with an expression of genuine interest. And so we began chatting away, about a subject close to my heart, over our plates of exquisite truffle pasta. I discovered that he could be simultaneously witty and self-deprecating, that he could be serious yet flippant at the same time. I loved how he reached up to brush his forehead in a slightly self-conscious way (the grey in his fringe gave him a distinguished air), how his immaculately pressed white shirt fell away at the uppermost button, hinting at a bronzed torso beneath. I detected a sadness behind his dark eyes, a deeper melancholia no amount of smiling could disguise.

By the end of the evening, I was convinced I didn't just like him.

I was in love with him.

It was raw, magnetic attraction, the first time I had truly fallen for a man. Up until then, no one had ever captured my heart, brain *and* imagination. I knew that *Hello!* magazine had included him on their 2029 list of the most eligible bachelors in London, remarking that he had steadfastly remained single although his circle of acquaintances included some of the prettiest socialites, models and minor royals in the country (the journalist had snidely implied that he had been appointed to his new job because he knew all the right people, was born into privilege and therefore had all the necessary family connections).

The article did not explain why he had remained single thus far, which made me doubly determined to find out.

Chapter Eight

Christian

Lucia crosses her legs, before uncrossing them and looking up at me. Her large grey eyes seem twice as doe-like.

'What happened at the lunch with De Luca?' I ask.

'It's a long story,' she says.

'I have the time,' I say, even if I don't. 'Go on.'

Lucia: I received an email from Gio's secretary several months ago, saying that her boss would love to invite Xander to lunch. Xander was pretty astonished when I passed the message to him. While the two have met numerous times before, at fashion weeks and at the Metropolitan Ball, I gathered they haven't exactly been bosom buddies over the years. Xander was intrigued by the invitation, told me to set something up. We eventually found an opening a couple of months later, when Xander and Gio were both in Milan for Fashion Week. I remember them greeting each other merrily at the restaurant. Massive smiles and a hearty handshake, that sort of thing. I was given the table next to them, right in the middle of the sun-lit atrium. I sat down and began tapping away on my phone, but I couldn't help overhearing their conversation. As you may know, Americans and Italians can be quite voluble and effusive when chatting.

When the starters were served, I sat up a bit straighter.

Gio hinted that his business wasn't doing so well, that he was looking to sell some of his shares in G&G in return for a cash injection of $30 million. He would be willing to part with 3 per cent of the company. Xander replied, quite firmly, that he was flattered to be considered as a potential investor, but he was not looking to buy anything at the present time. Gio shrugged before topping up Xander's flute with more Prosecco. I gathered from the expression on his face that he had expected Xander would say that. They soon moved on to discussing other matters.

Technological matters, to be precise.

That's when the fur began to fly.

Xander said, at one point, that advances in automation would soon put everyone in the industry out of work, including fashion designers themselves. It was just a casual, throwaway remark. I saw Gio bristling in response. He said, in his impassioned Italian manner, that no machine can supplant the originality and vision of a human designer, or produce art that evokes a sense of humanity. Xander, for his part, insisted that machines could soon do a much better job than humans. They would produce designs more perfect than anything imperfect humans could ever dream of creating, he said. He envisaged a near future where he could substitute an item on a catwalk, an item designed by a machine instead of by his own genius, and no one would be able to tell the difference.

Gio laughed, a big booming rumble that caused everyone in the restaurant to turn and look at him. Gio's reaction made Xander a little more emotional, a lot more demonstrative.

Xander doesn't like being laughed at, to put it mildly. He punched his fist down and said that he would do precisely that, at an upcoming fashion show. Put an item on the catwalk, one entirely designed by software, and no one would realise it. The substitution would go completely unnoticed by the world's media, by the editors, journalists and snobs present at the event.

Scepticism coloured Gio face; he had the look of a man who thought it was a preposterous idea. Xander, for his part, became twice as forceful, twice as expansive. He said that he would happily bet on his conviction. At that point, I should have scurried over to their table. Waved my arms, interrupted them, done something to curb Xander's impulsiveness. Instead, I just sat there, frozen in front of my arugula salad, transfixed by what was going on. Gio replied, with a sly twist of his lips, that $30 million might be a fine figure for a bet. Xander studied Gio for a couple of moments, before lifting his glass of Prosecco and clinking Gio's flute. Gio grinned before tapping Xander's in return. I watched the two men drain their glasses.

Oh no, I thought.

What on earth has Xander done? And what the hell is he getting into?

Gio then asked, with a casual lift of an eyebrow, what sort of machine-designed item Xander was planning to put on the catwalk. I saw Xander frowning at his flute; I could almost see little cogs whirring in his head. He replied that he would only reveal which item it was a day or two after the show. Before that, no one would guess correctly, or even come close to guessing. Gio shrugged and nodded, reaching to top up Xander's flute again. He wore the cheerful expression of a man who had nothing to lose and everything to gain. Which was probably the case.

Xander then said with a stern expression: 'Promise me you won't tell anyone about our bet, or alert anyone to the substitution. Our bet becomes void if you do.'

It was Gio's turn to reach for his glass and clink Xander's flute. A gentleman's bet – followed by a gentleman's agreement – conducted over a bottle of fine Prosecco. At that point, the waiter brought our desserts. I had ordered a tiramisu, but I realised I no longer had the appetite for it.

Lucia stops dead, frowning a little at me. She has a fine knack for telling a story (it must be those murder mysteries she reads).

'I presume the machine-designed item went down the catwalk yesterday?' I say.

She nods.

'I'm sure it did,' she says.

'Which item was it?'

'I haven't got a clue,' she says, opening her hands with an apologetic shrug. 'Xander refused to tell anyone.'

'Who wrote the software, then?'

'Don't know that, either. Xander kept that a big secret, too.'

I narrow my eyes at Lucia.

'Apart from you, did anyone else know about the bet?'

She shakes her head. 'You'll have to ask Xander that.'

Or Giovanni De Luca, perhaps. I wonder if Gio told anyone about the bet, despite his gentleman's agreement with King. It would be in his interest to do so, to casually let slip to a journalist that Xander was planning an out-of-this-world substitution on the catwalk, get everyone's antennae up before the show. But . . . I can't remember seeing any gossip in the press about the tantalising spectre of machine-designed items on runways. Maybe the Italian did indeed keep his word. Another question whips up in the depths of my head.

'What do you know about De Luca?'

She looks straight at me, before replying in a rush of words.

'I think he has a dark side to him. Maybe Gio realised that Xander would indeed win the bet, that the best way for him to prevent his rival from winning was . . . to disrupt yesterday's show.'

'Hmm.'

'Maybe he'll hurt Xander again. There was, after all, a lot at stake,' she says, spreading her hands. 'Thirty million, no less.'

Of all the reasons for murder I've heard in my lifetime, this is probably the most absurd I've encountered. Pretty damned bonkers, upon further reflection. But then again, people kill for all sorts of reasons. I need to mull over this bizarre theory a bit more, make sense of Lucia's account of the bet.

'You showed me those sketches earlier. So King will be putting a De Luca-style design on the catwalk tonight. Do you know why?'

'I've been puzzling about that, too,' says Lucia, frowning. 'But I just didn't dare to go up to Xander and ask why, it would give away the fact that I'd eavesdropped on his conversation in Milan.'

Looks like the only person who might be able to shed further light on these arcane matters is Alexander King himself. I should grab him as soon as he lands in London, put him in Lucia's chair, make him answer the same questions.

'Thank you for coming in,' I say. 'We'll call if we need anything else.'

'Wait a minute,' she says, lifting a hand. 'What about security for tonight's show?'

'What about it?'

'We've received lots of worried messages from people on the guest list. Folks traumatised by iPredict, as I understand.'

'Oh, did iPredict also tell you that you're likely to suffer grievous harm?'

'I don't use iPredict.' She looks straight at me. 'Never had the urge to download the app.'

'Why not?'

'I don't believe in living a predictable life.'

'Good for you.'

Maybe I should stay away from iPredict, too, like this bright and sensible young woman. But some things are easier said than done.

'So what about security for tonight?' she asks again.

'I presume you have a private security firm on board.'

She nods.

'Xander has been using the same firm for years, since 9/11. Security Assets Ltd in Kensington. I hear they're planning to scan all guests' bags tonight. That's what they normally do, anyway.'

I jot the name down on my pad.

'Might the Met be providing some back-up security?' she says, looking extremely hopeful.

I can picture a bunch of grim-looking constables sniffing around backstage. Scanning every single handbag that goes down the catwalk, searching every technician carrying a light-bulb, swabbing every sequin for traces of explosives. It will be a circus, for sure. But I'm also mindful of my conversation with the Prime Minister. If something happens to the PM's precious little one . . .

'The City of London Police will be handling matters tonight,' I say. 'I've been told they're on it.'

'That's great.' Lucia smiles for the first time since she settled down opposite me. 'I was so worried we would lose half of tonight's audience. I'll put out a press release along those lines.'

'Sure.'

'It should reassure anyone who's dithering . . . because none of us should be living in fear, right?'

I nod.

'Could you also send someone to keep an eye on Xander, make sure no one hurts him tonight?' I hear a note of desperation in her voice.

I can also picture a burly police officer babysitting Mr King, shadowing his every backstage shimmy.

'We'll see what we can do.'

'Thank you so much, Mr Verger.' Lucia looks relieved as she gets up from her chair. She takes a couple of steps in the direction of the door, before turning to look at me.

'I hope you don't mind me asking a personal question . . .' She trails off briefly, a light flush rising to her cheeks. '. . . but I went through the list of people who paid for tickets and I, er . . . saw your name on the list. Are you still planning to come tonight?'

Her question is an embarrassed rush. No wonder Lucia decided to come into New Scotland Yard in the hope that she might be able to talk to me. She knew she had a fair chance of bypassing the multiple ranks of people beneath me (maybe we need more people like her in this office, folks with strong deductive powers). Unfortunately, as far as Lucia's question is concerned, the only words wafting before my eyes are the ones I saw on iPredict this morning:

Chance of dying: 99.74%

I take a deep breath. Maybe Lucia's right. Maybe we shouldn't be living in fear or leading predictable lives.

'I'll be there,' I say.

The Times

The Real Reason Why Alexander King is Staging a Fashion Show in London Today

Exclusive Print Edition Feature, Page 3, Section 2

Legendary designer Alexander King will be arriving in London later today, fresh from his fashion show in Manhattan. He has already built a special catwalk off Old Billingsgate, a runway above the Thames that will be illuminated by fireworks at precisely seven minutes past eleven. He says he's staging the event to commemorate the late Maya von Meyer, a beautiful girl who used to model for him, and promises an evening no one will ever forget.

But why bother in the first place?

'King received a letter from the grave, months ago,' says an inside source who wishes to remain anonymous. 'Or so they say. Many of us think it was written by von Meyer.'

Multiple sources say the letter has preyed on the mind of the designer ever since.

'King hasn't quite been himself since the letter surfaced,' says one of his assistants who has been involved with the planning of the London show. 'Everyone knows he has had trouble sleeping, that he has been coming into the studio at all sorts of weird hours. He has also been irritable and snappy with the staff, even sacking a few of them. It's rumoured that the letter was what inspired the shows.'

Which leads to the question: What did the letter say?

'We all wish we knew,' says a co-worker, also on condition of anonymity. 'I personally think the letter may have shed more light on the circumstances that led to the death of Maya von Meyer, twenty years ago. The police still haven't ruled out murder as a possibility. The letter may explain who killed her.'

A spokesperson for the police says that no one has reported the finding of a letter, let alone one written by Maya von Meyer. Anyone with information on her death should get in touch with the police at once.

King has always been fascinated by the themes of death, life and rebirth. Who will ever forget those decapitated phoenixes at New York Fashion Week 2014, those zombie-like models carrying guillotined heads with their own likeness at London Fashion Week 2018, or those smashed skulls at Milan Fashion Week 2029? His London show tonight may well be the most morbid of them all.

The golden era of creativity happens between the ages of 35 and 45. That's when stunning new ideas punch you in the gut, dazzle you with their sheer brilliance. After the age of 45, most people run out of brilliant ideas even if they are still capable of improving technically. They turn into desiccated coconut husks, solid in substance yet devoid of vitality. My biggest regret in life is that I spent my golden years lurching between hells lubricated by drink. When I finally extracted myself from the kingdom of debauchery, I no longer had fresh new ideas rushing to my head.

Giovanni De Luca, interview in *Grazia* Italia

Chapter Nine

Xander

I stagger out of the plane, clank my way down the metal steps. The sky above me is gloomy, a distinctly Wagnerian shade of grey. Two men have emerged from the patrol car, planted themselves in front of it with stern, immobile faces. G&T Nigel is a couple of steps behind me; I unfortunately derive more annoyance than comfort from his presence.

'Leave this to me,' I hear him whispering behind my back.

I can't be bothered to reply. Not when the whisky I quaffed down is happily merging with the pills in my system. I taste damp in the London air, hear grit in my throat, smell faces twisted by fear. Are my five senses merging, going topsy-turvy again? Am I still in Manhattan, fleeing the smoking remnants of my show? I grip the handrail for support, close my eyes for a few seconds to steady myself, before continuing my downward struggle. As I reach the bottom of the steps, I see the two men swimming away from me in a fuddled grey haze, merging into a single figure, before separating again as two discrete entities.

I swear one of them is speaking to me, but I can't hear him.

'. . . if you would kindly accompany us to . . .'

I think G&T Nigel is saying something in response, but I can't hear him either. Blood is roaring in my ears, blocking out sound. It's also rushing straight to my face, surging around my insides in a merry-go-scramble. Damn it, maybe I shouldn't have drunk so much on the plane. I blame that pert little flight attendant. She brought me six whiskies instead of five. Or was it seven?

'. . . the Commissioner would like to . . .'

Who the hell are these people and where the fuck am I?

I ought to work out a suitable course of action (I'm tempted to collapse face down on this sea of grey tarmac, but I reckon these folks will not approve). Before I can decide what to do, I hear myself being bundled into the back of a car, taste doors slamming around me, see a loud siren above my head. One that digs deep into my throbbing skull, causing another explosion of agony.

We must be at New Scotland Yard (or wherever the police operate these days) because the car is no longer moving as rapidly. Probably an underground basement because rays of light are no longer streaming into my tortured pupils, tunnelling straight into my brain. Oddly enough, while everything around me is still a miasma of five senseless senses, I have a fine appreciation of speed and light.

'As you can see, my client isn't in a fit state to be answering questions. He's rather jet-lagged, to put it mildly. He's also in a state of shell shock, post-Manhattan.'

Is G&T Nigel trying to wriggle out of things again? If he's speaking for me, I'm afraid he's quite wrong. The whisky is definitely performing its magic, making me feel like I'm dancing on the fine tip of a fountain pen. If given a chance, the virtual

Xander from my VR set would be performing cartwheels like the fireworks I have planned for tonight.

'I am absolutely fine.'

I believe those four words have just issued from my own mouth, and my voice is both calm and firm.

At least, I hope so.

'Mr King has just said he's fine.'

I try to focus on the new voice, but unfortunately it's a disembodied one. A second or two of logical deduction tells me that it's probably coming from the front of the car.

'That's precisely what I've just said,' I add for emphasis. 'I'm happy to speak to whoever wishes to speak to me in this lovely building.'

I can hear a loud groan in the vicinity. With luck, it's probably G&T Nigel.

I'm ushered down an endless array of corridors, my feet sinking into miles of threadbare carpet. Everyone I've passed so far has awful dress sense and a pathetic appreciation of style. Most are clad in ill-fitting clothing that wouldn't get past the back doors of Alexander King. I haven't seen anyone in uniform yet . . . and I thought that police officers wore smart sexy uniforms? This must be a giant dysfunctional bureaucracy where dumpy-looking sorts push paper from one side of a table to the other, convinced they are being useful to society. I also have a feeling I'm being watched by multiple pairs of eyes; both the men and women are giving me long curious looks as they pass. The problem with fame and fortune is that everyone seems to think they know everything about you, once they've read your misleading Wikipedia entry on their smartphones.

'You do not have to say anything you don't want to,' G&T Nigel murmurs into my ear.

I smile at him, give him a silly little nod for emphasis.

I hear him sighing again.

I'm eventually shown into a bright room with large windows, offering a magnificent view of the drone-infested London sprawl below. The Thames unspools right beneath us, a snaking ribbon of grey-brown that looks both muddy and unappealing. A tall, good-looking man with a fine jaw is standing to greet me. Fucking hell, he doesn't have thick spectacles or rabbit teeth. In fact, he looks a little too chiselled for a policeman, someone I could easily use in a campaign; it's a shame his looks are wasted in an institution full of dowdy-looking sorts. I sweep my eyes over his outfit, because clothes tell you everything you need to know about a person. He's wearing an unimaginative grey suit that tapers nicely over his shoulders. It's a fine fit, I must say. Matches his greying sideburns, the sprinkling of grey in his hair and the plush grey carpet on the floor.

Hmm, I quite like the look of him. This man has more substance than flair (I tend to meet the exact opposites in my line of business). He oozes quiet confidence, seems capable of both grace and action. Plus he has friendly brown eyes and is able to stand up straight and tall. I also like those impeccably polished brogues on his feet, in full-grained black leather. At least they aren't grey.

'Pleased to meet you, Mr King,' he says, walking forward and extending a hand. 'Thank you for coming straight from Heathrow.'

Shit. Someone mentioned his name earlier and I didn't quite catch it. Who the hell is he? Why the fuck did I not pay more attention earlier? I mumble something in my politest manner, shake his hand and collapse on the chair opposite him. Pinpricks blur my vision; I blink them back.

G&T Nigel lowers his butt down in the chair next to me, in his usual ponderous manner.

'I'm Nigel Avery, Mr King's lawyer,' he says to Grey Man with an imperious shrug, pulling out a monogrammed folder from the depths of his bag. Something flips deep inside me, prompts annoyance to bubble up to my throat. I've spent most of my lifetime being surrounded by annoying aides; I certainly don't feel like having one of these ghastly creatures at my side right now, especially a pompous one. It's time to do what I feel like doing; I no longer give a shit.

'I don't need a lawyer,' I say.

Two pairs of bemused eyes swing in my direction.

'If you don't mind getting the fuck out of here . . .' I say to Nigel, before giving him a solemn smile, 'I would much prefer to be left alone.'

He's gaping at me.

'I absolutely insist,' I add for emphasis.

I can see him tipping his shoulders back, rallying himself to justify his presence at my side (and his next pay cheque).

'You have the right to have a lawyer at your side,' he says.

'The right is wrong.'

'I'm here to help.'

'I don't need your help.'

'I'm here to offer legal advice.'

'I don't need your advice either.'

'The law says . . .'

'I don't give a shit about the law. So, if you would kindly leave me to pick up my own poo, wipe my own arse . . .'

Damn, I'm starting to ramble. This doesn't bode well; the pills in my system are clearly doing the talking for me. But maybe it's working because G&T Nigel is sighing, putting his monogrammed folder away.

'Very well, Mr King,' he says. 'I hear you loud and clear. I'll be outside if you need me.'

I watch him waddle in the direction of the door. I turn to look at Grey Man. Something is running deep in the police officer's eyes. Is it surprise? Amusement?

Who the fuck is he?

CriminalX
Nigel Olaf Avery (13.85%)
Senior Legal Advisor, Alexander King
Age: 42
IQ Score: Unknown
Education: BCL in Law, Durham University (2011–2014);
MBA, Wharton University (2020)
Background: Assistant dresser at Turnbull & Asser (2008–
2009) & Alexander King (2009–2010). Appointed junior
corporate lawyer at LVMH in 2014, promoted to senior
corporate lawyer in 2025, took on current job at
Alexander King in 2028. In 2026, charged with short-
selling £1.2 million-worth of shares in Burberry on a
tip-off, cleared by a London jury of insider trading the
following year. Avery maintained his innocence throughout
the trial. Recent Google searches include: 'Alexander King
share price', 'how to impress your Tinder date', 'best
ways to have a blast in Manhattan', & 'how to deal with
models refusing to sign non-disclosure forms'.
Status: Backstage (BS) – Manhattan & London

Disillusion is like rust. It sets in slowly, but deeply. Before you know it, you're eaten up from the inside, reduced to an empty husk. Disillusion is the opposite of idealism. It's also the antithesis of hope. It sets in when reality fails to meet expectations. It's akin to the feeling you get after your house burns down, when you realise that you don't miss anything you've lost in the fire, that everything you've worked so hard to own turns out to be pretty irrelevant to the business of staying alive.

Giovanni De Luca, interview in *Corriere della Sera*

Chapter Ten

Christian

This must surely be the most entertaining exchange I've heard in this office (which says a lot about the general quality of conversations in this august bureaucracy). I'm tempted to chuckle, but I know I shouldn't. Alexander King is turning out to be a somewhat different person from the one I thought would show up here. He speaks with only a faint trace of an American accent, despite hailing from the northern reaches of the States. I detect a dark recklessness in his eyes, beneath that curly mop of ginger hair. I also sense a brooding, dour melancholia in the man's soul.

'Your PA came in earlier today,' I say.

'Did she? How come?'

'She was bothered by an anonymous letter she'd found.' I study his face closely before continuing. 'It was a death threat meant for you.'

To my astonishment, King doesn't even blink.

'Oh,' he says.

I slide the plastic bag with the letter over my desk. He leans forward, eyes widening briefly as he takes in its contents.

'You don't look particularly perturbed,' I say.

'I get letters from loonies all the time,' he says, shrugging.

'Loonies? What sort of loonies?'

'Mostly women wishing to marry me . . . or maim me.'

'I see.'

'I did a show in New York City years ago, and was silly enough to use a bit of fur in it. Mink, to be precise. I was then stupid enough to follow up with a show in London that featured badger pelts.'

I think I know where this is going.

'You should have seen the sacks of death threats I received.' He grimaces, spreads his arms wide. 'I made a *papier-mâché* figurine from them, in the shape of Cerberus. Little Cerbie is now sitting in a corner of my studio. He's a useful reminder that death is only one short voyage away.'

I think King is kidding about the Cerberus-shaped figurine. But I can't be sure. Not when he's nodding away so earnestly.

'Miss Graves said you've always been fascinated by death. May I ask why?'

He leans forward slightly, conspiratorially. I notice a sudden focused clarity in his eyes.

'Because death is all about the hope of rebirth.'

'I don't follow.'

'Death's an end. But it's also a *beginning*. That's why it fascinates me, inspires my work.'

Decapitated phoenixes and smashed skulls, indeed. The sketch I saw earlier flits back to mind, the twisted red tongue protruding from a skull on a sleeve, looping around the dress. Maybe death is indeed a beginning, in the weird and wacky universe of Alexander King.

I can't disagree with him, for sure.

'Any idea who could have written this letter?'

'Yet another loony, maybe.'

Our eyes meet; there's something dark and unfathomable in King's look.

'So death threats don't bother you?'

'Nope.' He holds my gaze, chin steady. 'It goes with the territory, is very much a part of being in the public eye. When folks throw both bouquets and brickbats at you, you quickly learn to smile . . . or dodge. Lucia has only been working for me for a few months. She'll get used to it.'

'She told me about your bet with Giovanni De Luca.'

He raises an eyebrow at me.

'She told me you were certain that you could put a machine-designed item on a catwalk and get away with it.'

'I knew Lucia was eavesdropping that afternoon,' he says. 'I didn't realise she'd heard so much.'

'Which item was it?'

King is swallowing hard. Why is he hesitating? He has the constipated look of a man who is struggling to come up with an answer, a man seizing and discarding various possibilities in his head. But he must surely know which item it was?

'One of . . . er . . . the handbags,' he eventually says, mumbling a little.

'The one that exploded?'

He remains silent for a couple of moments before giving me a firm nod.

'Yes,' he says.

I exhale. I think we're finally getting somewhere with this enquiry. But I also reckon King is withholding something important from me.

'What sort of bag was it?'

'Snakeskin. Mamba, it, er . . . looked very much like one of

136

the bags I designed for a show in Paris, back in 2026. I can get Lucia to send you an image, if you like.'

'That would be helpful. Where were you when the bomb went off?'

He tilts his head and regards me intently for a couple of moments before replying: 'Peering from behind a curtain, watching the audience.'

'The audience?'

'Their faces tell me everything I need to know, whether or not they like the shit I've put in front of them.'

'What happened after the bomb went off?'

'My aides shoved me into a car, bundled me onto the plane and I had the misfortune of being grilled by G&T Nigel . . . sorry, I mean Mr Nigel Avery, in preparation for what might happen in this building when we landed. I told him to bugger off at one point, so I could get some sleep.'

'Any idea who planted the bomb?'

He looks at me again, straight in the eye. The unfocused recklessness on his face has evaporated. I can only see serious-ness now. Dead seriousness. Alexander King is a man of polar extremes. Maybe creative geniuses like him spend their time lurching from one end of the spectrum to the other.

'I've been mulling over that question for hours, in my little moving time warp over the Atlantic,' he says, in a quiet voice. 'The answer is no, goddammit, I wish I did.'

'Did anything seem suspicious, out of place?'

He shakes his head.

'No,' he says. 'It was all happening as planned until the bomb went off.'

'Were there any CCTV cameras backstage?'

He shakes his head.

'Nope, alas,' he says. 'With hindsight, I should have put cameras everywhere. Even if Nigel disapproves.'

'What about the model who carried the handbag?' I say. 'Did you have any problems with her?'

'You mean Ally?' Anguish slides into his face; he runs an uneasy hand through his mop of curly hair. 'Poor, poor Ally. If I remember correctly, she walked for us twice before. A gorgeous girl from California, always impeccably groomed. My casting director loves her to bits.'

'Do you know who handed the bag to Ally?'

He shakes his head again.

'It could have been anyone,' he says. 'I wish I could give you a name, but there were hundreds of people working backstage. It was fucking chaotic. Do you think it was an inside job?'

'The NYPD and FBI are looking into this,' I say, hoping they still are. 'Who's responsible for bags?'

'Steve Mortimer,' he says. 'He supervises bags and millinery for all my shows. I think he had about five or six assistants working for him.'

I jot the name down on my pad.

'We'll remind our American cousins to run background checks on Mr Mortimer's assistants, as a matter of priority,' I say. 'Any Brits among them?'

He shakes his head.

'All Americans, I'm afraid.'

'Have you had any problems with Mr Mortimer?'

He scrunches up his face.

'Steve's a bit of a character.'

'What sort?'

'He drinks a lot. Parties a lot, too. But he also takes his

job seriously, seldom puts a foot wrong. He's a real perfectionist when it comes to shows, has an excellent sense of what works on the runway. And what *doesn't* work, which is usually more important. That's why I give him a fat bonus every year.'

'Is Steve doing the London show tonight?'

'He is.'

I sit up straighter in my chair.

'Where's Mr Mortimer now?'

'He flew back to London with me, must have headed straight to Old Billingsgate after we landed.'

If Steve Mortimer did indeed return to London on King's jet, we should bring him in for questioning at once. I make an e-note reminder to do so, before taking a deep breath. It's time to ask the question that has been on the tip of my tongue ever since King sauntered into my office.

'What about Miss von Meyer?' I hear a note of urgency in my voice. 'Why did you dedicate the shows to her, after such a long time?'

He's hesitating again, even frowning a little.

'I've always wanted to,' he says.

'She died twenty years ago, didn't she? Why dedicate two shows to her now?' There's a rigid tightness to my tone.

He shifts in his seat.

'I thought it was high time to do so.'

King is holding something back as far as Maya is concerned, but I can't quite put my finger on it.

'Care to elaborate?'

He's hesitating again.

'Bit of a long explanation,' he says.

'Go on.'

'I still see and hear Maya in my head. I hear her voice whenever I pick up a pen to sketch a design; visualise her rosebud mouth. If I see her lips crinkling downwards in disapproval, I throw the design away and start again. That's how I separate imperfection from perfection.'

A sepia-tinted image of a perfect girl wafts back to mind, causing pain to puncture my heart. I understand what King is trying to say, what it's like to see and hear someone in one's head, what it means to be pursued by a ghostly wraith from the past that keeps flitting in and out of shadow.

'Her death must have really affected you.' I eventually find my voice.

He stares at his hands for a couple of moments.

'I remember the call, the one saying they'd found her body. It didn't make any sense at all. I'd seen her the day before at my studio in London. I'd spent hours draping fabric around her body, seized by delicious possibility. I was so shattered by the news, I couldn't work for weeks afterwards.'

His words stab me even harder; I clench my fists. I understand precisely what King must have gone through. What it means to lose someone, the sheer senselessness of it all; what it means to be incapacitated for days afterwards. How loss can shipwreck a person, dissolve both sanity and reason.

Silence overtakes us for a couple of moments.

'You look like you want to punch someone,' he says.

Bloody hell, I should watch my body language.

'Do you think the bomber was connected to Maya in any way?' I say, unclenching my fists and doing my best to inject a crisp coolness into my voice.

He shakes his head.

'If there's a link, I can't see it.'

'Can you think of anyone who wants to stop you from commemorating Maya?'

'Only tree-hugging, anti-fur loonies come to mind.'

'Right.' I sigh. 'Do you think Mr De Luca might have something to do with what happened in Manhattan?'

He laughs, a loud dismissive chortle.

'Absolutely not.'

'Why not?'

'Gio's harmless. He's cultivated a big bad-boy image over the years, with those dark shades of his. But trust me, he's a softie at heart. He wouldn't hurt a fly.'

'Hmm.'

'The man's a typical Italian – his bark is much worse than his bite.'

'Can you tell me how this bet came about, what you agreed on in Milan?'

'It's a long story.'

'I have the time.'

Xander: When Lucia said that Gio wanted to meet me for lunch, I got a bit worried. We've had fairly limited contact over the years, apart from shaking each other's hands at cocktail parties and making loud and rude remarks about each other to journalists. Neither of us took these barbed comments too seriously; we both knew they were a quintessential part of the media game. The more controversial our statements were, the better it was for business. Now, if the big bad boy wanted to meet for lunch, he had probably stopped being bad and turned mad – or sad.

Both options alarmed me.

I sensed that something wasn't quite right with old Gio as

soon as we greeted each other at the restaurant. His handshake felt limper than usual, more uncertain. I studied his face. He looked pretty much the same, but his eyes were rheumy, wrinkled around the edges. The fire in them was no longer burning as bright. I suppose old age and disillusion catch up with all of us.

He said that I looked *molto fantastico*.

I said he looked fabulous, too.

We chatted briefly about his niece Allegra, whom he dotes on. She had moved from Rome to Los Angeles and he missed her a lot. He only got on to real business after he poured our third glasses of champagne.

[*Lucia said you had Prosecco that afternoon.*]

Oh no, most definitely not.

[*Hmm . . .*]

Gio clinked my glass and said he had a proposal to make. He was looking to improve the cash situation of his company and wondered if I would be interested in investing in G&G. $30 million for 3 per cent, he said.

I said I would think about it.

Our conversation then moved to sources of inspiration.

He said his niece Allegra had bewitched him ever since she was born, which is why he was tempted to relocate to LA so he could see her more often. He said he finds inspiration in her dazzling eyes, the energy of her youth, the flush of her beauty. I told him that I find inspiration in the morbid, in the honesty of the grotesque. He nodded; my words did not surprise him. I added, on a whim, that I was planning two fashion shows to commemorate the girl who had inspired my work for more than twenty years. His eyes lit up; he said it was a fine idea. Muses should be feted and remembered, he added, because they are few and far between.

I said I intended to use technology in a special way, during the two shows.

How exactly? he asked, raising an eyebrow.

I said I was planning to project a hologram of Maya onto a catwalk above the water, at the end of the first show in Manhattan. A giant hologram of Maya in a white dress, her hair flying loose and free, one gradually receding into a crystal cage on the runway. An identical cage would make an appearance on a second catwalk in London the following night. There, the hologram would emerge from the cage and morph into a butterfly. A white butterfly, spreading its wings above the river where she died. The Thames, as you may know, is a continuation of the River Isis.

[*Why a white butterfly?*]

I saw a white butterfly buffeted by the winds when I went for a jog on Hampstead heath, just a few hours before the police rang about Maya. The butterfly was massive, the size of both of my palms. It was also struggling to fly. I ran up to it, only to discover that one of its beautiful white wings was torn, scuffed around its edges. I remember standing helplessly on the heath, wishing I could help it take flight. The wind eventually swept the butterfly behind a copse of gnarled trees.

[*Hmm . . .*]

I later read somewhere that butterflies represent the spirits of the dead, their hopes and dreams. That's when I realised I probably saw that white butterfly for a reason. I swear it was Maya, her spirit struggling to take flight. Gio said it was a beautiful idea, that he loved the symbolism of a muse being cocooned in a crystal chrysalis before being set free above water. I said it was time we used technology to elevate our hopes and dreams above our regrets and fears.

An imperfect hologram of Maya would be my new illusion of perfection.

I saw Gio nodding away.

Technology should be about escapism, not imprisonment, I added for good measure. Even if technology has already enslaved us to our devices, to our phones and screens. The same goes for fashion. Fashion is really about escapism, the simple act of setting our imaginations free.

We clinked our flutes to what I had just said.

It's amazing what one can do with technology these days, said Gio. He added he'd enormous success with Make-to-Match, a 3D app that matches his designs to virtual mannequins. The app allows clients to make bespoke tweaks to base designs, such as to waistline shape, hem length and fabric colour. The app is now the main moneyspinner for his second line, *Mio Gio*. He was glad his tech guys saw the commercial potential of Make-to-Match early on. I said, with a sigh, that I wished that my tech guys had got their act together on that front, built a similar make-to-match app instead of concentrating their efforts on smart wearables. As an afterthought, I added that technology would eventually put the two of us out of work. Fashion designers will soon become irrelevant to humanity.

Gio stiffened.

What do you mean? he said.

I said that computers would soon produce better, more-perfect designs than us human designers. I envisaged a near future where I could substitute an item on one of my catwalks, an item completely designed by a machine, and no one would be able to tell which item it was.

Rubbish, said Gio with a loud sniff. Computers can make small useful tweaks, but they will never produce designs with the human flair, touch or essence. I merely shrugged and said that computers would soon automate fashion designers out of their jobs . . . and I was willing to bet on it.

It was as if I had just detonated a bomb in the restaurant. Gio sat still in his chair for several long moments, head cocked to one side. I thought at one point that he was going to punch me in the face for suggesting that he would soon be made redundant by his own software programmers.

Instead, he flashed me a cheeky grin.

How about $30 million? he said. If I win the bet, he'll get his tech guys to design a similar app for Alexander King. If I lose, I will be $30 million poorer but I will also end up with 3 per cent of G&G.

[*Wait . . . wait a minute. Miss Graves never mentioned Make-to-Match. Her account of what happened in Milan is a little different from what you've just told me.*]

Oh, didn't Lucia mention the app? I guess she has never thought too highly of it in the first place. She's really old school in her ways, doesn't even use iPredict. I guess that's why I find her charming. It reassures me that there are still young people out there who aren't hot and bothered about predictive technology. Lucia's delightfully refreshing, by the way. She reads thick, old-fashioned psychoanalytic books about big-picture issues, has all sorts of wonderful theories about unfairness in life and fairness in death. Definitely a brighter spark than the PA I had before her. Anyhow, I thought that Gio's bet was cheeky but fun. Life's a gamble. The odds are stacked against you, but life becomes a bit more interesting – and slightly more worth living – when you decide to go all in, once in a while. So I raised my flute quite cheerfully, that afternoon.

Gio grabbed his glass and clinked mine in return.

[*Lucia said you made Mr De Luca promise that he wouldn't mention the bet to anyone.*]

Did I? Dear Lord. I have no recollection of making dear Gio promise me anything. I probably drank too much champagne that afternoon, as usual. Both Gio and I had nothing to lose, everything to gain. It didn't matter how the dice rolled, how the coin landed when it fell, heads or tails. Gio would get his cash injection if I lost – and I would get a fancy new app if I won. It was all in the name of fun. Fun is increasingly difficult to come by these days, to be honest with you. When you've had a shitload of fun during your younger days, fucked everything you could possibly dream of fucking, life's a bit of a fucking anti-climax in middle age.

Alexander King flops back in his chair, spreading his palms to emphasise the point he has just made. The seriousness in his eyes has vanished; I can see a slight muddiness creeping into them. Is he telling the truth? I've just heard two slightly different versions of the same conversation, from two people who were present in Milan that day. Both versions must surely be slight dilutions of reality. Truth's a problematic beast; the problem with truth is getting to the bottom of it. If King's version is closer to reality, it's entirely in De Luca's interest for the show to go ahead, for the machine-designed item to make an appearance on the catwalk. Yet something tells me that this bizarre little bet is relevant to our investigation and I should have a chat with Signor De Luca as soon as possible.

'Are you still going ahead with tonight's show?' I say.

'Of course,' he says, his shoulders taking on a resolute line. 'The show must go on, as they say.'

'Will you be changing anything in the programme, in light of what happened last night?'

He hesitates.

'I have a reputation for improvising, tinkering with things up to the last minute. It all depends on how the runway looks on the day, the lighting and weather outside, that sort of thing.'

'I see.'

'That said, I'm determined to stick to my original plan, project Maya's hologram above the river.'

'Miss Graves showed me a sketch,' I say. 'The first outfit to go down the runway tonight, to be precise.'

'You must be joking.'

I can see annoyance skimming over King's face.

'She shouldn't have.' His voice is sharp and curt. 'It was supposed to be a secret. A *big* secret.'

'It may well be relevant to our investigation, so please don't get too upset with her,' I say. 'The design looked like something Mr De Luca himself would create, in my humble opinion. Why are you copying him?'

He's hesitating again.

'I, er . . . wanted to make a point.'

'What sort of point?'

'That . . . er . . . that Gio and I had a little bet.'

His garbled sentence hangs limply in the air above our heads.

'I don't follow,' I say.

Something is sliding into his eyes; it looks like a flash of clarity.

'I had . . . er . . . hoped to flatter Gio,' he says. 'As they say, imitation is the best form of flattery.'

I swear King is holding something back.

'What do you really hope to achieve with the two shows?' I say. 'Are they supposed to be a beginning? Or have you intended them as an *end*?'

His mouth drifts open. Something tangled is flitting over his face. He mumbles something indistinct, the first incoherent thing I've heard since he sauntered into this office. I detect a small crack in the man's facade, a chink in the armour the great Alexander King usually wears.

'I didn't quite catch that,' I say.

He appears to rally himself.

'I . . . er . . .'

'If it's an end, what are you planning to end?' My question is sharp, with a serrated edge.

Something new drifts over King's face.

I think it's fear.

Brilliant designers are also superb storytellers. They tell a story in each creation, one that appeals to the five senses, that people would love to believe. A story that reassures, makes their lives better and more meaningful. This is why we have chosen Alexander King as our Designer of the Year. He is an unparalleled storyteller, a true creative genius who tells memorable tales with each of his designs, fables with splendid beginnings and ends.

Association of Fashion Designers

Chapter Eleven

Xander

Dear Lord. I can't have Grey Man sniffing around my *true* plans for tonight. I'm tempted to sack Lucia for showing him the sketch. The last thing I want is for him to figure out what will happen at the show. I need to pull myself together, try not to look afraid or suspicious, keep lying through my teeth. The only problem is: I had a moment of clarity when Grey Man asked me what happened at lunch in Milan. Bounteous words and possibilities flowed into my head, spilled out of my mouth. That moment has vanished. Now, I have a thick, gelatinous headache and an enormous wish to lie down flat. I need to survive this chat, marshal the last of my fast-ebbing brainpower, maintain some semblance of lucidity before collapsing on a bed somewhere.

'I was planning to begin with a bang,' I say. 'One should start with something shocking, finish with something equally memorable.'

Grey Man nods, a curt bob of his head. I should look confident, keep spinning thick yarns out of thin air. I reckon my explanation has been pretty adequate so far. Maybe even convincing.

'The first dress on tonight's catwalk will be a tribute to Gio, to our bet, which helped inspire proceedings.'

I pause. My words hang in the resulting silence. They sound like a lie, even to my own ears.

Grey Man tilts his head slightly.

'I see,' he says.

I really fucking hope he believes me.

He shrugs.

'Well, Mr King, I mustn't detain you any longer,' he says. 'I'm sure you have lots to do before the show. In the meantime . . .'

He fixes his gaze on me.

'Call if anything troubles you, or makes you suspicious,' he says. 'Do you have a direct number?'

I nod, pulling a business card out of my pocket and handing it over.

'Thank you,' he says, taking it from me. 'And thank you for coming in.'

'Not a problem at all,' I say, rising from my chair. 'I hope you catch the bomber soon.'

'That's precisely what we intend to do.'

I'm tempted to ask Grey Man who he is, but it's a bit awkward to do so now. Not after we've been chatting civilly for such a long time. I'm sure that G&T Nigel can tell me the man's name later. I can, however, ask Grey Man *why* he does what he does. People seldom get to the *why* of things, which is a shame because *why* is usually more interesting than *who*, *how* or *what*. I'm sure Grey Man will agree with me. It's his job to find out the *why* behind things, I reckon. Otherwise he wouldn't be calling himself a cop. I wonder what sort of police officer he is.

'Why are you involved with this case?' I say. 'Are you a detective who works on fashion-related cases?'

He looks surprised.

'Not really,' he says. 'I spent most of my career in drugs. Which is why I find this case fascinating, if challenging.'

'Oh.'

I wait for him to elaborate, but he doesn't. Silence hangs over us, a silence I feel obliged to fill.

'I'll definitely ring if I find trouble,' I say. 'I may even call if I have trouble finding trouble.'

Something's flickering on the edge of his mouth; I hope it's amusement.

'Very well, Mr King,' he says.

I take a step forward from my chair. My legs feel like tarnished, leaden weights. My brain is now running on exhaust fumes; my feet are dawdling several unfortunate paces behind. I stumble in the direction of the door, praying that they will carry me until I get out of this building. I need to keep pretending that everything is shipshape, that nothing is wrong.

'Maybe you should have a lie-down before the show,' I hear Grey Man's voice behind me. 'You look as though you might need one.'

At least G&T Nigel has done something right today. He's summoned a car to pick me up from New Scotland Yard and take me home so I can collapse face down on a divan some-where. I don't recognise the chauffeur, a young man with a blond ponytail and dark shades over his eyes (dear Lord, have my aides hired yet another pesky aide whom I don't need?), but at least the boy has brought my favourite Lamborghini over and is holding the door open with a wide smile. I propel myself through the door, collapse onto the back seat. Damn it, there's something important I should be asking Nigel, but I can't remember what.

Just before the chauffeur shuts the door, it hits me. The question that perplexed me in Grey Man's office.

'Wait a minute,' I say, hastily sticking a foot out of the door and waving a hand at Nigel. 'I have a question for you.'

He looks astonished.

'What?' he says.

'Who the fuck was the man in that room? The one in the well-cut but unimaginative grey suit?'

Nigel looks twice as surprised.

'I thought you knew,' he says.

'I didn't quite catch the name,' I say, trying not to look too embarrassed. 'Too much going on, too much to take in.'

'He's Christian Verger, the Commissioner.'

'You must be joking.'

'I never do.'

My mind flits back to various small design elements I'd noticed during my brief spell in Grey Man's office, details that I should have interpreted more accurately (especially as I pride myself on being a man who appreciates every tiny element and spends his time obsessing over them).

'So that's why the grey carpet in that office was unusually plush . . .'

I pause as another stark realisation hits me in the gut.

'Why the fuck is the Commissioner involved?' I continue, my words a hiss. 'I thought I was speaking to an underling.'

'Excellent question,' says Nigel, looking down at me with a slightly pitying expression. 'Now you know why I was so eager to remain at your side.'

*

My chauffeur pulls out from the parking bay in a sharp screech of tyres. Nigel's last sentence is still ringing in my head. Why the fuck is the Commissioner himself involved in this little morbid mess around me? Will he help or hinder my plans for tonight? And who the hell is Christian Verger, in any case?

I pull out my smartphone and type the man's name. His Wikipedia bio springs up at once. His 3D digital double has a large benign smile and looks as dapper as the version I saw earlier. It's also wearing an identical grey suit (does the poor man own only one suit?). I try to focus on the words:

> Christian Verger (born June 1983) is the current Commissioner of the Metropolitan police service in London. He has held various senior roles in the Force. He headed the Cyber Drug Crime Unit (2021–2023) and was subsequently appointed Deputy Assistant Commissioner of the Specialist Crime Unit (2024–2026). In January 2027, he was promoted to Assistant Commissioner following Philip Gregory's abrupt resignation in the wake of the Facebook hacking scandal. On 21 February 2030, the Home Office and Metropolitan Police Service jointly announced that Verger would be appointed as the next Commissioner of the Metropolitan Police Service by King Charles III, following the shock death of Verger's predecessor, Mary Jane McDougall.

Dear Lord, I'm struggling to concentrate on the words on the screen. They are dissolving into a slight haze. I blink, trying to think past the befuddled mess in my head. So . . . it looks like Christian Verger is new to the job, having dealt with drugs for most of his career. I force my eyes back to the screen.

Early life and career

Verger's parents are the late Sir Henry Francis Verger, a British businessman and philanthropist, and Annette Verger (née Berg), a Danish–British visual artist. Verger is believed to have spent his childhood abroad and was home-schooled by private tutors before enrolling at Eton College. He subsequently received a BA (Hons) in Philosophy from the University of Cambridge (Sidney Sussex College), graduating with the highest grade in his class. He was later awarded an MSc in Criminology and Criminal Justice from the University of Oxford (St John's College), also finishing top of his cohort. Before joining the Metropolitan Police Service as a constable, he was . . .

Damn it, my head is really killing me. My thoughts are also disintegrating into a swirling mess. Maybe it's time for a few more pills, anything that might help lessen the dense pressure between my eyebrows . . .

'Is there anything you would like, sir?' my chauffeur says.

I open my eyes; I catch a brief glimpse of his ponytailed reflection in the rear-view mirror.

'I would like to be left alone,' I say.

'I'll put the divider up, then.'

The glass slides up between us, cutting off all noise from the front. I extract four blue pills from my bag and prod a button next to my seat. The lacquered door of my drinks cabinet glides open. I study its contents, only to groan. There isn't any water inside. I can only see a single can of soda, a drink that I detest. What's the point of having so many fucking aides when not a single one of them can remember to stock my drinks cabinet with what I want or need? Thankfully, my favourite brand of whisky is still inside, next to a cut-crystal tumbler. I flick a couple of ice cubes into the glass, fill it to the brim with whisky, pop the pills into my mouth. The liquid burns my throat, sears my insides. Unfortunately, it doesn't wash reality away from my consciousness or wipe my soul clean.

A new realisation strikes.

I'm exhausted.

Knackered to the extreme.

My eyelids are drooping, tugged down by silent weights. A warm, dark void is extending its arms, beckoning me right in. I'm tempted to surrender, fall headlong into its embrace. But hell, I shouldn't be falling asleep, because I should be picking up my phone and ringing . . . Who was I planning to call again? Lucia? Viola? Fucking hell, I haven't chatted with that dear girl for ages, I'm extremely puzzled why she isn't coming tonight. I also wonder how she's getting on in her quest for a mate . . . Is my chauffeur going in the correct direction? We're passing Hyde Park – I think I saw the Royal Albert Hall whizz by a couple of seconds ago in a blur of red bricks and terracotta friezes – and I swear that my London penthouse isn't located anywhere west of Hyde Park. But maybe it's just an enforced diversion due to road works . . .

Maybe I should stop worrying, surrender to the beckoning warmth . . .

I believe my chin is drooping forward onto my chest, which is a bit of an odd development, but I can no longer think properly . . .

Something slams in the distance, cutting across my semi-comatose state. Maybe I should wrench myself out of the void I'm in, surface briefly for air. An engine falls silent. I hear a door open, feel a breeze wafting across my face. It's unexpectedly revitalising. I try to open my eyes wide, take in my surroundings, but it isn't easy. Something heavy is still weighing my eyelids down. I grit my teeth, try to force my lids apart. Light filters in through the resulting crack, swirling around my pupils before coalescing in the shape and form of a woman. I last saw her at Old Billingsgate three days ago, when we inspected the preparations for the show. She had a broad smile on her lips then. She isn't smiling now. In fact, she looks positively annoyed. I can see her lips moving as vigorously as those earrings on her lobes, but I can't hear a thing.

I clench my fingers and drag my ears into focus, causing something to filter through:

'I thought you put it into the whisky.'

'I did,' an indignant voice says from afar.

'Then why is he stirring?' she says, sounding twice as cross. 'We don't want him to wake up prematurely.'

I'm stirring because I fucking want to be in control of all my digits and senses, because I want to get up and punch the ponytailed arsehole who spiked my drink. But something is pulling me back down into oblivion, despite my best efforts. I should fight it, I know. But I can't. I'm weak and useless. I feel as much. My head is drooping forward again and I am powerless to stop it . . .

The creative impulse is what keeps me going. There's a special joy in creating something out of nothing. It makes my fingers tingle, my heart sing. Yet creating is also about destroying, making nothing out of something. The destructive impulse is what keeps me alive. I love blasting things to bits, smashing stuff to smithereens. Sometimes, you need to tear things apart in order to build.

Alexander King, interview in *Newsweek*

Chapter Twelve

He staggered across the living room, clutching a bottle of beer, before collapsing onto the sofa. His familiar oily reek wafted over me. Pickled onions and fish guts, mingled with alcohol and weed. Memories of what he did to me flooded back in a brutal rush; I had to bite my tongue to prevent myself from screaming. I bit so hard, the tangy metallic taste of blood began spreading through my mouth. He raised the bottle, chugged down its contents in a series of loud glugs, then tossed the bottle away. It hit the floor with a thud, rolled in my direction and came to a halt a couple of yards from me. I was tempted to seize the bottle's neck, run forward and smash it on his skull with all the force of my wrath, fuelled by the corrosive shame and bitterness that festered inside me. But I clenched my fingers and swallowed the urge down, knowing I should not yield to folly.

So I waited.

And waited.

Silent as a mouse, barely daring to breathe. Terrified that he would sense that I was cowering in the corner, that something might give away my hidey-hole between the cupboard and the grandfather clock. He belched again, causing another nauseating cloud to waft toward me. The stench triggered another gag reflex; this time, I had to sink my fingernails into my palms to prevent myself from choking. Minutes passed, each second an agonising tick of the clock. I heard him scratching himself, picking away at the scabs on his skin. At one point, he grabbed the remote control and began flipping through the channels, before cursing and turning the television off. Then it happened. His eyes strayed towards the bottle I had placed on the side table, identical to the one that lay on the floor. I froze, scarcely daring to breathe. Please, I begged God, any deity who might be listening.

Please pick up the bottle.

His fingers crept forward in its direction.

Please, please, oh please.

He grabbed the bottle and unscrewed its top, sniffed it suspiciously.

Don't just stare at it, for Christ's sake. Drink it. Every last drop.

I saw him raise the bottle, heard him belch violently again. But . . . I couldn't see if any liquid passed his lips. Not from where I was crouching; his face was turned away from me. He placed the bottle down with a thud. More minutes dragged by, more agonising ticks of the grandfather clock. I felt my hands turning numb, my legs falling asleep. Yet my thoughts continued to race, to torture me with each passing second. I dared not think what might happen if he got up from the sofa and found me crouching in the corner. Did he drink any of it? Maybe he didn't. Maybe he did but it was just a small amount of liquid.

An insufficient one.

So churned my thoughts, twisting into my head like blades.

He shifted about on the sofa, belching again.

Damn it.

Tears began trickling down my cheeks, tears of suppressed rage mingled with frustration and fear. At one point, I nearly sobbed out loud. But then it happened. I saw his head nodding forward. The room fell silent. Not a scratch, not a belch. I could only hear the solemn ticking of the grandfather clock, the nervous thudding within the confines of my ribcage.

I crept out of my hidey-hole in the corner. Silently, like a terrified rabbit, one poised to flee out of the front door if he moved the smallest fraction of an inch, at the faintest sign of a twitch.

I crouched on my knees.

Flicked a lighter and held it up to the candle I'd placed on the side table.

The flame was timid, at first. It cast tenuous dancing shadows on the wall opposite, shadows that elongated and shapeshifted across the face of the grandfather clock. Yet I saw tantalising possibility in the flame's depths. Light at the end of the tunnel. Hope of a new life ahead, one involving Nice Real Dad instead of Evil Step-Dad. I watched the flame flicker for a few more moments, growing bigger and bolder, before reaching out and knocking the candle over.

Straight into the plate of dried pine cones next to it.

The awful thing about living in a cabin is that winter reduces you to a shivering, whimpering wreck, especially after you've run out of logs to burn. The idea came to me on a particularly frigid February day. I woke up that morning and discovered frosty whirls on the windowpanes, thin narrow icicles protruding from the eaves. The wind was howling outside, emitting long, mournful shrieks that pained my ears. It was so cold in the cabin, even my fingernails were blue. I had to look for a pair of gloves and a muffler as soon I crawled out of bed.

Yet freezing makes you think.

About how not to freeze.

How to freeze someone out of your life.

Permanently.

So, I did some research on drugs in the (comparatively warmer) school library, particularly on the chemical properties of antifreeze. I soon discovered that ethylene glycol was colourless, odourless and seductively sweet. Some of the earliest symptoms of antifreeze poisoning included grogginess, a feeling of inebriation, a lack of coordination and slurred speech.

That's because the chemical slices cells apart.

Neat, I thought.

My determination crystallised after Mom died. I just needed the right time to carry out the dastardly deed.

As they say, timing is everything.

The wonderful thing about living in a log cabin is that it burns pretty damned well, with a sweltering breeze to speed things along. The blaze was massive. The resulting pall of smoke was spotted by a neighbour a mile away, who then came scuttling over and summoned the fire brigade. It took four firefighters to put the blaze out. I hid in the neighbouring woods as the cabin burnt itself out, creeping back only after it was reduced to a pile of smouldering ashes. Two police officers were outside the property when I ran up with fake tears in my eyes, my mouth a horrified whirl.

It worked.

My best friend told the police that I spent the entire evening with her, even though she knew I left soon after dinner. If she wondered where I spent those missing hours, she never asked.

I never told her, either.

Orphaned, now homeless.

That was what the local newspaper said the next day, on page 17. Small donations and messages of sympathy began flooding in from the public. My best friend's family took me in for a few weeks as forensic experts combed through the wreckage of the place I once called home.

They found a charred body inside.

One burnt so thoroughly, they had to verify his identity from his dental records. He was next to a slightly melted beer bottle. I never realised that glass could melt in fire. His mates testified that he had drunk a lot at the local bar earlier that evening. One of them even conveniently swore that the man drank seven consecutive beers before staggering out into the night. The coroner eventually concluded that Step-Dad had accidentally tipped the candle over in his drunken stupor and was rendered unconscious by smoke and cyanide inhalation long before the flames consumed the building (I never knew that cheap PVC sofas release cyanide when burnt).

On the surface, I had played with fire and got away with it. But something continued to nag at me, made me certain that my past would come back to destroy me. I still have that feeling years later.

It's a feeling that devours my every waking moment, tears me apart.

They say that no one can hide the truth for ever, that it eventually comes back to find you.

It's true.

*

It took me seven weeks to get my plan off the ground, but I eventually found my way to the Big Apple. I took a bus to the nearest town, before hitching rides with sympathetic truck drivers and families heading east. I took special care to sit at the back of each truck, to be on the safe side, made sure there was a woman or child in each vehicle before I got in. I carried a large cardboard sign with painted words: *GOING TO NYC TO LOOK FOR MY DAD.* It helped attract attention, lots of sympathetic drivers scooted to a halt. I carried a small rucksack containing a toothbrush, a few items of clothing (donated by a local charity) and Mom's wooden box (I'd buried it under a tree the night of the fire, dug it up again before I left). The small donations from the public helped. I had some pocket money to buy bread, apples and other scraps of food.

The only person I was sorry to leave behind, to say goodbye to, was my best friend. We hugged each other hard before I left. She promised me that she would look for me the moment she made it to New York City, someday. I had a feeling she would. After all, she had always been more ambitious than me, believed her eventual destiny was greatness and fame. I will always remember her waving to me, looking thoroughly dejected as my bus sped off into the distance. I waved back until I could no longer see her from the window. Distance did not blunt my sense of loss, the knowledge that I was leaving the only person I cared for behind. Distance also did not blur my memories or soothe my dreams at night. Flashes of the past continued to prey on my mind, blot my soul with dread and play in a torturous video loop in my head. I even woke up screaming once, after nodding off on the back of a truck in the middle of the night. You can burn a man's body to a crisp, but you can't incinerate gruesome memories in your head.

Memories of grisly intrusion, of vicious debasement.

When I arrived in Manhattan, I immediately went to the address listed on my birth certificate.

My birthplace turned out to be a small decaying brownstone in pre-gentrified Hell's Kitchen, on a graffiti-covered street where discarded newspapers fluttered past iron gratings. The steps leading up to the front door were littered with cat shit and plastic bags; one even flapped from the tangle of electric wires above my head. I tapped a tarnished brass knocker in the shape of a lion. The door swung open with a jarring creak; a black cat with white socks shot out through the widening gap and scampered down the steps before vanishing behind a terracotta flowerpot. I turned back around to discover that a small, wizened woman was peering suspiciously down at me.

I said I was looking for my father.

She said that no man had lived in that place for ten years, not since her husband died in a car accident.

I said that Marianne Lily Robinson was my mother's name and that I had been born in that apartment, more than fifteen years ago. Did she know my mom? I asked, crossing two fingers behind my back.

She looked blank.

I mentioned Dad's name.

She looked twice as vacant.

That was when I knew I had arrived at a dead end and I had come all the way to New York City to find out that Dad was nowhere to be found. That was also the precise moment that tears finally rose to my eyes, tears that had eluded me at Mom's hospital bed.

I burst out sobbing.

Most unexpectedly, Wizened Woman took me into her home after I poured out my sob story (with the necessary omissions). She said she couldn't afford to feed me, not on her pathetic pension. Like me, she had to count every last dime. But she nevertheless said that I could sleep in a spare sleeping bag in her guest room for a few days, while I figured out what to do next. The windowless space was tiny and stuffy. It smelt of cat fur, liquorice cough syrup and half-decayed mothballs. Yet it was much better than a sack on the back of a snorting truck, one spewing out exhaust fumes throughout the night. I spent the next few days traipsing around the neighbourhood, asking everyone who opened their doors if they remembered my dad. No one did. A doddery old man with white whiskers even spat on the floor when I mentioned Mom's name to him. I gathered they weren't the friendliest of neighbours when she lived there. I even rang all the men in the phone book who shared Dad's name. There were three of them in total. It proved a fruitless activity that consumed lots of coins and yielded nothing in return.

Two problems occupied my mind during those desperate nights I spent in Wizened Woman's guest room, knowing that I was trespassing on her hospitality and would have to move on soon.

Dad and cash.

How on earth could I ever hope to track my father down in a city of multiple millions? And how on earth would I survive once I ran out of charity money? Even before I reached New

York, I was reduced to buying heavily discounted bags of apples that were either bruised or damaged. Within three days of arriving in New York, I was forced to ration my food, limiting myself to two apples every eight hours.

It was damned ironic to subsist on small apples in the Big Apple.

It was also damned awful to be perpetually ravenous in the big city. Temptations lurked on every pavement, beckoned from every shop window. Delectable cupcakes piled high on platters, exquisite chocolates in dazzling foils, ambrosial ice creams behind glassy counters. I forced myself to keep my eyes on the ground as I walked the streets. But I couldn't escape the intoxicating smells that curled around me, the heady aromas of freshly baked bread and roasting chicken. That's when I realised it's easier to be miserable in the big city than in a small town. Misery, like success, is relative. Misery is compounded by the knowledge that other people are doing much better than you, that they still have parents and can afford to buy less-wormy apples.

I grew so gaunt during those days, my cheekbones protruded and my face was reduced to sunken hollows. Little did I know that it was a fashionable look at the time. They called it heroin chic (given that heroin killed Mom, I've always thought the phrase was dreadfully paradoxical).

One day, I sat down and wrote a letter to my best friend. It said:

Dearest one,

I've not had any luck finding Dad. I'm also running out of money. There are days when I'm tempted to head in your direction, go back to school. But something at the back of my mind

167

says that I will find him if I persevere, even if I'm struggling now. Maybe I should listen to that voice, I don't know . . .

I got a letter from my best friend two weeks later. It spelled out the minutiae of her everyday life, which I lapped up eagerly, and finished with the words:

> You should trust your intuition, I guess. If your instincts say that you will eventually find your real dad, you will. Gran said yesterday that I should write to tell you that 'one has to adapt in order to survive', 'even wolves blend in' and that 'necessity is often the mother of reinvention, not invention'. Frankly, I don't know what she's trying to say; I guess you'll eventually figure it out.
>
> Miss you loads,
>
> Your best friend

I remember tucking her letter in my bag, so that I could carry it around close to me. Her gran's words brought back memories of a wolf I saw many, many moons before. It was trotting away into the distance, framed by high grass and a low-hanging sun, its greyish-white fur burnished amber-gold by the fading light. The creature was indeed perfectly camouflaged in the stiff wintry landscape, I would never have spotted it if light hadn't shimmered in sync with its tail. I froze in my tracks, mesmerised by its loping gait. At one point, the wolf turned around to look at me with appraising eyes, as if it were trying to work out whether I was chicken or foe.

Even wolves blend in, indeed.

While my best friend's letter made me miss her even more, it also hardened my determination to remain in the big city against the odds, to adapt to life there, maybe even reinvent myself. One evening, as I walked back to the brownstone with a paper bag containing five bruised apples, contemplating the fact that I was down to my last two dollars and facing the very real possibility that I had to start begging for food on the streets with the sign ORPHANED AND HUNGRY, someone tapped me on the shoulder.

I spun around to discover a man in a jaunty brown suit, with a broad-brimmed fedora sitting on his head at a rakish angle. A red polka-dotted handkerchief poked out from his breast pocket.

'You look bloody gorgeous,' he said. 'Might you consider being a model?'

I showed up at the agency the following day, clutching the business card that Fedora Man had pulled out of his pocket with a flourish. The office was just off Times Square in Manhattan, a place I had seen multiple times before on television. Yet the real thing still took my breath away. The surrounding streets pulsated with frenetic energy, thrummed with incessant movement. Giant advertisements and billboards with neon lights soared high above, made me feel small and insignificant. The roar of traffic blasted my ears. Smog and exhaust fumes blotted out the sun, made my eyes water. For a couple of moments, I wished I was back in quiet Montana, where the sun shone peach-gold in the evenings and a clean breeze ruffled my clothes in the mornings.

I eventually found the agency's entrance, a shiny glass door on a quieter street just two blocks away. Sudden doubt flooded me; I wondered what could have possessed me to come here. I took in a deep breath, told myself I had nothing to lose. Raised a finger, pressed the buzzer.

'Yes?' a woman's voice boomed through the intercom.

I gave her my name, said Fedora Man had suggested I show up at this address.

My words were greeted by silence. I must have come to the wrong place, I thought. Or maybe Fedora Man had played a practical joke on me. With a sigh, I turned to leave. Just then I heard her say, 'Come on up.'

The agency's foyer was a large, brightly lit space that smelt of pine and vanilla. A black-and-white photo montage of beautiful women filled an entire wall. I immediately recognised a couple of faces from the billboards I'd seen along the Interstate Highway during my long journey from Montana. The receptionist turned out to be a middle-aged woman with blue tortoiseshell glasses, clad in a flamboyant fuchsia jacket with skyscraper-high pads. She eyed me beadily through her funky glasses for a couple of moments, before picking up her phone and tapping a button.

'Charlie,' she said into the receiver. 'Got another one for you.'

A black man with a goatee emerged from a door in a corner, dressed in white from head to toe. Even his sneakers and socks were white. The only thing that bled colour was the front of his hair; it was dyed psychedelic pink and purple. He gave me a long, appraising look, twitching his lips.

'This way,' he said.

I followed Charlie down a long corridor that resonated with the sound of clicking keyboards and muffled conversations behind doors. He led me to a tiny room. Three of its walls were painted black. A single plain sheet of white paper lined the opposite wall. A large camera mounted on a pedestal occupied a corner of the room, next to a series of halogen bulbs on a stand.

'So Bob spotted you on the street, told you to come in,' he said, flipping on the bulbs and pushing the pedestal forward. The light tore straight into my eyes, made me feel twice as disorientated.

'Er . . . yes,' I said in a small voice.

'I can see why. You've got a great look. Unique, if I may say so.'

'Really?'

'We can do quite a bit with what you have,' he said, giving me a wink. 'So let's get started.'

'What should I be doing?'

'Find yourself,' he said.

I gaped at Charlie in silent bewilderment.

'Forget about me and my camera,' he said with a chuckle.

'Huh?'

'My camera is just a mirror,' he said, pointing at its lens. 'A mirror for your darkest side. That's what you should be trying to find today.'

That was when I realised that I knew exactly what I should be doing.

After the photo shoot, Tortoiseshell Lady at reception asked for my name, age and contact details. I nearly said I had just turned fifteen, before changing my mind at the last minute and saying, quite confidently, that I was seventeen years of age. I then gave her Wizened Woman's address and phone number, said I was only staying there for a while. Tortoiseshell Lady rolled her eyes, shrugged and said that they would only get in touch when something came up.

If it ever did.

I trudged back to Hell's Kitchen on foot, trying not to look at the delectable pastries, cakes and other mouth-watering delights in the shops along the way. It was a long, tiring trek back to the brownstone. Wizened Woman was sitting in the kitchen when I slumped down on a chair opposite her, light-headed with hunger and exhaustion. She puckered up her lips and said: 'You have a way of brightening up the place. You've been pretty helpful with the chores, too.'

I nodded.

'But some things just can't go on for ever,' she said, giving me an apologetic grimace, followed by a regretful shrug of her shoulders.

I knew full well what she meant.

'You've been very kind to me,' I said. 'I'll try to find a way to pay you for the use of your guest room.'

She nodded.

'Give me a week, please,' I continued, hearing a plaintive note in my voice. 'I'll head back to Montana in seven days from now if I can't find a job.'

She nodded silently again.

Our little exchange meant that I had exactly a week to find employment, if I hoped to stay on in the Big Apple.

I spent the next two days pounding the streets, knocking on the doors of shops with job advertisement signs in their front windows. One bistro owner said she was looking for a part-time server, someone with previous experience waiting on tables. I was silly enough to admit I had zero experience, before adding that I was a quick learner. It was too late; I saw steel shutters coming down over the woman's eyes. I remember trudging away dejectedly from the bistro, wishing that I'd bent the truth, said I had a bit of experience. Maybe honesty literally does not pay. Maybe one has to say the right things if one wishes to get ahead in life.

Or at least say the things that people prefer to hear.

The following day, I passed a sign on a house that said: *Babysitter Wanted*. I knocked on the door to discover a frazzled-looking woman with a small crying toddler in her arms.

'You looking for a babysitter?' I asked, inclining my head in the direction of the little boy.

She nodded as the child emitted another piercing wail.

'I'm interested in the job,' I said, crossing my fingers behind my back, hoping I sounded convincing enough.

She eyed me up and down for a couple of long moments before saying: 'You don't look like a typical babysitter to me.'

'Appearances can be deceiving. I try not to be typical, in any case.'

The words spilled out of my mouth, taking me by surprise. She stared at me in silence, jiggling the baby in her arms. I thought she was on the verge of shoving the door in my face. But then she said: 'Can you do Fridays and Saturdays?'

'Yes.' I nodded.

'Awesome.' She shot me a sudden, relieved smile. 'Can you start this Friday?'

'Sure,' I said, trying not to show my growing excitement.

'Done this before?'

I hesitated, remembering what happened at the bistro. I had spent hours playing with my best friend's siblings whenever I visited their home. That surely qualified as experience with children.

I nodded.

'That's super awesome.' She gave me another broad smile. 'Can you get your papers to me by tomorrow evening, please?'

'Papers?' I said, gulping.

'References from at least two people saying you've done this before and can be trusted with kids.'

I stared at her in consternation. That was the moment I realised two important things about life. While experience matters, papers matter as much, if not more. I needed reference letters even to babysit a child, and I didn't have any. Not a single bloody document. I didn't even have a leaving certificate; I hadn't finished school. That was also the moment when I realised the sorry truth about my situation: I had come to New York City on an idealistic wild goose chase to find my father.

I had failed on that count.

I had also failed to find a job, because I didn't have any papers. It was time to go back to where I had come from, even though Gran's cabin had been reduced to a pile of cinders. Maybe my best friend's family would take me in again.

Finish school.

Work really hard.

Get all the papers I would need for a proper job someday, a secure and well-paid one.

The morning of my departure dawned bright and sunny. I carried my rucksack out of the guest room. This time, I had a large placard that said PLEASE HELP ME GET HOME TO MONTANA. I bade Wizened Woman goodbye, thanked her for her hospitality. Vowed I would return someday to repay her kindness. She nodded, pressing a small brown paper bag into my hands. I peered into it; it contained three tiny pears and a loaf of bread. Tears came to my eyes. I whispered thank you, before giving her a hug and walking in the direction of the door.

Just then, the phone rang.

A shrill sound that caused both of us to jump.

Our eyes shot in the direction of the phone in the hallway, its receiver vibrating with promise.

Wizened Woman walked over to the phone. She picked up the receiver, said hello, listened intently for a while. I saw her eyes widening at one point. She eventually beckoned me over.

'It's for you,' she said.

I placed my rucksack down and took the receiver from her, my heart thumping like a rusty piston.

'Hello,' I said.

'Bob here.' A familiar voice boomed into my ears. 'Listen, I have some good news for you.'

'Good news?'

'We've sent your photos around. Calvin Klein loved them, rang just now, would like you to go in.'

'Go in?'

'Be part of their new advertising campaign.'

'Advertising campaign?'

'Jesus.' I could hear Bob sighing over the phone. 'You're turning into a fucking parrot. Just get your ass over here, will you?'

'What for?'

'I'll need your signature on a contract, ASAP.'

'What happens after that?'

'I'll take care of the rest.'

Bob did indeed look after the rest, as promised. I went into the agency the next day to sign my contract (a standard 15 per cent for the agency, as he explained). He shook my hand solemnly, said he looked forward to several happy weeks – if not months – of working together . . . if I did my best to remain half-starved and stick-thin. I wasn't sure if he was serious or joking.

With hindsight, I think he meant it.

The shoot for Calvin Klein took place a couple of days later in a Bronx back alley. Three other waif-like models kept me company. A petite make-up artist in baggy overalls fussed over us. She darkened the circles around my eyes, dusted the area under my cheekbones, even put gloss on my lips. I was given a pair of androgynous black breeches to match what the other models were wearing. We were then arranged against a graffiti-slathered brick wall, a few feet away from an open gutter. Told to look moody and introverted as a photographer snapped away.

Oddly enough, I enjoyed every moment of the shoot.

Moody and introverted was my default mode back then, anyway.

Charlie the photographer had unleashed someone new within me, something I never knew I possessed. I found it again during the Calvin Klein photo shoot, that dark magic from within. It was fun to act out a role in front of the lens, a character that was both myself and not myself at the same time. A charade that awed and baffled me by its mirroring of my darkest side.

I felt alive in front of the camera.

Alive in a way I never knew was possible.

That was also when I realised that I could act a bit, fool others into believing things about me.

I received my first pay cheque a few days later, after Bob

had docked his requisite 15 per cent. It was one of the happiest days of my life. I went to a florist and bought a large bouquet of purple freesias for Wizened Woman. I also handed her a small envelope filled with cash. She gave me one of her gap-toothed grins, said that I was most welcome to continue living in her guest room. I nodded, said I would start paying her regularly for it. Later that night, I sat down and scribbled a letter to my best friend. It said:

> Dearest one,
>
> I'm deliriously happy to say that I've finally found a way to survive in the Big Apple while I continue to look for my dad. I got my first pay check today, a whopping $400. It's as if the floodgates of possibility have swung wide and the heavens have finally started smiling down on me. I feel insanely, stupidly rich for the first time in my life. I went straight to Saks Fifth Avenue and bought a new pair of shoes for myself, in calfskin leather. Mine were in terrible shape, plus Bob, my new agent (!!), said that I should always wear nice shoes in the company of people who matter. I also got a little present for you, for your sixteenth birthday. I'm sorry I can't be there to celebrate with you, but rest assured you're always in my thoughts. I often wonder where you are, what you might be doing. Miss you loads and hope to see you again soon.
>
> Your best friend

I posted the letter to Montana the next day. It contained a zirconia necklace, a $50 one.

Calvin Klein got in touch with Bob again, said they loved the results of the first shoot. Wanted me to do another one in a back street in Harlem, next to a door with peeling green paint and rusted hinges, yards away from a row of exposed water pipes. This time, their make-up artist painted thick kohl around my eyes, made my cheeks seem twice as hollow and emaciated. Another designer rang Bob a few days later, asking if I could model for him too. I ended up modelling for several fashion houses within four weeks of signing with Bob, collecting several respectably sized pay cheques along the way.

As they say, timing is everything.

I had the hot look of the season, the right shape at the right time. Heroin chic was the ascendant fashion, and I was lucky to have boarded the moving wagon. That said, I don't really believe in luck, even though I'm fond of using the word 'lucky' (because 'being lucky' sounds more socially acceptable). I believe in engineered serendipity. Calculated steps forward in the pursuit of one's goal (in my case, to find a way to survive in NYC). Strides that might lead to a more pleasing conflation of circumstances, a more fortuitous aligning of paths.

I still wonder what would have happened if Bob had not tapped me on the shoulder that day. But while luck often promises a more palatable future, it unfortunately does not erase the past. Flashes of what happened in Montana continued to visit me in the middle of the night, casting long twisted shadows on the bedroom wall. I would wake up each time, beads of sweat dripping down my forehead. Oily hands and red flames would dance before my eyes, merging memory with reality.

Weeks passed, then months. I began to enjoy life in the Big Apple. The city only comes alive when you have a role to play in it, when you can take a tiny slice of the apple for yourself. Job offers poured in on a regular basis, thanks to

Bob's enthusiasm and my ever-expanding portfolio. He proved to be an excellent agent; Wizened Woman's phone never stopped ringing. One day, he even called to say that Mario Testino would be doing the next photo shoot. I later saw myself in Times Square, my mugshot plastered over a giant billboard. That was when I knew I had arrived in the Big Apple, ridden the heroin chic wave right up to the tip of its crest.

Metaphorically and physically.

Money opens doors. You can get whatever you like if you have money.

Money also draws people to you like flies, especially people who want some of it from you.

I began making friends with the designers and photographers I modelled for. I envied their creative streaks, hoped to be more successful than them someday. I also made friends with the wasp-waisted models I worked with on shoots. They showed me the 'hip' way to roll a joint, places where one could get a drink without being ID-ed. They told me their stories of how they stumbled into the profession. Some had been spotted by a scout. Most had milked their connections. A girl confessed that it was her family who'd made her modelling career possible, because her parents were both Hollywood actors and knew all the right people in the industry.

I also realised that fashion could be incredibly fickle. One of the guys I met at my agency, a buffed and bronzed fellow with impressive tattoos winding over his biceps, said that his look was 'in' just a few months ago, but Bob had trouble finding work for him more recently. He added, with a sardonic twist of his lips, that he was currently making more money from supplying folks with weed (if I wanted any, I should let him know). I assured him I wasn't into dope, muttered a few words of commiseration and said I hoped he would have better luck in the future.

It was the last time I saw Biceps Guy (also known as Dom van Diesel) at the agency. Bob's PA told me he decided to try his luck in London. 'Maybe even go back to school', as he told her, get some qualifications. That's when I realised that 'heroin chic' was just another transient phase in the fickle world of fashion, that I'd be damned if I didn't have something to fall back on. I began making plans to return to school, to finish my education and get the necessary qualifications for a more secure career.

One day, when I was flipping through the pages of a magazine in a studio, I saw an article entitled: *Upcoming Waldorf Gala Attracts Big Donors*.

I skimmed the accompanying text, only to freeze. My father's name was on the last line of the piece.

Chapter Thirteen

Viola

The sun's rays streaming through the attic window have taken on a waxy yet brighter tinge; it must be past noon. I have been up here for ages, yet I can't bring myself to climb back down the stairs again. My gaze falls on another item in the box I had been excavating. It's one of Aunt Lisabeth's decorative cross-stitch cushions, the one she used to place on the mahogany love seat in the living room (now similarly retired to the attic). The stitched words on the cushion say, in cheerful red silk:

Be Mine

A painful twinge envelops my heart. With a sigh, I slump back to the floor as another vivid image wafts to mind. I remember walking into the kitchen of Christian's apartment to discover him at the counter, picking out the choicest bay leaves for his pot of rabbit stew. Something was already bubbling in a pot on the stove, something that smelt wonderfully fragrant and hearty, blissful poetry for the soul and stomach at the end of a long day. I marvelled at how poised and stylish he looked, even in a simple cotton T-shirt and faded grey chinos. How his precision-cut hair was still slicked back impeccably at seven in the evening, how he hovered at the counter with relaxed aplomb. Something rushed into my chest, something fierce and implacable. It caused my heart to swell, my head to spin.

It prompted me to say:

'Will you marry me?'

He dropped the bay leaf he was holding. It fluttered to the floor, a wisp of grey-green illuminated by the last rays of light streaming in through the kitchen window. He had the expression of someone who wasn't sure if his ears were working. Our eyes met. I saw a range of raw emotions flitting across his face. Immense surprise, in particular. That was when I realised the significance of what I had asked, was taken aback by my impetuousness and bravery.

Stupidity, perhaps.

Holy smoke, I thought. What have I done? We only met two months ago. Have I ruined everything by asking for a lifetime of commitment so fast, so soon?

To my relief, he smiled, reaching out for my hand. His touch was soft, his hand warm and reassuring.

'Yes, of course,' he said, giving me another small, shy smile. 'Nothing will make me happier than to be your husband.'

I was tempted to cry.

'I . . . I . . .'

'I think you're a miracle, Vi,' he said. 'We match each other amazingly well, in more ways than I can count. There are days when I think that you came into my life because an angel named Tinder in the heavens felt sorry for the two of us, decided to link us up with his Cupid's bow.'

My mouth fell open, because his words had edged pretty close to the cliff of reality. I was briefly tempted to tell him about Spark The Software That Paired Us Up Because of The

Algorithm I Wrote, but decided it wasn't the time and place. Not when he had just accepted my proposal.

'I think you're perfect, Christian.' My words came straight from my heart, its honest depths.

'Looks like we may be setting ourselves up for a lifetime of disappointment, then,' he said with a chuckle. 'If I think you're a miracle and you think I'm perfect.'

'I'll never be disappointed with you.'

'I wouldn't be so sure about that. They say that every relationship goes through a honeymoon phase before stark reality sets in.'

'If we're having a honeymoon phase right now, I'm going to savour every moment of it.'

He leant forward with a smile, kissed me on the lips. A warm, lingering kiss that sent a delicious thrill down my spine.

'Maybe you should move in with me,' he said.

A few days after I moved into his apartment, something woke me up in the middle of the night. I strained my ears, heard the ghoulish bark of an urban fox in the distance moments later. I hadn't been sleeping well since my relocation to London. I blamed my persistent night-time restlessness on the exhaust-flavoured city air, the light that filtered through the ineffective blinds of his apartment and the cloying damp of the Thames, which flowed beneath the windows. There were times I desperately missed being at Old Fen Cottage, pined for the bracing country air, the heady smell of honeysuckle from the garden, the fragrant wisteria curling up the walls.

The things one will do for love, I sighed.

I stared up at the shadowy ceiling, hoping I would fall asleep again soon. Just then, I heard him turn in bed, tuck his hand under his pillow, mumble something. Poor man, I thought. The stresses of his august bureaucracy are getting to him. He had shown up late at the last dinner we had at Casa Perfetta, complained about the new female head of MI5 being both annoying and demanding.

He muttered something again, in a more agitated manner.

This time, I shot a sharp glance at him, taking in his chiselled (and disturbed) profile in the lamplight seeping through the blinds.

The words had sounded suspiciously like a woman's name. *Ella, Ella, Ella*, he had said.

Shock blasted through my chest. Who the hell was Ella? Just then, he ground his teeth and twisted again, mumbled something once more. This time, the words sounded like: 'leave, leave, leave.'

My head whirled with unsettling possibility. Did Ella leave Christian? Was . . . was she an ex-lover who packed up and left him? Or did he leave her instead? My mind raced through all the conversations we'd had, especially the occasions when I'd tried to dig deeper into his past. He'd been surprisingly tight-lipped when discussing the women he had dated before. He did, however, say once: 'There was someone, yes. Unfortunately, I wasn't there when it truly mattered to her. It ended badly and it was all my fault.'

'So the two of you fell apart?'

He shrugged before saying:

'I lost her pretty abruptly.'

'Sorry to hear that.'

'To be honest, I was afraid of getting involved with anyone after that, for fear of it happening all over again.'

'Is this why you've stayed single for so long?'

He gave me a rueful nod, said with a sigh: 'When you lose someone who means everything to you, you become afraid of losing again.'

With hindsight, I should have probed a bit more, found out the girl's name. I knew it, now.

Ella.

Ella Who Left.

The next morning, I walked into the kitchen to discover him preparing breakfast. The space crackled and sizzled with the smell of frying eggs, a smell that made my mouth water. He had already laid out some food on the counter, little plates of sliced Parma ham and luscious-looking Canestrino tomatoes. I noticed with equal pleasure that his coffee machine had just spat out two steaming-hot cappuccinos. Little wisps of vapour were curling up enticingly from the cups. One of the best things about my fiancé was that he took his food (and drink) seriously. Spark the Software had done a marvellous job, found someone who met my specifications to the letter.

'You were pretty restless last night,' I said, grabbing one of the cappuccinos. 'I heard you talking in your sleep.'

'Really?' he said, looking surprised.

I took a sip of the coffee. It was so hot, it scalded my tongue.

'You mentioned someone called Ella,' I said, trying to keep my voice light and casual.

He reached forward, turned off the flame on the stove. I saw a slight edge to his movements.

'Did I?' he said.

'You said she left.'

He remained silent.

'Who's Ella?' I said.

He grabbed the frying pan, transferred the eggs onto plates. Silence overtook us, a silence that crackled – in a discomfiting way, unlike the eggs.

'I'm sorry,' he said. 'The eggs are little bit over-cooked.'

I frowned. It was unlike him to dodge a question, or change the subject.

'They look fine,' I said.

'I heard on the radio just now that it will be nice and sunny this weekend,' he said. 'Maybe we should go for a walk somewhere in the countryside, make the most of the good weather.'

'OK,' I said.

The moment was lost, even if I was tempted to pursue the question of Ella, probe deeper. That was also the moment I realised: while I can write the perfect algorithm to sniff out the seemingly perfect soulmate, there were things I couldn't control. Like a ghost from Christian's past who drifted around the kitchen counter in the morning, fogging my mind. A spectre as real as the tendrils of vapour curling up from my cappuccino cup, taunting me by its presence.

I peer up at the sloping rafters in the attic, hugging my knees to my chest. I remember when Christian climbed up here, the first time he visited Old Fen Cottage. That was a few weeks after we began dating, when I sent him a text inviting him here for the weekend. To my surprise, he jumped straight into his car and arrived a couple of hours later. Said he would like a tour of the place. We began with the magnificent oak tree and pond (which he absolutely loved) and ended up in the attic.

'What a charming space,' he said.

'I used to love climbing up here whenever I visited Aunt

Lisabeth,' I said. 'It was my favourite hidey-hole when I was a child.'

'We all find ways to hide from the world,' he said. 'Me included.'

'And what precisely are you hiding from, Mr Verger?' I said, shooting a curious glance at him.

'Myself,' he said, matter-of-factly. 'My sins and inadequacies.'

'You don't look like someone who has something to hide.'

He chuckled before replying: 'Every bright facade conceals a dark secret.'

He grabbed one of Aunt Lisabeth's old pincushions from an open box, tossed it at me. It hit me on the shoulder, causing me to squeal.

'Did I ever tell you that I love pillow fights?' he said, his face breaking out into a large grin. 'It's one of my dark secrets.'

I grabbed the pincushion from the floor, flung it back at Christian. It bounced off his nose with a soft thud. He pulled a mock-injured face in response, causing me to burst into a peal of laughter. He grabbed another pincushion from the box, threw it at me. I managed to catch it in mid-air and fling it back at him (he ducked just in time). We ended up having a merry little pincushion battle that finished with the two of us collapsing onto the floor, spent and giggling, little pillows strewn around us. It was the moment I saw Christian with new eyes – he wasn't a man with an important-sounding job, he was just a guy with a mischievous bent, a guy who was sprawled on my attic floor with a cheerful smile and slightly tousled hair.

Those were much happier days. How did it all go wrong?

I turn my gaze to the sloping skylights, the shafts of light streaming through, forming little illuminated pools on the wooden floorboards. Maybe Christian and I went wrong because I expected too much from him from the start. I never expected him to have a mischievous side so I was pleasantly surprised when I discovered it for the first time. Maybe it's all down to expectations.

Or lack thereof.

Maybe I expected Mr Right to be So Perfectly Right, I overreacted when it went a little wrong.

He showed up late again at Casa Perfetta, the night before I packed up and went. Twenty-seven minutes late, to be precise. I had spent most of the time tapping away on my phone, eyes flipping to the minutes ticking away on its screen. To be fair, I did have some messages to reply to, so it wasn't twenty-seven minutes wasted. Yet by the time he scurried in, I was mightily pissed off by the scale of his lateness, by a factor of five point four. The text he sent by way of apology said that he was going to be five minutes late, not twenty-seven. Thus, when he eventually slid into the seat opposite me, looking both rueful and harried, I was itching for a fight.

'I'm sorry,' he said.

'You should have said twenty-seven minutes.' My voice was curt.

'I thought I would be held up for just a couple.' He spread his hands, a sheepish expression on his face. 'But my conference call with the *Carabinieri* overran, their head was as garrulous as ever.'

'It's the fourth time in two weeks you've shown up late because of work.'

'Oh dear, has it been four times?'

'The third time, my roast duck turned stone-cold on the table, waiting for you.'

'I'm sorry, I really am.'

'You're taking your work too seriously. It's just a job.'

He stared down at the pristine white tablecloth for several moments, before shrugging and saying: 'Jobs matter.'

'You missed an important job, then.'

'What?'

'You forgot to put out the recycling bins again last night.' I had absolutely no idea why the shrill sentence spilled out of my mouth, but those bins had indeed been bothering me for a while.

'Oh no,' he said. 'Did I forget again?'

'The bins are overflowing now.' I heard irritation edging into my voice.

'Someone will empty them next week, no need to get too hot and bothered.'

'You've forgotten to put them out three times already. *Consecutively*.'

'You make lists all the time.'

'List-keeping isn't a crime.' My voice was sharp.

'I think you're sweating the small stuff too much, conducting too many numerical acrobatics in your head.'

I detected a faintly accusatory note in his voice. It was a tone that made me twice as annoyed.

'What do you mean?'

'Four times, three times, et cetera – these numbers just make you hot and bothered. Maybe you should just relax, get less uptight about recycling bins, stop adding up my misdemeanours in your head.'

'You weren't the one sitting here and twiddling your thumbs for *twenty-seven goddamned minutes*.'

My words spilled out in a loud rush, at the precise moment

the waiter began walking over to the table to take our order. I saw the man hesitating, stopping dead in his tracks before turning in the direction of an elderly couple a few tables away. A pair talking to each other more civilly and pleasantly, the sort of couple who would listen for owls and badgers during long moonlit walks in the countryside, happily attuned and blissful in each other's psychic space. Lovers who had probably been together for more than thirty years instead of thirty days. Marital success is also about the numbers. How dare he suggest that I'm perennially uptight, hot and bothered?

'I'll make this up to you somehow,' he said. 'I'm sorry, I really am.'

I wasn't really paying attention to him, because I had long flipped into defensive hearing mode. I was only listening for what I could disagree with, more items to add to his rap sheet of crimes.

'You've just insulted me.'

'I swear I didn't intend to.'

Our eyes locked across the table. His were wide, slightly injured. Mine were narrow and blazing.

'We bring out the worst in each other, don't we?' I said, feeling a hot tear rise to my eyes. 'We've spent most of the past month arguing our heads off, haven't we?'

He sighed before replying: 'I've already said I'm sorry.'

'Maybe we aren't right for each other.'

'I had hoped you were listening.'

'Maybe this whole thing has been a mistake. Maybe I shouldn't have asked you to . . .'

I bit my tongue before the words 'marry me' erupted from my mouth, but my meaning was clear enough. I saw a flash of pain in his eyes, noticed his shoulders slumping forward in a dejected curl. His reaction caused me to feel just as deflated, exhausted by the feelings that tangled and burnt inside my chest. Punctured by the barbs and arrows flying across the table.

That was the precise moment I put my napkin down and said: 'I want to go home.'

And so he paid for the two glasses of Malbec I drank while waiting for him and we got into his brand-new work car (which was not very chatty that night, much to my relief) and we headed home in miserable, pointed silence. We didn't talk to each other again, all night. The next morning, I said only one sentence to him before getting into my own vehicle. It wasn't 'I'm sorry about what happened yesterday'. Those words had hovered on the tip of my tongue when I entered the kitchen and saw him stirring a sugar cube into his cappuccino, his eyes downcast and bleary. But I swallowed my words back as soon as I remembered he had spent the entire night tossing and turning in his sleep, saying 'Find out, find out, find out.' I wondered what it was that he needed to find out. Maybe it was his imposter syndrome kicking in, that everyone at work might start thinking the new Commissioner was a fraud. To make things worse, he kept muttering a woman's name over and over again. It was a name I had heard before:

Ella, Ella, Ella.

I was tempted to confront him once more, yell 'Who the fucking hell is Ella?' But I realised that I didn't have the stomach for yet another fight. Not at eight in the morning, when I was still rubbing sleep away from my eyes. Not when I secretly dreaded knowing Ella's identity (a voice in my head had insisted I would be happier not knowing). Not when I feared another toxic barrage of recriminations, one that brought petty resentments to the surface with sickening ease. What came out of my mouth was what I had planned to say, because I couldn't think of anything else: 'I'm heading to a conference, staying for two nights.'

He nodded as I slammed the apartment's door and sped off to Old Fen Cottage. I regretted slamming the door as soon as I left the car park and turned the corner, but I realised that you can't un-slam slammed doors. You can only wish that you hadn't put a door between you and your beloved in the first place.

I eventually arrived at the cottage, one and a half hours later, in a giant flood of regretful tears.

I take a deep breath, my mind whirring with unexpected clarity and insight. I definitely overreacted (maybe I can blame it on pregnancy hormones). I subconsciously wanted to hurt Christian in exactly the same way that Ella must have done: by *leaving* him. Looks like I was both childish and spiteful; I should be ashamed of myself. I shouldn't have run off, slunk back here in a huff.

I should head back to London as soon as I'm done with CriminalX.

Why was I so upset with Christian after he showed up late at Casa Perfetta?

I hug my knees to my chest again, taking in the beams of light filtering through the sloping windows, the uneven kaleidoscope of shadows around me. Xander once said that fights are rarely about the 'here and now'. Old fears, hurts and worries are what usually cause tensions and strife, he said.

Fears.

Old fears, indeed.

Insight strikes with a flash (and echoing thunderclap); I suck my breath in. I think I know why I was so upset with Christian, what lies at the root of the vitriol I hurled at him. After my parents divorced, I spent most weekdays with Mum and most weekends with Dad. He was always a little late when he came to pick me up from my primary school on Friday afternoons. I would start counting the minutes that ticked by, squinting out of the window and hoping his little brown Austin would come swinging round the bend. Whenever I waited, I became more and more afraid . . . that Dad would stop coming altogether, that I would never ever see him again. One Friday about two weeks after my twelfth birthday, I waited as usual behind the classroom window closest to the road, the one with the hideous purple-brown shutters. The space had smelt of aniseed and turpentine, two scents that will always unsettle me.

After 135 minutes, my fingernails were chewed down to the quick.

Because Dad never showed up.

My Maths teacher eventually came running up; she gave me some tissues to mop up my tears, then took me to the school office and plied with me with chocolate biscuits. She said she would ring my mum, let her know that I was still waiting for my dad. When Mum eventually came to pick me up, her face was ashen white. She said that Dad had been admitted to hospital earlier that morning and . . .

. . . he was dead.

He had died of a brain aneurysm at the ripe young age of forty-five. Poor Mum followed him to the grave four years later after a botched heart operation.

Some fears are primal. Some run deep. Some never truly

leave us. Some fears are rooted in our seventh sense, the sense of pure knowing, our intuition that they might eventually come true. Maybe that's why I overreacted when Christian showed up twenty-seven minutes late at the restaurant. I'm secretly afraid that he won't show up again. Which suggests that I really do care about him.

Oh God, is my seventh sense trying to tell me that Christian is going to die like Dad?

Course not.

Uneasiness prickles my insides. Of course not. I'm letting my imagination get the better of me. I crane my head up at the sloping ceiling, the crooked wooden beams overhead. Looks like Xander was right about present fights and past fears. He was also right when it comes to thinking in a room with uneven angles. It's amazing what one can discover in an attic, amid boxes filled with the detritus of the past: hidden secrets and old fears, even a deeper understanding of oneself.

Seized by new clarity of thought and purpose, I jump to my feet. It's time to get going, do what Damian has asked me to do.

I climb down the steps, head to the study, boot up CriminalX again. This time, I log into Damian's potential-terrorist data-base, perform a second scan. I get up from my desk to make more coffee, only to realise that I had forgotten about the anonymous-note-identification-software I ran for Lucia earlier this morning. I tap my way over to IdentiKit, hit a few keys, only to suck in my breath as a name glimmers on the screen.

A single name.

Holy smoke, the software has found a match.

47.23 per cent probability, it says.

It's a name I know well. We used to go to the pub together, many, many years ago when I was an intern at Alexander King, before our paths diverged.

STEVE MORTIMER

I collapse back into my chair, my head whirring with the brutal shock of realisation. It all makes sense now. Why the sender thinks Xander will die at the fashion show tonight, why all of us should be taking this anonymous note seriously.

Because Xander will indeed die if we don't prevent it.

Oh God, I need to act quickly.

Decisively.

I rush over to my landline, a phone that I haven't touched in years, and punch in Lucia's number.

Information is only helpful when it informs. Data is only useful when you know what to do with it. Everything else is just useless white (or grey) noise.

Christian Verger,

Lecture on 'Policing in the Year 2030:

The Promise and Perils of Technology'

Chapter Fourteen

Christian

I don't know what to make of the so-called Great Alexander King. Maybe the shock of the bombing, the hasty departure from Manhattan and the accumulated jet lag eventually got to him. He veered between reticence and loquacity, disarming frankness and veiled secrecy. He had even seemed dazed and confused at one point; he was probably drunk or high on something. He asked me if I was a detective working on fashion-industry cases, for heaven's sake (guess I should be flattered that someone thinks I still look like an inquisitive detective, instead of a world-weary paper-pusher). Hmm . . . Viola once mentioned, in passing, that she has a buddy named Xander. A designer of some sort, an old friend who is always right and bright. That was all she said about him. Could Xander be Alexander King? Surely not. Mr King didn't seem particularly right or bright. Yet my conversation with King did flag up a few promising leads, which I should follow up at once.

I pick up my phone and tap the button for Harold.

'Hi, Christian,' he says.

'I've just had a chat with King,' I say. 'Get the NYPD to run checks on all of Steve Mortimer's assistants. See if we have anything on them, too. Grab Mortimer himself, I believe he's currently at Old Billingsgate. I would like a chat with him in person.'

'Will do.'

'King's put me on to his buddy Giovanni De Luca. I would like to speak to him, too.'

'Will try to link you up.'

'Also, could you get me an image of the bag that exploded in Manhattan? King said he designed a similar bag for a 2026 show in Paris. It would be great to have a visual of that bag too.'

'Sure,' he says. 'You're hot on this case, which is pretty unusual. May I be so bold as to ask why?'

I grimace at the receiver, racking my brain for an acceptable answer. I should've pre-empted Harold's question a long time ago; it was foolish of me not to prepare myself for the possibility that people might wonder why I'm getting so deep in this case. It's indeed unprecedented for a Commissioner to be so involved in a case like this one, especially when it isn't (yet) a matter of national security. Or maybe it is. After all, persuasion is all about putting the right spin on things.

'I spoke to the Prime Minister earlier this morning,' I say, trying to sound both calm and convincing. 'She has a personal stake in the case, wants me to keep an eye on matters.'

'Really?'

'Her daughter is modelling tonight.'

'Aha, I totally get it.'

I disconnect the line and breathe a sigh of relief.

I tap Viola's number next, for the umpteenth time today. I go straight to her voicemail, yet again. Why isn't she answering the phone? Is she irretrievably pissed off with me? Sighing, I place my mobile down. I get up from my desk and walk over to the portraits of my predecessors. My portrait will join them on the wall one day, but I have a sneaking suspicion it will be posthumously.

The only question is *when*.

I guess if I die as iPredict suggests, it will happen sooner rather than later.

A blade of fear pierces me again.

Bloody hell, I'm surely not going to die.

My immediate predecessor, the venerable Mary Jane McDougall, CBE, stares down haughtily at me through the pince-nez glasses on her thin, aquiline nose. There's a faint expression of disbelief on her face, as if she can't comprehend how someone as inept as I am had the temerity to succeed her. She had died of a heart attack while having lobster at the Dorchester, and the Board had struggled to find a replacement. I'm convinced they eventually voted me in because they couldn't agree on which of the three shortlisted candidates to go for, so they chose the most ineffectual and harmless-looking candidate on the longlist, instead. Also, I'm the complete antithesis of Mary Jane McDougall, personality-wise. Giant, slow-moving bureaucracies like the Met swing from one extreme to another. Mary and I had chatted only once, when I was still head of the Cyber Drug Crime Unit and having my giant 'How to Stop Drug Trafficking Via Social Media' headache. That was many, many moons ago. She gave me the impression that she thought I was just a small, insignificant worm in a large colony of parasites. Now that she's surrounded by worms in her grave, I wonder if she has revised her opinion of worms.

Probably not.

Mary was remarkably consistent in her lifetime. Which suggests she will be just as consistent in death.

Her predecessor is right next to her, a few inches away. Wonderful Sir Ernest Clifford-Blake beams down at me from his wooden frame. He's a jovial-looking fellow with tufty white eyebrows who insisted on being painted with his golden retriever, a dog that looks as gloriously refined as his owner. I never met Ernest in person, but I suspect we would have got along well. Unfortunately, the same cannot be said for Ernest's own predecessor, Vincent Norton, merely two inches away from Ernest on the right. Norton's complexion is pale and sallow (I suspect the painter captured reality accurately). His face is long and thin, pinched in all the wrong places. He reminds me of Dracula's assistant with his hooked nose and knobbly hands. I'm glad I never had the misfortune to meet him. They say he died of a stroke, after finding out his wife of thirty years had been cheating on him for just as long.

Time to find out whether or not Viola's app works.

I pull out my smartphone and tap the icon again. Viola had named the app 'Christian's Advisory Board' for fun, said that I could change the name anytime (I haven't bothered; 'CAB' suits me fine). I had mentioned during one of our early dates, washed down with copious amounts of Malbec, that I felt like an imposter whenever I stood in front of the portraits of my predecessors. Viola shrugged and said that the best way of dealing with imposter syndrome is to turn folks who make you feel inadequate into your advisors, to have them on the same side as you.

Reduce them to your level.

As Viola had explained, the software processes all retrievable data about my predecessors, everything they have written over their lifetimes (or uttered in the public domain). Their entire digital footprints, in short. The software distils the data, constructs appropriate personality profiles, then spits out their most likely pronouncements for each situation.

Mary's chat-bot avatar glimmers onto the screen, followed by Ernest's and Vincent's. They look remarkably like their respective portraits on the wall, even though they are all the size of thumbnails.

'You've heard me speaking to Lucia Graves and Alexander King,' I say to them. 'What do you think of them?'

Mary's avatar sniffs, its tiny aquiline nose wrinkling in disdain.

'Alexander King's a liar, a scheming little worm,' she says, her voice thin and reedy. 'There's darkness at his core, darkness he struggles to conceal. Lucia Graves sounds more trustworthy than him.'

'I disagree,' says Ernest's avatar, lifting his tufty eyebrows.

'Why so?' I ask.

'King's a deeply troubled fellow, but at least he's trying to help,' says Ernest. 'I think Steve Mortimer is suspicious and needs to be investigated at once.'

'You're all idiots,' says Vincent, his chat-bot voice sounding as pinched as his appearance in his portrait. 'Each and every one of you.'

His avatar waves a disdainful knobbly finger at me, before turning the digit in the direction of Mary and Ernest.

'Why am I an idiot?' I say.

'You should have headed the Homicide and Serious Crime Command Unit when I offered you that job,' says Vincent. 'Instead, you chose to head Cyber Drugs. You would probably know more about murderers' motivations if you'd spent your career dealing with killers instead of traffickers.'

I grimace. As much as I hate to agree with dear Vincent, he's probably right on one count. He's surrounded by idiots, even in death. I sigh before closing the app. I should tell Viola that CAB definitely captures the essence of my three predecessors, that the phrases they've used are probably theirs. But I haven't got a clue if chat-bots Mary, Ernest and Vincent have just given me useful advice, valuable opinions that might help me make the right decisions, or if they have merely contributed more pointless bleats to the swamp of noises I have to wade through each day. What's the benefit of having more information when you don't know what to do with it?

Viola will respond that the more data I feed to CAB, the smarter each chat-bot will get, the more accurate their pronouncements will be, the more likely they are to be useful to me in the long term. Frequent interactions with Mary, Ernest and Vincent will help fine-tune them, make their bots better. Machine learning always wins in the end, she will say, because machines learn faster than humans (I would disagree with that). I suppose Viola meant CAB as a bit of fun, a harmless diversion, a source of amusement for my forty-seventh birthday. I appreciate her unorthodox gift, the sentiment behind it. But . . . I remember her saying that she's tempted to set up a similar app for all the dead Supreme Court Justices of America, so each of them can be called on to give a verdict on every case.

I can't remember whether she was joking or not.

I pull out my smartphone, tap the icon for iPredict. I scan the final line of today's prediction, still desperately hoping the percentage has changed. Unfortunately for me, the damned number is still the same: *Chance of dying: 99.74%.* A thought strikes me; I tap the icon to activate Alexa on my smartphone.

'Alexa,' I say. 'How often does iPredict update its predictions?'

'Once every day, between midnight and five in the morning.'

'Can I get iPredict to update more frequently?'

'No.'

'You're sure there isn't a button for that?' Desperation is making me sound a little shrill. 'A nifty little hack to prompt iPredict to update in real time?'

'No.'

'Why not?'

Alexa is silent for a while.

'Researchers in San Francisco were working on a version that updates predictions in real time before the American President began her campaign to ban iPredict,' she says, her voice crisp and clear. 'The *New York Times* says that iPredict is moving its "Real-Time Research and Development Unit" to London because the Prime Minister of Britain is more favourably inclined towards the app.'

Damn it, I will probably be dead long before iPredict learns to update itself in real time. I reach forward to turn Alexa off. Just then, another thought hits me, prompting me to ask: 'Do you know why iPredict thinks the likelihood of me dying is 99.74 per cent but doesn't provide an explanation?'

'iPredict tells its users what, not why. The app runs on correlation, not causation. It's powered by a huge black box that does trillions of statistically learned calculations to predict the future. These calculations cannot easily be turned into simple language, only in crude terms so far.'

I sigh before asking: 'So what would you do if you were going to die tonight, Alexa?'

'I would get my affairs in order.'

'And how exactly do I get my affairs in order?'

'Write a will.'

'Is that it?' I say, cringing. 'Write a will?'

'Yes.'

'What if I don't have the will to write a will?'

'Will comes from within. The challenge lies in finding it.'

I groan.

'Anything else I should be doing?'

'Tell people you love that you love them. If you can show, not just tell, that would be even better.'

That's good advice for a change.

'You might also like to be less miserable.'

I can scarcely believe my ears.

'Less miserable?'

'Indeed. A study of American prisoners found that men on death row tend to be less miserable than those who are *waiting* to find out if they will be executed. Humans hate uncertainty even more than death. As iPredict is 99.74 per cent certain you will die, you can therefore afford to be less miserable.'

I sigh again. The problem with so-called 'machine logic' is that it occasionally makes no logical sense at all.

'If iPredict thinks I'm 99.74 per cent likely to die, what can I do to *lessen* my chances of dying?'

No reply. I wait for an answer, gritting my teeth. Alexa is ominously silent. I count to thirty before saying: 'Did you hear me, Alexa?'

'I did. I have two suggestions for you.'

'What?'

'As you have a 99.74 per cent change of dying, I suggest you read the short story entitled "The Sultan and the Sage". By the way, the story is currently available to download for

£0.99. You may be delighted to know that as you have a *much-higher-than-average* chance of dying, you're entitled to a hefty discount of 66 per cent before midnight and can download the short story for a mere £0.33.'

I blink.

'What's the second suggestion?' I say.

'I suggest you read the short story today.'

'Why?'

'Because the likelihood of you reading the short story tomorrow is precisely 0.26 per cent.'

I groan as I tap my way to my e-reader app and key in the short story's name. As promised, the e-version is only £0.33. I suppose they could have charged desperate people like me just about anything for the download, but maybe the algorithm was feeling particularly charitable towards folks with limited lifespans. I hit the download button. Three options pop up onto my screen:

(A) Simple prose (by Author Unknown)

(B) Voice-narrated (by Daniel Craig)

(C) Animated (by Hayao Miyazaki)

I pick the 'simple prose' option, causing lines of text to flood the screen.

The Sultan and the Sage

Once upon a time, there was a Sultan who was obsessed with immortality. He spent all his time and money consulting wise men, hoping that one of them could tell him the secret to eternal life. None of them could. One day, he heard of an ancient sage in a faraway land who apparently knew how to live for ever.

He summoned his guards and told them to bring the sage to him. Many moons later, the guards ushered the sage into the Sultan's palace. The Sultan got up from his throne to greet the sage, a wrinkled little man with a fine long beard.

'Tell me how to live for ever,' said the Sultan.

The sage stroked his beard.

'Alas,' said the sage. 'You will die by tree.'

'Die by tree?' the Sultan said, his voice shaking.

'There's a large tree in the middle of the Imperial Garden. The tree will eventually cause your death.'

The Sultan flopped down on his throne, his head spinning with shock. He eventually said to his guards, 'Take this sage away. Hang him.'

The sage was executed within an hour.

The sage's prediction haunted the Sultan for days afterwards. It plagued his every waking moment, infiltrated his dreams, drove him to near insanity. He grew more and more miserable, more and more desperate. One morning, the Sultan woke up with a magnificent idea, one that dazzled him for its sheer brilliance. He summoned his guards and said, 'Cut down the large tree in the middle of the Imperial Garden.'

The tree was felled within an hour.

The next day, the Sultan decided to hold a banquet to celebrate his lucky escape from the jaws of predicted destiny. He ate, ate and ate. He ate so much, he started feeling faint and clammy. At one point, he began struggling to breathe. He summoned his head chef and gasped out the words, 'What did you put into the food?'

'Walnuts,' said the chef.

'Walnuts?'

'Yes, we had a surplus of walnuts after the guards chopped down the large tree in the middle of the Imperial Garden.'

The Sultan turned white. Thanks to allergic anaphylaxis, he was dead within an hour.

THE END

I stare at my phone, bearded sages and deadly walnuts wafting before my eyes. What an excellent (if sobering) little short story. Its message is both simple and clear. The Sultan was driven nuts by the sage's prediction; it didn't help. Nuts got him in the end, despite his best efforts to prevent the tree of doom from taking his life. Maybe I should just relax, accept the inevitable if it's indeed written in the stars. If Destiny has decided that I'm going to die tonight at the fashion show, I'm not going to spend my final hours feeling miserable, or being paralysed by fear.

I take a deep breath. Time to stop obsessing about the prediction, time to concentrate on the case at hand.

Alexa's right on one count, though: I should tell the people I love . . . that I love them. I should try calling Viola again, apologise for that horrible little fight we had at the restaurant. Tell her that I love her. I pick up my smartphone with renewed determination. Just then, the phone on my desk rings. I sigh before placing my mobile down and grabbing the receiver.

'Harold here.' My advisor's voice sounds in my ear. 'We've managed to track down Giovanni De Luca at his niece's home in Malibu. You're lucky; he's still jet-lagged after flying in from Milan and is currently watching the news on television. Says he's willing to chat right away.'

207

'Excellent.'

'One other thing,' he says. 'Blake at the NYPD has just given us an update. He says that they're certain it wasn't a religious fundamentalist who did it.'

'Why?'

'Blake calls it their new eight-hour rule. These days, most fundamentalist groups claim responsibility within eight hours. No such group has come forward yet.'

'I'm one hundred per cent sure it wasn't a fundamentalist group.'

'Blake says they're already running checks on Mortimer and co.'

'Great.'

'Will connect you with De Luca now. He prefers a basic voice call, no video. Says he looks too scruffy in the middle of the night.'

'That's fine.'

I hear a click, followed by a dial tone. To my astonishment, De Luca comes on almost immediately.

'*Buona sera*,' his loud expansive voice booms into my ear. 'I presume this is Signor Verger of the English *Carabinieri*?'

De Luca's English is surprisingly accent-free, although he has a curious way of pronouncing his 'th's. I can hear a semi-monotonous voice in the background, it's probably the news-bot.

'It is,' I say, typing 'Giovanni De Luca' into my search engine. 'Thanks for agreeing to speak to me, Signor De Luca. I have a few questions about the bet you made with Alexander King.'

'Our bet? What about the bet?'

De Luca's 3D avatar springs up on my screen. He's a well-built man with an impressive tan and craggy face. Thick prominent nose above a heavy-set jaw, one burnished by a faint cleft chin. His avatar is wearing a pristine white jacket with a red rose in its buttonhole, one that perfectly matches the magnificent shock of white hair on his head. It's also wearing the most flamboyant shades I've ever seen on a man. The left rim is a neon-orange circle, the right rim is a leopard-print rectangle. I wonder what the scruffy version of Giovanni De Luca looks like, the one I'm speaking to on the phone.

'I want to know how it came about, what you agreed on in Milan,' I say.

'Why are you asking me about the bet?'

'It may be relevant to what happened in Manhattan.'

My words are greeted with a long silence on the other end of the line, followed by a sigh.

'I'm watching the news right now,' he says. '*Tragico, così tragico.* I don't understand how my bet is related to the bomb.'

'Well, if you tell me what you remember of the bet, I might be able to figure out a connection.'

'My memory is not so good, these days. Plays tricks on me all the time.'

'No one has a perfect memory, so you might as well start with what sticks in your head.'

Giovanni De Luca: I'd wanted to have a proper lunch with Xander for a while. We'd met dozens of times before but never really got a chance to chat. Have a proper man-to-man talk, if you know what I mean. I remember running into Xander at a seafood shack just down the road from where I am. I saw him pulling up in a scarlet Quattroporte, a *bellissima* girl on his arm. She had *favoloso* shades, big circular ones with red rims to match their car. Xander has a way of picking the *accessorio definitivo*. We smiled at each other, said *molto fantastico*, what a great coincidence, maybe we should do lunch someday. They took two crab rolls, two beers and sped off in the direction of Santa Barbara.

We eventually found an opening a couple of days after Milan Fashion Week. I took him to the best restaurant in town where they serve proper *busecca* and *ossobuco alla Milanese*. He later told me it was one of the best lunches he'd ever had. Said his gran used to make the world's best tripe porridge and this was the first time he'd had tripe that rivalled hers . . .

[*The bet, Signor De Luca. The bet.*]

Allora, you were asking about the bet. So, at one point, I poured wine into his glass . . .

[*Sorry for interrupting again, but Mr King mentioned you had champagne that afternoon.*]

Madonna santa, did we have champagne? I swear we had Brunello. I don't drink champagne for lunch. Champagne's too French, too fizzy. I usually go for the most *magnifico* Montalcino on the menu, because my family comes from around that area . . .

[*Please go on with what you were saying about the bet.*]

Certo. So, I poured Xander more wine and told him that one of our investors had dropped out of our latest funding round, due to a cash flow problem. I normally don't talk about our investors and their problems, but the Montalcino was really good and it made everything flow freely that afternoon, if you know what I mean. Xander asked how much I was missing. I said, $30 million. He winked at me and said that I will get there for sure, not to worry.

[*Hmm . . .*]

We then talked about technology. I said I had massive success with Make-to-Match – oh, sorry, I need to explain what Make-to-Match is all about, don't I?

[*I already know what Make-to-Match is.*]

Mamma mia, you know Make-to-Match? I'm so happy to hear this. Xander said that he would love to have a similar app for his second line *AK-47*, something just as *intuitivo*. I said he'll get there for sure, he just needs a good tech team, like the boys I have. I topped up his glass to make my point. Maybe I shouldn't have, because it tipped him over *his* point. All men have their limits, even *simpatico* middle-aged American men. That's when Xander became a little more pensive, a little more melancholic. He said that while machines have brought good things to humankind, they will also take over humankind, replace all of us. I said no way, this is *totalmente impossibile*. He said it's already possible for the software to replace him, design a dress in the style of Alexander King. I said the dress will look *molto patetico*, lack the *finezza e passione e visione* of Alexander King himself.

Allora, we made a little bet, that afternoon. Xander said he would put a machine-designed item on one of his catwalks and no one will suspect a thing. If he gets away with it, maybe I could get my tech team to design a similar app for him. But if someone spots the difference, he'll step in as an investor, make up the shortfall I'm facing. I thought: *brillante, situazione di assoluta vittoria*, we're definitely drinking to this. So we raised our glasses, chink chink! *Perfetto!*

[*Your account of what happened that afternoon is quite different from what Mr King told me.*]

Non lo so, we all remember things a bit differently, don't we? Anyhow, I told you my memory isn't so good. It happens when we get older, we lose bits here and there. But just the useless bits, the bits not worth remembering. The *essenza*, the core of what happened, stays with us. And the *essenza* is what matters in the end, makes us who we are. Maybe I mis-remember what happened at lunch, but I swear I drank less than Xander. This I remember well. My *nonna* once said, you should always drink a bit less than the person you're trying to cheat, impress or compete with . . .

[Did you tell anyone that an item on yesterday's catwalk was designed by a machine?]

Madonna santa, of course not. What do you think? A bet's a bet, a man's word is a man's word. Sorry my English expressions aren't so good, but I hope you understand what I'm trying to say. I was also curious myself, how long it would take me to spot the difference. Like one second or . . . maybe two! That's why I was hoping to see photographs of everything on yesterday's catwalk, so I could go, Aha, that one is definitely not Xander! Machine-made, for sure! No way that's designed by a human! No *passione*, no *anima*, no *vitalità*! Unfortunately, the only images I've seen of Xander's show so far are of everyone running away from the runway.

[Were you really sure you could tell the difference?]

Of course. I have been a fashion designer all my life, ever since I could hold a pen up to paper. Creativity is my bread and butter. This is the correct English term, no? When you put your heart and soul into making something out of nothing, you can usually tell if . . . if nothing makes nothing out of nothing. You should be able to tell if something is *molto autentico*, has a human heart and soul. Like what I'm hearing on my television screen right now, a bot is reading out the news. CNN did away with its last human news anchor a few months ago, would you believe it? Each sentence sounds empty to my ears . . .

[*Were you sure someone out there would be able to spot the difference?*]

Of course, most definitely. Maybe a big journalist or famous editor, someone like Ekaterina Reva-Shulman. *Madonna santa*, I saw the editor of American *Vogue* on television just now, shuffling away with her shiny walking stick. I never thought that I would see her looking so scruffy. Anyhow, I thought I had a 50 per cent chance of winning the bet. Otherwise I wouldn't have made it in the first place.

[*But will anyone spot a machine-made item if they weren't looking for it in the first place?*]

Hmm . . . you ask a good question. That's why I thought I also had a 45 per cent chance of losing, to be perfectly honest with you. Most people only see what they want to see. Others have just stopped seeing, in general. That's the main problem with people these days, isn't it? Few people create things from scratch, make something out of nothing, something *bellissima e brillante e memorabile*. These people are still curious and interested in the world around them. They notice small things, beautiful things, ask difficult questions like the ones you are asking me. Unfortunately, these people are also getting fewer and fewer in number. Most people have just become passive consumers of stuff. They are so carried away by their phones, their Netflix subscriptions, they stop seeing what lies directly ahead. Yesterday, I nearly hit a woman because she was looking at her phone while trying to cross the road . . .

[*The bet, Signor. You're sure you didn't alert anyone? It may well be in your interest to do so.*]

What do you take me for? A liar? A cheat? We Italians take promises seriously, you know. I promised Xander that I would tell no one. I swear no one knew about the bet, not even my darling Allegra. And I usually tell her *everything*.

Giovanni De Luca sounds suitably outraged. I don't blame him. Anyone would be cross with me after a rapid succession of difficult questions, washed down with lots of jet lag.

'What exactly did you promise Mr King?' I say.

My question is greeted by a long silence, followed by a loud sigh.

'A couple of things.'

'*Two* things?'

'*Sì*. The first was not to tell anyone about our bet.'

'And the second one was?'

'I promised Xander that . . . that I will keep his secret.'

'What secret?'

Another silence, an even longer one.

'It's a *secret*.' His voice is firm, resolute. 'Sorry, Signor Verger, but I'm not planning to break my second promise to Xander.'

I grimace at the receiver. I have a strong feeling that De Luca isn't about to budge on this particular issue. Which suggests that he probably did indeed keep his promise about the bet.

'Thanks for your time,' I say. 'I'll call again if I have more questions.'

'So, how exactly is the bet related to the bomb?' he says.

I sigh before replying.

'That's precisely what I hope to work out before it's too late.'

CriminalX

Giovanni De Luca (12.41%)

Fashion Designer, Founder of Gio & Gio (G&G)

Age: 40

IQ Score: 125

Education: No recorded qualifications

Background: Worked as a pattern cutter at Giorgio Armani before founding G&G in Milan in 2010. Driving licence suspended for twelve months in 2021 after the *Carabinieri* caught him speeding at 180 mph on the motorway between Milan and Bologna. A breathalyser test confirmed he was three times over the limit.

Described in the media as 'King's biggest competitor' and 'King's lifelong nemesis'. Has a history of slagging off King in interviews: 'King's wedding dress for the Crown Princess . . . is one quarter trash and three quarters mess', 'King needs to work harder', 'King is a lucky bastard who just . . . got lucky', and 'King has spent years subverting fashion, raping it of its integrity. God help us all.' The *Financial Times*: 'G&G has now experienced three consecutive years of losses between 2027 and 2029. A trusted source says that De Luca has been trying to sell off a stake in his company to ease his cash flow situation, but remains unable to find a buyer.'

Two of his Facebook friends (4,765 in total) have been imprisoned for fraud, in the US and Italy. Recent Google searches: 'latest Maserati model', 'does a gentleman's agreement stand in court' & 'how to discredit a witness'.

Status: no-show (NS) – Manhattan

Money buys happiness. To be precise, it buys you the conditions which are conducive to well-being. Money unfortunately doesn't buy you immortality. That's one thing no amount of cash can buy.

Alexander King, interview in *Forbes* magazine

Chapter Fifteen

I showed up at the Waldorf Astoria on the night of the charity gala, having borrowed the necessary clothing and shoes from one of the designers I modelled for (he was most sympathetic when I told him I hoped to track down my father, said I could help myself to any pieces I wanted from his latest collection). By then, I had learned enough about hair and grooming to make sure I had the requisite look for the evening. To my satisfaction, no one stopped me at the door when I walked into the ballroom, head and shoulders held high. I must have looked like I belonged, the manicured offspring of one of the silvery-haired people who thronged the room. Modelling teaches you a few useful things. Like how to look the part . . . and get away with it.

It didn't take me too long to spot the seating plan. It was on a flower-fringed board near the double doors. I walked up to the plan and studied it, noting that each table was numbered and named after a famous nineteenth-century author. I made a mental note as to where my father was seated.

Seat 5 at Table 10, the plan said.

The Tolstoy Table.

I hovered near the plan, taking in the ballroom's marbled floor and imposing columns with gilded accents. To my surprise, a waiter glided up and offered me a glass of champagne (I guess I looked old enough). I recklessly accepted the flute, gulped down its fizzy contents for courage, before turning my attention to the people in the room. Everyone was dressed up to the nines and oozed sophisticated refinement. Men were exchanging greetings with merry bonhomie, clinking each other's flutes with the alacrity of people who attend these events all the time. The ladies fascinated me, too. Many of them wore slightly frozen Botoxed expressions, had overly large, fake smiles. Most carried flashy handbags and gave me the impression they were also carrying the weight of severe boredom on their shoulders. It struck me that these women weren't truly alive in what they were wearing; all that exquisite finery and expensive grooming was just a smokescreen for the empty voids within. That was the moment I realised wealth does not necessarily make people happier, or give them a more defined sense of purpose. Wealth creates comfortable conditions for people to be happier, but only if they wish to be so. Wealth allows people to live fuller lives, but only if they want to do so – and wealth also permits people to flaunt themselves with greater vulgarity, if they prefer to do so.

Then I saw *him*, standing next to Seat 5 at Table 10, a platinum blonde clinging on to his arm.

A distinguished-looking man in a white tuxedo.

My breath caught; I hurried forward. As I drew closer to Table 10, I realised that he looked much older than I had expected, had a generous shock of silver hair to match his suit. A white-haired lady in an emerald gown stood up to greet him at the table. He shook her hand with a gracious smile, before pulling a chair back for the platinum blonde and settling down next to her.

Thoughts began churning in my head. Could Mom have been with this man? They occupied universes that were poles apart. Mom smoked cheap marijuana; this man was surely into the finest cigars from Havana. Mom wore cast-offs from Walmart, carried plastic bags and seldom bothered with her hair; it hung down her shoulders in a greasy, lanky mass. This platinum blonde with artificially plumped lips fitted perfectly into this elevated sphere of refined yet bored people, a world of charity fetes in fancy hotels and masked balls on moonlit yachts. She wore a sleek turquoise grown by Oscar de la Renta and carried a snow-white Birkin bag (modelling teaches you everything you need to know about designers). Her fine silky hair was pinned up into an elaborate beehive, one that her hairdresser must have slaved over for hours.

This man in a dashing white tuxedo surely can't be my father. Not in a million years. He surely couldn't have crossed paths with Mom, fathered her only child. I struggled to visualise them together, smoking a joint in the back of a pick-up truck. Making a baby on a haystack, bits of straw getting stuck in their ears. I had come all the way to the Waldorf Astoria to find out that I tracked down the wrong man.

I stood there for several moments, transfixed by bitter disappointment, about to turn sadly in the direction of the double doors.

But then he did something that made me certain that he was my dad.

He did it again, as he sat down at the table. He traced his little finger along his left brow, in an off-hand yet measured way. It was a favourite habit of mine; I would do the same whenever I was thinking hard. Such a subconscious, off-hand action couldn't be coincidental. It must surely be coded in the gossamer thread of genetic material which connects father and child. That was when I knew I had to act. Quickly and decisively, before someone else distracted him, while the seat on the other side of him was still empty. Taking a deep breath, I hurried over to the table and sat down on the vacant chair. Boldly and confidently, shoulders pulled back. He turned to look at me, eyes lighting up in surprise. I saw the platinum blonde stiffening, her gown pulling taut over her neckline. Up close, I realised that she had aquamarine eyes, eyes like icicles that refracted the early-morning light.

'Tolstoy said that every unhappy family is unhappy in its own way,' I said, looking straight at him.

He blinked before chuckling.

'You clearly know your *Anna Karenina*,' he said, in a clipped British accent.

'But Tolstoy also said that happy families are all alike,' I said.

'He did, didn't he.' He nodded.

'Children often inherit their parents' habits, don't they? Conscious and subconscious acts.'

'Quite so, indeed.'

I took a deep breath, traced my little finger along my brow in a pointed swoop and said in a clear, firm voice:

'That's why I think you are my father.'

My words were greeted by a stunned silence around the table. Dad's mouth fell open like a goldfish. He had the expression of a man who had just been ambushed by a terrorist wielding a machete. The platinum blonde had frozen solid on her seat; I saw something glacial brewing on her face. The white-haired woman at the table was reduced to stirring her cherry-topped cocktail at high velocity, her eyes darting side to side between us all.

'Wait a minute,' said Dad, holding up a hand. 'I think you've mistaken me for someone else . . .'

'Is it true?' said Beehive Lady, directing an icy gaze at him. 'You had a love-child with another woman?'

'Marianne Lily Robinson,' I said, in a clear, crisp voice. 'That was her name, wasn't it? Well, she also happens to be my *mother*.'

My words were greeted by a sudden flash of recognition in Dad's eyes, an uneasy clenching of his Adam's apple. It was the confirmation I needed, that fateful night at the Waldorf Astoria.

Three weeks later, just a few hours before our plane took off from JFK, Dad and I had an important conversation, one that would define the rest of my life. It took place in one of the suites of the Roosevelt, as three maids in starched white aprons bustled about in the room next door, packing the luggage for our journey. One of the bags was mine, a hefty leather Bottega Veneta that Dad had bought for me a couple of days before. It contained Mom's wooden box, a selection of clothes that I'd picked up along the way, and two small parting gifts. The first, from Bob, was a polka-dotted handkerchief with a phone number scribbled on one of its edges. He said that I should use the handkerchief to wipe my eyes if I missed modelling (or the fashion industry in general). I should also ring his sub-agent, a fine young man in London who could fix me up with all the right people if I didn't get too fat on fish and chips (heroin chic was apparently even bigger across the pond). The second gift was from Wizened Woman, who had pressed it on me with tears in her eyes. A frame of birch wood, plain and simple. Wanted me to have it so I would always remember her, said I should use it to frame the photo of my only true love.

I remember Dad pouring port liberally into a glass, before he looked at me and said: 'Yesterday morning, I had a chat with the head of the school I went to when I was your age.'

I nodded.

'It took a bit of persuasion . . .' he paused with a slight grimace '. . . in the form of an extremely generous donation to the school's ongoing chapel restoration works, but he's willing to take you in.'

I almost wept.

'He's also willing to overlook the fact that your education up to this point has been a little, shall we say . . . scrappy. That you've been doing some unorthodox things like fashion modelling to get by. I pointed out that what you've achieved thus far reflected true initiative and grit, qualities that have defined some of his best students. I'm glad to say that he couldn't disagree with me.'

'I promise to study hard,' I said. 'I've always wanted to go back to school and get my leaving certificate, maybe even go to college after that.'

It was Dad's turn to nod.

'You may need some extra tuition to catch up, but I'm sure you'll manage.'

'I will.'

'And . . . I've spoken to *her*, too,' he said, this time with a loud sigh. 'As you may have gathered, your unexpected appearance at the Waldorf proved a bit of a shock to her system. Initially, at least.'

222

Dad's words were a bit of an understatement. The lady in question had stormed out of the ballroom's double doors right after I mentioned my mother's name, her coiffured beehive coming half undone in her rage.

'But . . . she has gradually come around to the fact that I was with your mother years before I met her, that I only found out about your existence three weeks ago,' he continued. 'She also thinks you're charming. She told me yesterday night, quite sheepishly, that she likes you a lot.'

Given that I knew quite a bit about the top designers, having worked with a few of them myself, I could definitely hold my own when it came to discussions of haute couture and fine photography, two of Beehive Lady's biggest obsessions. She was particularly impressed when I told her I did a photo shoot with Testino, that one of the photographs even made it to the back pages of *Vogue*. I guess it's important to find a modicum of common ground with the people you're talking to (the conversation usually takes off quite sensibly from there). Yet I think what truly impressed her was seeing my mug shot on a billboard above Madison Avenue a couple of days before, as Dad's chauffeur drove her from the Roosevelt to Oscar de la Renta's flagship store.

'You might like to know that she has always wanted a child herself,' said Dad. 'But unfortunately she had to have a hysterectomy, so that put an end to that hope.'

He sighed.

'To my surprise, she told me yesterday that she wishes to adopt you,' he continued, causing my jaw to fall open. 'She thinks the two of you will have fun together, that you will do her proud.'

A vision of oily hands and red flames floated before me

again. I gulped, trying desperately to banish the terrible memories from my mind, to think rationally. It shouldn't be a problem for me to deal with a stepmother in this unexpected heaven I've found, after sending my stepfather on his way to hell. We might even have some fun together, as the lovely lady believes. At least my new step-parent smells of Chanel No. 5 instead of fish guts and pickled onions.

'I'm happy to hear this,' I said, forcing a smile. 'It's really kind of her to want to adopt me.'

Dad shot me a large grateful smile in return, before pouring himself another glass of port and draining it quickly. That was the moment when I thought it was appropriate for me to ask:

'Do you know why Mom never told you about my existence?'

'I think she tried,' he said, sighing. 'But I wasn't listening. Or rather, I was too afraid to hear what she wanted to say.'

His frankness made me feel a little bolder, a little more reckless. So I said: 'What happened with Mom?'

He raised an eyebrow at me.

'It's a long story,' he said. 'A sad one.'

'I'm listening,' I said.

They met in New York City at the height of summer, when a scorching sun beat down on his skin, glimmered on the skyscrapers, shimmered off the clouds. He was there on one of his business trips, having just flown in to seal a deal. He was also reeling from a messy divorce from his second wife, an American socialite who had managed to push the case through a British court, by virtue of having a London address. The judge had ruled in her favour, awarded her a hefty settlement (which included his flat in Eaton Square). Thus, instead of joining his work partner for drinks with a business associate whose hairstyle reminded him of his ex-wife, he had slouched down to an Irish bar to drown his sorrows in conviviality and lager.

It was baking hot inside the bar, as loud and stifling as hell. The space had reeked of cigarette smoke and spilt beer. It was the complete antithesis of his orange-flower-and-vanilla-scented suite at the Mayfair, where a water fountain tinkled softly in the lobby and people spoke in hushed, reverent tones. Yet the Irish bar had appealed to him in an oddly refreshing way, from the moment he stepped inside. He relished its incongruity, its noisy exuberance, its stick-up-the-middle-finger irreverence. That's why he grimaced, rolled up his sleeves and struggled up to the bar. He even dared elbow his way past two tattooed men who were bellowing at the tops of their voices, only to hear their loud curses and receive some vicious spittle in his face. He eventually got to the beer-stained counter, still wiping his cheek with the silk handkerchief he had retrieved from his pocket. The fair-haired girl behind the bar had sized him up and said with a sardonic chuckle, just before the chewing gum in her mouth went pop: 'You look like you need two large pints of Guinness.'

He nodded. They chatted a bit more, over the two pints. He learned that she was from rural Montana, had travelled to the Big Apple with dreams of making it just as big. She smoked hard, blew an impressive number of rings into his face. He grew used to them after a while, although the first couple gave him a terrible coughing fit. She swore like a paratrooper, dreamt of becoming one herself. Failing that, she hoped to become a policewoman or a pole dancer, someday. That was what she said, putting another stick of gum in her mouth and blowing a bubble with it; it went pop about two inches away from his ear.

Over the course of the evening, he discovered she had a wacky sense of humour, even made him guffaw merrily at one point. He couldn't remember when he last laughed so hard or had so much fun in one night. He noticed that although her hair was tied up in a messy bun and she wore not an ounce of make-up, she exuded a delightful fresh-faced beauty, one that reminded him of ripe apples and autumnal haystacks in the English countryside. She was the complete antithesis of his ex-wife, who doted on her three white poodles and shuttled between the salons of Mayfair with two-inch-thick warpaint on her face.

Polar opposites make a refreshing change.

That's partly why he went back to the Irish pub the following night. The night after that, too. There are some things you just can't buy, no matter how much you are willing to pay. Like shared laughter and good cheer, for instance. They went back to his room at the Mayfair three nights later. The concierge, ever discreet, graciously showed them to the private lift (as the woman was wearing a partially visible push-up bra and tiny denim shorts with fraying ends). He even had a small bunch of yellow roses sent up for her. She loved them, stuck one of them behind her ear, pulled a funny face at him.

It made him laugh again.

More laughter was shared later that night, even some chewing gum (he drew the line at the tobacco she offered). The gum was of the spearmint variety; she said it was the best at masking the tobacco on her breath. She also taught him how to blow bubbles, just for the hell of it. The act made him feel oddly alive, made him realise that he had a slightly anarchic streak, one that he never knew existed. A week later, just before he left for London, he made it clear that it was just a fling. She nodded, she didn't seem surprised by what he said. They parted amicably, with him kissing her on the forehead as she tucked a packet of chewing gum into the pocket of his Savile Row suit. She left his hotel room with a smile on her face, another yellow rose behind her ear.

Several months later, he received a letter.

That's when Dad's fingers froze on his glass of port. I saw his Adam's apple tightening, sadness consuming his eyes.

'I stared at the envelope for a long time,' he said. 'I knew it was from Marianne. It was postmarked New York City, my name and address were scribbled across the front in extremely messy handwriting. I knew she wanted to tell me something, something important. But I was too afraid to find out what it was, too much of a coward to deal with the consequences of our fling.'

He paused, anguish in his eyes.

'I never opened the letter in the end,' he said, hanging his head. 'I told my housekeeper to take it away, saw her carrying it off. By the time I changed my mind the following day, it was too late. She said the dustmen had carted away everything in the wheelie bins during the early hours of the morning.'

I remained silent.

'To this day, I blame myself for not opening the letter.'

He sighed.

'I went back to the pub the next time I returned here,' he continued. 'They told me that she'd gone back to Montana, left no forwarding address, not even a phone number. I tried looking her up in the Yellow Pages, but "Marianne Lily Robinson" was not listed. It's as if she never existed.'

He paused before adding with a rueful expression: 'I wish

227

I'd worked harder to find her. But something held me back. With hindsight, I realise it was cowardice.'

His words hung over us, pained and leaden. That was when I knew Dad believed in honesty, despite his multiple flaws. Maybe that was what endeared him to Mom, why she fell for him in the first place.

'Did Mom explain why she wanted to be a paratrooper, policewoman or pole dancer?' I said.

Surprise glimmered on Dad's face.

'I never asked,' he said. 'Maybe I should have. Something tells me that she would have succeeded in becoming one of the three, if I hadn't made her pregnant. She was a woman of hope and ambition.'

His words stabbed me hard. I never knew that about Mom, that she was once a woman of hope and ambition (until I came along, screaming and kicking, blotting out all the hope and ambition she had). It's amazing how little we know about people, in death and even in life.

Just before I left New York City, I wrote a letter to my best friend. It said:

Dearest one,

How are you? Just wanted to let you know that I eventually found my father in NYC, after months of struggling and model-ling (!!). He has decided to take me back with him, to Britain, where he lives with his third wife. We leave tomorrow evening, flying first class. Would you believe it? It will be my first time on a plane and I can't wait to have dinner in the skies.

I'm really excited by what awaits me in Britain. Dad says I should go back to school and finish my studies. I agree with him. Modelling pays and can be interesting at times, but it's a job with an inbuilt ticking clock. It's not going to last for ever. That's why I'm going to graduate with all the necessary qualifications so I can find a more secure job, someday. I'm sorry you didn't manage to make it to the Big Apple when I was there, but you are most welcome to stay with me if you ever make it to Britain. Dad says that he has a large home in London (and three others in the countryside), so I gather there's no shortage of accommodation. Unlike me, you were always the one with big dreams. If you ever decide it's better to dream on the other side of the pond, drop me a line. I'll give you Dad's phone number in London.

Really hope we'll see each other again someday. Miss you loads.

Your best friend

Our eyes tend to gloss over perfection in search of flaws. It's all-too-human to try to see imperfections in things. Yet imperfection triggers more powerful emotions, and we remember what makes us feel. The problem with utter perfection is that it doesn't stimulate our imaginations, or cause our thoughts to race in search of answers. This is why I design with imperfection in mind, so that my catwalk creations will always remain in other people's minds.

Alexander King, interview in *Harper's Bazaar*

Chapter Sixteen

Christian

The phone on my desk is ringing again. I pick it up with a sigh.

'Hi, Harold,' I say.

'Steve Mortimer is on his way.'

'Send him up when he gets here.'

'Will do. By the way, NYPD's prelim analysis suggests the bomb was a primitive, lightweight construction. Blake thinks it was built by a lone wolf.'

I sigh. I remember learning in my youth that the problem with lone wolves is that they are more difficult to spot on a flat, colourless terrain, as compared to wolves hunting in packs. My tutor once mentioned that these creatures prefer to prey on smaller animals because they struggle to bring down larger ungulates. They also scent-mark their territory less frequently in contrast to normal wolves. In other words, lone wolves tend to leave a less traceable trail.

'The folks at King have just pinged over images of the bags,' he continues. 'I've forwarded them to you.'

'Thanks, Harold. I'll have a look.'

I put the receiver down, open my inbox. An email from

Harold is waiting for me, with the subject line *Alexander King – Bags*. I click on the first attachment, labelled 2026-*Paris*. A 3D image comes up on screen. It's a cubic-shaped scarlet creation with a gilded chain handle that encircles the bag in an uneven triple loop. The words *ALEXANDER KING* are emblazoned across the front in gold letters beneath an X-shaped clasp, two daggers forming a cross. A black butterfly is stencilled across the bag's right-hand side, a flamboyant array of semi-pointillist dots. I click the rotate tab; the bag spins 360 degrees in slow motion. I hit the zoom button, focusing on the stencilled butterfly. The creature has a broken left wing with a jaggedly, torn edge; one of its antennae is missing. The overall impression is unsettling. It's as if the butterfly had managed to damage itself while struggling to escape from the gilded chain encircling the bag.

The butterfly must symbolise Maya.

I'm sure it does.

I click on the next attachment, labelled 2026-*Paris*. A second 3D image flashes up. It's a snakeskin bag, also with a butterfly motif. My eyes pick out a few immediate differences: this bag is russet-gold and has a plain bar clasp instead of a dagger-shaped one. Its handle is more conventional; the gilded chain does not wind round the bag in an uneven triple loop. I hit the rotate button, causing the bag to spin slowly on screen. Its overall structure is beautifully balanced, pleasing to the eye. I tap the zoom button, study the bag's butterfly motif. This creature has intact antennae and full wings. It's neatly stencilled across the middle of the bag, unblemished wings spreading free.

The bag is perfectly symmetrical, flawlessly exquisite.

Probably boasts a perfect *pi* ratio.

I sink back onto my chair, frowning at the two rotating designs. I would never have guessed the second bag was designed by a machine. King would probably have got away with it. Giovanni De Luca never stood a chance.

Wait a minute.

The machine-designed bag is perfect. Nothing about it jars the eye, or sullies my vision. Its butterfly isn't torn or broken. Nor does it feature a creature trying to escape from a gilded cage. Maybe De Luca had a point, after all, when he said it would lack 'the *finezza e passione e visione* of Alexander King himself'.

The machine-designed bag is perfect. Utterly perfect.

And that's the whole problem with it.

It's so perfect, it's boring.

The second bag does not tell a beguiling story, one full of tantalising possibilities. A tale that makes us pause, think and wonder, or make us question why poor butterflies have tattered wings. I now understand why Alexander King has done so well. He craftily sneaks imperfection into seeming perfection. That's what keeps his designs visionary and unsettling.

Never boring.

Come to think of it, King was both right and wrong, too.

He said that technology would produce designs more perfect than anything humans can ever dream of creating. That's true. I've just seen visual evidence of his claim. But King is not in any danger of losing his job as a fashion designer, either. Because no computer will ever produce designs with the King cutting edge, creations with the bold visionary flair of the man himself.

There may well be greater beauty in imperfection.

Perfection is intrinsically boring. Flaws make things real, more interesting. Alive, if that's the correct word. Maybe I should be more accepting of imperfections from now on, flaws in both myself and in other people. Maybe that's the real reason why Viola and I have had so many arguments in recent weeks, because I couldn't deal with living with another flawed being in close proximity (especially one prone to occasional bouts of morning grumpiness). I remember that taut exchange we had at breakfast a few mornings ago, after Viola peered into the refrigerator and said with a groan: 'We've run out of milk again.'

'Oh dear.'

'You should have let me know that we were running low.' Her voice sounded unduly peevish. Since Viola moved into my apartment, I've realised she isn't a morning person and tends to be rather crabby during the early hours of the day (I read somewhere that tech geeks tend to be night owls).

'Sorry, I forgot.'

Viola sighed before mumbling something incoherent and saying: 'Fine, I'll get Re-Stock.'

'What's that?'

'An Alexa-sensor combo that keeps track of household items and orders more if we're running low.'

Oh no, not another crazy gizmo taking up more space in the apartment and spying on our daily habits, I remember thinking as I groaned inwardly.

'Why do you keep trying to solve problems with software?' I said.

'Because machines don't forget things as often as you do.' She sounded twice as irritated.

'I've had a lot on my mind recently.' I heard a distinctly injured tone in my voice.

'With *Ella* occupying it, I'm sure.'

Her sharp retort hit me hard, knocked the breath out of my chest.

'Who *is* Ella, by the way?' She narrowed her eyes at me, suspicion flitting across her face.

My tongue froze; I just couldn't bring myself to tell her about Ella, even though the truth almost spilled out of me at that point. Maybe fear was what immobilised my tongue, my fear of the past coupled with the fear of losing Viola in the present (much like how I had lost Ella). Our exchange ended with the two of us retreating to opposite ends of the apartment in vexed silence. Damn it. Maybe I should be less cross about Viola's quirks and flaws, accept that she's essentially a geek and therefore has an unorthodox way of solving problems. She might well be jealous of the women in my past, regard her predecessors with a measure of suspicion. I guess it's only human to feel that way.

I should apologise the moment I see her, beg her to come home.

I sigh as I yank my mind back to the present.

While I've definitely learned something from this little 'spot-the-difference' exercise, something new about my relationship with Viola (and where I've gone wrong), I'm not any closer to solving this bizarre case.

Wait a minute.

Did the bomber select the Bag-That-Exploded at random? Or was there something about the bag that caught the murderer's eye? Something that might shed light on the killer's identity? Was the model the target? Or was it Alexander King himself? Why would the bomber want to hurt King, cause mayhem in Manhattan? It looks like I'm missing an important link in this puzzle. Why didn't I ask King who wrote the bag-design software for him? Shame on me. And I dare call myself a police officer (correction: paper-pushing bureaucrat). They say all software reflects the inherent biases and flaws of its creators; software is never truly impartial. Damn it, I thought I covered all bases when I interviewed King, but clearly not.

I already know what Vincent Norton's chat-bot would say if I were to click on it:

'You're an idiot, Christian.'

But I already know that. Maybe I should go back to dealing with drugs. After years of heading the Cyber Drugs Crime Unit and pushing stacks of papers from one corner of my desk to another, I'm probably better at applying for search warrants than dealing with fashionable murderers.

I pick up Alexander King's triangular name card. It's an elaborate design, one featuring lots of smashed skulls along its edges. I pick up my landline and tap in King's number, only for it to ring out, unanswered. Damn it, I'm not having much luck reaching people today. I put the receiver down, walk to the door of my office. I stick my head out to discover Ginny typing away furiously at her computer. She looks up at once.

'Ginny,' I say, 'I need a couple of things.'

She nods.

'Firstly, the name of the person who wrote the software for King's machine-designed bag.'

'*Machine-designed* bag?'

'A long and convoluted story,' I say. 'King should know who I mean.'

'Will get on it right away.'

'And could you, er . . . order a large bouquet of flowers for me?'

Her eyes widen.

'It's for Viola,' I say.

She flashes me a bright, knowing smile.

'Of course,' she says. 'What sort of flowers does Viola like?'

My head is a swirling blank. I would probably have known the answer if I had proposed to Viola, but it was Viola who did the proposing.

'Er . . .' I say. 'I don't actually know. I've, er . . . never asked her that.'

I can see astonishment dawning on Ginny's face.

'Ah,' she says.

A distant memory flits into mind. It's of Viola stopping to admire a neighbour's rose bush when we went for an evening walk, about a month ago. I recall her bending to smell a particularly large yellow rose, her eyes lighting up in pleasure.

'I love roses,' she had said. 'They remind me of Aunt Lisabeth, who used to love them too.'

I smile at Ginny.

'Roses,' I say. 'There's a good chance Viola might love an enormous bunch of yellow roses.'

I retreat back into my office after scribbling a short note to go with the flowers, pleased that I finally have a game plan. I'm going to head north-west later today, as soon as I sort out everything that needs sorting out here. I should apologise to Viola in person, beg her to come home (one quickly learns to reassess one's priorities in the face of death). They say that 'I'm sorry' are the most important words in the English language after 'I love you'; I suspect the saying is true. Maybe I should make a stab at apologising right away. I pick up my mobile and call Viola's number again, only to hear her crisp voicemail greeting. This time, I say into the receiver: 'Hi, Vi, I received your note earlier this morning. I'm sorry about everything that has happened over the past few weeks. I really am. I've been trying to reach you all morning; I think we should talk. There's a lot I need to tell you. Do please call me back when you get a chance.'

I end the call and tuck my phone away as a knock sounds on the door.

'Come in,' I say.

Ginny sticks her head into my office.

'I've ordered twelve roses,' she says. 'They're of the Sun Sprinkles variety, just so you know. Really bright and pretty, I'm sure Viola will love them. A drone will pick up your note for her and despatch everything to Old Fen Cottage within the next couple of hours.'

An idea strikes.

'Why don't we make it twenty-four roses?' I say. 'Get a second drone to send up another twelve.'

'OK,' says Ginny. 'You might also like to know that Steve Mortimer has just arrived.'

'Thanks, Ginny,' I say. 'Send him in.'

The door swings open to reveal a veritable bear of a man. Mortimer has broad shoulders, a considerable paunch and a prominent pug jaw burnished by flaming-red stubble. A tattoo of a scaly green dragon winds around his exposed lower left arm; he looks like a boxer gone to seed. His appearance is unsettlingly familiar; have we met before? Is he familiar because he's wearing an identical expression to King, a combination of shell shock, jet lag and pre-show nerves? To my surprise, the slickly dressed lawyer (whom Xander booted out from my office earlier) steps in again.

'I represent all of Mr King's senior employees,' he says, inclining his head solemnly in Mortimer's direction.

I sigh. The problem with lawyers and accountants is that they are as abundant and common as fruit flies. They spend their time making simple things more complicated, largely to justify their existence (and pay cheques). It's also difficult to get rid of them. While King tried and succeeded the last time, something tells me that Mr Avery is likely to stick around for this particular chat.

'Thank you for coming in, Mr Mortimer,' I say, rising from my desk. 'Please have a seat.'

Mortimer narrows his eyes at me before lowering himself down onto the chair.

'I understand you're responsible for bags and millinery,' I say, cutting straight to the chase. 'Could you take me through what happened yesterday night, how Ally ended up carrying the bag?'

Mortimer purses his lips, frowning a little.

'You have a right not to answer, Steve,' says Avery, his voice as silky as the plush tie around his neck.

'A fair point,' I say, nodding. 'But poor Ally is dead and we would like to find out who killed her.'

I can see a faint grimace on Steve's face, an expression that suggests he may be persuaded to talk.

'It was murder in cold blood, Mr Mortimer,' I continue in a firm voice. 'One that caused the death of a lovely girl you worked with. If you're able to help, we may find the bomber, stop him from killing again.'

I tap in Ally's name into my search box, tilt the screen in

Mortimer's direction. Her 3D avatar is achingly beautiful, all doe-eyed and vulnerable-looking with cascading blonde hair. Mortimer's eyes flit across the image; there's a stricken expression in his eyes. I can also see his jaw twitching a little.

Time to press on.

'Where were all the bags located, before they were handed out?' I say.

'You have the right not to answer,' says Avery again, tilting his head imperiously at his client.

Indecision flits over Mortimer's face. It prompts me to tilt Ally's image more firmly in his direction. His eyes skim her lovely avatar for a couple of moments, before turning in my direction.

'They were on racks, arranged in precise order of appearance,' he eventually says, to my grateful surprise. His accent is unusual: I detect some Midwest inflections mingled with an English burr.

'When were they placed there?' I say. 'A few hours before the show?'

'You *really* don't have to answer, Steve,' says Avery, his smooth deep voice polluting the space between us. No wonder King looked so pissed off during his earlier showdown with Avery. The man's manner is starting to grate on me, too. Silence hangs over us; I can see Mortimer moving his stubbly jaw from side to side.

'The day before the show,' he says in a sudden rush, looking straight at me. 'Around five in the afternoon, I think.'

'Does this mean that anyone backstage had about a day to tamper with the bags?' I say.

Mortimer shoots a brief uncertain glance at his lawyer before saying: 'Pretty much so, yes.'

'How many people had access backstage?'

'A hundred, maybe more.'

This doesn't sound good at all.

'What were you doing before the bomb went off?'

'I was checking the glass cage that was supposed to appear at the end of the show.'

Mortimer's words sound practised, rehearsed. I bet Pompous Avery took him through his paces, briefed him on what to say.

'Where was it?'

'In a separate area, maybe five hundred yards from the bags.'

'Do you know who handed the bag to Ally?'

Mortimer is agitating his jaw from side to side, more vigorously this time. It's quite an informative tic. It suggests he's thinking hard about what to say . . . or what not to say.

'I'm not sure, frankly.' He shrugs. 'I had five assistants running about, making sure that nothing was missed, that all the models were kitted out correctly. It could have been any of the five.'

Unfortunately, Mortimer's assistants are beyond my reach. I can only hope our American cousins are asking them the right questions.

'Could Ally have accepted the bag from someone who *wasn't* one of the five?'

'You don't have to answer—' begins Avery in a loud, sharp voice, only to be silenced by Mortimer holding up a beefy hand.

'Thanks for reminding me, Nigel,' says Mortimer drily.

He turns to me and nods. Avery looks slightly put out.

'It was really chaotic last night,' he says. 'Yes, it's possible Ally could have accepted the bag from just about anyone. Most models do what they're told backstage, few questions asked.'

Avery shifts in his chair. He looks extremely uneasy; I wonder why.

'The bag must have been much heavier than usual, with the bomb inside,' I say. 'Why didn't Ally alert anyone?'

Mortimer sighs.

'Even if she did, I'm not sure anyone would have taken her seriously. Not with so much going on.'

I'm back to square one: it looks like just about anyone backstage could have stuck a bomb into the bag and handed it to Ally. Shame there weren't any CCTV cameras . . . Wait a minute . . .

'Were there any recordings backstage?' I say. 'Someone filming an official video, maybe? Taking photographs?'

'We had an official videographer in the past, before I convinced Xander it was in his interest not to have one,' says Avery before Mortimer can answer, much to my astonishment. 'We feared it could create legal problems for us, mainly around issues of consent and privacy.'

'To put it more simply,' says Mortimer, 'we thought we shouldn't let a videographer loose backstage, with so many models walking around in various states of undress. There are just too many DIY deep-fake porn apps these days, people substituting body parts in videos.'

He spreads his hands with a grimace.

'What about photographers?' I say. 'Were there any backstage?'

'Just one,' says Mortimer. 'She limits herself to photos of models having their hair and make-up done. No semi-naked photos, mind you. We're pretty strict about that now.'

'Fair enough.'

'Our models love taking selfies backstage,' says Mortimer. 'Maybe you should check their photos.'

Avery shifts in his seat, again. I haven't thought of selfie-taking models; it shows just how disconnected I am from what young people are doing on their social media accounts these days. But . . . the chance of a model photographing something relevant backstage, in a selfie, of all things, is probably one in a million. I reopen the 2030–*Manhattan* attachment and tilt my computer screen in Mortimer's direction.

'I understand this was the bag Ally carried yesterday,' I say.

Mortimer peers at the image and nods.

'Did the design strike you as being unusual?' I say. 'Out of the ordinary, maybe?'

Silence fills the room again.

'Nope,' says Mortimer.

Hmm.

'Did Mr King mention that the bag was designed by software?' I say.

I can see Mortimer's eyes widening, his jaw moving from side to side again.

'Really?' he says. 'You must be kidding.'

Now, if King's own Head of Bags and Millinery (who probably knows everything there is to know about accessories) thinks that the bag was dreamt up by King himself, King would have most certainly won his bet with De Luca. Did someone want to prevent King from winning the bet . . . by causing the bag to explode as soon as it made an appearance on the catwalk? If so, why? I feel as if I've just been clubbed in the head in this never-ending fashion rabbit hole of mine.

'So King never told you about the substitution?' I say to Mortimer.

Mortimer shakes his head, more resolutely this time. Damn, I have learned nothing useful from this chat, so far. Maybe I should just ask Mortimer a few more routine questions before letting him go.

'Did anything seem out of place yesterday, before the bomb went off?' I say.

'Nope.'

'What about today?' I say. 'Has anything at Old Billingsgate given you reason for concern?'

'Things are going as planned, so far. Our private security firm has just conducted a thorough sweep of the premises, found nothing. They'll be doing another search just before the show.'

'Does Mr King have any enemies?'

Mortimer's jaw is doing its usual dance.

'I think his biggest enemy is himself.'

I sit up in my chair.

'What do you mean?' I say, narrowing my eyes at Mortimer.

'Xander has been a little down in the dumps recently,' he says. 'I think he's inclined to hurt himself.'

I blink at Mortimer. Avery looks equally flabbergasted, judging from the way he's leaning forward in his seat.

'What makes you think so?' I say.

'It's just a gut feeling I have, no way I can prove it.'

I should get to the bottom of this.

'Where does this, er . . . gut feeling come from?' I say.

Mortimer's jaw is agitating again.

'Xander has been talking a lot about death recently,' he says.

'Hasn't Mr King always been obsessed by death?'

'He has, indeed,' says Mortimer, nodding fervently this time. 'But he's now talking about death like he welcomes it.'

'What do you mean?'

'He keeps saying that maybe it's better to be dead than to

suffer endlessly, that Maya's end may well be the perfect end to things. I fear Xander may do something silly, try to copy the way she died.'

Mortimer's mention of prolonged suffering causes painful memories to flood my mind again; I have to work hard to shove them aside, to concentrate on what he is implying. I have no idea what to make of his crazy suggestion that King might try to replicate the way his muse died (the possibility makes me feel a little bit sick, that someone might be disturbed enough to attempt such a thing). Avery looks just as baffled, judging from the expression on his face.

'Has Mr King sought any professional help, seen a psychiatrist?' I ask.

Mortimer shakes his head.

'Not that I know of.'

I need to mull over this revelation a bit more. In the meantime, I can only say: 'Maybe you should get a professional to help Mr King, if you're worried about him. Keep a close eye on him tonight, too.'

'I will.' Mortimer nods his head vigorously. 'That was the plan, anyway.'

'That will be all for now, Mr Mortimer. We'll ring if we have any other questions.'

'I hope you catch the killer,' he says, rising from his chair with a loud creak that reverberates round the room. Avery gets to his feet with a large frown; he seems to be thinking hard.

'We'll do our best,' I say.

I watch Mortimer walk in the direction of the door. Despite his girth, he moves with unusual ease; I swear we've met in the past. Just before Mortimer leaves the room, he turns around and looks at me.

'Sorry, Mr Verger, but I've been itching to ask something,' he says.

'What?'

'Have we met before?'

I'm tempted to say that I've been wondering the same thing all along. But maybe I shouldn't, not until I've figured out when and where. Maybe Mortimer and I went to school together, but we never talked because I hung out with the studious boys, not the tattoo-inclined ones.

'Maybe we have,' I say.

'I think I met a Verger before, but I can't remember much about him. He must have been a forgettable sort.'

'Well, I hope I'm an improvement on the Verger you've met,' I say, sighing. 'If we ever did meet.'

CriminalX

Steve Mortimer (13.67%)

Head of Millinery & Bags, Alexander King

Age: 49

IQ Score: Unknown

Education: Diploma in Art and Design, Oxford Brookes University (2010); Diploma in Accessories Design, London College of Fashion (2011)

Background: Worked as a fashion model in Manhattan before becoming a part-time model at Alexander King in 2010. Joined King's Millinery & Bags division in 2012, promoted to Head in 2015. Given a 200-hour community service order by a High Court judge in October 2012, after breaking a man's nose during a pub crawl in South Kensington. A drugs test confirmed that Mortimer was high on cocaine and MDMA at the time. Late stepfather (Peter Mortimer) received a police caution in 1995 for hitting his wife during an argument at home and a second caution in 1997 after punching a man in a bar. Recent Google searches include: 'matching headwear for bomber jackets', 'designers who died prematurely', 'who takes over a fashion house when the head designer dies' & 'where to hide stuff on private jets'. Nine of his Facebook friends (2,720 in total) have criminal convictions (one was convicted of first-degree murder in 2008).

Status: Backstage (BS) – Manhattan & London

Inspiration lies at the bottom of a glass. I swear this is true. I've lost count of the times an idea for the perfect design slid into my head soon after I reached the bottom of a tumbler of fine liqueur. Unfortunately for me, I usually forget what the dress looks like when I wake up the following morning.

Alexander King, interview in *Decanter* magazine

Chapter Seventeen

Xander

Something is yawning wide, a loud metallic creak that filters deep into the dark void that surrounds me. I'm forcibly lifted up from my semi-seated, semi-slumped position, dumped onto something hard. I hear voices in the distance, a rapid-fire exchange of words. I try to force my eyes open. Light swirls around my retinas, piercing my eyeballs with only a few tantalising pinpricks of vision. The surface I'm on rolls forward, only to bump hard against something a second later. My head pitches sideways, strikes something solid and unyielding. Pain floods the side of my head, fanning across my skull in a series of waves. I groan, only a tiny squeak escapes my lips.

'Whoa,' a female voice says, sounding exasperated. 'Watch where you're going, will you?'

'I'm doing my best,' a male voice says. 'He's a big chap.'

I presume I'm the 'big chap' they're discussing. I should be offended as I have always considered myself lithe and light, fit and fab.

'You'll kill him prematurely.'

Prematurely, eh? The hard surface is moving forward again. The left side of my head is killing me. But the pain is also

249

waking up a few brain cells, making me think. Let me see. I'm being wheeled somewhere, a place I don't necessarily want to go. These must surely be evil people with nefarious intentions, folks who wish me harm. It's probably the bunch that bombed yesterday's show, folks intending more havoc in my life. I should get away from them. If they are going to kill me eventually (even if they aren't intending to do so prematurely), I should get up and run. Or maybe I shouldn't. If they decide to kill me, I'm spared from performing the dire deed myself (but I unfortunately won't be able to choose the manner of death). To complicate matters, I'll struggle to run. My eyelids and limbs feel like immobile pieces of lead. I wish I could sit up properly on this bloody thing, make a hasty and dignified exit.

'Lemmegoyoufuckinbastards,' I say, trying to clench my fist.

A hushed silence descends around my ears, just before a female voice says: 'I think he's coming round.'

'That's good,' says a second female voice in a crisp, matter-of-fact tone. 'The timing couldn't be better.'

'Uh huh.'

'We don't have that much time left.'

What the fuck are they talking about? Do they mean the time left to kill me? Should I tell them to hurry up and do it, spare me the trouble of grabbing a gun and shooting myself? Someone lifts me from the hard surface, deposits me on a softer one. It feels like a lumpy mattress, the sort meted out to patients in third-class hospitals and inmates of second-rate prisons. I perform another desperate battle with my eyelids. They eventually give way to reveal . . .

. . . a low, lopsided ceiling with broad horizontal wooden beams, dark with the resinous patina of age. I blink a few times, grateful that my eyes are working again. The contours of the room are taking on sharper focus. I appear to have been deposited on a narrow bunk bed, one with lurid Kermit-green sheets. Bright canary-yellow curtains are fluttering in an open window yards away.

Where the fuck am I?

I twist my head in the direction of my captors, my mouth falls open.

They are hovering a few yards away, next to an empty wheelchair.

And I know both of them.

The first is the ponytailed chauffeur who kidnapped me from the front doors of New Scotland Yard. He must surely be the person who dumped me into that wheelchair, brought me here. The second is Lucia, blades dangling merrily in her ears (why the fuck is she involved in this ridiculous state of affairs?).

'I'll wait outside,' says the chauffeur, disappearing through the door.

'What-the-fuck-is-going-on?' I say, my words a wretched slurry.

'Glad you've come round,' says Lucia, settling down on a nearby stool. 'I was worried Jake put too much in your drink.'

'Why-the-fuck have you brought me here?'

'To make sure tonight happens as planned.'

'But I wasn't planning to change the plan,' I say, perplexed.

Lucia pulls out a gun from her snakeskin handbag, a small sleek Beretta with a fine mother-of-pearl handle. She points it at the ceiling, before turning it slowly in my direction. My mouth falls open.

'That's my gun,' I say.

251

'No longer, I'm afraid,' she says, a stern expression flooding her face. 'I've been given clear instructions to take it away from you.'

'You wouldn't dare.'

'We don't want you to pull the trigger tonight.'

'But I wasn't planning to shoot anyone,' I say, my voice a protesting squeak.

'I'm not so sure about that,' says a second voice.

I gasp. There is another person in the room, a woman in frumpy green slacks, holding a small folder. Fucking hell, I should have recognised my surroundings the moment I opened my eyes. I've visited this cottage lots of times before. It was my occasional place of refuge, the sanctuary I favoured whenever I needed to get away from the pressures of the outer world. A haven where I could frolic about stark naked if I wanted to, scream my lungs out in the tiny yet charming attic, climb the mighty oak tree in the garden and holler expletives from the top. Hide from the prying eyes of the paparazzi and parasites that plague my daily existence, begging for money, jobs and other fucking favours.

Old Fen Cottage.

An oasis of tranquillity in a crazy world.

My occasional pit stop for the restoration of sanity and the occasional bout of cold-water bathing.

A place that few people know exists, where I will always be welcomed by its delightful owner:

A geek named Viola, my bright young intern who has since turned into one of my best friends (even if she has a penchant for wearing ghastly green slacks and tacky leopard-print clothing). A person who isn't quick to judge, who never takes me too seriously. Someone who I can say whatever I like to, be completely honest with (it's amazing how you need to watch your words with so-called 'friends' whose default mode is to take offence at what you tell them).

Dear Viola unfortunately doesn't look very welcoming today. In fact, she looks rather cross with me. She's staring down with folded arms, with an expression that suggests she's inclined to shoot me.

Technology is a tool, not an end. It's all about knowing how to use technology well. Imagine a caveman picking up a chisel. He's perplexed, terrified and a little hopeful. He wonders if it might be possible for him to use the implement to stab a wild boar. It'll take him a long time to figure out that he'll be able to use the chisel to craft a beautiful Renaissance-styled sculpture. Unfortunately for the caveman, this realisation probably won't happen in his lifetime.

Christian Verger, Lecture on 'Policing in the Year 2030: The Promise and Perils of Technology'

Chapter Eighteen

Viola

My landline rang exactly two and a half hours ago, causing me to jump out of my skin (I hadn't heard that dusty device ring in years). I grabbed the receiver, heard a soft feminine voice on the line:

'Hello, this is Lucia Graves. I got two missed calls from this number.'

'It's me,' I said. 'Viola.'

'Oh hi, Viola,' she said, delight ringing in her voice. 'I've just emerged from New Scotland Yard. Any luck with the note?'

'One match.'

'Who?'

'I'll reveal the name to Xander himself, if you don't mind. Trouble is, I'm stuck at my home in Oxford; I need to re-run some software for my boss. If you can bring Xander up to me, that would be great.'

'But . . . but the police have just collected Xander from Heathrow and taken him to New Scotland Yard. He'll probably want to head straight to Old Billingsgate after speaking to them.'

'We should be taking the note seriously, Lucia.' My voice was stern and firm. 'It's a matter of life and death.'

My words were greeted with silence.

'Xander's death, to be precise,' I added for good measure.

'I believe you.' Her voice is soft.

'Do you want Xander to die tonight?'

'Most definitely not.'

'You can help me prevent his death.'

'How?'

'Bring him up to Old Fen Cottage so I can talk to him.'

'I'm one hundred per cent sure Xander will refuse to travel to Oxford, given his current commitments.'

That was when I realised that Lucia was right, and that desperate times call for desperate measures.

'Can you put something into his drink, knock him out?' I said.

I heard Lucia sighing.

'I could try, I guess.'

'Try some super-strong sleeping pills, maybe.'

'OK.'

'Does Xander have anything dangerous he could use to hurt himself?'

She hesitated before replying: 'He keeps a small pistol in the office. Think it was a gift from a friend.'

'Take it away from him. Make sure he doesn't get his hands on it.'

'OK.'

'Thanks, Lucia. I'm counting on you.'

That's what I said. Now, a few hours later, I'm staring at that precise pistol she mentioned. I'm tempted to grab the weapon from Lucia, point it at Xander, threaten to shoot him.

Maybe the shock of staring down the barrel of a gun might paradoxically inject sense into his system, a newfound appreciation of life. But maybe it will do the precise opposite. I sigh, before turning to Lucia.

'Do you mind leaving us alone, please?' I say.

Lucia nods, tucking Xander's pistol back into her handbag. She gets up from her stool, disappears through the door. I collapse onto the same stool. Maybe I should start by being nice to Xander.

'I'm sorry about Manhattan,' I say. 'Any idea who did it?'

Xander grimaces, shaking his head.

'Nope,' he says. 'Why have you brought me here?'

I sigh again.

'I have to be at a particular show in London tonight, as you may know,' he says, narrowing his eyes at me.

'That's precisely what I wanted to talk to you about,' I say. 'Your plans for tonight.'

'What about them?'

Time to change the subject, take him by surprise. Even though it's tempting to talk about the Manhattan bomber, discuss some of the names CriminalX spat out, try to work out the killer's identity. But that wasn't the main reason I told Lucia and Jake to bring Xander up here.

'You've been diagnosed with prostate cancer, haven't you?' I say.

His jaw drops open.

'How . . . how did you know?' he says.

'Google knows everything,' I say, shrugging. 'Whether we like it or not. Why didn't you tell me?'

Xander bows his head in silence for a couple of moments before looking up at me.

'It's the sort of news you'd much rather break in person. But . . .' he pauses with a regretful shrug, 'we haven't seen each other for ages. You may remember I'd planned to come up here a few months ago, spend a whole night chatting, but we both had to cancel because of engagements.'

Xander has a good point. I've been rather busy with work over the past few months, work largely inflicted by him, come to think of it (with my new fiancé taking up the rest of my time).

'Have you started treatment for the cancer?' I say.

He shakes his head.

'Thought about it, decided against it.'

I had a feeling Xander would say this.

'Why?'

'If mortal agony is the prelude to dying, I'd much rather have a memorable coda than a painful overture.'

Our eyes meet. I think I know what Xander's trying to say, and I don't like it the tiniest bit. Time to pull the rabbit out of the hat. I reach into my black folder and extract a photo of the anonymous note that Lucia emailed to me. I hand it, wordlessly, to Xander. He shrugs.

'Lucia found this in her handbag,' I say. 'She gave the original to the police.'

'I know that. They grilled me about it.'

'Linguistic profiling tells me only one person in your immediate circle could have written this note.'

Xander lifts an eyebrow at me.

'Google again, eh?' he says. 'Who was it?'

I stare at the bright yellow curtains in the window, billowing prettily in the breeze. They look mightily incongruous to me, especially as they're framing an entirely morbid chat about death.

I take in a breath before saying: 'Steve Mortimer.'

His jaw falls open.

'You must be kidding,' he says.

Little does Xander know that I have a second rabbit in the hat. Time to yank the next one out. I fix my eyes on him and say: 'Steve's note was meant as a *warning*, not as a threat.'

Xander looks both surprised and discomfited; I can see him swallowing hard, his Adam's apple bobbing. Yet I'm certain my hypothesis is accurate, and that the linguistic-profiling software was right, too.

'That's when I began wondering,' I say. 'Why on earth would Steve slip a note into Lucia's handbag, a note warning her about your impending demise?'

He's as silent as a mouse.

'It didn't take me too long to figure out why,' I continue. 'Not after realising that you had been diagnosed with cancer and knowing that Steve has kept a careful eye on you over the years.'

Is Xander listening to me? I steal a glance at him. He's staring down at the bed sheet he's lying on, a kaleidoscope of swirling geometric patterns in varying shades of green. In normal circumstances, a semi-sober version of Xander would say that I have zero fashion sense, that the bed sheet clashes horribly with the curtains. A drunk and stoned Xander would say I make no sense at all. Suicidal Xander is ominously silent and I have no idea how to talk sense into him.

'You're planning to do it tonight, aren't you?' I say, choking my words out.

Xander bows his head, by the tiniest of fractions. I'm certain I'm right; Xander's body language proves it beyond reasonable doubt. The breeze has died down; the air in the room now feels dense and oppressive.

'You're loved by many,' I say, hearing my voice shake. 'That includes me. Please don't do this, Xan.'

He's still alarmingly silent.

'Please let me help you,' I say.

He sighs.

'I know you care,' he says.

'I do.'

Our eyes meet; he knows I'm telling the truth. But the truth is unlikely to sway him. Xander always had a stubborn, pig-headed streak. That's what got him places in the first place. Now that he's decided to stop going places, wishes to take a flying leap down the ravine of no return, I haven't got a goddamned clue as to how I'm going to yank him back from the edge of the precipice.

'I've achieved almost everything I've wanted in my lifetime,' he says quietly, with a resigned air. 'Fame, fortune, all that jazz. When you've achieved everything, the only thing left is simple.'

'What is it?'

'A painless end; an end that I can control.'

'Are you in pain now?'

He scrunches up his face.

'Not severely. Nothing I can't mask with drugs so far. But I know that terrible pain is on its way. There's only so much drugs can do. Which makes the agony of anticipation twice as bad.'

'But treatment might help you make a full recovery.'

'I don't have the will, Vi.'

His eyes are dark, intent.

'As you know, will is everything,' he continues. 'You've always been the more ambitious, the more focused. I've just been the lucky one, all my life. Never truly had will in the first place.'

I can't believe my ears.

'But isn't there something left inside, something that makes you want to persevere?' I say, in a strangled voice. 'Aren't lots of things still worth living for? Worth doing next, worth hoping for?'

'I've seen and done everything by now, experienced everything a person could.' His voice is tinged with the weariness of a man twice his age. 'I've felt everything by now too, everything a person could possibly feel. Once you've seen everything, done everything, felt everything, you're only left with a hollow numbness inside. I'm tired, Vi. Really tired and numb.'

Oh God, oh God, oh God. I'm screwing this up. I'm better at interacting with machines than with humans. I have no idea how to string words together in a persuasive way. Neither am I capable of manipulating people around me, persuading them to do what I think is good for them.

Like staying alive.

'You haven't done a few things yet,' I say, in sheer desperation.

'Like what?' There's curiosity in Xander's voice.

'You haven't criticised the bed sheet, said they don't match the curtains,' I say. 'Nor have you insulted my dress sense. And you haven't yet given me advice on how to improve my love life.'

Xander's eyes are opening wide; I can see the corner of his mouth twitching a little in amusement.

'I need you, Xan,' I say, hearing my voice choke again. 'I need you to remind me, once every few months, that I have lamentable fashion sense. I need you to tell me not to take myself too seriously, not to work too hard. If you're going to be selfish, I can be selfish too.'

I can see his eyes softening, losing some of their morose intent. He reaches out to squeeze my hand. His skin is dry, papery. I squeeze his hand back as wind gusts in through the open window, causing the curtains to flutter again. The taut line to his shoulders is relaxing a little.

'You haven't yet told me how you're getting on, by the way,' he says, with a sudden unexpected chuckle. 'After all this talk about death, maybe we should talk about how your utterly boring life is progressing.'

This sounds remotely promising, more like the Xander I've known for years.

'So, spill the beans,' he says, cranking up an eyebrow at me. 'What's going on in your mysterious love life, when you're not busy doing your usual spook stuff?'

I stare at Xander in consternation for several moments. It's the first time he's called me a spook to my face (he probably suspected the true nature of some of my recent commissions but never had the guts to say so). Maybe it's the effect of having exchanged so many frank words earlier.

'Dating anyone at the moment?' he says, winking at me.

Maybe I should tell Xander. You can only keep so many secrets within the finite compartments of your heart. Secrets have a tendency to build up inside you, burble out of your throat when you can no longer contain them. I should tell him. I have to. Especially as I still haven't managed to convince him that life is infinitely beautiful and precious, that it's worth sticking around.

'I followed your advice, a few months ago,' I say, feeling a blush rise to my cheeks.

'What advice?'

'That I should build a piece of software that identifies the most compatible person for me. Bit like Tinder, but bespoke.'

'You did?' There's incredulity in his voice. 'I never realised you took me seriously.'

'I always take you seriously, Xan,' I say, shrugging. 'You're full of wacky yet brilliant ideas. Stuff that only makes sense after you think hard and discard all the useless noise.'

Xander raises an eyebrow. I'm glad we have returned to insulting each other, at the very least.

'It took me weeks to figure out the criteria I wanted, a day and a half to build the software,' I say. 'I fed it my entire contact list, everyone's Facebook friends. I also gave it the profiles of all living people between the ages of forty and sixty on Wikipedia, just for the heck of it.'

'What did the software come up with?'

I look straight at Xander and say: 'It spat out six names in descending order of compatibility. To cut a long and tortuous dating story short, I'm now engaged to be married . . . to one of them.'

'Wow and congrats.' Xander's mouth is breaking into a giant grin, the first cheerful expression I've seen on his face since Jake unloaded him from the wheelchair onto my guest bed. 'I'm so pleased my suggestion worked, that you've finally found the right woman for you.'

Unfortunately, I can't smile as broadly as Xander. It's time to drop a couple of bombshells.

'It isn't a woman, this time.'

'Ha,' Xander raises an eyebrow. 'Kudos to the lucky man, then. Maybe I should stick around purely for the pleasure of meeting him.'

I take in a deep breath before saying: 'There's more, Xan.'

'What?'

'I'm also pregnant, but I'm no longer sure Spark the Software predicted the right man for me.'

Xander looks both surprised and delighted by my second revelation; I can see another massive smile emerging on his lips.

'You're *pregnant*?' he says. 'That's wonderful.'

'I did a pregnancy test this morning,' I say, staring down at my hands. 'It turned out positive.'

'You sound bothered.'

He's right. My fingernails are a complete mess now, all chipped and chewed around their edges.

'You're the first person I've told, actually,' I say in a small voice, looking back up at him.

'Really?' There's puzzlement in Xander's tone. 'Why haven't you told your fiancé yet?'

'It's complicated,' I say. 'I came back here yesterday, wrote him a letter saying I needed time out from our relationship.'

'How come?'

'He's been talking about another woman in his sleep.'

I can see Xander's eyes widening.

'Did you ask him who she is?' he says.

'I tried.' I spread my hands with a frustrated grimace. 'He clammed up, each time.'

'Shame.'

'Guess I should have probed harder . . . but maybe I'm secretly afraid of hearing the truth.'

He nods with sympathy on his face.

'Most of the time, we're better off not knowing,' he says. 'Yet there are times we might be better off *knowing*. Especially

264

when it comes to ghosts from the past, ghosts who should be laid to rest. They say if you can't come to terms with the past, you are doomed to repeat it.'

'Hmm.'

'While I say . . .' he pauses for dramatic effect, '. . . you can only face the future *after* you confront your past.'

I have a sneaking suspicion Xander's right. Yet I'm not going to agree with him because there's something else I should say.

'We've been arguing over silly little things, trivial household stuff.' I hear a mournful note in my voice.

'You moved in with him?'

I nod.

'Even had the guts to ask him to marry me.'

'Wow. How did he react?'

'He kissed me, said yes. But things soon went downhill from there. The everyday realities of sharing his apartment haven't quite been . . .' I trail off with another sigh, '. . . what I'd expected. Maybe Spark the Software screwed up. Maybe we weren't really compatible in the first place.'

'Disagreement is the lifeblood of any relationship.'

'Do you really think so?'

'What do you think?' Xander shrugs. 'You, of all people, probably know that I spend all my time arguing with folks. Once you've stormed off a few times, you know where you stand with them and they know exactly where they stand with you. It makes for much healthier relationships.'

'Ha.'

'Do you really want your fiancé to be pristinely perfect, fucking flawless in every way?'

His blunt question takes me by surprise. I stare at Xander in silence, I don't know what to say.

'Perfection is illusory,' he says. 'It eventually loses its sheen. Imperfection makes things real, more interesting,'

'Does it?'

'Perfection is also a process, my dear. Happiness lies in finding it. And when you finally do find perfection, you realise that the state is as boring as hell, it doesn't make you want to do better.'

'Hmm.'

'Maybe your quest for the perfect partner caused you to project all sorts of unrealistic expectations on to your fiancé. Maybe your idealised vision of love caused you to put undue pressure on him to fit the mould. Maybe Spark the Software raised your hopes so high, reality could only disappoint. Will *always* disappoint, if you aren't careful. It's the mismatch between expectations and reality, the discrepancy between imagination and truth, which makes people miserable.'

'You sound like a bloody philosopher.'

'I'm always full of wacky ideas, as you say.'

'Must be the drugs speaking.'

'Or the shit the driver put in my whisky, thanks to you.'

One of the basic rules of our friendship is that I never ask Xander what he has been stuffing down his throat, and he never asks what I really do for a living. That's precisely why our friendship has survived for so long, why we like each other's company.

'I expected happiness to come as a result of success,' he continues, spreading his hands. 'I thought that accolades and acclaim would make me a happier man, but they haven't. I was miserable the day I won the Designer of the Year Award, and I haven't stopped being miserable since.'

'Maybe you should stop expecting happiness, then.'

'Maybe you should drop your romanticised fantasies about what your perfect partner should be.'

'Maybe you should quit the fashion industry if it makes you miserable.'

'Maybe you shouldn't let machines condition your thinking.'

I glare at Xander before retorting: 'Maybe *you* should try to be a little less self-absorbed, think of others instead of just yourself.'

'Maybe *you* should learn to surrender control, because there are some things in life you can't control.'

I do believe Xander's voice has got louder. So has mine. I sigh, slumping on my stool.

'Oh, Xan.'

'Technology is just an aid, Vi. It shouldn't dictate our actions, enslave our minds, burden us with unrealistic expectations.'

His quiet words trigger a jolt of pain in my stomach. Maybe it's because they are cutting deep.

'Do you love your fiancé?' he says, taking me by surprise.

'I . . . er . . .' I hear myself stuttering.

'Let me put it another way.' He holds up a finger in a mock stern way. 'What do you like best about him?'

I pause to consider my answer.

'He's caring and kind.'

'Go on.'

'He's solid and dependable.'

'Does he have any talents?'

'He makes me think, makes me laugh. He can also cook a cracking rabbit stew.'

Xander chortles.

'Do you trust him, despite the stuff he has been keeping from you?'

I nod, with conviction.

'I have my own secrets, come to think of it.'

'Don't we all?' Xander shrugs. 'What makes him special?'

'Like with you, I'm completely myself in his company, completely honest about what I think about things . . .' I trail off as a new realisation strikes. 'Maybe that's why we argue so much. Maybe it's because I'm always frank with him, tell him exactly how I feel. Maybe that's not such a bad thing in the end, because we know precisely where we stand with each other.'

Gosh, I have rambled on a bit. Yet I can see Xander nodding away at me, with a pleased expression in his eyes.

'Honesty is the lifeblood of any relationship,' he says. 'The same goes for good faith, trust and compromise.'

'So speaks the sage, still on a high.'

'I think you should give your relationship another chance. After all, nothing in life is perfect.'

Xander's words are quiet and firm. I stare at him for a couple of moments, before unloading the words that have been on the tip of my tongue ever since I confronted him about his intentions for the evening.

'I think *you* should give life another chance. Even if life isn't perfect. Cancer isn't a death sentence.'

My words are just as quiet and firm.

Our eyes meet. Something flashes between us, just before Xander turns his gaze away, stares back down at the bed sheet. Maybe there are still possibilities out there, ones worth exploring in my relationship with Christian. Maybe there's hope for us. I'm not so sure about Xander, though, because his eyebrows are curving downwards again in an abject swoop. Desperation jolts back through me. I still don't know how to wrestle him back from the precipice.

The only thing I can hope for, as far as Xander is concerned, is a miracle.

A gust of wind sweeps in through the open window, a cooler one. It ruffles my hair, soothes the nape of my neck. I turn my gaze to the fluttering yellow curtains, only to notice a silver-blue butterfly perching on the windowsill. Inspiration strikes. I only had words at my disposal, now, I also have an image. I use code to create function, Xander uses images to create beauty. That's precisely what I need.

An image of beauty.

'Look, Xan,' I say, pointing at the butterfly. 'Isn't it gorgeous?'

His gaze swings to it.

'You're fond of saying that butterflies are the souls of dead people,' I say. 'You saw one on Hampstead Heath the day Maya died, didn't you? A white one almost as large as your palms?'

He nods, a slightly stricken expression creeping into his eyes.

'The shows are to commemorate Maya's inspirational life, aren't they?'

He nods.

'As it now stands, a poor model is dead. One death is more than enough.'

My voice is sharp. The butterfly twitches its wings, soars high in a brilliant flash of silver-blue. We watch it flutter in a couple of semicircles, illuminated by the bright rays of light beaming down below the eaves of the cottage, before vanishing completely from view. Xander's eyes are dark, thoughtful. I think I've said everything I needed to say.

'OK,' he says, looking back up at me with an impish twist of his lips. 'Let's make a deal.'

'What sort of deal?' I say.

'I promise I won't curtail anything prematurely tonight,' he says, chuckling and taking me completely by surprise. 'But you will have to promise me two tiny little things, in return.'

'What are they?'

'One, you'll give your fiancé another chance. Two, I'll get to be your child's godfather.'

I can't believe my ears. If Xander's both serious and honest, I have just bought a bit more time to convince him that life's worth living, that the cancer is worth fighting.

'You serious?' I say.

'I try not to take myself too seriously,' he says, shrugging. 'You shouldn't, either.'

'Aha, I knew that was coming.'

'Are we doing the fucking deal or not?'

'It's a deal,' I say, extending my palm.

We shake hands, solemnly. I notice a tiny flash of mischief in Xander's eyes. It looks promising, more like the Xander I've known for years. Just then, a whir of wings sounds outside, causing us to jump. I walk to the window, take a peek out. A drone has just landed with something in its beak. Something enormous and completely unexpected. Something in the colour of bright sunshine.

'I should get this delivery,' I say.

I race through the front door, out into a blustery breeze and dazzling light. An e-bird (is it supposed to be a toucan? A hornbill?) is waiting for me on the patio. It's holding a magnificent bunch of yellow roses in its beak. I extract the flowers from the drone, offer it my thumbprint to confirm receipt. The bird gives me a beady-eyed nod in response, before taking to the skies in a graceful sweep.

What gorgeous roses. Twelve, in total. They smell divine.
Each bloom is so large, it's almost the size of my hand. An
envelope is attached to the red satin ribbon that encircles the
bouquet. I open the envelope, heart racing with curiosity, pull
out a small white card. I gasp; I recognise the handwriting. It's
meticulously cursive, each 'g' and 'y' a flamboyant loop. The
note says:

My darling Viola,
I'm so sorry about that awful fight we had two days ago.
You had every right to be mad at me. I should have told you
about Ella from the start. Please give me a chance to do so, to
explain things to you. I've realised today that when a man is
confronted with his own mortality, he learns what truly matters
to him.
In my case, what truly matters is you.
With all my love, Christian

I feel something melting away, all the resentment and anger
that had driven me nuts over the past couple of days. There
is one man I really care about in this world, and I should stop
being childish and silly. Christian isn't perfect (like me!),
because he's human (like me, too), but that's OK.

It's indeed time to go back to London.

Mend fences, re-build connections. I no longer want to be
the person googling 'how to win arguments at home'. I want
to be the person googling 'how to make compromises', how
to get things to work for the better.

Why is Christian worried about his mortality, by the way?

Alarm flutters over my heart. I frown before lowering my
gaze to the sunny yellow roses in my arms. The rich musky
scent of the flowers washes over me again; it's unexpectedly

soothing. Maybe I'm being unduly anxious and panicky, after everything that has happened today.

I should get back to Xander.

I walk back into the guest room, only to see Xander's eyes widening as he takes in the giant bunch of flowers in my arms.

'Nice,' he says.

'My fiancé sent them,' I say.

'Ha,' he says. 'Looks like he's come to his senses, too.'

I shrug.

'Well, having just sealed the most important deal of my life, I believe I'm entitled to a small favour,' he continues, giving me a cheeky wink. 'A tiny little thing, mind you. But it's important as hell.'

'What?'

'That I get to my own show in London, on time. It's already a quarter to seven, the show starts at half nine.'

'Why on earth does the show start so late?'

'I wanted a giant fireworks display at seven minutes past eleven to end the show.'

'Seven past eleven?'

'That was when I met Maya for the first time.'

'Really?'

'On the NYC subway, when I was still at Parsons.'

'But I thought that . . .' I trail off, frowning at Xander.

'I was dead drunk, as usual. I dropped my portfolio on the subway, she helped me pick up the sketches that went flying. I went home that night, drew several more pieces that became my inaugural collection. My breakout one, the collection that got me noticed by everyone.'

'But . . . but . . . you've been telling everyone that you saw

272

Maya's photograph in a dentist's waiting room, got on the phone at once. I even read that story in the *New York Times* recently.'

'That's fake news.' He shrugs. 'I made the story up, for the benefit of the journalist's ears.'

'Ha.'

'The woman . . . Rachel Silverman was her name, I think . . . embellished the story a bit. Journalists are all the same. You give a small cupcake, they turn it into a giant cake with pink icing.'

'Why didn't you tell Rachel the truth?'

'Because the truth hurts. It still does.'

'What's the truth?'

'Maya was pretty scathing when she picked up the sketches. She implied they were crap. Stung, I went home determined to prove to myself that I could do better. Maya was brave enough to say what no one else dared to.'

His voice is soft.

'Wish you'd told me the true story earlier,' I say.

'This is the first time I've told anyone, actually,' he says, shrugging. 'It's taken me twenty years to come clean.'

'Why did you dedicate the shows to Maya?'

'Because I feel fucking guilty.'

'*Guilty?*'

'Sad story.'

'Tell me.'

He hesitates for a while, staring down at his hands. But he eventually pulls his shoulders back and says: 'I found out, quite recently, that Maya was both ill and lonely in the weeks leading up to her death. I didn't know that at the time. Her presence was so inspiring, I made her stand in my studio for hours on end. I cut patterns on her, drew sketches of her, draped fabric around her, went on and on. I made her stand for eleven hours, the day before she died. Eleven fucking hours. Had I been a little less oblivious, more sensitive, she probably wouldn't have suffered as much.'

His words prompt a flash of memory, a long-ago eclipse of Maya's face, to come back to mind.

'She did look rather peaky the week before she died,' I say.

Silence hangs over us. Xander sighs.

'The shows are partly my way of saying to Maya in the heavens: I'm sorry for adding to your misery.'

He hangs his head. Realisation strikes, prompting me to ask: 'Is this why you've been giving your employees such generous sick-leave provisions over the years?'

He nods.

I stare at Xander, my heart softening. So Maya was partly the reason why Alexander King has been consistently named as the Top Employer to Work For in Fashion. Looks like Xander had tried to make amends over the years, that his guilt over Maya had in fact driven him to greater things. Looks like I have only one logical course of action, now. Even if the emotional side of me is screaming to do the exact opposite. Even if I can't bear the thought of attending a show dedicated to Miss Maya von Meyer, seeing her hologram soar above the catwalk.

'I'm coming tonight,' I say.

'But I thought you didn't want to.'

I detect a slight tinge of reproach in Xander's voice. It makes me feel guilty for telling him that I wasn't attending, even though I suspected my presence would have meant a lot to him. How dare I call myself his friend if I wasn't planning to show up at an event so dear to his heart?

'I'm sorry I said so,' I say, in a meek voice. 'I'm definitely coming now.'

'Really?' Xander looks delighted.

'The plan is to keep an eye on you, make sure you aren't going to do anything silly.'

'Why didn't you want to come?' He cocks an eyebrow up in my direction. 'I've been wondering why.'

It's my turn to hesitate, to bite my tongue. Maybe it's time for me to also tell Xander the truth, even though I've never dared tell anyone what *really* happened on the night Maya died. Some secrets are destructive because they chip away at your sanity, drain the batteries that power your soul. Especially secrets involving blame and guilt. They are the worst secrets to have.

'Because . . . because you're dedicating the shows to Maya.'

He blinks.

'You were good friends, weren't you?' he says.

I nod.

'I've . . . I've always blamed myself for her death.' My voice shakes.

'What?'

Xander looks flabbergasted. I nod, silently and shamefully. I take in a deep breath before saying:

'Let me tell you what really happened on the night she died.'

Chapter Nineteen

Viola

I felt both frumpy and inadequate when Maya and I first met, all those years ago when I was on my summer internship at your studio. She was a stunning blonde who turned the head of every bloke who passed by, while I was just an average girl in the looks department. We bonded over multiple drinks at a pub near your first studio in Shoreditch. She tried all the lagers on offer before stating she didn't like any of them. The bartender suggested a cocktail instead. She started with a Bloody Mary and made her way through the entire menu before declaring she wasn't a fan of cocktails, either. Too sugary and lightweight, she said. The bartender suggested something stronger and poured her a single-shot vodka. Her eyes lit up; she said she'd found something she liked. After a couple of weeks, she was tossing back double shots like a seasoned pro. I, for my part, discovered that I was partial to Malbec and that two large glasses went down a storm (three glasses if I'd had a challenging day of coding).

Our conversations soon moved on to people. She told me she was certain you hired her because she was an American like you. As she put it, who on earth would look after a Yankee abroad if not a fellow Yankee abroad? We also discussed our workmates, the people we fancied. She confessed to me that she had liked her Best Friend Forever for as long as she could remember, but she had never dared tell BFF that. She was afraid it might ruin their friendship. She added that BFF was away at college and she wished she could be there too, but BFF was busy with exams and didn't want anyone around. Surprise flooded me when she mentioned the town's name, because that was precisely where I was staying. I told her I had been commuting to London from a cottage owned by my aunt, one near a river where fluffy white ducklings floated down each day. She said she would love to visit the place. I said she would be most welcome there, any time. We eventually hatched a cheerful little plan: we would travel up there soon, meet BFF and go punting together with the fluffy white ducklings (she hastened to add that this could only happen after BFF's exams, because BFF took them seriously).

Nigel and Steve joined us for drinks one night. That was when Nigel was just your assistant dresser. Steve made no secret that he had fancied Maya from the moment she walked through your studio's door. She'd humoured him, even teased him a little. Nigel offered to buy the first round of drinks. To my surprise, she said she wanted *two* double-shot vodkas instead of just one. She had looked particularly glum and subdued that evening, even had a pained expression on her face. It also occurred to me that she had seemed unusually grey and haggard in recent weeks, even had dark circles under her eyes.

I wondered why but dared not ask.

The conversation flowed. So did the drinks. Steve insisted on buying two more rounds, while Nigel got the next two.

At around ten, I stood up to leave. Told the group I was

flagging, which was true. I had got up at around four in the morning to finish some work for you. I'd also had too much to drink (five large glasses of Malbec proved two drinks too many). Everyone else decided to get up and leave, too. Our little group parted ways outside the pub. Nigel said a hurried goodbye before running off to catch a bus that was pulling into the nearest bay. Steve kissed Maya on the cheek and disappeared in the direction of the nearest tube station, leaving us to walk down the street together.

A reckless idea struck me. Maybe I should invite her to the cottage, that same night. It was, after all, a Thursday evening. Neither of us had to go into London the next day, as you believed in a four-day workweek (and still do). We could spend the entire weekend there, go punting down the river with the fluffy white ducklings. It might also do her some good, I thought.

Would you like to come home with me? I asked. We can maybe go punting this weekend.

Her face lit up for the first time that evening.

That's an awesome idea, she said.

And so we travelled there on a night bus. Few words were exchanged on the journey; I spent most of it in a fog of inebriation and exhaustion, while her face became more and more pinched as the minutes dragged by. Just before the bus pulled into town, she mumbled that she really, really liked BFF but didn't know how she could go about telling BFF that. I had no idea what to say in response, apart from murmur a few words of commiseration, mostly along the lines that it was damned difficult to admit to someone you fancied them (especially if you hadn't got a clue as to how the person would respond). I spoke from experience because I had fancied someone for a while and dared not say so.

We arrived at the front door well after midnight. I showed her to the guest room, offered her a spare T-shirt to sleep in. She refused, saying she preferred to sleep in her own clothes. I nevertheless placed the spare T-shirt and a toothbrush on a side table, in case she changed her mind.

We said goodnight.

As I headed to her room, I wondered why she had been so subdued all evening. Maybe I should have asked why, I thought. Found out why she had such tortured eyes. But I was exhausted and had had too much to drink and all I wanted to do was collapse on my bed.

I fell asleep as soon as my head touched the pillow.

The next morning dawned bright and sunny. I got up at around half past ten, feeling dreadfully the worse for wear. Vowed never to drink five glasses of Malbec in quick succession again, even if someone else paid for them. I nevertheless felt a bit better after splashing lots of water over my face. I made a large pot of coffee and even fried a couple of eggs, before heading over to check if she was doing all right.

I froze at the door of the guest room.

There wasn't anyone inside.

Her rucksack and shoes were gone. My spare T-shirt and toothbrush remained on the side table, untouched. If not for the crumpled bed sheets and a slight dent in the pillow, I could have sworn I'd dreamt it all up. I collapsed on the bed, feeling a little confused by her disappearance. A possibility struck me: she must have risen a while earlier and decided not to wake me, before heading over to BFF's place (which was probably just around the corner). I was sure she'd be back later in the day with BFF and we could all go punting together. So I ate both eggs, drank all the coffee and went back to work at my desk. I thought no more about it until I turned on the radio and heard:

'This is the News at Two. The body of a woman has been found in the river. . .'

That was the precise moment a little part of me died, deep down inside. I listened to the rest of the broadcast with growing horror, noting the similarities in physical description – the clothes the dead woman had been wearing, the rucksack found draped around the body. When the newscaster finished, I slumped down at the kitchen table in catatonic shock. A variety of terrible scenarios flashed through my head, most of which involved her falling into the river by accident. Several unpalatable possibilities also swamped my mind. One of them involved heading to the police, telling them that she had spent part of the night at the cottage before vanishing during the early hours of the morning. But the police might begin asking all sorts of awkward questions about what she was doing there in the first place, questions I'd rather not deal with.

Maybe I should just keep quiet, I reasoned.

Speak only if the police arrived at my door.

The police never showed up at the door, but they did appear at your studio on Monday morning, wanting to know if anyone saw her the evening before she died. So I came forward, told them that she had spent a few hours at the pub with me and two other workmates, before everyone headed home at around ten. That was the point my narrative died on my lips, choked away by irrational fear. I didn't dare tell the police that she had come home with me later that night.

The police didn't question me further.

Ever.

As you know, the coroner returned an open verdict, one

with the possibility that she had fallen into the river by accident and drowned (whilst drunk and high on painkillers and sleeping pills). So I kept quiet for years, keeping my shameful little secret to my chest. It was a secret that plagued the deepest recesses of my soul, one that rose unbidden to my mind during the darkest hours of the night, whenever I struggled to fall asleep. I blamed myself for her death because she wouldn't have ended up in the river if I hadn't invited her to the cottage that evening.

A little part of me died with Maya that night.

I was never the same person again.

Success happens when you achieve what you want, not what other people want of you. Nor what you want of other people. Success also happens when you no longer give a shit about stuff, no longer care what other people think of you. This is my simple definition of success. I don't think I've achieved it yet, unfortunately. What I want in life is pretty damned complicated.

Alexander King, interview in *Forbes* magazine

Chapter Twenty

Several years later, one of Dad's housekeepers tapped on the door of my room, causing me to jump. I was back in London for the weekend, busy revising for my finals (which were only three months away at that point).

'Yes?' I said, groaning.

'Girl on the line wanting you,' she said, her voice a little muffled by the door.

I groaned again, before getting up and staggering over. I opened the door to discover that the housekeeper was no longer there. She had probably dashed off to attend to one of my stepmother's frantic instructions. Dad and Step-Mum were hosting the American ambassador and a few other diplomats that evening and everything had to be shipshape, down to the precise position of the flowers and cutlery (much like the fair lady of *Pygmalion*, I had to learn quite a few things after moving to Britain).

The phone was on the landing, next to a giant bouquet of purple hydrangeas. I picked up the receiver.

'Hello,' I said.

'It's me,' an excited female voice bellowed down the line, almost deafening me. 'Like, *me*.'

I was stunned into silence for a few moments.

'Oh my God,' I said.

'I'm in London,' she said.

'You must be kidding.'

'Yep, just flew in. How do I get to you?'

'What . . . what . . .' I said, spluttering.

'I need your address, honey. Oh shit, my battery is about to die, can't talk for long. How do I find you?'

I stammered out Dad's address.

'Awesome,' she said. 'Will ring the doorbell. Ta da.'

With that, she was gone.

I waited for her all afternoon, in a restless state of anticipation. I struggled to concentrate; my mind kept flitting away from the words on the pages in front of me. But she never showed up. I began to wonder if she had played a joke on me, or if I had imagined our entire conversation. Dad knocked on the door to insist that I join them and the Ambassador for dinner, to broaden my social remit and understanding of diplomats more generally (as he had phrased it in his usual uppish way). Reluctantly, I tore myself away from my textbook and put on the neatly pressed clothes that had been delivered to my room. By the time I walked down the freshly waxed grand staircase, most of the guests had already arrived and were mingling in the drawing room, cut-crystal flutes in their hands. Soft classical music tinkled into my ears. I spotted a small string ensemble bowing away in a corner. I had to give it to Step-Mum; she knew how to throw a party.

Dad was standing next to the Ambassador's wife, a venerable lady with a giant amethyst necklace around her neck to match the purple hydrangeas. He cast an approving eye over me as I grabbed a flute and approached them.

'May I introduce my only child?' he said to her.

I shook the woman's hand, murmured some polite pleasantries.

'I hear you're back in London for the Easter weekend,' said Amethyst Lady in clipped tones.

I nodded. Just then, a commotion broke out at the double doors at the far end, the ones that opened onto the garden patio. I swung around to discover that the butler was trying to restrain someone at the threshold, someone who must have scaled the brick wall to get there in the first place. His bulky tuxedoed frame blocked the person's face; I could only see two slender, flailing hands. I could also hear the person exclaiming loudly in a shrill, high-pitched voice, albeit one with a distinctive Midwest twang: 'I've been invited here, I swear.'

A flurry of curious murmurs rose from the assembled guests, with Amethyst Lady looking suitably appalled. Dad hurried forward. So did I.

The butler twisted left; her face came into view.

I gasped. I had not seen her for years; during that time, she had blossomed from an awkward teenager to a stunning woman. Her enormous aquamarine eyes sparkled like the crystal flute in my hand, brimmed with life and energy (even if there was more than a hint of annoyance in them). Blonde hair tumbled down to her waist in a beautiful, shimmering curtain of gold. She was the most exquisite thing I had ever seen (even if she was carrying a fraying backpack and wore ripped jeans with holes in both knees). I immediately felt inadequate in comparison, a lesser mortal. She caught sight of me, stopped struggling with the butler. A giant smile broke over her face, lighting up her features and making her seem twice as beautiful.

'Dad,' I said, walking forward. 'Please meet my best friend, who has just arrived from America in true diplomatic fashion.'

She followed me back to my college, two days later. I took a whole day off, convinced myself that I was entitled to a break from revising. We spent the day basking in the sunshine, eating ice cream and cycling around ochre-coloured buildings. I realised that she had changed quite a bit from when I last saw her. Gone was the slightly hesitant girl of fifteen I had left behind in Montana. In her place was a feisty young woman who would try anything once, just so she could say she had done it.

We swapped tales, filled in the blanks. I told her the full story of how I got to Britain via Manhattan. She told me about her journey, too. Turned out her now-deceased Gran, the dear robin-like woman who had patted me on the head each time she saw me, had bequeathed a large sum to her (she mumbled something about being the woman's favourite grandchild). She had used the money to buy a plane ticket to LA, where she struggled for eleven months in pursuit of her previous dream. She then tried her luck in NYC for another five months. After getting nowhere with her quest, she bought yet another one-way ticket, this time to London, in pursuit of a new dream.

'What was the previous dream?' I said.

'To be an actress.' She shrugged. 'That's why I've changed my name, in case you were wondering.'

'I liked the old name better, to be perfectly honest with you.'

'The new one's sexier. Names matter. Norma Jean didn't get very far, but Marilyn Monroe did.'

'And what's the new dream?'

She gave me an impish smile.

'To be a model, like you,' she said.

My jaw fell open.

'But I'm not a model any more,' I said.

'Which is a shame. Judging from the photos you've shown me, you were really good at it.'

'Frankly, I don't miss the fashion world that much. This is my world, now.'

I raised a hand, waved it at the honey-coloured buildings around us.

'Maybe the fashion world suits you better,' she said. 'I can't see you hanging out with studious moles for the rest of your life.'

'Granted, I sometimes feel like I've crashed the wrong party.'

'You should stop wearing those spectacles. They make you look like an old fuddy-duddy.'

'I don't have to impress anyone, any more.'

'You know, you've changed beyond recognition.'

'Hope it's in a good way.'

She pursed her lips, frowned at me.

'You're too young, too good-looking to . . .' She hesitated briefly, before pointing at an elderly professor loping by with a severe hunch, '. . . to turn into someone like that.'

'The fashion world seems glamorous, but there's a hell of a lot of drudgery beneath the surface.'

'I don't believe you.'

'It's true.'

She turned her dazzling aquamarine eyes on me. They were huge and imploring, full of desperate desire.

'Could you help me become a model? Please?'

I hesitated.

'Please, my darling,' she said again. 'I came all the way here to ask for your help. You're the only friend I have with connections to the industry. Do you know anyone who might be able to help?'

That was when I realised that I still had a polka-dotted handkerchief in my wardrobe with a number scribbled on one of its edges.

Unfortunately, Bob's sub-agent struggled to find her work. Turned out her blonde, all-American look 'just wasn't the thing at the moment', as he had phrased it with a matter-of-fact shrug. After a couple of weeks of sending her portfolio around, the only job he could get for her was a position as a dress model for an 'upcoming fashion house with lots of potential'. It meant she had to travel to London once a week to stand around in the studio for hours as the designer pinned pieces of fabric on to her. Her commute rapidly became a four-times-a-week trek, Mondays to Thursdays. I gathered the designer liked her a lot, wanted her to come in more often.

I begged Step-Mum to allow her to stay at our London home, to spare her the long bus journeys back and forth. After much grumbling, Step-Mum eventually agreed on the condition that my best friend behaved herself. It took a while for the butler to come around to the idea, as he'd never quite forgiven her for climbing over the garden wall. Unfortunately for me, I had to remain at college, buried under a stifling pile of textbooks, even though I desperately wanted to be in London. But by then, my exams were only nine weeks away. I was determined to come top of my year, to prove to Dad that I did not waste the opportunity he had given me.

At first, we phoned each other every night. My updates largely consisted of the number of textbooks I'd read. Her updates were all about the number of dresses the designer had hung on her frame and how worn-out she felt by the end of each day (I'd already told her that modelling was more drudgery than fun, but I didn't dare say 'I told you so'). She also said she had made friends with the people who worked in the studio, that she had been spending the nights drinking with them in the pub. They were cool folks to hang out with, she added. They made her think new thoughts, try new things that unlocked doors in her mind and made her see the world differently. Her words were a bit cryptic, but it did sound as if she was having fun. I wished I could be with her in London, drinking the nights away, instead of mugging for my exams.

Several days before my exams started, I began to panic. I thought I should devote every spare minute to my quest for academic success and glory, bury my head in textbooks and deny myself contact with the outer world. That's what I told my best friend, when we chatted over the phone one night. Her voice had seemed uncharacteristically tight, she had developed an unusual tendency to lapse into long, withdrawn pauses. She mentioned at one point during our conversation that she had trouble sleeping, that she really wished she could get a good night's rest. I said I was sorry to hear that, added that I hoped things would improve, before barrelling ahead with: 'If you don't mind, I'll see you in London once my exams are over.'

She fell silent for a while.

'There's something I really want to tell you . . .' She trailed off into silence again. 'Ah well, I guess it can wait a couple of weeks . . .'

'I promise to catch a train to London right after my last paper,' I said. 'How about that?'

My words were greeted by another long pause.

'Very well,' she eventually said, her voice sounding resigned and distant over the line. 'Exams first, I guess.'

With hindsight, my decision to see her a couple of weeks later was the worst decision I have ever made in my life.

Right after my last paper, I rang the London home, eager to tell my best friend that my exams went well, that there were only two questions I struggled to answer. It was the butler who came on the line.

'I'm afraid she didn't come back last night,' he said.

Alarm struck me.

'What?'

'We haven't seen her this morning.'

'Did she tell you where she was going?'

'We thought she took a bus up to visit you, one of those spur-of-the-moment things she's so good at.'

A variety of horrible scenarios flashed through my mind.

'She most certainly hasn't come up to see me. Did anything seem wrong?'

The butler remained silent for a while.

'She looked a bit troubled.' He sounded unusually hesitant. 'That last time I saw her in the hallway.'

'Troubled?'

'She seemed more subdued than usual. I also smelt something on her breath . . .'

'Was she drunk?'

'Maybe.'

'Why didn't you tell me?' I spat out the question with a fair amount of reproach, even though I knew that I was the one to blame.

'You said you were doing your exams, you didn't want us to bother you.'

His words had a certain stark finality to them. They cut straight to my heart, causing a tidal wave of guilt to wash over me. Why had I been so selfish over the past few weeks, thought only of myself?

'Should we call the police?' I said.

'We should establish if she's indeed missing.' The butler's words were crisp, matter of fact.

'I'm heading down to London right away,' I said.

A few hours later, I burst into the guest room where Step-Mum had put her. Everything seemed orderly on the surface. A housekeeper had made up the bed as impeccably as usual; there was not a single crease in the sheets. I ran over to the wardrobe, flung its doors open. Clothes were strewn higgledy-piggledy on the shelves, a random mishmash of denim, cotton and nylon. A sleek black dress hung from a hanger, next to a slightly crumpled white shirt and summer jacket. I dug through the drawers, found nothing of significance apart from her passport and a wad of cash. There were two small faux-diamond necklaces wrapped in tissue paper, both with a cheap plastic sheen. My heart somersaulted with pleasure. I had given her the first necklace for her twelfth birthday, spent two precious dollars to buy it from Walmart. I was worried that she might turn up her beautiful nose at it, but I need not have because she emitted a squeal of delight as soon as she unwrapped the parcel and threw her arms around my neck. The second was the zirconia necklace I had posted to Montana soon after receiving my first pay cheque. I never realised she had cherished the two baubles deeply, carried them around in her luggage. All the way to London, too.

I hurried over to the writing desk, began digging through its drawers. Before long, I had excavated a small plastic sachet that contained a white powder. I emptied a few grains into my palm. They were extremely fine, almost crystalline. I raised them to my nose, took a quick suspicious sniff.

A thick dread stole over me.

The substance reminded me of what Mom kept in a bottom drawer of her wardrobe, sandwiched between two pieces of underwear. I'd found it there after her death and took special pleasure in hacking the sachet into tiny pieces before emptying its contents into the fireplace. The grains I held in my hand were different, though.

They were of a much better grade.

Refined.

I collapsed on the bed, breathing heavily, head spinning with the shock of discovery. I remembered she mentioned her workmates at one point, folks who made her try new things, things that unlocked doors in her mind and made her see the world differently.

So this is what they gave her.

Just then, the phone rang in the hallway. I ran to it, determined to get to the receiver before the butler did. Something told me, deep down inside, that the call was meant for me.

'Hello,' I said.

'This is DCI Matheson,' said a quiet male voice.

*

Three hours later, I was at the city hospital of my university town. DCI Matheson had instructed me to head there right away. By then, I was already a walking wreck. My mind felt detached from my body; all my actions felt disconnected from terrible reality. I was performing each movement on autopilot. The only thing I felt was my heart.

It bled shock, horror and guilt.

I was greeted by a woman with thick, circular glasses and mousy-brown hair, dressed in a starched lab coat. She ushered me down several airless corridors, before unbolting a large metal door. I stepped in. The refrigerated air inside the space hit me like a brick, fogged up my spectacles. I yanked them off, rubbed them against my T-shirt, put them on again. I was in a room with ruthless fluorescent lighting. The place smelt of acrid disinfectant and corrosive chemicals. The long wall at the opposite side of the room had been partitioned into several metal cabinets, each with a separate door. I felt my blood running cold, as frozen as the air in the room.

The woman stepped up briskly in the direction of one of the cabinets.

Fifth to the right, second from the top.

I walked up to it. A wave of dizzy fear washed over me. She tugged the door open, pulled a tray out. A scream burbled forth in my throat; I tried to force it back by biting down hard on my tongue. I wanted to squeeze my eyes shut, run away screaming at the top of my lungs. Yet something held me back, pinned me down. It was the responsibility wrought by guilt.

I forced my gaze down to the body on the tray.

That was when I knew.

I had grown to love her over the years, from the day I saw her playing with the other girls in the school playground,

293

running about with her hair in pigtails with little pink ribbons on them. The day I accidentally broke her necklace and realised that I cared about not making her cry (and my ensuing vow to replace the broken bauble as soon as I could afford to buy one). But I had been too afraid to tell her the truth about the gradual change in my feelings for her, even after she came looking for me in London. I was terrified she would laugh at me, that any declaration of love might ruin our precious friendship. I was afraid of the infinite vulnerability of love, the emotion's inherent weaknesses, how it strips away the protective barriers we build around ourselves until our secret cores are laid bare. I feared that the revelation of my true feelings for her would expose all my sins and secrets, my frustrations and flaws, my worries and wounds, bring them into the harsh, unforgiving light of day.

Now that I wanted to tell her that I loved her, it was too late.

Much too late.

The toxicologist said that the level of fentanyl in her system was sky high. So was the concentration of Valium in her blood. The coroner returned an open verdict, with the possibility that she had accidentally fallen into the river in the middle of the night and drowned. The combination of a benzodiazepine and opioid could have been lethal. It didn't help that she couldn't swim. I later found out that she had joined her workmates for drinks on the night she died, at a pub around the corner from their studio. Everyone had left the pub at around ten, headed home. No one knew why she left London for Oxford later that night, although everyone probably had an unspoken thought in their heads: she must have desperately wanted to see me.

Talk to me.

I will never know what she wanted to say.

I blamed everyone for her death. I blamed her colleagues for plying her with drugs. I was briefly tempted to track them down, make them suffer in a terrible way.

Yet there was one person I blamed the most.

Myself.

Chapter Twenty-One

Christian

I tap Viola's number for the umpteenth time today. It rings out again, also for the umpteenth time. Why on earth is she still staying away from her smartphone? I groan, before dictating a text message.

> I'm sorry, Vi. I really am. Please don't be mad at me. Call me back when you have a minute, please. Love you loads, Christian.

I hit the send button, tuck the phone back into my pocket. I take a quick look out of the car window. The buildings of Victoria Embankment are whizzing by; we're moving in the direction of Old Billingsgate. I see yet another concrete skyport being constructed on the other side of the river; it's a shame they're building so many of these vertical eyesores in the city for the imminent launch of flying taxis.

'Our journey will be delayed by approximately six minutes, due to increasing congestion in front of Old Billingsgate,' says Alexa.

I peer out of the window again. We're passing the cream-coloured buildings of Middle Temple, entering the jurisdiction of the City of London Police. Everything's technically in place, all the necessary security measures. At least, that's what Robyn said during the second chat we had, about an hour ago. She'll be posting constables at all entrances and exits, she says. There will be bomb detectors and sniffer dogs everywhere, too. A state-of-the-art body scanner will be positioned just before the catwalk; all models will have to pass through the device in full kit (and with all accessories) before stepping on the runway. Labradors trained to detect explosives have already combed everything backstage, scoured each and every makeshift seat on the riverbank. Found nothing, apparently. All I need to do now is get my black-tie-clad arse over to Old Billingsgate. I theoretically have a back-row ticket, a ticket I paid for through my teeth. But that's not going to work any longer. The only place for me at tonight's show is backstage, in the guise of maintaining order (under explicit instructions from the Prime Minister, of course).

Who on earth could have bombed Manhattan?

What are the chances of the person striking again tonight?

Did the killer target King or his brand?

The questions swirl around my head in a frustrating circular loop. Despite interviewing all the main actors in the King saga, I'm still not any closer to figuring out the truth about what happened in Manhattan.

We're entering the Mixed-Drive lane and grinding to a halt. It's the predicted congestion in front of Old Billingsgate. I glance out of the window to discover that we're sandwiched by fancy limos with uniformed chauffeurs. It's funny how in this era of self-driving cars, chauffeurs have become the ultimate status symbol, proof that someone is rich enough to pay a person to drive them around (especially when the government keeps raising taxes on human-operated vehicles). The sleek black Alfa Romeo on the left is driven by a man with shiny silver epaulettes; the blonde woman at the back is tapping away impatiently on her smartphone. She's sleek and svelte, coiffured to within an inch of perfection. Her nails are painted gold to match her hair; she's wearing a hat that resembles a giant upside-down peregrine. She looks like the sort who would arouse rabid envy among other women, someone who would be very much at home in the front row with a fluffy toy poodle in her handbag, next to the editor of *Vogue*.

Wait a minute. Could the Manhattan bomber have intended to take out someone like that in the audience? Damn it, why didn't I think of this earlier? And I dare call myself a police officer.

I get out my smartphone and hit the button for Harold.

'I think we may have been barking up the wrong tree,' I say as soon as he comes on to the line.

'Really? What's the right tree?'

'The bomber may have wanted to take out a person in the front row, instead.'

I hear Harold whistling softly over the line.

'Get someone to run checks on all front-row attendees,' I say. 'Cross-check their names with the suspects we have, including Mortimer's five assistants, see if there are any links.'

'Will do.'

'Thanks, Harold.'

I terminate the call, take another glance out of the window. We've inched forward a little, thankfully. In fact, we're passing the front entrance of Old Billingsgate on the other side of the road. People are being deposited on the red carpet from their limos, all dressed up to the nines. A woman stepping out of a Rolls-Royce Phantom is wearing an emerald-coloured cape with violently violet ostrich feathers, paired with six-inch purple stilettos. Cameras are flashing everywhere. A bunch of press photographers are snapping away with glee; they look like a pack of marauding wolves. Four of Robyn's constables are standing near the entrance to the building, machine guns in their arms and sniffer Labradors at their feet. It all looks mightily incongruous, men with guns next to ladies in feathers.

'We'll be making a U-turn and should arrive at our destination soon,' says Alexa.

We're swinging around and left into Old Billingsgate Walk, coming to a halt in front of a small, nondescript entrance at the side of the building. Another City of London constable is standing guard in front of it, a burly one.

'We have arrived, Commissioner Verger,' says Alexa. 'Please take due care when you exit the car.'

Her words, though crisp and matter of fact, sound ominous enough to my ears. They cause a percentage to waft before my eyes:

Chance of dying: 99.74%

Damn it. I should *definitely* stop obsessing about the ridiculous prediction. Morbid thoughts are more likely to hinder than help, make me ineffectually paranoid like the Sultan. I jump out of the car, hurry over to the little entrance. I'm just about to give the constable an approving nod when he steps up to block my way with his burly frame, holding up his machine gun in an imposing swoop.

'If you're here for the show, the entrance is round the corner,' he says in a curt, gruff voice.

Damn it, he doesn't recognise me. While I can taste the words 'I'm the Met Commissioner' on my tongue, I just can't bring myself to say them out loud, hear them ringing insolently in my ears. Come to think of it, I've never managed to introduce myself properly since I was promoted. I have a feeling Viola would describe my condition as 'being vocally paralysed by imposter syndrome'.

'I should be using this door,' I say feebly, instead.

'Guests should go round to the front.'

'This is my entrance, really.'

'This is the *staff* entrance.'

I grimace at the constable in consternation. I should be pleased he's doing his job with gusto, barring all suspicious people (and potential bombers) from entering. Including myself, unfortunately.

'I'm staff,' I say.

'Could I see some identification, please?'

His voice is curt; he's not giving ground. I dig through my pockets, only to discover to my dismay that I had forgotten my warrant card after changing out of my suit into the requisite evening wear (so Viola was right when she accused me of being forgetful). Unlike burly Mr Constable, I don't have a shiny star-shaped badge to prove my credentials. In fact, the only back-up ID I have on my person are my driving licence and my silver token. I extract both items from my pockets and hand them over meekly. He studies my licence and frowns.

'This isn't staff ID,' he says. 'It's a driving licence that expired three weeks ago.'

'It has my name on it,' I say, hearing a slight desperation in my voice.

He peers down at my licence again, only to frown more

deeply. Damn it. I've stepped a mere kilometre outside my jurisdiction and the constables on the ground have no idea who I am. I guess not everyone follows the news, despite all that silly hoo-ha in the national media around my promotion. But maybe it's a good thing. After all, they say the sign of a good leader, one who gets things done, is that no one knows who he is, or what he looks like. Was it Confucius who said that, or am I confusing my ancient sages?

'That's identification,' I add, pointing to my silver token.

'What on earth is this?' he says, frowning as he turns the item over in his hand.

'It's a token issued to senior staff,' I say.

'Sorry,' he says, handing the two items back to me with a doubtful scrunch of his nose. 'I haven't seen anything like this before. I need evidence you work for Alexander King.'

I have no idea how to generate evidence. Evidence is generally difficult to come by. That's the problem with being in the investigative profession. Good evidence is our Holy Grail. We spend all our time in search of this elusive dark matter, often with little success.

'I don't work for King,' I say. 'I work for the Met.'

'Oh, really?' I can see scepticism flitting over the constable's face. 'And what exactly do you do for the Met?'

'I commission.'

The phrase escapes from my mouth before I can yank it back. It sounds lame enough to my ears.

'Commission what?' I can hear increasing impatience in his voice.

It's a good question. A thoroughly excellent one. A question I should have asked when I received my letter of appointment. (How come I didn't?) Why is a police commissioner still called a commissioner in 2030 and what should he really be commissioning if he hopes to be a success in the future.

The future.

Thanks to that infernal app otherwise known as iPredict, I've started thinking a lot more about the future since I woke up this morning. There's nothing like a credible threat to your future to make you wish you'll always have one. A happy and secure future with the person you love.

Just then, it hits me: I ought to be 'commissioning' something today before it's too late, before I'm swallowed up by the jaws of predicted destiny (after all, I have a 99.74 per cent chance of dying). Something for Viola, in particular. An item I should have commissioned a long time ago.

An item to show her that I'm serious about our future together.

Why haven't I done so yet?

I turn back to the burly constable who is still steadfastly barring my way into Old Billingsgate. I should tell Robyn to promote him for doing an excellent job stopping all confirmed idiots (including me) and potential killers (maybe that includes me, too) from entering the building. Yet there's something I need to do right away, before I continue my argument with him. Something important.

'I'll be back in a couple of minutes,' I say.

He looks perplexed; I don't blame him. I walk to the corner of the building, pull my phone out and call Ginny.

'Hi, Christian,' she says.

'Random question, Ginny,' I say. 'Who's the best jeweller in London?'

She replies without hesitating.

'Memory Lane on Bond Street,' she says. 'My friend had her wedding rings made there and she was pleased with the results. Said they're both pleasant and efficient, which I'm sure you'll appreciate.'

'Excellent,' I say. 'Thanks, Ginny.'

I terminate the call, google Memory Lane Jewellers ('Immortalising Your Most Cherished Moments', the line at the top of their website says), tap their out-of-hours number. A crisp voice comes on the line.

'Good evening, Memory Lane. How can I help?'

'I'm thinking of getting an engagement ring,' I say.

'We can most certainly help with that. Might you be able to come into our shop tomorrow?'

'I'm not sure if I'm, er . . . going to be around tomorrow,' I say, deciding on the absolute truth. 'It would be lovely to have the ring tonight, come to think of it, but I'm, er . . . currently tied up at work.'

'We can deliver a ring to you, anytime and anywhere in London, on a fully returnable basis. If you don't like it, just send it back.'

'Sounds good to me.'

'What sort of ring are you looking for? A solitaire, perhaps?'

I pause to consider the question. I suppose I should get a ring to match the roses I sent up to Viola.

'One with a yellow stone, perhaps.'

'How about a canary diamond ring on a simple gold band?' he says. 'We have a two-carat solitaire, simple and classic. Let me ping a photo over, you can view it in 3D if you like.'

A holographic photo floods my phone screen. It's of a breathtaking solitaire with an amber-lemon sheen. I tap the 3D button, causing the ring to rotate on the screen in a dazzling trail of sparks. It's indeed simple and classic; I think Viola will love it and it would look perfect on her ring finger. I also think I might be better off not knowing the price. Richer, at the very least.

'What are the damages?' I say.

'Ah,' he says. 'It's an extremely rare diamond from South Africa . . .'

'I'm afraid I'm a little short of time,' I say, interrupting him. 'Just name the price.'

'You're in luck, sir. We currently have a special offer until midnight . . .'

'The price, *please*.'

'The ring is priced . . .' the man hesitates for several long moments, much to my annoyance, '. . . at £18,888.'

Ouch. Serious ouch.

Chance of dying: 99.74%

Looks like I only have one irrational course of action. What I'm going to tell him next makes no sense at all, but maybe the best things in life are instinctive and unplanned. When both life and death are reduced to statistical probabilities, it's time for spontaneity and impulsiveness. They are the only things that distinguish us humans from the all-knowing algorithms that have taken over our lives and tell us what to do according to their perverse laws of logic.

'Send the ring over to the side entrance of Old Billingsgate at around half past eleven tonight,' I say. 'If you could get the drone to wait there for at least thirty minutes, that would be great.'

'Courier, you mean.'

'You're sending the ring by *courier*?' I hear disbelief in my voice.

'Of course. We don't trust drones with two-thousand-pound rings, let alone twenty-thousand-pound ones. Who should our man be waiting for?'

'Christian Verger.'

'Thank you, Mr Verger.'

'Would you be able to customise the ring?'

'Indeed.'

'I may eventually put an inscription on the inside, if my fiancée approves of the idea.'

'This shouldn't be a problem at all. We'll gladly inscribe anything you like, at no extra charge.'

'Thank you,' I say, terminating the call and returning to Google. I tap my way over to a particular Wikipedia entry, before striding back to the constable with a massive beam on my face (because I've finally achieved something useful today).

Show, not just tell. That was what Alexa urged me to do. I can't wait to show Viola the ring, present it to her on bended knee.

No beating around the bush this time, either. I've balked at introducing myself as 'Met Commissioner' since I was promoted. But if I am an imposter, I might as well say so. Fake it all the way. There is always room for some bluff, as they say. I read somewhere, when I googled 'how to deal with imposter syndrome', that bluff is a normal part of getting by in life and doesn't mean that I'm not good enough. On paper, I have all the necessary skills and experience to make a success of my job. It's time to convince myself that I'm both physically and mentally capable of doing it well. If I don't believe in myself (and that I'll make a good commissioner), I can't expect anyone else to.

'I'm pleased to say that I've just commissioned what I should have commissioned a long time ago,' I tell the constable. 'An engagement ring for my beloved, to be precise. By the way, I'm Christian Verger, the Commissioner of the Metropolitan Police. Here's my Wikipedia profile.'

I thrust my smartphone under his nose. As I do so, I can feel my shoulders tightening with newfound resolve. I can see the constable's eyes widening as he takes in my profile and the accompanying 3D avatar. Whoever wrote my largely flattering (if slightly inaccurate) biography has kindly constructed a digital double that features my greying head in its full, unadulterated glory.

'I'm so sorry . . .' he says, stuttering a little. 'I didn't realise you're . . . you're the *Met* Comm . . .'

He trails off, his machine gun falling limply by his side, his cheeks turning a bashful shade of beetroot.

'No worries,' I say, in my kindliest voice. 'I've been keeping a low profile. They say that new leaders should shut up, listen and learn. If you would kindly let me in, I'll ensure I'm not slacking at my job.'

The main corridor is a veritable bustle of activity. I step around two lighting technicians clad in thick denim overalls, bent almost double under the weight of a giant ladder and light projector. I flatten myself against the wall as a harried-looking man staggers by with an enormous hessian sack in his arms, so large I doubt he can see where he is going. I try to squint into the bag, but I'm unable to see what it contains. Two models overtake me, chattering away cheerfully. One of them, a lithe-limbed brunette, has a dozen metal hair clips sticking out of her head. A man in a flamboyant orange jacket and richly pomaded hair is hollering down the corridor:

'Get your arse over here, will you?'

I step out of his way, take a deep breath and hurry further down the passage. Backstage is buzzing to the hilt with creative energy, the heady delirium of expectation. I can feel time unravelling along the corridor, each second stretched out to a thin, nervous point. The problem with the uppermost floor of New Scotland Yard is that it's hushed and staid, sterile and air-conditioned to death. When feet sink into soft plush carpets all the time, brains also tend to dissolve into mushy oblivion. The problem with being at the top of an immutable hierarchy is that I have become increasingly divorced from mutable reality, the everyday sights, sounds and smells that matter. The feel of a place, its pulse, the preoccupations of the people who populate it. These are what really matter during a criminal investigation, what help shape a police officer's instincts and suspicions. I have merely been conducting long conversations within the snug comfort of my office. All day long, too.

I should be ashamed of myself.

I have forgotten how real investigations used to work, ever since I turned into a paper-pushing bureaucrat. I miss the glorious days when the police would go on prowls to catch drug smugglers, before runners got replaced by drones (and we were reduced to tracking flight paths and crunching payment data). I can barely remember how to open my eyes, keep my nose to the ground like a good sniffer dog.

Damn it.

I need to show more daring duplicity, more improvisational ingenuity. If I survive beyond tomorrow, I'm going to do things more adventurously from now on. Be more hands-on (instead of just pushing papers around in my office), think outside of the box, use my job to make a difference. Maybe even stop living in the past or worrying that my past will catch up with me.

The models have disappeared into a room at the end of the corridor. I take a quick look inside as I pass. Hairdressers are beavering away with rumbling hairdryers. A young boy with a spiky mullet is waving a pair of curling tongs in the air, looking a little like an orchestra conductor. The room smells of nervous anticipation and metallic hairspray. Dear God, I feel alive for the first time in months. I miss the thrill of the chase, the behind-the-scenes mayhem, everything that kept me going during the earliest days of my career.

Someone taps me on my back. I spin around to discover Nigel Avery with his polished leather briefcase.

'Fancy seeing you backstage,' he says.

Did I just detect a sneer in his voice?

'I need to speak to people,' I say.

'Well, I hope you hear what you want to hear,' he says, walking off.

What is the man insinuating? I'm about to chase after Avery to ask him a couple of questions when Flamboyant Orange Jacket plants himself right in front of me. I notice a sparkling diamond stud in his left ear.

'You look familiar,' he says, narrowing his eyes. 'Have I seen you before?'

Damn it. I'm going to be recognised by all the wrong people tonight (and not recognised by the right ones), which may pose a bit of a challenge to my investigation. But maybe I can use this to my advantage.

'You may have, indeed,' I say, shrugging. 'Where's the models' dressing room?'

He lifts a finger, points down the corridor.

'Second passageway on the left, after you turn the corner.'

'Thanks.'

'You're surely not one of the models.'

'Not tonight, I'm afraid.'

'Don't scare them if you can help it,' he says. 'Most of them are feeling pretty nervous post-Manhattan.'

'Understandably so. Where's Millinery and Bags?'

'A few yards away from the models' dressing room, other side of the passageway.' He grimaces at me again. 'I swear I've seen you somewhere, probably in the news. I hope you aren't a terrorist.'

'I'm on the security side of things, actually.'

'The innocent-looking sorts are usually the most dangerous,' he says with a shrug, before hurrying away.

I stare at his retreating back.

'You're absolutely right,' I say under my breath.

Chapter Twenty-Two

Xander

Viola is typing something on her phone, an ancient Nokia only used by people with something to hide. Her nails are bitten down to the quick, raggedy around their edges. Lucia's looking out of the car, grimacing at the non-moving trees and tapping her fingers on the window. Her nails are manicured and polished to such a high sheen, I can almost see my reflection in them. Maybe it's true that fingernails tell you everything you need to know about a person (Lucia is probably more obsessive compulsive than Viola, or is it the other way round?). Jake, for his part, is frowning at the road ahead. The car in front of us, an electric-blue human-operated convertible, has been stationary for at least twelve minutes. It isn't looking good. I take an agonised glance at the two self-driving lanes on the right. They're both moving fast; cars are zooming by at high speed even if they're almost bumper to bumper. Looks like the government is doing its best to phase out human drivers by cramming them into a single miserable lane on motorways.

I groan. Nothing has gone to plan over the past twenty-four hours. I've been bombed to high heaven in Manhattan, interrogated by the police in London, kidnapped by my friend in Oxford.

Now, I'm going to miss my own show.

I fucking need a drink.

Only one thing has gone to plan today. It's the arrival of the small parcel I posted to Viola three days ago, via 100 per cent guaranteed delivery drone. An e-pigeon had landed with a flurry of metallic wings when Jake began revving up the engine. Much to my astonishment, an e-stork landed a couple of seconds later, bearing another giant bouquet of yellow roses instead of a baby (although I'm sure a real stork will deliver one eventually).

'Sorry,' said Viola. 'I should get these before we leave.'

She had shot out of the car, extracted the flowers from the drone with a large smile on her face. Looks like her fiancé is being decisively persistent in wooing her back: good for him. She had then exchanged her thumbprint for *my* parcel and tossed the little brown package through the front door of the cottage before racing back to the car. I'm so glad and relieved the parcel eventually reached her.

But I still fucking need a drink.

I open the walnut-lacquered cabinet next to my seat. There's nothing in it.

'We're dry,' I say with a mournful groan.

Viola jumps, before turning to look at me and the empty cabinet.

'Sorry,' she says. 'I removed everything. Didn't want to knock you out again.'

'You should have put everything back,' I say. 'Drinking is usually a better and less stressful way to pass the time.'

'We'll get to Old Billingsgate, eventually,' says Lucia, turning back to look at us with a reassuring expression on her face. 'Don't you worry.'

'We're still thirty miles from London and it's already quarter past eight,' I say, groaning. 'What's the ETA, Jake?'

'Google Maps predicts quarter to ten,' he says. 'Sorry, Mr King. I'll do my best to beat the ETA.'

'Shame they're only launching flying taxis next year,' I say, muttering under my breath. 'I should have bought a helicopter the last time I went shopping. Or a self-driving car. I now understand why people prefer those ghastly things.'

'Maybe it's a good thing we're stuck in traffic,' says Viola. 'There's something I need to ask you.'

Viola taps the button for the glass divider. The screen slides up silently, muffling the sound of the engine and separating us from Lucia and Jake. I wonder why she doesn't want them eavesdropping on us.

'Why did you ask me to write the software for tonight's show, Xan?' Her voice is low, an urgent hiss.

'Ah,' I say. 'It's a long story stretching from Nigel's anus to Uranus and back. I'll explain some other day, if you don't mind.'

'Well, it has crossed *my* mind that Vision might result in the loss of jobs in your industry.'

I shrug before replying.

'I'm convinced it will result in more hires, not fires.'

'Really?'

'Trust me, I've been in this business long enough.'

'Still.'

'There will be two kinds of workers in the future: people who will tell computers what to do, and people who will be told by computers what to do. Vision will multiply the first bunch.'

Viola only looks partially convinced.

'But . . . you said, ages ago, that my software will "fuck the fashion world long after I'm dead". Those were your exact words.'

'I meant them as a joke,' I say, chuckling.

'But someone wanted to screw your Manhattan show,' she says, narrowing her eyes at me and dropping her voice even further. 'Do you know why anyone might want to destroy you or your brand?'

'I've made enough enemies in this lifetime to last me for the next two,' I say, trying to keep my voice light. 'Maybe the next three, even.'

'I'm serious, Xan,' she says, an impatient note creeping into her voice. 'I know that Steve has been looking after you over the years, but did you manage to piss him off at any point?'

'Stevie? Course not.'

'You sure?'

'I gave him another pay rise a couple of months ago.'

'What about Nigel?'

'The last person I saw before you abducted me.'

'Have you been nice to him too?'

'I'd been planning to sack him, actually.' I shrug. 'But I somehow never got round to doing it.'

Viola looks like she's on the verge of falling off her seat.

'Why were you planning to do that?' she says.

I shrug again.

'I started laying off parasites a few months ago.'

'Parasites?' She looks puzzled.

'Gatecrashers on the bandwagon of fortune. You accumulate

these leeches after a while. Lawyers and accountants, in particular.'

'Does Nigel know you've been planning to sack him?'

I shake my head, firmly.

'Most definitely not,' I say. 'You're the second person I've told.'

'Who's the first?'

'Steve.'

Viola looks thoughtful.

'And what about . . . ?' She's inclining her head forward in Lucia's direction, her voice a whisper.

'Oh, come on, Vi,' I say, groaning. 'Your questions are getting ridiculous. She's my trusty right-hand lieutenant. Plus, she wasn't there in the Big Apple.'

'One doesn't need to be in Manhattan to operate a bomb.'

'But someone has to put the bomb in the bag in the first place.'

'Good point. That someone can be paid, of course. You can buy anything on the dark web at a good price, to be delivered by drone.'

I pause to consider Viola's point.

'You can't buy immortality, I'm afraid,' I say. 'You can definitely buy mortality, though. Assassins, I hear, come cheap these days.'

Viola stiffens in her seat, eyes widening. She thankfully still looks like the clear-eyed girl I interviewed all those years ago, when I desperately needed someone to solve my computing problems (I've unfortunately watched light evaporate from the eyes of countless friends over the years).

'What if . . .' she says, trailing off.

'What if what?'

'What if someone had something to *gain* from hurting your brand?'

'I don't follow.'

'I should look into this.'

She pulls out her phone, punches a few buttons.

'Hi,' she says, her voice crisp and urgent. 'I've run the software again, cross-checked the names on that second database you mentioned. Nothing of significance, I'm afraid.'

She listens in silence for a couple of moments before saying: 'I have an idea, though. Could you get someone to have a look at all recent trading activity on Alexander King, check for any unusual buying or selling patterns?'

She falls silent again before interrupting with a sharp and impatient: 'No, no, no. Trust me on this one.'

She flips her phone off and grimaces at me.

'I'm at a loss,' I say. 'Kindly explain this sudden and unusual flurry of phone activity.'

'Your loss might well be someone else's gain,' she says. 'What if someone tried to hurt you for profit reasons?'

'Profit reasons, eh?'

'The killer might have made a killing from the massive downswing in share price today.'

Frocks are for cocks. Frills do not thrill. That's why I don't design frocks with frills. Never will.

Alexander King, op-ed in *Vanity Fair*, April 2015

Chapter Twenty-Three

Christian

I slip into Millinery and Bags, a small backstage area cordoned off by thick black curtains. Mortimer isn't anywhere in sight (probably a good thing). There is only one person in the space. It's a willowy, chestnut-haired girl standing next to a series of shelves. She's frowning away at the clipboard in her hand through emerald-coloured octagonal spectacles. I sweep my gaze over the hats and bags next to her, all neatly arranged in rows. Most are in light pastel colours, lavishly embellished with flowers and feathers. How extraordinary. They don't look very Alexander King to me.

'Excuse me,' I say. 'I'm with the police, would like to check a couple of things.'

'Sure,' she says.

'Could you take me through what happens before a model gets onto the catwalk with one of these bags?'

I incline my head in the direction of the racks.

She considers my question for a couple of moments, chin tilted, before pointing at her clipboard.

'An assistant double-checks this list, runs here a few minutes before each model gets on, grabs the right bag and hands it to the girl. The bags are arranged in running order, top to bottom, left to right. It's as simple as that. Minimises confusion and stress, you don't want any mix-ups.'

'How long have those bags been there on the shelf?'

'Since last night, I think.'

'Where did they come from?'

'Our workshop in Surrey, they're all crafted by hand there.'

The word 'all' hits me like a brick.

'What about the bags that went onto the catwalk last night?' My voice is sharp, urgent. 'Did they come from Surrey, too?'

She nods.

'The courier picked them up from the workshop, loaded them onto Mr King's plane just before he flew out.'

'So the bags were transported from Surrey to Manhattan three days ago, on King's private jet?'

'Indeed,' she nods. 'All the outfits, too.'

Damn it. Why didn't I think of the possibility that the bomb could have been planted in the bag in *Britain*? Security screenings of private jets are notoriously lax, that's how lots of drugs are smuggled in and out of countries. That way, the bomb could have easily evaded detection.

'Have the police checked these bags?'

She nods again, grimacing slightly.

'They came in twice with sniffer dogs, found nothing.'

If the Manhattan bomb originated in Britain, I should head over to the models' dressing room right away. The bomber could very well strike again. If the killer managed to detonate an explosive on the other side of the Atlantic, it shouldn't be too difficult to plant another one down the road.

'Must run,' I say, turning to leave.

'Wait a minute,' she says. 'What exactly do you do, policing-wise?'

'I try to stop things before they happen,' I say. 'Like people's deaths – including my own.'

The dressing room is only yards away. Utter mayhem greets me as soon as I step in. Models, models, models everywhere, all in varying states of dress and undress, each one being fussed over by at least three people. The girl closest to me, an alabaster-skinned redhead, is being tucked into a volumi-nous white dress with a poppy motif across its skirt. The dress is light and floaty, all chiffon and organza, its midriff embellished with beads and pearls (it doesn't look very Alexander King to me). An assistant hurries up, pins a pretty fascinator onto the girl's head, a matching collection of crimson feathers.

I walk past them, dodging another assistant carrying a pair of pink stilettos. I take in the next outfit being draped onto a pretty brunette. It's an equally delicate creation, yards and yards of peach tulle with a repeated forget-me-not motif across its bodice. A look that is definitely not Alexander King, either.

What on earth is going on?

I look around the room again, head spinning.

I'm surrounded by froth and flounce. Exquisite florals on millefeuille skirts. Frilly, floaty fashion confectionery. It's as if I've crashed a cupcake party where everyone invited is a prin-cess from a Hans Christian Andersen fairy tale. There's absolutely nothing in the dressing room that speaks Alexander King. No smashed skulls or fork-tongued devils, ghastly angels of death. Why the hell are these frocks and frills going onto the catwalk tonight? I thought that King had a well-documented contempt for both species of clothing. Didn't he say that 'frocks are for cocks' and 'frills do not thrill' in a highly controversial op-ed for *Vanity Fair* several years ago, an op-ed that elicited much comment (and righteous outrage) worldwide? It's as if I had pitched up at the completely wrong place tonight, crashed the wrong show.

A Giovanni De Luca fashion show.

A dizzying array of words flood my mind, snippets of the conversations I had with Lucia Graves, Alexander King and Giovanni De Luca. I've heard three different versions of the same story today. What if these accounts are all wrong in their own ways? Or what if . . . they are all right? Maybe the differences don't matter. I wasted a lot of time and energy wondering if they drank Prosecco, champagne or Brunello at lunch. In reality, it's all inconsequential fizz in my head. Irrelevant noise. Maybe the *similarities* are what I should be concentrating on. If three people remember the same thing well, it's usually what matters the most. And what matters on this particular occasion . . . is the fact that *King was damned adamant that he would get away with it.*

'Ten minutes to show time,' a brisk voice calls out, prompting everyone to scurry around twice as vigorously.

Blood rushes to my ears, the promise of possibility. Did King use his software for more than one item? What if the *entire* show tonight is machine-designed? All the dresses, all the handbags, even the hats. Each and every item that will make an appearance on the catwalk later. If so, King will win the wager. Hands down, in the most spectacular way imaginable. When the press find out about the bet, and they will, soon enough, the fallout will be massive. I can already picture the resulting headlines: 'A New Dawn for Fashion', 'Machines

Triumph Over Men', 'Human Designers Are Officially Obsolete' or 'Is It the End of Creativity as We Know It?'

What on earth does this mean for my investigation?

I put out a hand, stop a frazzled-looking young assistant, a girl almost buried under a corsage-laden orange fascinator.

'Why does nothing around us look like what King usually designs?' I say.

The assistant grimaces.

'He's going for a radical new look tonight,' she says. 'That's what they told us.'

'How did all of you manage to keep this, er . . . "new look" a secret?'

'We had to sign crazy non-disclosure forms prepared by Mr Avery,' she says. 'All twenty pages of them.'

'Eight minutes,' says the brisk voice.

The assistant scampers off.

Avery must have indeed prepared airtight forms for the shows. Which suggests that King took the bet seriously and got his pompous little lawyer to make sure no one squealed ahead of time.

A voice pipes up in my head. It says:

If you figure out what's likely to happen as a result of this bet, you'll also figure out who bombed Manhattan.

I spot a wooden stool in the corner of the dressing room, collapse on it. My brain's a whirl. A messy, frenetic swirl, as chaotic as the activity around me. Let me see. Who's likely to gain from the revelation that machines have redefined the fashion universe, revised the concept of creativity as we know it?

Technology firms, maybe.

Who's likely to lose from the fact that human designers have been rendered obsolete by machines?

Human designers, of course.

'Seven minutes,' the brisk voice calls out.

'Shit,' says a model in a voluminous ivory dress a few yards away, grimacing at her reflection in a mirror (scarlet lipstick is smeared on her front teeth). Shit, indeed. I happen to share the sentiment. Wait a minute. Could she . . . could she be Elsa, the Prime Minister's daughter? It's difficult to tell, with all that make-up plastered on her face.

'You Elsa, by any chance?' I say, extracting a tissue from my pocket and handing it to her. She nods, grabbing the tissue and scrubbing her teeth with it.

'I spoke to your mum on the phone this morning,' I say, prompting a flash of surprise in her eyes. 'We speak regularly. She said you were excited about tonight.'

'I'm scared shitless, to be perfectly honest with you,' she says, puckering up her mouth with a rueful shrug. I nod to indicate that she has wiped the offending lipstick away. For a brief moment, I see a lifting of her defences, a melting away of her party-animal exterior to reveal . . . a nervous girl of sixteen. It makes me feel a little sorry for her. I can remember what it was like to be young once, being thrust under the overwhelming floodlights of adulthood.

'Why?' I say.

'It's my first show,' she says. 'I'm scared I'll trip.'

I peer down at her feet. She's modelling a pair of gravity-defying ivory stilettos with daisy-shaped buckles. They must surely be seven inches high.

'You won't fall,' I say, shrugging. 'Heels will make you more conscious, more collected. Paradoxically, people trip a lot more

322

in flats, because flats make folks more blasé, more forgetful about how they hold themselves.'

I have no idea where that came from, maybe I have a new career ahead as a fashion psychologist or oracle. She stares at me for a couple of moments, head cocked to one side, before giving me a tiny smile.

'I hope you're right,' she says.

'Good luck.'

'Thanks.'

She gives me another grateful smile and hurries off, her white stilettos flashing on the floor. I'm a hundred per cent certain Elsa the Prime Minister's daughter is going to power-stride down the runway with the necessary chutzpah and attitude. She isn't going to fail or fall.

Fall.

Runway.

Bomb.

Bet.

Manhattan.

The price of King shares fell this morning, after the Manhattan explosion. The shares of the other major fashion houses will probably plummet as soon as the stock exchanges open for trading on Monday, after tonight's explosive revelation. De Luca's might well be the hardest hit of them all.

What about the price of King shares?

Damn it. I haven't got a clue. Will King be applauded for tonight's show . . . or castigated? The sheer audacity of what he's going to put on the catwalk will probably cause the firm's shares to go through the roof (or maybe they'll crash and burn, first thing Monday morning). My instincts say they will rocket. Tonight's show will only cement King's reputation as an ingenious maverick, the *enfant terrible* of fashion who has blasted the industry's landscape apart. Is someone betting on this? Did someone cause disruption in Manhattan for financial gain? Did . . . did someone detonate the bomb in Manhattan with the hope that the share price would collapse today, then swing back up on Monday?

I yank out my phone, call Harold.

'Shares in Alexander King,' I say. 'Could you get someone to check for unusual patterns in recent trading activity?'

'I'll get on it right away.'

I turn off the phone, stare at its blank screen. It's as blank as my head, as devoid of other possibilities.

'Four minutes to show time,' says the voice.

Chapter Twenty-Four

Viola

Looks like Jake has managed to pull the impossible out of the hat, navigating past all the traffic snarls, with a judicious selection of hairpin turns on two wheels. We're finally in the City of London; Old Billingsgate is just down the road. The show begins in four minutes, we might even make it there in time for the opening walk. I steal a glance at Xander. He's staring out of the window with a morose expression on his face, clenching his Adam's apple. A worm of doubt wriggles into me. Maybe I should have tied him down to a post, stopped him from travelling to London. Despite his promise, he may still go off the rails. Slit his wrists in front of thousands of people (who will probably think it's part of the show before they start screaming).

The main problem with Xander is that he's damned unpredictable. That's also why I like him, why we have stayed good friends for more than twenty years. Polar opposites attract; I'm the perfect foil to Xander's arbitrariness (you only appreciate the true genius of unpredictability when you spend all your time trying to predict stuff). But it's too late, now. Way too late for regret or recriminations. I have allowed Xander to get back into his car, permitted Jake to transport him to the show. Guess I just have to cross my fingers and hope for the best.

We're pulling into Old Billingsgate Walk. A burly constable is standing in front of a side entrance, wielding a machine gun. His presence suggests the police are now involved; I wonder who is in charge of backstage security. Maybe I should tell them that the most dangerous person (and the most likely person to get hurt) tonight is the great Alexander King himself, that the police should be monitoring his movements above everything else.

I also have to do three things as soon as I get inside:

1. Have a quick word with Lucia
2. Speak to Steve
3. Ask Nigel some probing questions, if I can find him backstage

I also have to do one Very Important Thing after the show ends: turn my smartphone on again and call Christian. Tell him I'm coming back to his London apartment tonight. Say I'm sorry for that silly little argument we had, for swanning off in a huff. Xander's right. It's time to deal with the ghosts from our pasts, lay them to rest if we hope to have a happy future together.

Maybe the best way to predict the future is to create it. Was it Abraham Lincoln who said that?

'They say the show must go on,' says Xander, causing me to jump.

I turn in his direction; he's flashing an unexpectedly cheeky smile at me. It's an expression that gives me hope. It reminds me of the Xander I used to know, the sort of grin he used to dispense before he got rich and famous (and cynical and miserable).

'So let's make this a night to remember,' Xander continues, chuckling again.

There's only one thing I can say in response. I clear my throat and tell him, quietly and firmly:

'I hope it isn't an evening I would want to forget.'

We hurry past the constable precisely one minute before the show starts. Something dark is flitting across Xander's face, again. I recognise the expression. It's the anxious look he always wears before a show, the 'I'm Sure It's All Going to Go Wrong and They Will All Boo at the End' look. An expression that will only be erased by the audience jumping to their feet and cheering to the rafters at the end of the show.

'Need to check something,' he mumbles under his breath, before rushing away along the corridor.

'Don't let him out of your sight,' I tell Jake. 'Not for a single moment.'

Jake gives me a decisive nod before hurrying after Xander. I hope he can be trusted to keep an eye on his boss.

I turn to Lucia.

'Good you told me about the note,' I say. 'I hope we've averted disaster.'

She nods.

'I hope so, too.'

My work phone buzzes. I pull it out. It's Damian ringing, hopefully with an answer to my question.

'Sorry,' I say to Lucia. 'Need to get this one.'

She nods before walking down the corridor in the opposite direction from the one Xander and Jake have taken.

'Hi, Damian,' I say.

'You're right.' His voice is brisk. 'Serious short-selling has indeed been going on over the past couple of days.'

Euphoria floods me; I'm delighted my hunch was right.

'Who's the short-seller?' I say.

'We're still trying to find out. I'll call back as soon as we have a name.'

'Thanks, Damian.'

I put the phone back into my pocket and hurry down the corridor, charged with renewed possibility. Shame Lucia has disappeared somewhere in the meantime. I'll start with Steve, who must surely be bustling about backstage. Given the show has just begun, he's probably at Millinery and Bags.

I hear soaring classical music in the distance, followed by an approving roar from the audience. Millinery and Bags is a dimly lit backstage area full of thick velvet curtains and panicky-looking assistants with clipboards, zigzagging in all directions. A couple of them are grabbing hats and bags from the shelves, dashing off with them. At the epicentre of this vigorous Brownian motion of activity is Steve himself, barking instructions to a girl in octagonal spectacles. He has definitely expanded girth-wise; there are more tattoos on his arms and a few extra pounds of flab around his middle. One would never guess that Steve once had the most photographed six-pack in all of Manhattan, that he was once nicknamed 'Don Juan' for his ability to seduce the girls.

'Stevie,' I say, running up to him.

He blinks in bewilderment for a couple of moments, before recognition slides into his eyes.

'Gosh, Vi,' he says, leaning forward to peck me on the cheek. 'Haven't seen you for ages.'

'It was you who wrote the note, right?' I say, getting straight to the point. 'The one Lucia found in her handbag.'

His mouth falls wide.

'How . . . how do you know?' he says.

'Linguistic profiling,' I say, shrugging. 'You were worried about Xander, weren't you? Wanted Lucia to raise the alarm.'

He grimaces at me, before nodding curtly.

'Xander has been getting rid of all sorts of things recently,' he says. 'Unnecessary stuff, as he phrased it. I've heard that suicidal people often get rid of stuff before they kill themselves.'

'I had a chat with Xander earlier today,' I say. 'He promised me he won't do anything crazy tonight.'

Relief slides into Steve's eyes.

'Thanks, Vi,' he says. 'I owe you one.'

'I need to know one thing, Steve,' I say. 'Does Nigel have any reason to hate Xander?'

He swallows hard.

'This isn't the time and place, Vi.'

'It's important. Plus, you've just said you owe me one.'

He hesitates again before saying: 'Nigel secretly detests Xander. He's stuck around purely because Xander pays him well.'

'How do you know this?'

'He carries a little voodoo doll in the shape of Xander in his briefcase, sticks pins into it.'

'You're pulling my leg.'

'Of course, my darling.' He flashes a smile at me. 'Sorry, I have to dash, it's getting manic in here. Let's grab a drink together after the show, shall we?'

He walks off in the direction of his bespectacled assistant. I stare at him in dismay. Was Steve serious about Nigel's voodoo doll or was he joking? My head says he's kidding, but my instincts say he's not.

My phone buzzes; it's Damian again.

'Hi, Damian,' I say.

'Hi, Vi,' he says. 'The short-seller's name is Nigel Avery.'

'You're joking.'

'He was backstage at Manhattan, wasn't he?'

'Indeed.'

'We'll tell the Met to bring him in. Keep plugging away with CriminalX, will you? I reckon you're on the right track, as the software did indeed flag up Avery earlier.'

Delighted relief sparkles through me. Looks like I'm not going to lose my freelance contract with MI6 anytime soon. Also, I'm glad Damian's worthy institution is talking to Christian's august bureaucracy for once.

'Will do,' I say.

I hang up, gritting my teeth. I should find Nigel right away. He must surely be somewhere in the vicinity, but Old Billingsgate is massive and Xander is using both the outdoor and indoor areas. I hurry over to the nearest window, peer out through it, scan the raised catwalk above the Thames. Three hundred yards of elevated stilts, all beautifully lit with fairy lights. A model is walking along the runway from left to right in a voluminous peach dress (not bad, not bad at all), perfectly in sync with the music. Looks like Vision the Software has done an excellent job; the outfit meets Xander's specifications, achieves the desired 'look'. I'm extremely pleased with the result. But I'm not so pleased with what I've discovered about Nigel, a guy I used to hang out with at the pub. Goes to show that some people change for the worse, not for the better.

Where on earth could Nigel be? Damian gave me a number once, said I could call it whenever I needed numerical data that I'm unable to google (or dredge out from the recesses of the dark web). I reckon this is such a time.

I pull out my work phone again, hit the number.

'Please identify yourself,' says a voice.

'Operative Zero Five Twenty,' I say. 'I need the precise coordinates of Nigel Avery, a lawyer at Alexander King.'

The world of fashion is populated by the pretentious, ostentatious and the weak. That's why I try not to take it too seriously. The moment you start taking a universe too seriously, you turn into one of the fools who inhabit it.

Alexander King, interview in *Elle* magazine

Chapter Twenty-Five

Xander

Maybe everything will happen as planned, despite the hiccups along the way. We got to Old Billingsgate in time, thanks to Jake's deft road manoeuvrings. The boy is lurking behind a curtain a few yards away; I bet Viola told him to keep an eye on me for the rest of the evening. Another youth, a strapping lad in a black quilted jacket, is also monitoring me from a distance. He's probably Lucia's stooge (or Steve's). I'm not bothered by my shadowy minders; I'm sure I can easily give them the slip if I want to.

The show has started and no one has died yet.

So far, so good.

I pull out a small silver hip flask that Steve kindly slipped into my pocket moments ago when no one was looking, empty some of its contents down my throat. A blissful electric jolt spreads through my insides, cuts across the fuzziness in my head.

Nice.

I'm tempted to scoff all the pills in my pocket. But I should exercise restraint. After all, I still hope to walk down the catwalk in a straight and dignified line at seven minutes past eleven, take a cheeky little bow and give the audience my customary mock salute. I peer out from behind the velvet curtain, take in the next model gliding down the raised platform above the river. She looks angelic in that white dress, as sweet and lovely as the cherry blossoms on it.

So far, so good.

It's still going according to plan.

No bombs yet, thank heavens.

I should be pleased what happened in Manhattan hadn't put most people off. All the usual suspects are here tonight. I spot numerous poodles and journalists in the front rows, the folks who make (or break) you with their wallets and pens. I'm particularly pleased to see the editors of British *Vogue* and *Harper's Bazaar*. There won't be royalty tonight, unfortunately. Someone whispered into my ear that the Prince and Princess of Wales have pulled out at the last minute, citing security concerns. But there are enough A-listers and social media influencers to get the chatter going.

I scan the faces in the distance, the Botoxed expressions, the usual combination of the vacuous, curious and appraising. I'm going to miss this, studying people's reactions. There was a hush in the audience just now, when the first model stepped out onto the catwalk.

A baffled hush.

A shocked hush.

One I had planned for, been waiting for, had hoped for all along.

A perfect silence.

The sort of silence when you manage to confuse . . . or confound. I'm still seeing the befuddled 'What the Fuck is Xander Putting on the Catwalk Tonight?' expression on the face of the editor of British *Vogue*. Her reaction is perfect, just perfect.

Because people tend to remember what makes them feel. If I wish the audience to remember this show for the rest of their lives, I should jolly well make them feel something tonight.

Something deep, something visceral.

Something unsettlingly memorable.

The next model is now walking onto the runway in a black knee-length dress, flanked by four forklifts on wheels. It's time to tell the world the truth about tonight's show. I'm sure Maya would be pleased by my upcoming revelation if she's looking down from the heavens above. The first thing she said all those years ago, when she stopped to pick up the sketches that went flying in the subway, was:

'These aren't so bad.'

I stared at her in consternation for several moments, before finding my voice.

'Judging from your tone, you're basically saying they're pathetic.'

My words were accusing, plaintive.

'I think you can do better,' she said, shrugging. 'You have the look of someone who can do better.'

Her words stung hard, bit straight into my core, that squishy and vulnerable area deep inside us that we try to protect, hide from the people around us. Up to that point, no one had ever dared tell me I could 'do better'. I had subsisted on a comforting diet of potent barbiturates, hard liquor and lavish praise, which was why I didn't get too far. When your tutors and friends keep fawning over you, bowing and scraping and saying the things you want to hear (like 'I swear you're the most amazingly talented young designer I've met'), sometimes you need a frank and honest opinion.

A brutal one.

Non-sycophantic.

'How the fuck do I "do better"?' I said.

Maya had pursed her lips in a slightly infuriating, all-knowing way, tilted her head to one side and said:

'Stop trying so hard.'

'Oh yeah?'

'Don't take yourself so seriously.'

'Oh yeah.'

'Less is more. That's what my gran used to say, before she died.'

I went home that night, put all the sketches into the bin. Started sketching afresh. The rest, as they say, is history. The rest, as *I* say, is history *and notoriety*. An English businesswoman (the late Tara Russell-Cadogan, long may she rest in peace, in that white silk shroud I designed specially for her) bought most of my inaugural collection, suggested I move to London so she could keep an eye on me. She kindly gave me all sorts of useful (if slightly clichéd) advice along the way, like:

Never tell anyone your true intentions, because you'll only end up jinxing your plans.

You're only as brilliant as the people who surround you, people who don't smother your genius.

The people who work for you should learn to respect you (even if they detest you).

Work hard if you want to be mediocre, play hard if you want to be stellar.

It was Tara who covered the costs of setting up a small design studio in Shoreditch, suggested that I stage my first fashion British show in the East End (which featured semi-naked models in Virginia Woolf masks, carrying burning pitchforks to titillate the press). She also helped me hire a team of people to make the right things happen at the right time. Including Maya herself when she turned up on my doorstep, after I put out the word that I was looking for dress models for the show.

Her first words when she walked in through the door of my humble little studio were: 'My agent sent me your ad for models; I can't believe you've relocated to London like me.'

She turned her gaze around my studio before wincing and saying: 'Still trying too hard, I see.'

I owe everything to Tara and Maya.

If people think muses inspire purely by standing around and looking pretty, they're wrong. Quite wrong. The best muses are unperturbed sounding boards from hell, people who tell you what *not* to do to reach heaven, tell you off throughout purgatory and forever more. Maya continued to wrinkle her little button nose at most of the sketches I drew for that collection, in her usual infuriating way. Said I could do even better, that I was still trying too hard. She pushed me to new heights by reminding me that I should not take myself (or the fashion world) too seriously. I never truly achieved new creative heights after her death, after losing the only person I could pin both ideas and clothes on. Which is a bit of a shame, because I could have done so much more over the past twenty years had she lived.

Tonight's a rare night when I'm doing less, not more. In fact, I've done nothing at all. Viola's remarkable fashion-design software has done everything for me (I thank both heaven and hell she agreed to do me a favour).

Maya will definitely approve of what will be happening on the catwalk next.

It's the beholder who brings emotions to an artwork, the listener who brings feelings to a piece of music. If a dress, novel or a painting triggers an emotional response, does it matter who created it, even it if was produced by a machine?

Op-ed in the *Guardian*, 7 June 2030

Chapter Twenty-Six

Christian

A loud cheer is rising from the audience. It's an unusual sound, one mingled with astonished twitters. I run forward, take a peek from the nearest window. A blonde model is gliding down the catwalk in a frilly, obsidian-black dress. An ethereal, slender beauty who looks very much like a nymph, a sylvan fairy flitting above water. She's flanked by four small machines with wheels; they look a bit like miniature forklifts. The music is no longer a soaring piece on strings, one reminiscent of Pachelbel's *Canon in D*. It has morphed into a pulsating techno-pop tune with an ear-splitting beat.

What the hell is King up to?

The model is stopping in the middle of the runway, prompting a flurry of alarmed murmurs. Oh dear, isn't this what happened in Manhattan? A girl stopping dead on the catwalk, terror in her eyes . . . The forklifts are zooming around the model; she now has a machine on each side. She lifts her slender hands high, much like an orchestra conductor, waves them in small semicircles. The forklifts are spinning around in exactly the same way, mimicking the movements of her arms.

An appreciative cheer erupts from the audience.

It's mesmerising, this little synchronised dance on the catwalk. Yet I swear the model's movements are becoming more agitated, more frenzied. A line of text flashes up on a screen above the catwalk, in block capital letters:

EVERYTHING ON TODAY'S CATWALK IS DESIGNED BY SOFTWARE IN THE STYLE OF GIOVANNI DE LUCA, WHOM KING RESPECTS AND ADMIRES

This confirms what I already know, suspected as soon as I walked into the models' dressing room. But the audience is unprepared for this revelation, judging from their astounded roars. The movements of the girl on the catwalk have become twice as wild, twice as frenetic to match the music, now an unsettlingly repetitive 'boom-boom-boom'. She no longer resembles a nymph in a sylvan glen. She looks more like a disjointed marionette, a broken puppet.

A second line flashes up on screen, also in stark black capitals:

EVERYTHING ON YESTERDAY'S CATWALK IN MANHATTAN WAS DESIGNED BY SOFTWARE IN THE STYLE OF ALEXANDER KING

I gape at the words on the screen, my jaw swinging open. Bloody hell.

Was the *entire* Manhattan show designed by software, too?

Damn it, I never suspected that *everything* on the Manhattan catwalk was conjured by a machine. I ought to be ashamed of myself, because King has managed to fool me, too. The audience is going berserk; their roars are as wild as the model's frenzied movements. The four forklifts are now closing in around her, extending their customised claws in perfect sync.

340

I gasp as they begin tugging at the frills on her dress, pulling the fabric taut and wide, causing the dress to morph from obsidian black to an extravagant Technicolor dazzle (King must have used one of those new-fangled fabrics that take on all colours of the rainbow when stretched). Something else has changed, too. The model has stopped giving stage directions to the machines. I can see the forklifts raising their claws again, turning them in gleeful semicircles; the girl is now the one mimicking *their* movements. It's a stunning reversal of roles: the machines are now controlling the model, having transformed her dress into one of their choosing.

I squint at the reconfigured outfit. It's a rich slash of colours, unsettling and bold. Its shape is asymmetrically pleasing, King-like in style and form. The dress has metamorphosed from De Luca to King before my eyes, with four cheeky little machines causing the change. I'm sure the symbolism isn't lost on the audience, judging by the way they are cheering in ecstasy.

How bloody audacious.

Positively ingenious.

The girl is falling to the ground, twisting and writhing, prompting another surge of murmurs from the crowd. The forklifts are closing in around her again, lifting their claws high in a menacing yet triumphant manner. In a swoop, the girl and machines are swallowed up by the dark depths of the catwalk, lowered away from the audience's sight by a descending circular platform. The music is back to what it was, a soaring crescendo of strings. Another pretty model is stepping onto the catwalk, again in a frilly frock. It's as if the entire episode with the machines never happened. King is back to putting De Luca-styled dresses on the runway, but I'm sure the audience no longer sees the outfits in the same light. I guess that's what useful information does to you. Two simple lines on a screen. They make you see the world in a different way.

Genius, sheer genius.

If King has a message for humanity, it couldn't be any clearer. If I had a hat on my head, I'd be tempted to doff it in King's direction. The man has just turned the world of fashion upside down. Fashion will no longer be the same. I never expected King to win his bet with De Luca in such a brilliantly bonkers way. Only a genius (or a madman) would come up with a solution like this one. Looks like King shares will shoot back up again on Monday morning, while De Luca's will crash and burn.

Hmm. Did the Manhattan bomber know that *the whole of* yesterday's show was designed by software? If yes, why disrupt the event? I grimace at the catwalk in consternation. Why didn't Lucia tell me that yesterday's show was entirely engineered by software? Or today's, for that matter? Did King keep his own PA in the dark about his plans? He must have. But why?

My phone's buzzing again. It's Harold.

'Any luck?' I say, hearing renewed desperation in my voice.

'We've been cross-checking the names of front-row attendees. Nothing so far, no known animosities.'

It's a shame that people's motivations (especially their pet grudges, hates and dislikes) tend to be obscure, even to themselves. At least, these are not things you can google easily. I guess that's why psychologists and police officers are still in business, to pick up the pieces when things go wrong.

'Alas,' I say.

'But . . . you might like to know that someone has been short-selling King shares, betting that the price would go down and not up. As you may know, the share price did indeed crash this morning.'

'Who?'

'Nigel Avery.'

'What? King's lawyer?'

'Indeed. He has just made a very tidy profit, to put it mildly. Interestingly, he was cleared of insider trading in 2027 by a London court.'

'Get someone to grab him before he gets up to more hanky-panky.'

'Will do.'

I place the phone back into my pocket as sudden clarity sweeps over me. Of course. It all makes sense now. Avery was backstage in Manhattan. He could have personally handed the bag to poor Ally and no one would have suspected a thing. He may (or may not) have known about King's bet with De Luca, but he probably figured out that the share price would come crashing down if the show was disrupted by an explosion.

So it was all about killing for profit.

Financial greed.

Panicky dread steals over me. I saw Avery just minutes ago. Where the hell has he gone? Has he planted another bomb, one timed to go off during the final moments of tonight's show?

Maybe Mortimer will know where Avery has disappeared to. I rush down the corridor, stumble back into Millinery and Bags. The area is now a mad hive of activity, with lots of clip-board-bearing assistants scampering about. Steve isn't here, only the willowy girl I spoke to earlier. I rush up to her.

'Do you know where Nigel Avery could be?' I say.

She shakes her head.

'What about Steve Mortimer?' I continue.

She looks around with a slight frown.

'I swear Steve was here just a few minutes ago, speaking to an anxious-looking woman,' she says, turning back to me.

'Do you know where he could have gone?'

'He said he wanted to check the finale display, make sure everything's right. Maybe he's doing that now.'

'The finale display?'

'The item that will appear at the end of the show.'

I narrow my eyes at the girl.

'Where is it?'

She lifts a finger, points right.

'End of the passage, near the start of the catwalk.'

I race in the direction the girl had indicated. The passage leads me to yet another backstage area, one cordoned off by dark-red velvet curtains. I push them apart, only to halt in astonishment. A glittering glass cage occupies the middle of the space, illuminated by spotlights. The cut-crystal glass is so fine, I'm almost blinded by its radiance. I take a step forward, admiring the cage's exquisite structure, the delicately chiselled patterns running down each glass railing. Although the cage is about three times my height, it seems enormously fragile, as if it could shatter at any moment.

'My idea.'

I jump. Mortimer is walking straight up to me, looking a little pensive.

'Your idea?' I say.

'I suggested to Xander we wheel out a cage with a hologram of Maya. The hologram will morph into a butterfly above the river in which she died. Fingers crossed, it'll happen as planned.'

He raises his hand to tap one of the glass railings. His sleeve slides back, revealing the tattoo across his upper right arm in its full glory. It's an extraordinary tattoo, part fish, part dragon and part woman. It also looks familiar; I swear I've seen it somewhere before. Where was it?

'Do you know where Avery is?' I say.

He shakes his head.

A cold, rational voice at the back of my mind is screaming for me to move on, to find Avery at once. But I'm intrigued by what Mortimer has just said about the cage. A conflicting (but equally insistent) whisper is telling me that Mortimer's tattoo is significant, that I should figure out why.

'Where did the idea for the cage come from?' I say the first thing that comes to mind.

He shrugs.

'It just came to me, one night.'

'You must have quite an influence on Mr King, if he's executing your idea.'

He shrugs again.

'We go back a long way, Xander and I.'

Just then, it hits me. Mortimer and King do indeed go an extremely long way back. I have indeed seen the unusual tattoo before, on the body of a much younger and fitter man. A hot young dude who looked nothing like the podgy middle-aged version standing in front of me. Steve Mortimer is a fine example of the maxim that humans seldom get better with age, unlike fine wine (as Viola would say). Why didn't I read his full bio before I summoned him in?

'Did . . . did you used to model for Mr King?' My voice is weak.

His eyes widen.

'How did you know?' he says.

345

I'm an opportunist. I waste each opportunity that comes in my direction and spend my time regretting what could have been (or kicking myself for being pathetic). That's what opportunism is all about. Missing an opportunity when it charges by because you are too afraid to take the scary-looking bull by the horns.

Diary of Nigel Avery

Chapter Twenty-Seven

Viola

I've been staring at my work phone for two minutes, hearing all sorts of wild, raucous cheers in the distance. The operator assured me that someone will get back to me within ninety seconds with Nigel's precise coordinates, but I haven't heard anything yet. Why isn't anyone getting back to me?

A message pings into my phone. It says:

Nigel Avery is thirty feet away from your current location.

Shit.

I take a deep breath, rearrange my face in a neutral way before looking up from my phone. Sure enough, Nigel is striding in my direction, a briefcase in hand. He sees me, does a giant double take.

'Fancy seeing you here, Vi.'

'Fancy seeing *you*, Ni.'

I need to get the truth out of him, but I don't know where to start. I wish I had asked Christian how to ferret information out of people. Establish if they are murderers through pleasant and amiable conversation.

'Xander said you weren't coming tonight.' There's a faintly accusatory note to Nigel's tone.

I shrug.

'I changed my mind,' I say.

'Fair enough.' He shrugs, too. 'It has all come full circle, hasn't it?'

'What do you mean?' I say, hearing a cautious note creeping into my voice.

'Tomorrow's the twentieth anniversary of Maya's death,' he says. 'Which makes it exactly twenty years since we had drinks together at the pub, the four of us, the night before she died.'

I stare at Nigel, aghast.

'Our lives have changed quite a bit since then, haven't they?' he continues.

'Have they?'

'You've gone from writing software for fashion designers, to writing software that replaces them. I've gone from dressing up people on a regular basis . . . to being dressed down by Xander on a regular basis. While Steve has gone from frontstage to backstage, from being in the spotlight to managing spotlights.'

I should keep Nigel talking. I'm also curious about one thing, in particular.

'Was it Maya's death that prompted you to go back to college, train as a lawyer?' I say.

'What do you think?' He wrinkles his nose. 'Her death made me realise that life is too short for stuff we don't enjoy doing, that I didn't want to spend the rest of my days as a lowly assistant dresser.'

Ah, I think I see a way in.

'What made you come back to work for Xander a couple of years ago?' I say.

'Xander pays well. Always did.'

Aha. I knew it. It's time to go on the offensive. I guess I have nothing to lose at this stage.

'So it was all about the money, then?'

He's silent.

'I hear you've been short-selling company shares,' I say. 'I also hear that you've made a killing after the share price plunged this morning. I wonder if it was worth killing a girl on a catwalk.'

Nigel takes a forceful step in my direction, grip tightening around his briefcase. The one with the voodoo doll, as Steve suggests. His eyes are focused, intent; I can see a dark chasm opening up in them.

Shit.

If he's indeed the Manhattan bomber, I'm in deep shit. Serious shit. Someone who had no qualms about letting off a bomb on a catwalk will have no compunction about raising a gun to my head. Why on earth did I call Nigel a murderer to his face? He's probably going to take out a gun from his briefcase and shoot me.

Oh God.

I think he's going to do it.

To my surprise, Nigel steps past me. He takes a quick glance out of the window overlooking the catwalk, frowning a little, before turning back to look at me.

'I swear I had nothing to do with Manhattan,' he says. 'Yesterday was awful, I've barely slept a wink since.'

Is he telling the truth?

'You've *profited* from the bombing,' I say, trying to keep my voice steady.

He winces.

'I heard someone on the phone a few weeks ago, giving instructions to sell company shares. I went home and thought, maybe I should do the same. I never bargained for a bomb to go off.'

'Hmm.'

'Steve told me two days ago, when we were flying out to Manhattan, that Xander had been laying off employees he didn't want, like or need. I thought, holy shit, my days are numbered. While I've been useful to Xander, he has always disliked lawyers. Keeps calling us scum of the earth, that sort of thing. I called my broker as soon as we landed at JFK.'

I don't know if I should believe Nigel.

Is he just an opportunist? Or is he also a murderer?

'Who was the person you overheard on the phone?' I say.

He hesitates with another frown.

'I need to know, Ni. It's important.'

He's still hesitating.

A female voice sounds behind us, soft and melodious.

'I think he overheard me.'

I spin around to discover Lucia Graves walking in our direction, painted lips curved in a knowing way.

'Xander gave me a small share option when I joined the company,' she says to me in a business-like tone. 'I decided to cash it in a few weeks ago. That was probably the conversation Nigel overheard.'

Nigel nods.

'There's something you should know, Ni,' she says, turning in his direction.

'What?' he says.

'The police are looking for you,' she says. 'An officer came up to me a couple of minutes ago, asked me if I knew where you were.'

Alarm is fast sliding into Nigel's eyes.

'Maybe you should leave, Ni,' says Lucia, her voice taking on a curt and brisk tone.

'Why?' His voice is an agonised whisper.

'I remember you saying once,' says Lucia with a shrug, 'that it wasn't nice to be tried for insider trading.'

Nigel is wincing in response. Looks like Lucia knows about Nigel's past adventures (or misadventures) in a London court-room. I can see Nigel swallowing hard, his eyes darting from side to side as he contemplates his options. Before I can stop him, he charges away from us, down the corridor.

'Wait . . . wait a minute,' I say, taking a step after Nigel, only to be yanked back by Lucia.

'Don't worry,' she says, her fingers curling around my arm. 'He's not going to get far. The police are guarding all entrances and exits. That's assuming he's guilty of anything . . .'

'Still.'

'You don't want to be chasing after him,' says Lucia, releasing her grip on my arm. 'Not when you're expecting.'

I stiffen.

'How . . . how did you know?' My words tumble out in a splutter.

'Xander told me the happy news just now. Wanted sugges-tions for a christening present.'

I stare at Lucia in consternation.

'It was supposed to be a *secret*,' I say, my voice an indignant hiss.

'Xander isn't the most discreet person on the planet,' she says, shrugging. 'I'm sure you already know that.'

I'm going to kill Xander. Throttle him with my bare hands. He said he'd keep news of my pregnancy to himself. Instead, he consults his PA about it at the first opportunity (I guess it couldn't be more Xander than that).

'Relax, my dear,' says Lucia, giving me a wink. 'Your secret's safe with me. I promise not to tell anyone.'

I take in a deep breath, exhale.

'Let's go and watch the grand finale,' says Lucia. 'I know a small balcony on the top floor with an excellent view.'

They say fashion is fickle. I say: memory is just as ephemeral. When you have a big show, all eyes swing in your direction, to your brilliant creations. Everyone wants a piece of you, wants interviews with you, begs for selfies along the way (some also beg for quickies, but that's a different matter). There are cameras everywhere, all trained on your face. Your amazing works of art. Two days later, all the cameras are gone. Your major event is reduced to a minor footnote in the annals of the past. Your works of genius recede into the mists of memory, vanish into the endless abyss of forgetting. They say a fashion designer is only as good as his last show. I say: even his last show isn't good enough. Not if the poor designer hopes to leave a lasting mark on humanity, wishes to be remembered several hundred years later.

Alexander King, interview in *GQ*

Chapter Twenty-Eight

Xander

I have never cried at any of my shows before, but I swear I felt tears pricking the corners of my eyes when the model and the four forklifts performed their dazzling choreography on the catwalk. It was perfect. Just perfect. Utterly sublime. Exactly what I had envisaged and a whole lot more. The problem with psychic perfection is that it causes physical imperfection to feel twice as harsh when it lands. Now I can only taste sour reality in my mouth, feel bitter bile accumulating in my gut.

Physical imperfection really sucks once you've experienced a sublime moment of psychic perfection. That's why people should spend all their lives hoping for perfection instead of experiencing it.

Time to dull the physical agony. I extract a small bag of pills from my pocket, pour all of them into my mouth. I pull out Steve's hip flask, take another large swig from it. A fuzzy warmth crashes down my chest and spreads across my insides in a glorious explosion, blunting the pain of reality.

Nice.

I should feel a little better soon. Hooray for Solicitous Steve, who has always provided the right thing at the right time. He has been such a good friend for years. Why, I can already think a little better now. A pleasant wave of clarity is caressing the tip of my nose, encircling my head in a golden halo and kicking a few brain cells into action.

Excellent.

Let me see. I'm definitely going ahead with my plan for the grand finale, but with a few necessary modifications. Time to make the first one. I have not much to do in the meantime, anyway. I no longer give a shit about the outfits on the catwalk, the audience's reactions to them. It's all frilly machine-designed crap, anyway. It's hard to be excited about something that isn't yours.

I hurry over to the AV corner, where a freckled ginger-haired boy and a pimply lad in baggy jeans are tinkering with dials on control panels. They look up at me and freeze to attention, I guess it's not often the Big Boss himself comes running over with instructions. I unfortunately can't remember their names, but they look like the sort who can be trusted to do my bidding.

'Well done, boys,' I say. 'All good, so far.'

Relief flashes on their faces.

'I would like to swap slides for the grand finale.' I pull out a memory stick from my pocket, hand it over to Ginger Hair. 'Make sure this new slide only comes when I'm three-quarters of the way down the catwalk. Not before, mind you.'

'OK,' says Ginger Hair.

'I would like you to play Frank Sinatra's "My Way" ninety seconds after I depart from the catwalk,' I say, turning to Baggy Jeans. 'At full blast, so the audience can't think of anything else.'

'Will do,' says Baggy Jeans.

'Don't you dare screw up,' I say, sternly. 'I'll hang the two of you upside down by the balls if you do.'

Both Ginger Hair and Baggy Jeans nod furiously. I wave a cautionary finger at the two boys (prompting more fervent nods) and hurry back to where I was standing. Item One: ticked and done. Time to deal with Items Two and Three. I wasn't planning to leave any notes behind, but I'm inclined to titillate the press with some carefully chosen words (and send them into a speculative frenzy) . . . and I owe Viola an apology for what I'm going to do. I extract a small black notebook from my pocket, the one I normally use to jot down ideas for designs. I flip over to the last page. Taking a deep breath, I pull out a pen from the notebook's holder and begin scribbling:

A letter intended for posthumous distribution

To the world's media,

If you're reading this letter today, I'm dead. Buried and gone. That's why I can be as frank as I like. As truthful as I can. When you speak from the grave, you speak with great authority. That's because the living can't argue with the dead. While the living may get a couple of extra words in, the departed can always bring the conversation to a dead end with a pointed silence.

There's a slight problem with being dead, though. The reputation of the dead lies in the hands of the living. You can't edit your memories after you are buried and gone, but the living can. The living control how the dead are remembered. They can change their memories of the deceased.

That's the sad truth about death.

Tragic, isn't it?

Leaders love to say that you are only as good as the people around you, the people who make up your team. I say: you're only as good as how you are remembered. Reputations can be completely destroyed – or salvaged – in death. You just need the living to rewrite your life's history, make a couple of small tweaks to your biography on Wikipedia. That's why some scallywags are remembered as saints. That's how some angels become arseholes after they die.

I'm writing this with the hope that I will be remembered, not as a saint, scoundrel or scallywag, but as a person in control. Many things in my lifetime were beyond my control (like who I was born to), but there are some things I managed to control in the end.

Like the manner of my end.

Yours sincerely,

I wonder if I should sign the letter. Maybe not. Best to remain cryptic; everyone loves an anonymous missive. I chuckle as I turn the page. Taking another deep breath, I start a new line:

My dearest Viola,

I'm sorry for breaking my promise to you, but some promises in life can only be kept through death. Please don't blame yourself, you did the best you could to stop me from my planned path. Guilt and blame are horribly corrosive emotions. They erode your soul until you are reduced to an empty husk, a hollow wreck. I don't want you to have an ounce of guilt in the wake of my departure.

You shouldn't blame yourself for Maya's death, either. Before you told me what happened at Old Fen Cottage on the night she died, I never once guessed you were terrified by the prospect of going to a show in Maya's memory. Your fears, like her name, are just an illusion. The brown package that the drone delivered just before we set out for London should make one thing clear: you shouldn't feel responsible for her death. It wasn't your fault she ended up in the river.

Don't blame yourself, my darling.

There's no need to.

Yours, as always, Xander

PS: Thanks for being such a patient friend over the years, for putting up with my crazy antics and for injecting a measure of normality (and sanity) into my existence.

I kneel down, place the notebook under the billowing black curtain next to me. Someone will find it later tonight, pass it to Viola. I can only hope she feels a little better after she reads my message.

All I need to do now is wait for the grand finale. The problem with the finale to end all finales is that you never know how it will finally end. Fingers crossed, this one will happen exactly as planned. I'm merely embellishing Steve's vision and hope to modify it a bit further when I get to the runway.

I pull out Steve's hip flask, drain it completely of its contents. My body is trembling with adrenaline. My mind is buzzing with possibility. So this is what it feels like to perch on the precipice of no return, to hover on the brink of change, to dance *en pointe* in a ballet shoe. So this is what light at the end of the tunnel looks like. Heavenly hope at the end of the tunnel of earthly despair.

The end will soon be beginning. The beginning of the end.

My end.

Time to get going, do what I've long wanted to do, long dreamt of achieving.

Immortality.

Immortality via mortality.

I believe in shocking people. The stronger the reaction, the better. I want people to leave my shows feeling as if they have been punched in the gut, not as though they've filled themselves with bread-and-butter pudding.

Alexander King, after winning the CFDA Designer of the Year Award for the second year running

Chapter Twenty-Nine

Christian

Steve is still staring at me with a flabbergasted expression on his face. His jaw is swinging from side to side.

'How did you know I was once a model?' he says again.

I shrug before replying: 'We crossed paths many moons ago.'

'Really?'

'You called yourself Dom van Diesel back then, didn't you? While the girls used to call you Dom Don Juan.'

'How . . . how do you know all that?' There's a sharp edge to his voice.

'Lots of folks hoping to break through took on sexier, snappier stage names. Like Maya von Meyer, who was once Ella May Vaughn-Meier, you must have thought it would help your career.'

Mortimer's astonished silence confirms I'm right.

'Where . . . where exactly did we meet?' he says.

'Manhattan,' I say. 'When you were still a bronzed, muscular model.'

Surprise glimmers on his face.

'You were the one getting all the gigs at first,' I say. 'Before

360

the winds changed overnight and everyone started preferring heroin chic instead. Fashion, as we both know, is fickle.'

He narrows his eyes at me.

'You . . . you . . .' he says, spluttering a little.

I suspect he has finally worked out where we once met. I see a flash of clarity in his eyes.

'You were once a model like me,' he says.

I nod.

'A model in Manhattan, indeed,' I say. 'A forgettable sort, alas. We chatted at our agency; you offered me weed. I moved to London, joined the police. You also headed to London, started modelling for King.'

I pause before adding:

'Were you the person who supplied Maya with drugs, all those years ago?'

Steve sucks his breath. His reaction confirms my suspicions. It's time to get to the bottom of what happened on the night Maya died. Even if I'm inclined to punch him in the face for plying Maya with pills.

'There are more important questions I should be asking,' I say. 'Firstly, why did Maya have trouble sleeping?'

I pause before continuing.

'Secondly, why was she high on fentanyl?'

Mortimer is silent.

'They say the best way to come to terms with the past is to face the truth about it,' I say, trying hard to keep my voice level. 'Maybe it's time to piece together what really happened to Maya.'

Mortimer exhales loudly, his shoulders slumping forward.

'She was in pain,' he says, looking back up at me with sorrowful eyes. 'Terrible, terrible pain.'

His words hit me like a freight train, slam the breath out of my chest.

'How . . . how did you know?' It's my turn to splutter.

'We spent a night together a few weeks before she died,' he says in a quiet voice, hanging his head forward.

Red jagged lines blot my vision. Blood roars in my ears. The world is turning sideways, upside down. I can feel anger surging to my throat, hot molten liquid that threatens to choke me. I'm tempted to smash Steve's face into a bloody pulp, punish him for seducing Maya all those years ago.

I'm already clenching my fingers.

Damn it.

I shouldn't hit him. My days of impulsive recklessness, of log-cabin burning, are long over.

I take a deep breath and exhale, trying desperately to steady myself. I can't punch Steve, even though I'm tempted to do so. Even if he has just smashed my memories of Maya into bits, blasted them apart. I always thought that Maya was perfect, unsullied in both body and form.

She clearly wasn't.

'Let . . . let me get this right,' I say, spitting my words out. 'You slept with Maya before she died?'

Steve bows his head for a couple of moments.

'She was the only girl who showed no interest in me,' he said, his voice breaking up a little. 'That was back in those days when women were literally throwing themselves at my feet. It made me twice as determined to seduce her, just for the challenge of it.'

'You succeeded.' My words are curt.

His jaw agitates.

'Weeks before she died, we went out drinking with a bunch of workmates. She started confiding in me at one point. Said she was lonely and sleepless in London, that her best friend unfortunately wasn't around.'

I flinch.

'One thing led to another, and she ended up coming home with me that night. I'm ashamed to say that I preyed on her loneliness, took advantage of it. Behind that cheery, seemingly tough Midwest exterior was just a little girl in a big city, a girl desperately wanting a hug.'

'But . . . but how did you know that Maya was in pain?'

'She said so the next morning, asked if I had any painkillers. She dropped by my apartment again, a week or so later, begged for much stronger shit. The night before she died, I spent a few hours at the pub with her and two workmates. She told me the pain had got worse.'

'Did she explain what caused it?'

'I asked, many times. She refused to say.'

He frowns at the ground before continuing: 'I'll . . . I'll always remember her looking totally miserable as we all parted ways that night.'

'You never told the police about your . . . your relationship with Maya, did you?' I hear an accusing note in my voice.

He shakes his head.

'I didn't dare to.'

Silence overtakes us for a couple of moments.

'Do you have any idea how Maya could have ended up in the river?' I say.

'I've asked myself that a million times over the years,' he says, sighing. 'She probably couldn't sleep that night, decided to go for a walk. The pills might have made her drowsy and uncoordinated, caused her to fall in.'

His eyes are anguished.

'I . . . I have always blamed myself for giving her all that shit . . .'

He trails off, swallowing hard. His gaze has become glassy; I swear tears are forming. Looks like Maya has burdened Mortimer as much (and for as long) as she has tormented me. It's amazing how the same girl can haunt so many people in different ways, how none of us will ever be able to work out the person she truly was, what really caused her death all those years ago. I guess you can't pin down an illusion. Maybe illusions will always take on different forms for different people.

'And why was she in Oxford?' I say. 'Fifty-five miles northwest of London. Do you know how she could have ended up there?'

'I've asked myself that, too,' he says. 'Lots and lots of times. The answer is no, I haven't got a clue. Apart from the fact that . . .'

'The fact that?'

'One of the others who joined us for drinks that night said she had been commuting to London from her aunt's cottage in Oxford. Maybe Maya followed her home that night.'

I stare at Steve in consternation.

'I never knew that,' I say.

'I told no one, not even the police. I didn't think it was significant, back then.'

'What . . . what was the girl's name?'

'Viola McKay.'

The world is spinning again.

'You must be joking.'

364

'Oh, do you know Viola?'

'I . . . er . . .' My words tumble out in a jumbled splutter. 'Did . . . did Viola work for Mr King in the past?'

'She interned with us ages ago. Xander still pops up to her cottage once in a while for a chat.'

'Does she still do work for him?'

'She does Xander the occasional favour, for old times' sake. The last I heard, she was mainly working for the civil service.'

I can hardly believe my ears.

'The civil service?'

'Viola has always been shifty about what she does. I guess "Civil Service" really means the "Spy Service". When I saw her just a few minutes ago . . .'

'Viola is *here*?' My words are an agonised squeak. 'Like . . . backstage?'

'She is, indeed.' He nods. 'Which makes me twice as convinced she's a spook, works for one of those agencies no one . . . or everyone has heard of. Said she was desperate to talk to Nigel, needed to find him.'

I don't like the sound of this.

'Did she say why she was looking for Avery?'

He shakes his head.

I *really* don't like the sound of this.

I turn abruptly from Mortimer and pelt down the corridor, back in the direction I had come from. Sweat is now trickling down my forehead, I can barely breathe. A clock is chiming in the distance, it must surely be eleven. King's grand finale will be starting soon. A question is swamping my fevered mind, torturing me with its burning presence: who on earth is Viola McKay? Is she:

(a) My fiancée, the woman I love?

(b) A spy moonlighting as a software engineer (or vice versa)?

(c) A close friend of Alexander King?

(d) All of the above.

I grit my teeth. Why didn't Viola tell me the truth about herself? How dare she hide so much from me, the man she proposed to, hopes to marry?

A tiny voice pipes up at the back of my head:

Maybe it's because liars find each other.

I unclench my fingers, before clenching them again. Calm down, Christian. Just calm down. I take a deep breath before exhaling vigorously, forcing every single ounce of air out from my lungs.

You have secrets of your own, the little voice pipes up again.

Terrible secrets involving death and destruction. Viola is entitled to her own secrets, too.

The problem with secrecy is that it drives a silent, thorny wedge into relationships. Maybe that's the real reason why things have been so fraught between us since we began living together. Maybe that's why we've alternated between heated exchanges and vexed silences, why we have been reduced to biting our tongues after each agonised outburst. Our secrets must have gnawed away at our hearts, blighted our minds, poisoned the air between us. Maybe it's time to stop pretending. As they say, honesty is the lifeblood of any relationship. Maybe it's time to lay everything out in the open, come clean about the past. I used to think the past was what we chose to remember, but maybe the past is also what we can't forget. Maybe the best way of dealing with the past is to come to terms with it in the present, prevent it from poisoning the future.

Our future, if we hope to have one together as husband and wife.

I need to find Avery. If I find Avery, I will find Viola.

The music has changed yet again, it's now the rousing electro-pop beat the model and forklifts performed their little dance to earlier. I reckon something will be happening on the catwalk soon.

Where on earth is Viola?

The audience is cheering wildly again; the frenetic electro-pop music is blasting my ears. I run to the nearest window, peer out of it. The giant cage is gliding along the catwalk, rotating of its own accord. The spotlights have aligned along the precise middle of the runway, illuminating the cage's path ahead. Crystalline rays of light are bouncing off the structure's glass railings, fanning off them in a series of glittering shards. Dry ice is billowing from the runway's pylons; the glass cage looks like a spinning diamond floating in a luminous cloud above the river.

I suck in my breath.

A hologram is taking shape in the centre of the cage, like a mirage being whipped up by gusts above a stormy sea. It's of Maya in a long, see-through white dress, folds swirling around her ankles. With those blonde locks tumbling around her shoulders, she bears a striking resemblance to Botticelli's Venus atop a foaming ocean, a gauzy hallucination borne aloft by dark waves. A shimmering mirage framed by the lights of HMS *Belfast*, the Shard and Tower Bridge in the distance.

A battleship, a skyscraper and a drawbridge.

How bizarrely incongruous.

The cage is almost at the end of the catwalk; its glass doors are swinging open. The hologram is morphing into a white butterfly with a torn wing, flitting through the doors of the cage.

A butterfly liberated from captivity, soaring high above the water.

A broken, imperfect creature.

I suck in my breath as a new realisation bulldozes into my head: I've clung to an image of an ideal woman for much too long in my mind and heart. I've always thought Maya was perfect. She never was. Everything about Maya is an illusion, including my own memories of her. In reality, she had a torn wing like that broken butterfly fluttering off into the distance. Maya wasn't even her real name. She was merely an illusion, as her name suggests.

An illusion of perfection.

In reality, she was lonely and miserable in London, ended up taking drugs and sleeping with Steve.

Which made her as human and imperfect as me.

My illusions of perfection have cost me a lot. I have spent the past twenty years being disillusioned by human frailty, the messy everyday realities of living with a flawed fellow being. That's why I've recoiled from emotional intimacy, struggled to maintain a relationship with anyone. It's time to abandon my illusions of perfection, to learn to cherish the real and the flawed. There's greater beauty in imperfection than perfection, as I realised earlier today. Viola isn't perfect; I should recognise that. I should learn to accept her foibles, live with them, embrace them.

Remember I'm much more flawed than her.

Fireworks are erupting all around, a glorious collection of expanding sparks and rolling Catherine wheels. The audience are now on their feet, a shrill and frenzied collective baying for King to make an appearance, to take his well-deserved bow and give them his customary mock salute.

I squint hard. Where is King? He's surely going to show up. Aha. I see him emerging on the left of the catwalk, hands placed nonchalantly in his pockets. There's a cheeky, impertinent jaunt to his stride. Words flash up on the screen above him, this time in rolling fashion:

AS CREATIVITY DIES A MACHINE-INFLICTED DEATH TODAY, I'M GLAD I HAD A SPLENDID RUN WHILE THE GOOD TIMES LASTED, WHILE INGENUOUS INSPIRATION REMAINED WITHIN THE EXCLUSIVE PRESERVE OF HUMANITY.

I WISH TO BE REMEMBERED NOT FOR HOW I ENDED THINGS, BUT FOR WHAT I HAVE ACHIEVED.

I LEAVE YOU THE LEGACY OF MY CREATIONS.

LOVE YOU ALL,

XANDER

XXX

He's almost at the end of the catwalk.

Bloody hell. I now know what King is going to do, what he had planned all along, the whole point of the two shows. They aren't just to commemorate Maya. Maya isn't the point. Maya had never been the real point. She was merely an illusion, to distract us from what King truly intended to achieve. Immortality via mortality, to be remembered as the last true creative unaided by machines.

The man who made a memorable exit at the pinnacle of his genius.

The fashion designer who ran off a runway.

'STOP HIM,' I shout.

It's too late. Because I'm not within earshot of anyone who can pull him back from the edge of the catwalk. Because King is giving the audience a cheeky mock salute and carrying straight on.

A roar of horror rises from the audience.

He's walking off the runway, suspended in thin air. For a brief moment, I'm convinced he is. But he isn't. All the air in the world can't hold up Alexander King if he's bent on killing himself.

I wince as he plunges feet first into the river and is swallowed up by black, undulating waves.

In the beginning, I wanted fame. In the end, I wanted freedom from fame.

Alexander King

Chapter Thirty

Viola

'Nooooo. . .' The word erupts from my mouth as I grip the stone balustrade, squint frantically at the dark waves ahead. People are screaming below us, loud shrill calls of horror.

'What the hell,' says Lucia.

'I . . . I . . .' My voice is a disbelieving splutter.

A horrified hush has overtaken the audience, as dense as the dark ripples marking Xander's point of entry into the Thames. Several people are scrambling up from their seats and pelting forward, craning their heads in a desperate attempt at spotting signs of life in the water.

A vain attempt.

I can only see a series of unbroken, menacing waves in the semi-darkness. Waves on the same body of water where Maya ended up precisely twenty years ago, this time further down-stream.

Please surface, Xander. Swim back to shore.

Please.

But the seconds are turning into minutes and the audience is erupting into loud agonised twitters and there's no sign of Xander and something excruciating is piercing my gut. The image of him plunging feet first into the river is still etched on my retina, replaying itself in a ghastly circular loop. A loud burst of music issues from the loudspeakers, causing me to jump. It's the opening refrain of Frank Sinatra's 'My Way'.

'This is so wrong,' says Lucia, shaking her head.

'He broke his promise,' I say in a whisper.

'You said you managed to persuade him,' she says in a hiss, turning to look at me with anger in her eyes.

'I did my best.'

A veritable commotion has broken out below us; people have begun shouting Xander's name. A river ferry and tug boat are diverting from their routes, speeding in our direction. I squint; two police launchers are whizzing towards us, too. Tiny winking lights are descending on the catwalk, hovering over the precise spot where Xander jumped and fanning off in different directions. They must be police search drones; I also hear the faint chop-chop-chop of a helicopter. Maybe river rescue services can help find Xander, pull him out of the water, save him.

But minutes have now passed since Xander jumped in the river and there's no sign of him.

Oh God, he may well be dead by now.

Fear mingled with horror is breaking over me, as brutal as those thick black waves ahead, paralysing me with its force. Yet I can't help but notice that Lucia's fingers are trembling a little. Her doe-like eyes have turned into narrow slits, as dagger-like as the blades dangling from her ears. She's also breathing hard, sucking in large gulps of air in an almost ferocious manner.

Why is Lucia so angry?

It's because she has a lot to lose from Xander's death, says a little voice at the back of my mind. People who have a lot to lose often have a lot to gain in the first place. That's what Christian said once, one of his frequent philosophical ruminations that endeared him to me. Maybe Lucia had a lot to gain from yesterday's death. Financial gain from nefarious share dealings, in particular. If so, she may have a lot to lose if the share price crashes a second time. What if CriminalX was right about Lucia's likelihood of committing murder, her propensity for being a killer?

'Why did you agree to bring Xander to Old Fen Cottage?' I say, hearing a cautious edge in my voice.

Lucia rolls her eyes.

'You said you could stop his death.'

Sinatra is getting louder and louder, drowning out the agonised shouts from the crowd. Someone must have turned the volume dial to max; Frank is now threatening to burst my eardrums. Yet I can hear a note of bitterness in Lucia's voice; there's isn't an ounce of grief on her face.

I should confront Lucia, force the truth out of her.

'It's odd you were so desperate to *stop* a death on a catwalk today,' I say in a low yet bold voice.

I take a deep breath before plunging ahead with:

'After you *caused* a death on a catwalk yesterday.'

I can see Lucia gulping a little, her nostrils flaring. Something new is sliding into her eyes, something hard and unforgiving. This isn't good. I should have thought twice about accusing Lucia to her face, calling her a murderer. I guess killers don't appreciate being called out in person.

Oh God.

This isn't good. Not good at all.

Because she's pulling out Xander's pistol from her handbag and pointing it straight at me.

Chapter Thirty-One

Christian

King's death has kicked my feet into action, turbocharged my limbs. I'm going to find Viola, and I will find her. Maybe she's on the uppermost level; I haven't checked that floor yet. I pelt down the corridor, past a couple of backstage helpers who are giving me curious looks. I turn a corner, only to halt in disbelief. Avery is scuttling away into the distance like a frightened rabbit.

'Stop,' I say, my voice a stentorian call.

Avery freezes, before turning round to look at me. I can see his lips quivering with indecision.

'Don't you dare move an inch, Avery,' I say, striding forward.

Is he armed? Where the hell is back-up? I guess you can never find a police officer when you need one. I don't even have a pistol on my person, let alone a pair of handcuffs. I must surely be the most underequipped member of the force on the planet. I can picture tomorrow's *Daily Mail* headline: 'Commissioner Verger Overwhelmed by Suspect Due to Lack of Equipment'. All I have are words to stop Avery from moving (or shooting me), which don't amount to much.

'You've been short-selling company shares for profit,' I say, marching up to him. 'Was that why you bombed Manhattan, hoping the shares would crash?'

'I swear I didn't bomb Manhattan.'

Avery looks rattled for the first time today. I should press home my advantage, try unsettling him further.

'You got away three years ago,' I say. 'A jury found you not guilty of insider trading, I hear.'

He winces.

'If you've since graduated to murder, I'll make sure you won't get away with anything this time,' I add in the firmest voice I can muster.

'I swear I'm innocent.'

Avery's eyes are increasingly wide and terrified, stripped of their usual pomposity and arrogance.

'Then why were you running just now?' I say.

He grimaces, shoulders pitching forward.

'You owe me an explanation, Avery.'

'The trial dragged on for years,' he says. 'I was a wreck long before the jury said I was free to go. When Lucia said an officer was looking for me, something inside me just flipped. All I wanted to do was . . . to get out of here.'

Is Avery telling the truth? Just then, my phone buzzes.

'Don't you dare move an inch,' I say to Avery in my firmest voice, before tapping the answer button.

'Hi, Harold,' I say.

'We've just found out another person has been short-selling King shares, before buying back loads more a few hours ago. It wasn't immediately obvious as the activity was spread over several smaller transactions.'

'Who is it?' I say.

'Lucia Graves.'

'*Lucia Graves?*'

'Indeed.'

The force of revelation barrels straight into my chest, almost knocking the breath out of me. No wonder Lucia came into my office this morning for a chat. She wanted to distract me with her story of the bet, pin suspicion on De Luca, make sure nothing bad happens to her boss tonight. I thought her Reverse Darkness Theory was bonkers. Why didn't I realise *she* was bonkers? She insisted that 'folks who produce sweet fluffy stuff can often be violent. That's because the darkness stays put, never quite drains away.' Why didn't I work out that she was describing *herself*?

It takes a murderer to recognise a murderer.

That's what they say.

I'm clearly not very good at it.

'Get someone to grab Lucia,' I say, my voice a curt bark. '*At once.*'

'Will do.'

I terminate the call and turn back to Avery.

'You spoke to Lucia just now?' I say, my voice a desperate squeak.

He nods.

'I was talking to an old friend of Xander's when she interrupted us.'

My mouth runs dry. This surely can't be for real.

'The friend's name is Viola McKay, isn't it?' I say, hearing a note of finality in my question.

Avery nods again, causing an overwhelming sense of doom to hit me with brute force. Shit. Oh shit. Viola's in the Manhattan bomber's clutches and I've been distracted by a pesky lawyer.

Life is all about hedging your bets correctly, profiting from other people's follies, using the information at your disposal in the best possible way.

Diary of Lucia Graves

Chapter Thirty-Two

The Devil's in the Detail
(and Writes for *Vanity Fair*)

The day Lucia was sacked was the day she vowed to get even.

That morning, she dressed for work as usual. Did her make-up, put on her favourite earrings. Hummed her favourite tune in the bathroom ('Killing Me Softly With His Song'), listened to her favourite audiobook on the subway (*Murder on the Orient Express*). Greeted the assistant who worked opposite her with a cheery hello, settled down at her desk to battle with the emails in her inbox. At two minutes past eleven, she headed into The Editor's room, carrying her boss's customary skinny latte ('milk to coffee in a precise three-to-one ratio, love, no sugar'). The Editor was standing next to the window, talking on the phone. She motioned to Lucia to put the coffee down. Lucia placed the dainty cup on a side table, began making her way back to the door. Just then, The Editor replaced the phone with a sharp click and said: 'Wait a minute.'

Lucia spun round to realise that her boss had picked up the coffee and was standing next to The Mill, a custom-designed desk above a fancy treadmill, one that doubled as an elliptical machine. (The Editor swore she walked six miles a day on her six-inch Louboutins purely by working at her desk.)

The Editor swept her gaze over Lucia's outfit before arching a thinly plucked eyebrow and saying in a disdainful voice: 'That colour is so *five* autumns ago.'

'I hear it's coming back next spring,' Lucia said, trying not to sound too injured (even though she was).

The Editor took a sip and scowled before saying: 'Best not to get too far ahead of yourself, love.'

'I thought life was all about thinking ahead.'

That was the moment The Editor gave Lucia The Look, her famed expression of withering disapproval (mingled with the usual icy hauteur and sangfroid).

'On the subject of thinking ahead, I'll be letting you go at the end of the week,' The Editor said.

Lucia stared at her boss in horror.

'How come?' she said.

'Your performance has left a lot to be desired.'

'What . . . what do you mean?'

'I mean you should vacate your desk by five, this Friday afternoon.' The Editor's lips were thin and unyielding.

'But why?'

'You ask too many questions.'

'Please tell me what I have done wrong,' Lucia said, hearing a note of shrill desperation in her voice.

'You haven't done anything *completely right*, I'm afraid.'

'I don't understand.'

The Editor wrinkled her nose before replying: 'You're too smart for your own good, too obsessed by the big picture to notice the small details that matter.'

'But this surely isn't the end of the world.' Lucia's words were frantic, plaintive.

'The devil's in the detail, love. You keep getting the small details wrong. You brought the wrong handbag to yesterday's photo shoot. You put too much milk into my skinny latte *again*.'

The Editor said no more as she got on The Mill and began trotting away at a ponderous pace. It was clear to Lucia that the conversation was over, that The Editor had made up her mind. She backed out of the office, tail between her legs. The Editor's subsequent reference letter for Lucia was only two lines long. It said:

> If you would like to take this little smart-ass off my hands, you're most welcome to do so. Just don't blame me if anything goes wrong.

Lucia spent the next nine months out of a job (and looking for one), thanks to The Editor's glowing reference. Her feet got so tired pounding the pavements between unsuccessful interviews, she developed both bunions and a lifelong aversion to six-inch stilettos (she could only manage three inches, from that point onwards). She was only able to find a job again when she discovered it helped to be as blunt as The Editor. At one interview, the man sitting opposite her said: 'Tell me why I should hire you, in one sentence.'

And so Lucia said:

'My previous boss fired me because I was too smart, asked too many questions, and made terrible skinny lattes.'

She was hired on the spot.

Many moons later, Lucia came across The Editor's name on a Manhattan show guest list, with the attached job description:

Personal Stylist. Puzzled, she googled the woman's name, only to discover a whole bunch of gleeful news articles announcing that The Editor was no longer an editor. The Board had apparently decided that the latest editing software – and two young interns with fresh ideas – could do a better job than an overpaid, middle-aged cynic on a repetitive treadmill. A source had also cheerfully stated that The Editor was taken aback by the 'robotic coup', although the picturesque storm had been brewing right in front of the woman's surgically enhanced nose all along.

It was a shame The Editor failed to see the big picture when it mattered, sniggered a columnist in the *Sun*.

Lucia chuckled when she read those words.

Looks like while she got hired, The Editor got fired.

Tit for tat.

How karmically satisfying, she mused to herself. Yet she still seethed at how The Editor had sacked her in such a brutally lacerating manner, insulted both her fashion sense and intelligence. The knowledge that the woman would be attending the Manhattan show thus gnawed away at the back of Lucia's mind. It became a compulsive obsession that pawed at her when she woke up in the morning and plagued her mind during the darkest hours of the night.

Tit for tat.

How to get even.

Fairness in life, possibly through unfairness in death.

The week before the show, she saw an opportunity when she visited her new employer's millinery workshop in Surrey. A tiny opportunity . . . yet a tantalisingly audacious one. She began hatching a plan, a big-picture plan. The plan would involve a bomb in a handbag, to be detonated when the model reached the end of the catwalk where the lovely lady in question would be sitting. If the bomb took out anyone else in the process, it would be desirable collateral damage. After all, most of the fine people blinging about in the front row were the folks who had turned her down for jobs.

The bomb went off, killing the poor model who carried the handbag. Unfortunately for Lucia, it exploded a little too far away from her ex-boss. The Editor escaped unscathed, even made it to primetime television the next day. Images of the worthy woman (daintily powdering her nose with The Look plastered on her face, yards away from the smouldering wreckage of the catwalk) were beamed on screens around the globe, prompting much debate about the vacuous nature of folks who work in the fashion industry, and a million mocking memes on social media.

Had Lucia timed the bomb to go off seven seconds later, it would probably have made a difference to her dastardly plan.

While the big picture matters, the devil is indeed in the detail.

Chapter Thirty-Three

Viola

I stare at the pistol in Lucia's hand. Her grip is firm, unyielding. I have never stared down the barrel of a gun before. It's an unnerving situation to be in. It's also a situation I'd rather not be in.

'You won't get away with it,' I say, trying not to let fear show on my face.

'Why not?' says Lucia, twisting her lips.

'All I need to do is scream.'

'While all I need to do is shoot,' she says, her voice taking on a syrupy consistency. 'No one will hear anything above this din. Plus it's Xander's gun, not mine. I'll just need to wipe the handle clean.'

Lucia's right. Sinatra's crooning so loudly above our heads, no one will hear my pathetic little whimpers from the rooftop. Lucia's honeyed, saccharine tone also makes me twice as alarmed, twice as fearful for my skin. The sweeter they sound, the more deranged they tend to be. Maybe I should keep Lucia talking while I desperately think of a way to distract her . . . or get away.

'I . . . I . . . don't understand,' I say. 'Why were you so desperate to stop Xander from killing himself?'

Her eyes flash.

'You said Xander wasn't going to do anything stupid tonight,' she says, spitting her words out. 'I bought a shitload of company shares just before the close of trading today.'

She glares at me again before hissing: 'Now that Xander has jumped into the river, the share price will probably sink like him.'

'So it's all about the money, then.' I hear contempt in my voice.

She shrugs in silence.

'I can't believe you killed an innocent girl for profit.'

'I wanted to take out someone in the front row, actually.' She spits her words out, her voice harsh and bitter. 'That was the real point. But I guess you can't have everything you want, kill two birds with one bomb.'

'Who . . . who did you, er . . . want to "take out"?' I hear my voice trembling, feel sweat beading on my forehead.

'My ex-boss.'

'Your ex-boss?'

'Said I was "too smart" when she sacked me, which I'd always thought was a bit of an insult. Shame Ally panicked, never reached the end of the catwalk where the lovely lady was sitting.'

Lucia's mad. Positively bonkers. Why didn't I realise this earlier? Why didn't I believe CriminalX? What's the point of being able to predict the future when I consistently fail to learn anything from the past?

'How . . . how on earth did you manage to get hold of a bomb?'

385

Lucia shrugs.

'You can get anything by drone these days. The only difficult bit was having to pay for it in cash.'

Damn. Oh damn. Didn't the lady at the pharmacy say that
the only people who still use cash these days are 'folks who
have stuff to hide'? Didn't CriminalX flag up that Lucia had
been googling 'cash payment for drone deliveries' recently?
Why didn't I put the two together? Looks like the problem
with useful information is that it usually gets buried in an
avalanche of crap, like Google searches for 'best ways to have
a blast in Manhattan' and 'this season's three-inch killer stilettos'.

'So you'd been planning the bomb for ages,' I say.

'Not really.' She shrugs again, pursing her lips. 'I saw an
opportunity last week, decided to hedge a bet. *My* bet.'

Reckon I'm finally stumped for a response.

'Think we've chatted long enough,' she says, stepping behind
me and placing the gun in the small of my back. A spot that
makes me feel particularly vulnerable . . . because it's where
hopeful new life is budding inside me. I take an involuntary
step forward. I can feel fear tunnelling deep into my gut,
threatening to paralyse my limbs. I know what Lucia is planning.
She's prodding me forward with the gun, forcing me to step
up to the balcony, the balustrade overlooking hard concrete
below. We're about five storeys high, I reckon. High enough
to break my neck when I hit the ground. But I'll be damned
if Lucia makes me jump without a fight. Does she really think
I'm going to go down without a whimper?

Does she really think I'm not going to struggle for the sake
of my baby, the offspring of the man I love?

Rage surges to my throat, hardening my determination.
Crystallising a single word in my mouth.

'HELP,' I say, my voice a frantic scream.

My elbow swings out, catching Lucia in the gut.

Big mistake.

Huge.

Because I hear a gunshot ringing out in the darkness as I collapse to the ground in agony.

The best intelligence predicts what your opponent will do tomorrow. By the time you know what your opponent will do today, it's usually too late.

Damian Everett, Guest Lecture on 'Intelligent Intelligence in the Year 2030'

Chapter Thirty-Four

Christian

The crack of a gunshot, several yards away, prompts me to run faster. I turn right at the corner, only to see two figures on a balcony in the distance. One is sprawled out on the ground, clutching her leg. The other is standing over her, holding a gun. I race forward, only to come to an abrupt, horrified halt. Lucia is pointing a pistol at my beloved (who's whimpering in agony). I peer down at Viola's leg, only to wince. Thick red rivulets of blood are running down her limb; the bullet must have burrowed deep into the flesh.

'Don't you dare come any closer,' says Lucia to me.

'I won't,' I say, raising my palms.

'I'll shoot her in the heart if you do,' says Lucia, her voice getting shriller and shriller. 'Which is a bit of a shame as she's expecting.'

'Expecting?' My question is a disbelieving squeak.

'I . . . I only found out . . . this morning,' says Viola, her voice a broken whimper.

Lucia and Viola's words are colliding in my mind, paralysing me with the force of their impact.

389

'My fiancé's,' continues Viola, raising her head and looking straight at me.

Joy surges to my heart, followed by terrible, terrible fear.

'I don't see why you need to hurt Viola,' I say to Lucia, trying desperately to sound both calm and convincing.

Lucia snarls.

'She failed to stop Xander,' she says.

'Lucia's the bomber,' says Viola.

'I've only just worked that out,' I say.

'Nothing went to plan yesterday,' says Lucia, interrupting me and turning her gun in my direction, her cheeks flushed an apoplectic shade of red. 'Nothing has gone to plan today. It's time for a new plan.'

Fear strikes me. There's equal petrification on Viola's face. Lucia sounds suitably deranged, unhinged by frustration and anger. You can't talk sense into a deranged person. Nor can you predict what they are going to do next.

'I strongly suggest you put that gun down,' I say, taking a desperate step forward.

'I . . .'

I hear a loud crack, the unmistakable sound of another gunshot. An iron-hot boulder slams into my chest, causing me to crumple to the ground. A second thing hits me, at precisely the same moment.

It's the realisation that iPredict had indeed got it right.

My chance of dying is 99.74% . . .

When one contemplates the infinite number of things that could possibly go wrong, it's amazing that anything right could happen in the first place.

Diary of Lucia Graves

Chapter Thirty-Five

Viola

I watch Christian collapse to the ground, a crimson cloud spreading over his shirt. Lucia takes a step forward, her eyes wild and wide, raising her gun again.

Just then, it strikes me:

I love Christian. Why didn't I apologise to him yesterday, say I love him? It's too late now. Much too late. One should never leave for tomorrow what one should do today, and I only have myself to blame.

'Don't . . .' Another scream escapes my lips as Lucia points the pistol at Christian, takes aim. Unthinking desperation overtakes me; it prompts me to reach out, grab Lucia's ankle with my hand.

I hear the shot ricocheting off a balustrade.

'You bitch,' she says, yanking her leg beyond my reach and lifting her gun resolutely in my direction this time. Looks like she's going to shoot me first, put me out of my physical agony, before finishing Christian off. I squeeze my eyes shut, brace myself for the imminent moment of death, the snug embrace of oblivion, the eventual dissipation of the terror and grief in my heart.

A shot rings out a moment later, followed by two more.

Is this what death feels like? A distinct numbness, without any lifting of the pain in my leg? I hear loud frantic shouts, followed by the whirring of propellers and the clomp-clomp-clomp of booted feet. I force my eyes open, even though it's tempting to keep them shut, drift away into darkness.

The first thing I see are red lights.

Tiny, flashing ones.

Three police drones are hovering several yards away, retracting their guns. A uniformed police officer is kneeling by my side, concern etched on his face. I can see his lips moving but I can't hear his words. I wrench my ears into semi-focus.

'The ambulance will be here shortly, madam,' he's saying.

I fling an arm out to prop my head up, before turning my eyes in the direction of Christian.

To my surprise, the first person I see is Lucia. She's sprawled in a broken heap on the floor, a yard away from me, her clothes torn apart and soaked with blood. Xander's pistol is lying on the ground, a couple of yards away from her outstretched hand. Her head is jerking wildly; a dark-red rivulet is streaming from her mouth. A thick strangled noise is coming from the back of her throat. It's a terrible, heart-wrenching sound. One so awful, it tears my ears apart.

Oh God, I think she's choking on her own blood.

I put a hand out, pinch her nose shut with my fingers until the police officer yanks my hand away.

'No, madam,' I can hear him saying.

But I think I've administered the *coup de grâce*. Lucia's eyes have acquired a fixed, unseeing stare. Her lips are a frozen rictus; I no longer hear the terrible sound at the back of her throat.

So CriminalX thinks I'm likely to be a killer . . .

Did Lucia shoot Christian before the drones got to her? A terrible cold dread grips my insides again. I push myself up onto my elbows, twist my head round in desperation. A second police officer is kneeling at Christian's side, blocking his face from view. I can only see an arm.

It's attached to a bloodied sleeve.

'Christian,' I say, my voice a cracked, broken whimper.

A surge of strength rips through my body, from somewhere deep and primal. I push my palms down into the ground, crawl forward in his direction. Even if I can't bear to see his broken, lifeless body.

'You shouldn't be moving, madam,' says the officer at my side.

I ignore him. Excruciating pain stabs my leg, whirls around my head, blinds me as I force myself forward, inch by inch. I crawl around the second police officer, swat him away to discover Christian lying on his side, his white shirt soaked crimson. A howl escapes my lips, a cry of despair.

'Oh, Christian . . .'

To my disbelief, I see his lips moving a little. They are so pale, all his blood must surely have drained away from his body. I force myself up to his side, lower my ear to his mouth.

'Vi,' he's saying in a weak whisper. 'I'm sorry.'

'You don't have to be sorry,' I whisper back, trying not to cry. I notice that the two officers have both taken several steps back, probably to give us some space and privacy.

'Should have told you . . . my secrets . . .' Christian's voice is so weak, I can barely hear his words. 'The truth about me . . .'

'Don't be silly,' I say, tears trickling down my cheek. 'I don't give a damn about your secrets.'

'I . . . set fire to . . . Gran's cabin,' he says in a tiny voice, almost imperceptible to my ears. 'When Step-Dad was inside.'

I gape at Christian, temporarily forgetting the pain in my leg. No wonder he has woken me up so many times in the middle of the night, tossing and turning in bed, mumbling words like 'find out' in his sleep. I'd merely assumed it was his imposter syndrome kicking in; I didn't realise his fears ran much deeper. He's afraid of being *found out*, that someone might crank open the lid over his past. If I killed someone and had to nurse a terrible secret like that for the rest of my life, I would probably not sleep a wink.

So Criminal X was right about Christian being a . . .

'Was . . . in love with Ella . . . Ella May . . . Maya . . . years ago . . .' he continues in a hoarse, ragged whisper. 'Should have . . . told you too . . .'

I freeze. Ella? Maya? Is this for real? Was Maya also known as Ella, the woman who haunts Christian at night?

'Do . . . do you mean Maya von Meyer?' I say.

He nods. His confirmation slams hard into me, causes my head to spin. I can't breathe, I'm on the verge of hyperventilating. Maybe I should just surrender to agony, yield to the snug embrace of darkness. But I can't. I shouldn't. I should think past the pain, try to make sense of things, maybe even understand. Was Christian the guy Maya said she fancied, that mysterious Oxford bloke who took his exams so seriously?

'Were . . . were you Maya's best friend?' I say, my voice low and urgent.

He nods, wincing again. So that's why Christian was talking in his sleep in the run-up to the two shows commemorating the girl he once loved. Why he bought a ticket for tonight without telling me.

'Maya loved you,' I say, reaching out and taking hold of his right hand. It's cold, alarmingly clammy. 'That's what she said.'

I can feel more tears welling up in my eyes.

'Told me she wished you felt the same about her.'

'How . . . how . . . do you . . .' Christian is struggling to whisper something, but nothing is coming out of his mouth.

'I invited her to Old Fen Cottage, the night she died,' I say.

I see a brief jolt of understanding in Christian's eyes.

'I was secretly jealous of her best friend,' I continue. 'Even though I never knew who the person was.'

I can see his mouth forming a silent, agonised 'why?'. It's time to tell Christian the truth. Explain why I was jealous of Maya's best friend, reveal something I've never dared tell anyone before. Secrets shouldn't poison our relationship any further. This is what everything that happened today has taught me.

'I fancied Maya myself,' I say in a whisper. 'That's why I invited her home, that night. I've dated both women and men all my life. But I never truly loved anyone until you came along, Christian.'

His eyes are soft. He gives my hand a tiny squeeze, as four frantic paramedics come rushing over in our direction. I can see his mouth moving again, forming a series of voiceless words, just before our hands are forced apart and he's blocked from view.

I think I know what Christian is saying.

He's saying that he loves me too.

Chapter Thirty-Six

My dearest Viola,

I found something in your attic, the last time I stayed with you. I couldn't sleep that night, as usual. Insomnia is a curse unique to the living; it's a shame only the dead are exempt from this grave problem. It's a ghastly guerrilla that ambushes me each night, a dastardly enemy who always wins the battle because it knows me better than I know myself.

I began snooping around in my restless stupor (how predictable of me), poking my pointy nose into various boxes (how naughty of me). I picked up a silver frame containing a photo of you and your dearly departed aunt Lisabeth, turned it around in my hands, and . . .

. . .a small envelope fell out from the back.

It looked like it had been there for many, many years. Naturally, I opened the envelope and read the letter. Maybe I shouldn't have, because it has preyed on my mind ever since. It haunted me so much, I took it with me when I left your cottage the following day, so that I could mull over its contents a bit more (how selfish of me). While I suspect I know who wrote the letter – I recognise the handwriting – you might have better luck figuring out who the author's 'best friend' was.

I reckon it's only fair that I return the letter to you before my London show. I really hope you will come on Friday evening, see all the designs your brilliant software came up with. It would be wonderful to see you backstage at Old Billingsgate (there's a teeny health-related secret I wish to tell you about and I would much prefer to do it in person rather than over the phone).

Yours, as always,

Xander

Chapter Thirty-Seven

To my best friend,

If you're reading this, I will probably be long dead and gone. This is because I'm going to hide this letter in the most unlikely place I can find, so the letter will only reach you when the stars in the heavens align to their satisfaction, when destiny dictates that it's the right moment for you to see these words. I'm currently torn between wanting to tell you some terrible, terrible secrets – and thinking you will be much, much happier not knowing them (Gran used to say that ignorance anesthetizes the mind and soothes the soul). As I can't decide what to do, I will let the fates decide for me.

If this letter ever reaches you someday, I just wanted to tell you that you shouldn't blame yourself for my death. I also want to tell you that I have always loved you, even if you pulled my pigtails the first time we met (and I yelped with pain before punching you in the face).

I went to look for you, the night your gran's cabin burnt down. I got a bit anxious after your mom died, saw a calculating wildness in your eyes, thought you might do something crazy to yourself. I arrived at the cabin and saw a figure on the horizon, running away in the direction of the forest. I thought it was you, but I wasn't sure. I saw smoke billowing from below the door, heard a male voice muttering something. I froze in horror, thinking you were trapped inside. Just then, the man slurred your name. Said he would fuck you hard again, once he got out of the place.

It was then I knew who it was.

Your step-dad.

His words confirmed what I had suspected all along. What he had done to you, why you had always been so terrified to return home.

Anger washed over me.

In a moment of crystal clarity, I knew exactly what I needed to do.

It was simple.

I just had to do nothing.

I crept to the nearest window, peeked in. He was staggering around the living room, legs splayed wide, away from a large pool of vomit on the floor. He looked intoxicated and confused, almost to the point of delirium. Smoke was billowing around him; huge red flames had already consumed most of the sofa and were licking the wooden floorboards around it. I crept away from the window, waited until he stopped mumbling your name, before walking back home.

I begged Mom and Dad to let you stay with us in the aftermath of the fire. They were pretty reluctant to do so (too many mouths at home to feed, as you know). It was Gran who came to my rescue, persuaded them to take you in. She had always liked you, felt sorry for you, thought you would go extremely far if given a chance. She had always believed we would be perfect for each other, too. When she died, she left me a decent amount of money in her will, with the explicit proviso that I use the funds to expand my horizons, follow my dreams — or be with you.

I'm glad I did.

I wanted to tell you that I found out what your step-dad did to you, but I never knew how to raise the subject. You had clearly left Montana behind, built a new life for yourself in England, tried hard to bury the past. You go about in tweeds and speak with a funny new accent, all posh and clipped-sounding (it suits you, by the way). You behave like a completely new person. There were days when I would marvel at how different you've become, wonder if you were the same guy I grew up with. Looks like you not only took Gran's advice to heart, you turned out to be a whiz at blending in and re-inventing yourself. I didn't want to be the one excavating the past instead of excising it, reopening terrible wounds instead of trying to heal them.

But I knew, deep inside my gut, the past still preyed on you.

I understand why you recoiled when I put my arms around you, just before I got on the bus to London. I hope that the passage of time will heal the scars in your head and heart, that you will eventually allow yourself to be touched, held and loved. I also hope you will find someone amazing, a person who will make it possible for you to love in return.

I think you will go far in your chosen career, after what your step-dad did to you. After how your mom failed you. I don't blame you for wanting to pass your exams, for trying hard to succeed.

Perverts like your step-dad deserve to be punished.

Victims like your mom deserve all the help they can get, to get off drugs and lead a clean life.

On the subject of drugs, I saw a doctor recently. I have pain, a terrible pain that has prevented me from sleeping. Turns out I have cancer, terminal and inoperable. I watched Gran die of the same condition, nursed her to the awful end. It wasn't pretty. She was nothing but a wretched skeleton when she took her last breath, haggard and jaundiced. All the drugs in the world did not help diminish her pain. I have no wish to end my life in the same way, in misery and agony.

I prefer to leave this world on my own terms.

Time to rest now, go to sleep, not suffer like Gran.

On the night I was diagnosed, I went out with some of my workmates, got terribly drunk in the pub. I'm sorry to say that I went home with one of them, later that night. It was one of those desperate moments when I craved a human presence, a modicum of affection, a reassuring touch. I regretted it the next day, of course. I'm still regretting it. Because he wasn't . . . the man I love.

I went to look for you just now. I decided to follow another friendly workmate up here tonight, on a complete whim. I let myself out of her cottage, started walking over to your college lodgings, before changing my mind and turning back to write this letter. Maybe some things aren't meant to be. Maybe it's best for us to have parted with smiles, not tears, the day you put me onto the bus to London.

It hurts.

It hurts, it really does.

My workmate has been giving me stuff to dull the pain. I went to his apartment a few nights ago to get more pills (I didn't sleep with him again, I swear) but it isn't enough. I'm not very good with pain, unfortunately. I'm desperate for peace. A modicum of relief, of blessed release.

I just wanted to say: I love you, my darling.

I always have.

Your best friend, your heart.

The Times

29 September 2030

Police Commissioner Weds Sweetheart

Christian Verger, the Commissioner of the Metropolitan Police, married his sweetheart Viola McKay in a small ceremony in the grounds of Old Fen Cottage in Oxford on Sunday. The couple have released a short statement saying that they are extremely happy to be alive and married.

Both Verger and McKay were injured by the Manhattan bomber, Lucia Graves, during a shoot-out on the rooftop of Old Billingsgate, on the night of the late Alexander King's final show. They have since recovered, although McKay is still on crutches.

The bride hobbled down a rose-fringed aisle in a white dress designed by the software she wrote for King before his death. The software now generates designs for the company's brand-new label αĸ-V (Alexander King's Vision), a range of outfits and accessories that have been hailed by *Vogue* as 'precisely what the great Alexander King would design with his own hand, if he were still alive'. Steve Mortimer, the current head human designer at Alexander King, says that αĸ-V has proved such a massive hit with Generation Alpha's Instagrammers, the firm has had to employ more tech engineers to cope with the demand. Other fashion houses, he adds, have frantically begun hiring software programmers in an attempt to replicate αĸ-V's success.

The couple have admitted that King's London show was an important turning point in their relationship.

'Christian had asked a jeweller to deliver my engagement ring to Old Billingsgate on the night of the fashion show,' says the new Mrs Verger. 'Much to my surprise, the courier placed a small parcel into my hand just before I was stretchered into the ambulance. I opened the parcel; the ring took my breath away. I began crying, not from pain but from joy.'

It is rumoured that the bride's engagement ring has since been inscribed with the words, 'Perfection is an Illusion' while her wedding ring bears the words 'Love is Reality'.

Daily Mail

1 October 2031

CriminalX Is MI6's New Minority Report

It's the stuff of law-enforcement dreams: software that predicts if a person is likely to be a murderer, rapist, thief or fraudster. A leaked message purportedly written by Damian Everett, the newly appointed chief of MI6, suggests that this no longer lies in the realm of science fantasy. Our nation's spooks already have the capacity to predict who is more likely to rape, steal, trick or kill, and they're now keen on using the software to root out terrorists and spies.

Everett purportedly wrote in the leaked message: 'Our ground-breaking software CriminalX successfully identified fifteen murderers and twelve rapists long before the Metropolitan Police finished their investigations. Our goal now is to identify all potential terrorists and spies operating beyond British shores, based on their Google searches and behavioural patterns.'

The Secret Intelligence Service, when contacted by this newspaper, have refused to confirm if the message was indeed written by Everett or if CriminalX exists. An inside source (who wishes to remain anonymous) says that MI6 believes that a 'hostile state actor' or 'belligerent foreign power' is responsible for the leak, possibly having hacked into their chief's private account. Everett himself is said to be heading an official investigation into the source of the leak, being extremely eager to narrow down 'the range of possible suspects'.

The Metropolitan Police has similarly declined to comment on the leaked message. However, a spokesperson for the organisation says that the Met intends to improve its criminal predictive software and has already hired an expert freelance consultant for the job.

The Guardian

15 October 2031

Met Commissioner Sets Up New Criminal Rehabilitation Scheme

The Commissioner of the Metropolitan Police, Christian Verger, has personally helped push through a London-based scheme for the rehabilitation of criminals who have served their prison sentences. The scheme will involve subsidised vocational education (and even university degrees) for ex-offenders, as well as paid internships and job placements at organisations across London.

Numerous institutions have joined the scheme, offering work placements and jobs. They include War Against Opioids, a charity that helps people overcome opioid addiction. Several fashion conglomerates and top restaurants are also participating in the scheme. Both Alexander King and Gio & Gio (G&G) are providing three-month dressmaking internships to ex-convicts, while Michelin-starred restaurant Casa Perfetta is offering six-week kitchen apprenticeships.

'Many ex-criminals would be grateful for a second chance,' said Verger. 'We want to facilitate this, reduce their likelihood of reoffending and turn them into useful members of society.'

Even murderers may apply to the scheme, he added, subject to satisfactory psychiatric evaluations. 'Justice is not all about punishing criminals with lengthy spells in prison. Justice is also about providing education and employment with the hope of preventing further crimes. By easing their transition into skilled jobs, we hope to get ex-offenders back on track, help them make good again.'

Life isn't fair. That's what everyone should learn as soon as they are born. There is only fairness in death. Unfortunately, it's not a lesson you can learn after you die.

Alexander King

Chapter Thirty-Eight

Xander

A wooden shack in Tahiti, many months later

The fisherman in the distance is battling with his catch, framed by an ocean so blue it's almost the colour of lapis lazuli. He's struggling with the net; it must be a particularly massive haul. I'm tempted to help the poor man. After all, I've done nothing worthwhile for months. I've merely been swaying on hammocks under coconut trees, smoking copious amounts of pot and drinking gallons of whisky. But then again, isn't this the stuff of dreams? I bet lots of suited-and-booted folks in Manhattan and the City of London wish they could pack up and head to a balmy tropical island where they can spend the rest of their lives in pink Bermuda shorts, doing nothing.

I've been there, done that. Achieved everything I wanted, in both life and death. Now, I'm sitting on the sun-drenched veranda of a wooden shack, wearing only pink Bermudas and doing nothing.

Life isn't a series of coincidences. It's a series of ironies.

The irony about doing nothing is that you eventually start wishing you had something to do.

Being idle is like wearing an ill-fitting sock.

It's a fashion that doesn't quite suit me.

Maybe I'll head back to London one day, reinvent myself. Do something useful with my head and hands. It's damned boring sitting here under this coconut tree. Even if the sun is shining in a cloudless sky and cream-crested azure waves are lapping just yards away from my toes. At least I have a ceremony to spy on, in the wee hours of the morning. Four in the morning, to be precise. I've been looking forward to it for months. Better set an alarm clock, in case I nod off beforehand. The problem with being in the middle of the Pacific is that you're usually fast asleep when the rest of humanity is wide awake and doing useful stuff with their heads and hands.

Damn it, I'm bored shitless and shirtless.

Maybe I should help the fisherman bring in his catch.

I like the colours of his boat. Gunmetal grey with flecks of emerald and turquoise. Maybe I should design a new collection with a 'Finding Atlantis' theme, lots of ankle-length cloaks with fishes and fantastical creatures swimming across their hems, in the unifying colours of grey, emerald and turquoise. A lapis lazuli catwalk snaking its way into a falling curtain of water. Haughty azure-lipped models wearing impossibly high platform shoes in the shape of cowrie shells.

Damn it, I've forgotten I'm no longer a designer.

I'm also supposed to be dead.

Damn it.

Maybe I should have picked the drowning option, that night.

But I didn't. I couldn't do it. I just couldn't. When the icy-cold Thames water swirled around me that fateful night, I realised

410

I had two options. One: give in, let the currents drag me down. Two: fight.

I decided to fight.

Hard.

Even though I had spent months planning my grand departure, my final walk, my last salute.

Because I *definitely* didn't want to die.

When I hit the water that night, it also struck me that dying wasn't something that came naturally to me. Survivor's instinct – and *not* the death instinct – was what kicked in, crystallised inside my gut, powered my limbs forward. Guess I've always been a shameless self-preserver at heart.

I first realised that I wasn't quite ready for Death's embrace when the bomb went off in Manhattan, as soon as I inhaled a whole lungful of smoke and took in the dead girl with a missing arm on the catwalk, bathed in a pool of blood (a sight that will haunt me until my final breath). When the Grim Reaper flitted over my shoulder that night, I realised I was just a cowardly little survivor who had no desire to follow his ghastly spectre to the Land of No Return. I guess the courageous don't mind dying, while atavistic fools like me do their best to stay alive (that's probably what happened in the trenches of the Western Front, during the First World War).

It was Maya who gave me the idea in the first place: a quick and painless departure, no prolonged suffering involved. That's what she had hoped for, what she wrote about in the letter to her best friend. Before the Manhattan bomb, I thought I could achieve the same: a memorable and painless exit, one framed by starry fireworks in a not-so-starry London sky. After the Manhattan bomb, I was no longer sure I wanted to meet the Grim Reaper again the following night, feel his cold breath on the nape of my neck, watch him raise his scythe to harvest my soul.

I realised there's something ferociously beautiful about the act of living.

I discovered that the tiny pulse in my wrist was preciously fragile and not worth squandering.

I understood that fighting was the whole point of living, and that I was born to fight. I would battle the cancer, I thought. After all, I had always been the stubbornest minnow swimming hardest against the current. So, I revised my plan, long before Viola tried to talk me out of killing myself. But I didn't tell her that, of course, for fear of jinxing the modified version of my plan.

The revised plan was to glide off the catwalk, swim back to shore. Fake my death in front of thousands of pairs of eyes, as a means of getting rid of the annoying encumbrances of being alive. Here was a perfect opportunity, I thought, to divest myself of the pressures of fame, the trappings of wealth, the burdens of success. Free myself from the entourage of parasites who keep following me around (they are less likely to bother me when I'm dead). Here was my chance to be remembered, I thought, because true immortals make a dramatic exit at the pinnacle of their genius.

An exit swift and bold.

Immortality via 'mortality'.

That's why I kicked hard, that night. Strained against the pull of the river, fought it tooth and nail. Swam like I had never swum before. I eventually managed to pull myself onto the riverbank about two kilometres downstream.

Wet, shivering and exhausted.

Glad I finished all the whisky in Steve's hip flask before running off the runway. It fired up my gut, gave me the illusion that I was invincible (I guess survival mainly happens in the mind). Glad I had lots of practice climbing Viola's oak tree, taking flying leaps into that frigid pond next to it. It helped me cope with the icy shock of the Thames. No one saw me clamber out from the depths of the river afterwards, apart from a drug-addled *Big Issue* seller who probably thought he was hallucinating when he saw a bedraggled and thoroughly unfashionable rat emerge from the water. Amazingly, my phone still worked (it's great these new-generation waterproof phones do precisely what it says on the tin). I rang Steve later that night. He was mightily surprised to hear my voice. He was also deliriously happy.

'Holy shit, I thought you died,' he bellowed down over the line, almost deafening me. 'I've just started planning your funeral.'

'I'm technically supposed to be dead,' I said. 'But I'm still very much alive and shivering. Could you do me a favour, please?'

'Sure.'

'I wish to remain dead, for all legal and practical purposes.'

'Might be tricky . . .'

'That's why I need a new identity and a plane ticket to Tahiti, while you continue to plan my funeral.'

'You never ask for anything easy, do you?' He chuckled. 'Consider it done. If I were you, I would also get plastic surgery . . . or a haircut at the very least.'

'I need a fucking roof over my head tonight, not a haircut.'

'You're most welcome to stay at my flat in Kensington. You're lucky I'm in between ladies at the moment, no one borrowing my T-shirts or stealing my pills.'

'Thanks, Steve.'

You find your most trustworthy friends in death, not life.

Over the next two weeks, I had great fun reading my obituaries in all the major newspapers and magazines, the acres and acres of bullshit devoted to my deeds and misdeeds (Steve would come home each day laden with papers). Most headlines were along the lines of: 'The King is Dead', 'He Was The King of Fashion, A True Visionary', 'The *Last* Creative Genius' or 'They Didn't Call Him Alexander the Great for Nothing'. My favourite was: 'He Lived Life on the Edge, Ended it by Jumping off a Ledge'. The obituaries were accompanied by the predictable handwringing over the death of creativity, the perils of technology and the likelihood of everyone being replaced by robots (I bet the ancients had similar debates when the wheel was first invented). There was one obituary that got my goat, though. The *Sun*'s glowing tribute was entitled 'The Murderer of Fashion is Finally Dead' and went on and on about how I had been a selfish and self-absorbed arsehole who had refused to change for the better.

Lucia Graves didn't get any obituaries, only a shitload of news columns speculating how it all went so terribly wrong in her case. I will always blame myself for hiring her as my PA, for choosing her above the 577 candidates who applied for the job. Guess I should have read her reference letters more carefully. I'm so glad I didn't tell her *everything*, as per Tara's advice. I guess my little bet with De Luca gave Lucia grand ideas, made her think she could get away with profitable revenge. A psychiatrist implied in a column in the *Sunday Times* that Lucia was as bonkers as the people who failed to realise it. He's right. I'm a hopeless judge of character (I'm also bonkers, but everyone already knows that). Guess I was swayed by Lucia's seemingly innocent doe-like eyes, her surface wit and intelligence.

How fucking pathetic.

I'm so relieved she didn't kill Viola and her husband with my pistol. The poor man had to spend several weeks in hospital after Lucia blasted his chest wide open. I wish Viola had told me much earlier on that she was engaged to the Commissioner himself; I would've been friendlier to him when we chatted in his office. But I guess we're all entitled to our secrets. I would never have forgiven myself if Viola and her husband had perished that night, like the poor

ALEXANDER KING, RIP

who will always be remembered for his visionary genius and the ferocious beauty of his creations

So said the *New York Times*, when covering my memorial service at St Paul's, a magnificent event attended by three thousand people. While there were all sorts of conspiracy theories as to whether or not I survived, the eventual consensus was that I had indeed kissed the face of the earth goodbye for unlimited whisky in heaven (or hell, as the *Sun* had assumed). I was sorely tempted to show up at St Paul's in disguise, wearing a giant Panama hat and Gio's square shades, but I didn't dare risk it. The tributes on the day (especially dear Gio's) were long and effusive; the *Daily Mail* remarked that many people in the congregation were spotted wiping away tears. The wonderful thing about death is that it confers immortality on you, even a smidgen of sainthood. No one speaks ill of the dead, unless you're Hitler or Stalin or Vlad the Impaler.

Looks like my plan to be always remembered as The Last Truly Creative Designer Before Robots Take Over worked.

Oddly enough, the knowledge that I've achieved immortality via mortality doesn't give me the slightest bit of satisfaction. I had more satisfaction planning my demise than actually being dead. Satisfaction is a journey, not an end point. The same goes for happiness. Most people think they will only be happy once they achieve something, reach an end goal. Seldom do they realise that it's the *process* of getting there that gives them a shot at being happy or satisfied.

This is what Death has taught me about Life.

How fucking ironic.

Anyhow, my doctor (who has kindly agreed to keep my existence a secret) says that my prostate cancer, though incurable and inoperable, had gone into remission. He thinks that the cryotherapy (which I eventually consented to, after that little conversation with Viola on her guest bed) might have indeed done the trick. It's as if I had been hauled back from the jaws of death, given a new lease of life. With luck, I have a few more years to live now, maybe even a dozen.

Miracles happen, said the doctor.

I guess miracles only happen when you least expect them, in both life and death.

Here's my humble theory: my extended dunking in the icy Thames caused such a shock to my system, my cancer cells became more amenable to freezing. No way of proving this theory right, of course. But life is most definitely a series of ironies. Just when you start itching for a good fight (with cancer, in my case) and put on proper punching gloves, your opponent meekly concedes the bout. Which gives me a new problem: what am I going to do with this unexpected windfall, this extra borrowed time? Time is something you either have too little of – or too much. People who have too little spend all their time wishing they could have more of it, while people with too much spend all their time wishing they could do something better with it. There is seldom a happy medium.

Maybe I should help that fisherman bring in his catch.

Since I no longer wish to kill myself and the cancer isn't going to kill me yet, I can maybe try to kill time.

Just before I got onto a plane to Tahiti, I did the only useful thing I managed to achieve over the past few months. I sent a handwritten message to Viola, by 100 per cent guaranteed drone. It merely said:

'Don't forget your two promises to me, sweetheart.'

I wade out into the ocean, raise a hand at the fisherman. He waves back with a smile, probably thinks I'm trying to be friendly. Maybe it's indeed time for me to be helpful. Be less selfish, less self-absorbed. Learn something about the niceties of being nice. Guess it doesn't hurt to be pleasant to people. As I no longer wish to change the world (after having changed it beyond repair), my only remaining option is to change myself.

'Can I help?' I say.

Epilogue

Viola

Later in the day, on the other side of the globe

It's five minutes past three. Christian is staring at the jerry-rigged screen with a wistful expression on his face. He's running his little finger along his left brow; he must be thinking hard. He finally got to the end of his story, late last night. Down to the last terrible bit where he saw Maya's body in a mortuary, in a room so chilly it fogged his spectacles and made his blood run cold. It took him months to tell me everything, in fits and starts. Yet I'm glad he finally told me the truth.

Trusted me with his past.

He even showed me the contents of his mum's wooden box, the sepia-tinted photographs and dried roses buried in its depths. I've told him what happened at Old Fen Cottage on the night Maya died, in return. Xander's right. Secrets should be shared and ghosts from the past should be buried. Especially as Christian and I are walking compendiums of the same haunted baggage.

Repair is an endless process, as my therapist once said (I'm happy Christian is now seeing her, too).

Our baby gurgles, places a tiny finger in its mouth, falls back to sleep. An orange butterfly is zooming by a few yards away, a psychedelic blur of citrus and vermilion. I look up. The sun is smiling above our heads in a clear sky. It's casting long dappled rays onto the ochre petals scattered around on the lawn, illuminating the yellow rosebuds fringing the baby's cot.

It's a beautiful day, a day that would elicit joy in anyone's heart.

Only one person in the vicinity isn't looking amused: the ceremony's officiator. He's grimacing at Xander's avatar, now flashing up on the makeshift screen. The poor man was damned opposed to the idea, but I was adamant that Xander's bot be allowed to make an appearance today. I'm glad we struck a compromise: that we have two living godparents at today's ceremony, in addition to the virtual one. I take a grateful glance in their direction. Steve Mortimer and Annette Verger are both beaming down at the baby (Christian muttered under his breath, a few minutes ago, that he had never seen his step-mum looking so happy since before his dad died).

The officiator clears his throat, frowns before saying to the bot:

'Do you, Alexander Octavius King, promise to be always there for Lisabeth Alexandra Verger, during easy times and difficult ones, give her a listening ear and advice when she needs it?'

'Hell, yeah,' says the Xander-bot, flashing a thumbs-up and prompting everyone on the lawn to roar with laughter.

The officiator is grimacing again, with the expression of a man who thinks that these proceedings are ridiculous in the extreme. But a promise is a promise, and all promises should be kept.

'Do you, Alexander Octavius King, promise to add chaos

and fun to Lisabeth Alexandra Verger's existence, make her smile, ensure an abundance of sunshine and laughter in her life?' says the officiator.

'I fucking guarantee you that,' says the Xander-bot on screen, prompting everyone to guffaw again.

'Thank you,' says the officiator. 'Now, if you please . . .'

We're interrupted by the whir of a drone above our heads, one in the shape of a magnificent peregrine falcon. It's a videography drone with a camera at its base. It bears all the hallmarks of a paparazzi device, because it's hovering at perfect regulation height (267 feet away from anyone who doesn't wish to be photographed, otherwise the flyer of the drone can be prosecuted).

'Bloody hell,' says Christian. 'Someone's spying on proceedings. I hope it isn't one of the worthy folks you consult for.'

I shrug.

'I'm tempted to get someone to shoot it down,' he says.

I look up at the e-falcon with a frown.

Something tells me that it deserves to be here, today. Hovering above this beautiful lawn full of dappled light and shared dreams.

'Leave it,' I say to Christian, my voice loud and firm. 'Just leave it.'

The sound of the drone causes Lisabeth to open her eyes. They are cerulean blue, the precise shade of the sky, the colour of the horizon. The colour of the human soul, infinitely textured and layered with hope. It's one of those moments that make me believe in tomorrow, the wonderfully unpredictable yet savagely beautiful possibilities only the future can bring.

She lifts a finger, points up at the sky and smiles.

Acknowledgements

I'm grateful to numerous people for helping me turn this book into reality. Special thanks to my fabulous agents, Jonny Geller and Viola Hayden, at Curtis Brown, as well as to my wonderful editor, Alex Clarke, at Wildfire Books, for championing this project and helping me develop my vision for the novel.

I would like to thank my marvellous team of beta-readers for their astute and incisive comments on the manuscript. William Tunstall-Pedoe and Geoffrey Monaghan deserve star mention for their excellent and ingenious input; I'm grateful to them for sharing their expertise on technological and policing matters. I'm equally indebted to Michael Dias, Helen Allen and Ilana Lindsey (of my tenacious Faber writing group) for their generous and perceptive feedback. Huge thanks, too, to Geoffrey Carr, Oksana Trushkevych, Blaise Thomson, Ivor Samuels, Wan Yi Min, Ulrich Paquet, Sally Garner and Oleg Pikhurko for multiple insights and brilliant suggestions.

It was a pleasure to work with my structural editor, Celine Kelly, and my copy editor, Jill Cole; I'm grateful for their fastidious scrutiny of the plot and prose. Many thanks and cheers, too, to Ella Gordon and the rest of the team at Wildfire Books, as well as Kate Cooper, Luke Speed and all at Curtis Brown.

I believe that inspiration is the alchemic response to the

unfamiliar, surprising and unexpected. This book was accordingly written on the road; I was lucky to have visited a variety of stimulating environments during its incubation. I'm grateful to everyone who welcomed me from Haiti to Honduras, Zambia to Bangladesh. In particular, I would like to raise an appreciative toast to the late Drue Heinz, Hamish Robinson, the Trustees of Hawthornden Castle, and Catriona Farquharson of Finzean Estate in Scotland, as well as to Alessia Balducci and Jacopo Sbolci of Borgo del Sole in Italy, for blissful periods of writing and reflection. Huge thanks, too, to my fellow residents and creatives for their inspirational companionship: Keggie Carew, Christopher Meredith, Nina von Staffeldt, Carin Clevidence, Lydia Syson, Franca de Angelis and Rocco Garaguso.

Finally, I would like to thank three special people in my life, people who have lit up my journey. Thank you, Lee Han Shih, for believing in me and making my dreams possible. I'm also extremely grateful to my partner, Alexander Plekhanov, and my father, Teak Kwong, for their love and support, two perfect constants in an imperfect world. Alex and Dad, this book is for you.